Disturbing
the Dead

Books by Sandra Parshall

The Heat of the Moon
Disturbing the Dead
Broken Places

Disturbing
the Dead

Sandra Parshall

Poisoned Pen Press

Poisoned Pen Press
6962 E. First Ave., Ste. 103
Scottsdale, AZ 85251
www.poisonedpenpress.com
info@poisonedpenpress.com

Printed in the United States of America

For Jerry

Acknowledgements

My critique partners deserve special thanks for patiently sticking with me through many versions of this story and its characters. I couldn't have written the book without Cat Dubie, Carol Baier, Janet Bolin, Cristina Ryplansky, and Daryl Wood Gerber. My thanks also to Babs Whelton, Lorraine Bartlett, and others who read early versions. Members of the Sisters In Crime Guppies Chapter have always been there with inspiration and encouragement, as well as expertise on herbal remedies, flesh wounds, legal dilemmas, imaginative uses for feminine hygiene products, and virtually any other topic that might come up in a mystery novel.

I'm grateful to my husband, Jerry, for his help with this book and for seeing me through the shock-to-the-system changes that come with publishing a book; and my agent, Jacky Sach, for her insightful suggestions and her work on my behalf. My friend Dr. Carole Fulton checked the veterinary medicine details and prevented me from inadvertently blowing up an animal hospital.

At Poisoned Pen Press, I'd like to thank my editor, Barbara Peters, for helping me make the book stronger; publisher Robert Rosenwald; Jessica Tribble, Marilyn Pizzo, Nan Beams, and the rest of the staff who work so hard to produce beautiful books for their authors.

Disturbing the Dead is a work of fiction, set in a fictional Virginia mountain community, but the Melungeon people of Appalachia are real and their history as "tri-racial isolates"–a mixture of white, Native American, and black—is as I describe it. The Melungeon Heritage Association, based in Wise, VA, has been an invaluable source of information about the lives of Melungeons, past and present, and several individuals have generously shared their personal stories and family photos with me. Because the Melungeons' skin was often dark and no one could say for certain where they originated, they have battled prejudice and legal discrimination for centuries, but since the founding of the MHA a few years ago, many have embraced their heritage and begun to explore family histories that were previously hidden. To learn more, visit www.melungeon.org.

Chapter One

He wanted the skull.

Captain Tom Bridger and the deputies under his command had been gathering bones on the wooded mountaintop for three hours, but snow was rapidly burying the search area and they still didn't have a complete skeleton.

Tom crouched under the trees and pawed through brush and weeds and leaf litter. Without the skull and teeth they might never put a human name to the bones. If this was Pauline McClure's skeleton they were reassembling, he had to know.

He couldn't see a damned thing anymore. At one in the afternoon, the January day was dim as twilight and Tom was afraid the team might overlook dirt-encrusted bones in the deep shadows among the trees. Unhooking his flashlight from his utility belt, he stood and yelled to the other ten deputies in the woods, "Use your flashlights, guys, so you don't miss anything. Another half-hour, then you can quit."

From somewhere nearby he heard a groan, loud and drawn out.

Dennis Murray, a lanky sergeant working six yards from Tom, said, "That's the sound of a man freezing his balls off."

"Hang in there, guys," Tom called. "I'll buy a steak dinner for the man who finds the skull." Tom's own fingers and toes had gone numb an hour ago, but he wanted that skull more than he wanted to be warm. *Hell, I'm young and strong,* he told himself grimly. *I'll survive a little frostbite.*

As if to test his resolve, a gust rattled bare tree limbs above him and dumped snow on his head. His high-crowned, flat-brimmed deputy's hat made Tom feel like Dudley Do-Right, but at the moment he was grateful for its protection. He shook off the snow and settled the hat back over his thick black hair.

"You think it's her, don't you?" Dennis asked. "The doc was sure that pelvis we found is a woman's."

"It could be anybody." Tom tugged up the collar of his uniform jacket to keep melting snow from snaking down his neck. "Maybe a hiker who didn't know the area and got lost." Dropping to a crouch again, he dug through an inch of snow to a fresh patch of ground. The search had begun that morning, after tree-cutters clearing the mountaintop for construction discovered the skeleton of a human hand and alerted the Sheriff's Department.

"If a hiker got lost anywhere in the mountains," Dennis said, "we'd know about it. Besides, these bones are old and all chewed up. They've been here for years. And we've only got one outstanding missing person case."

"Let's just wait and see, Denny." But he was right. Mason County, small and rural and tucked into the foothills of Virginia's Blue Ridge, had a single enduring mystery, the subject of gossip and speculation ten years after the fact: What happened to Pauline McClure? A beautiful, wealthy widow in her forties, she'd vanished from her country estate and no clue to her fate had ever turned up.

Tom glanced over to find Dennis watching him through the falling snow.

"I'd think you'd be real excited about finding her." Dennis swiped flakes off the lenses of his wire-rimmed glasses. "Considering how long your dad spent on the case."

Dennis had worked with Tom's father, John Bridger, but probably had no idea what a toll the unsolved McClure case had taken on him and his family. "Whoever it is," Tom said, "our job's the same—find out how she ended up dead on top of a mountain."

He bent to his work again, scraping away snow and lifting decayed leaves layer by layer. His gloved fingers brushed something solid.

He kept digging, carefully, a little at a time. Definitely something there.

Leaning closer to the ground, he focused the flashlight beam and pushed aside bits of crumbling leaf matter. A set of human teeth grinned up at him.

"Jesus Christ." He sat back on his heels.

The skull was stained as dark as the earth, and a colony of lichen covered the forehead. Tom cleared off debris until the skull was fully exposed. The mandible was still attached. The lab would have a complete set of teeth to compare with dental records.

"Welcome back to the world," Tom whispered. In the gaping eye sockets he saw all the lonely seasons the bones had lain here under the trees. "Let's find out if you can tell us your name."

He looked over his shoulder toward the clearing, where Dr. Gretchen Lauter, the medical examiner, was tagging and bagging everything the deputies uncovered. "Gretchen," Tom called, "I've found the grand prize."

The doctor, a small woman in her fifties, picked her way through underbrush to his side. Dennis joined them. Together they stood in silence for a moment, watching snow collect on the skull at their feet.

A sour taste rose in Tom's throat. This was a hell of a way for anyone to end up. He'd seen bleeding bodies and dead ones, in Richmond and here in Mason County, but nothing had ever gotten to him like this slow gathering of dismembered bones. All of them were darkened by exposure and most bore the marks of wild animals' teeth.

Gretchen tugged her knit cap lower over her salt-and-pepper curls. "Get some pictures before we move it."

Dennis retrieved a small digital camera from inside his jacket and stooped to snap a few shots while Tom illuminated the skull with his flashlight.

"Let's get it up," Gretchen said, "so I can have a closer look."

When Tom lifted the skull, the mandible dropped off. "Aw, Christ."

"Not to worry." She scooped it up. "The human jaw doesn't break all that easily."

Tom's gaze was riveted to the back of the skull he held. "What about the cranium? What would it take to cause this kind of damage?"

He turned the skull, showing them the long cleft down the back, angled from the top past the right ear opening to the base.

"Holy crap," Dennis said.

Gretchen pulled in a deep breath. "Oh, my lord. First thing that comes to mind is an ax. It must have gone well into the brain."

Tom fingered the split and a shudder of horror moved through him. He imagined an ax blade slicing through scalp, cracking bone, coming to rest in the coils of the brain. Obliterating with one blow every thought and emotion that had made the woman who she was. "No chance it's animal damage? Or maybe it was caused by freezing and thawing."

Gretchen shook her head. "A break that long, that wide—not likely. I'm very much afraid you've got yourself a murder case."

A knot tightened in Tom's gut. "But is it Pauline McClure?"

"All I can give you is a guess," Gretchen said. "Let me look at the teeth." She examined the mandible, then handed the jawbone to Tom in exchange for the skull. "Not many people have as much dental work as Pauline did. I haven't seen her chart in ten years, but I remember all these bridges and crowns. And you know what this is, don't you?" She ran a finger around a small bony protrusion a couple inches up from the base of the skull.

Automatically Tom's hand went to a similar lump of bone at the back of his own head, but when he realized what he was doing he yanked his arm down. "Anatolian bump."

"The Melungeons are the only people around here who've got that, right?" Dennis said.

Gretchen nodded. "And Pauline was Melungeon."

"So it is her," Tom said. "She was lying up here all the time, just a few miles from her house." *While my father nearly drove himself crazy trying to find her.* If an out-of-state millionaire hadn't decided to build a vacation home on top of Indian Mountain, Pauline's bones might never have been found. Now she was Tom's problem. This wasn't the end of Pauline's story, a neat wrap-up of his father's work. This was the beginning of a murder investigation, and the case was as cold as the victim's bones.

"I'll have to check the teeth against her dental records," Gretchen cautioned, "and the state lab will have to verify it—"

"Good God almighty," came a voice behind them.

Tom turned to see Sheriff Toby Willingham bracing himself against a tree at the edge of the woods. He breathed in hard gasps and pressed a hand to his chest inside his uniform jacket. His jowly face was blanched as white as the snow.

The old man couldn't leave them to do their work, he had to huff and puff his way up here to remind everybody who was boss. Tom waded through snow and brush to Willingham's side and gripped his arm. They were of equal height, six feet, but lately the sheriff had lost a lot of weight and developed a slump to his shoulders that made him look like a little old man to Tom. "You all right?"

"Of course I'm all right. I just need to catch my breath." The sheriff shook off Tom's touch, his eyes locked on the jawbone in Tom's other hand.

"Well, you look awful, Toby," Gretchen said as she joined them. "A man with your heart condition has no business climbing a mountain."

When she passed the skull to Tom and tried to take the sheriff's pulse, Willingham wrenched his arm away. Irritation brought color to his cheeks. "I'm in charge of these men, in case you forgot. And I'm not a damned invalid, so stop treating me like one."

Tom almost grinned at Gretchen's elaborate eye-roll, but he pulled a straight face before the sheriff could take offense and start ranting about insubordination. He should have built up immunity to the sheriff's alpha male routine, but it still rankled more than he liked to admit. The only bond between them was the memory of Tom's father, who had seen qualities in Willingham that eluded Tom's best efforts at detection.

"Rest a little and catch your breath, Toby," Gretchen said. She seemed as surprised as Tom was when the sheriff accepted the order and plodded back to the clearing, brushed snow off a tree stump and sat down.

Leaving Dennis to continue searching, Tom and Gretchen followed the sheriff into the clearing. Tom held the skull while Gretchen rummaged through a bin filled with plastic and paper bags for one of the right size. The bones gathered earlier were stowed in a long cardboard box that was collecting snow on the ground next to the sheriff. Everything would be driven to Roanoke for examination at the western laboratory of the Virginia Division of Forensic Science.

"Did you know Pauline well?" Tom asked Gretchen. For most of his adult life he'd despised the ghost who had haunted his father's last years, but with Pauline's skull very likely in his hands, her bones piled in a box, he felt a surprising stab of pity for a woman brutally robbed of life.

"Not all that well," Gretchen said, "but she went to high school with your dad and me, and I saw her a couple of times later on when her own doctor wasn't available. I gave her Valium once." She sighed and shook her head. "Pauline went through hell with those in-laws of hers."

"Yeah, I heard they weren't crazy about a Melungeon girl marrying into the family."

Sheriff Willingham muttered, "Damned narrow-minded…" His words trailed off.

Gretchen shook open a plastic bag, placed the mandible in it, and began filling out a tag with the date and location of the discovery and a description of the item. "Do you remember when Pauline disappeared?" she asked Tom. "You were just a kid—"

"I was twenty."

Gretchen's smile was indulgent, almost motherly. "Like I said, you were a kid. I thought maybe you were so wrapped up in your own life, you didn't pay any attention to what your father was working on."

"I paid attention." Memory swept Tom off the frigid mountain, back to a time when the countryside lay tired and dusty under the heat of summer. "It was the end of August, right before I left for Charlottesville for junior year."

Had Pauline been killed and hidden up here the same night she went missing? Looking around, Tom tried to see Indian Mountain the way it was before construction workers gouged a trail to the crest—steep and densely wooded, the foliage nearly impenetrable in late summer.

The killer must have been a man. Tom pictured a tall figure, bent under his burden, fighting his way up the incline through the brush with only moonlight to guide the way. Even a strong man would have stopped every now and then to lay down the body and rest before he slung the stiffening form over his shoulder and resumed the trek to the top.

Tom asked Willingham, "Wasn't this mountain searched after Mrs. McClure disappeared?"

"Of course it was, and those caves at the bottom too." Willingham rose and flung his arms wide. "But look what we were dealing with. We couldn't cover every single inch. Somebody carrying a grown woman's body to the top through all that underbrush—well, it was so unlikely we didn't even consider it."

"Somebody managed it."

"Your dad was a damned good cop. This was the only case he wasn't able to close, but I know he did everything right. You gonna start second-guessing him now?"

"He would expect me to second-guess everything about the original investigation. He'd do the same in my shoes."

"Maybe you ought not to be handling this. I'll take charge of it myself."

For a moment Tom was too surprised to answer. The sheriff hadn't headed up an investigation in years. Tom was chief deputy, lead investigator, and this was his job. If the case was left to Willingham, weakened and distracted by illness, it would never be solved. Tom made an argument that he knew would sway the sheriff. "My dad put a lot of effort into this case, and he'd want me to finish it for him."

Willingham turned mournful eyes on the leafless trees and blew out a breath that hung in a frosty cloud before dissolving. "I wish John could be here now."

So do I. God, so do I. Tom didn't say it aloud because he knew the sheriff wasn't inviting him to share a mutual grief. Willingham seemed to believe he'd personally suffered the most from the death of his longtime friend and second in command, and he played chief mourner even when John Bridger's son was standing right in front of him.

His voice level but flinty, Tom said, "You'll have to make do with me."

Willingham met his gaze for a moment, and Tom saw accusation and resentment in the sheriff's pale blue eyes. In the end, though, Willingham relented grudgingly. "Well, you can't tie up every man we've got on a cold case."

"Just give me Brandon Connelly. He seems pretty sharp."

Willingham waved a hand, agreeing, but his face hadn't lost its belligerence. "You watch your step with Pauline's family. And I don't mean the McClures. She was a Turner from Rocky Branch District, and those people don't like cops poking around in their business. You might be half Melungeon, but they won't forgive you for wearing a badge. Remember you're not in—"

"—Richmond anymore. Yeah, I know."

"And don't believe everything you hear, either. Well, I'm going on back to town." As Willingham started down the mountain, he said over his shoulder, "Stop standing around with that woman's head in your hands."

Tom kept an eye on the sheriff's slip-sliding descent, ready to spring to the rescue if Willingham fell. "What does he mean," Tom asked Gretchen, "don't believe everything I hear?"

"Oh, good heavens," Gretchen said, "don't ask me to explain Toby."

She said it a little too lightly, and Tom was about to press her on it when somebody yelled, "Hey, Captain!"

Two young blond deputies, the Blackwood twins, hustled out of the woods into the clearing. In the gloom the brothers' wide grins made them look like Cheshire cats.

"We found this." Kevin held one of the cardboard boxes the deputies were using to collect evidence. "We thought it might—"

Before Kevin got all the words out, Tom looked to Keith for the rest of the sentence.

"—tie in somehow," Keith finished.

Tom handed the skull to Gretchen and pulled an ax head from the box. Thick rust coated the iron wedge, but he thought he detected a darker stain along the cutting edge. No. Not possible after so many years. But his pulse quickened and he barely caught a jubilant laugh before it escaped. "Oh, yeah, it might tie in. Good work, guys."

Keith and Kevin beamed.

With a glance at the sky, Tom added, "The snow's getting too heavy to work in. Go string the tape at the foot of the mountain before you take off."

"Will do," the twins said in unison.

Gretchen tilted her head to look beyond Tom. "Here comes Brandon. He's got something too."

Deputy Brandon Connelly trotted toward them with a cardboard box clutched against his chest. He'd come hatless, and his short sandy hair dripped with melting snow. "Hey, Boss," he said, holding out the box, "look at this."

"Good God," Tom said.

The box contained another skull, stained brown and coated in spots with mud and dark green moss.

Gretchen peered at it and gasped.

"Is it human?" Tom asked her.

"I'm very much afraid it is."

Tom glanced at the skull in Gretchen's hands, looked back at the one in the box. "If that's Pauline McClure, who the hell is this?"

Chapter Two

Rachel Goddard adjusted her stethoscope and leaned into the cage to check the bulldog's heart and lungs. She got a sloppy lick on the chin in greeting. "Oh, yeah," she said, laughing, "I think you've fully recovered, lover boy."

Tom Bridger's English bulldog, Billy Bob, was ready to go home after his teeth cleaning, but Tom hadn't kept his pickup appointment. Delayed at work, Rachel assumed. Clients had been telling her all day that something mysterious was happening on Indian Mountain north of town and the whole Sheriff's Department was up there. Couldn't be a lost child—thank God—because if it were, the whole county would have been alerted and half the adults would be helping with the search. What, then? A dead body? A murder victim? With a shudder, Rachel shook the thought away.

"Dr. Goddard?" Shannon, the chubby young receptionist, stood in the doorway. "You've got a call. A woman named Leslie Ryan. She said it's urgent."

Aware of her suddenly racing heartbeat, Rachel gave the bulldog a quick scratch on the head and closed his cage. What on earth could Leslie be calling her about? She strode up the rear hallway to her office, and as she walked she brushed her auburn hair off her cheeks and smoothed her lab coat, almost unconsciously putting herself in order to face bad news.

In the office, she stood for a moment looking out the window, her attention caught by the procession of deputies' cruisers moving up Main Street in the snow. Whatever had happened, it must be over now. She would find out what was going on when Tom picked up Billy Bob.

She was procrastinating. *Pick up the phone and find out what this is about.* She ran her tongue over dry lips and lifted the receiver. "Leslie?"

"Hello, Rachel. How are you? How are things going at the new animal hospital?"

Definitely bad news, if the straightforward assistant prosecutor couldn't bring herself to get right to the point. Rachel envisioned Leslie in her spartan office in Fairfax City, clad in a plain suit, her blonde hair restrained in a severe twist at the nape of her neck. "I'm very busy," Rachel said. "Most of my staff's out with the flu. But you didn't call to ask how I am. Tell me what's wrong."

She heard Leslie sigh. "Perry Nelson is petitioning for unsupervised weekends with his family, and his doctors are supporting the request. The hearing is week after next."

The news hit Rachel like a kick in the gut and left her breathless, light-headed. "My God, he's only been there seven months. They can't turn him loose. He could go anywhere, do anything."

"My reaction exactly," Leslie said. "It's absurd. The doctors claim that trips outside the hospital are essential to his recovery, but the man is a menace to society in general and to you in particular. I wanted you to know that I'll go before the judge and oppose the request in the strongest possible terms."

Rachel sank into her desk chair and closed her eyes for a second while she breathed deeply. It couldn't happen. The thug who'd nearly killed her had no right to walk free again. But Nelson was a good enough actor to persuade a jury he hadn't been responsible for his actions when he'd shot her. Now he'd apparently conned the doctors at the state hospital into believing he was no longer a danger. He might be able to win over the judge. He might get out. Then he would come after Rachel.

"Rachel? Are you all right?"

"No, I'm not all right. I'm mad as hell." An alarming thought struck her. "Has this been on the news?"

"If it hasn't yet, it will be by the end of the day."

She didn't want her sister to hear about it from a news report. Right now Michelle would be at work, unreachable while she was busy with her young autistic patients, but Rachel would have to catch her as soon as possible. "I knew he'd try to get out someday," Rachel told Leslie, "but I didn't expect it to happen so quickly."

"I hate to say it, but this is only the beginning. If we're going to keep him locked up, and keep you safe, we'll have to fight him every inch of the way."

Keep me safe. What a laugh. Six months before, Rachel had left Northern Virginia—and a man she loved—because she'd thought the peaceful countryside would make her feel safe. But violence could follow her anywhere.

She stared out the window at the bleak day. The last of the police cars had moved out of view, and snow was already filling in the tire tracks on Main Street.

Chapter Three

The search team retreated to the Sheriff's Department headquarters, a low concrete building in Mountainview that hunkered behind the imposing neo-classical Mason County Courthouse like an outhouse attached to a mansion.

They had no idea who the second skull belonged to, but Gretchen Lauter compared the teeth in the first skull to the dental records in the old case file and assured Tom that they'd found Pauline McClure's remains. The discovery would be the talk of the county within hours and Tom wanted to reach Pauline's mother, Sarelda Turner, before she heard the news from an unofficial source. He and Brandon Connelly grabbed a couple of burgers for a late lunch and ate them in the department's old Explorer as they set out in the storm.

Mrs. Turner lived in western Mason County, where the narrow roads twisted like spastic snakes around the mountains. Most of the county's poor, and its dwindling population of Melungeons, lived in the hills and hollows of Rocky Branch District.

Brandon, excited over being involved in a murder case, chattered nonstop for half an hour. When he suddenly shut up, Tom was surprised enough to glance over at him.

"Captain," Brandon said, a new tentative note in his voice, "can I ask you a question without you taking offense?"

Taking offense? What on earth— Oh. That. Has to be. "You want to ask me something about Melungeons?"

"Well, uh—" Brandon stopped to clear his throat. At twenty-one, he was the youngest member of the department, a deputy for only a few months, and he seemed painfully wary of getting on the wrong side of his superiors.

Tom laughed. "Spit it out, Bran. Ask me anything you want to."

"Well. Okay." He sounded relieved to have permission to speak freely. "Mostly, I was wondering how a girl from Rocky Branch ended up married to a McClure. I mean, the McClures are snobs with a capital S."

"I have to agree with you on that," Tom said. "The way I've always heard the story, Pauline went to work at Mason National Bank in some low-level job right out of high school. Adam McClure had just become president of the bank, after his father dropped dead from a heart attack. Adam spotted Pauline and the rest is history. A bachelor in his thirties and a girl like her—you saw her picture, it's not hard to understand."

"Man, she was really something. It's hard to believe one of those skulls we found is the same person." Brandon was silent a moment, then said, "You know, I can see why the McClures wouldn't want their son to marry a poor girl. They probably thought she was after their money. But I heard they hated her mostly because she was Melungeon, and I don't understand that."

"Come on, Bran," Tom said. "Things are a hell of a lot better than they were thirty-five years ago when Pauline married Adam McClure, but there're still plenty of people who need somebody to look down on. Are you telling me you never knew any kids in school who treated Melungeons differently? Called them wild or peculiar—or niggers?"

"Well, yeah, that happened sometimes," Brandon admitted with obvious reluctance. "But look at you. You're half Melungeon, and you're a cop, your dad and your brother were cops, and you were a big basketball star in high school."

"My dad got his job because he saved Willingham's life in Vietnam. And I had to be a great player to get on the basketball team at all. The coach used to call me a half-breed, and he didn't give a damn whether I heard it or not. My father threatened the Board of Education with a lawsuit and they ended up firing the bastard." Tom's hands tightened around the steering wheel as the old, aching anger spilled through him. Christ, why was he dredging up this stuff?

"Wow," Brandon said, and for a moment he seemed at a loss for words.

Through the billowing curtain of snow, Tom saw the evidence of poverty in the little houses they passed. Tin roofs, peeling paint, sagging porches. His father's family had once lived in this district, but they'd become tenant farmers in another part of the county when John Bridger was a child. He'd never lost his connection to the area, though, and its residents had trusted him to settle their disputes because he was one of their own. They didn't know Tom, never sought his help, and when he came out here on the job he was just another cop, unwelcome and resented.

"Your mother's family didn't try to stop your mom from marrying your dad, did they?" Brandon asked.

"No, the McGrails are great people." They were the ones Tom meant when he used the word family. His Bridger relatives had left Mason County long ago in search of work. Occasionally Tom wondered if he still had distant Melungeon relatives in Rocky Branch District, but somehow he'd never gotten around to finding out.

"How come Pauline McClure had blue eyes?" Brandon asked. "If Melungeons are Portuguese and Indian—"

"And other things. They're all over the mountains, and they've married whites, blacks, Indians. There've always been some Melungeons with blue eyes, or green, even if they had dark skin. These days they've mixed in so much that a lot of them don't have dark skin anymore and they might not even know they've got a Melungeon background." Tom smiled ruefully. "But you'll still see plenty like me. When I was working in Richmond, I just let people think I was Cherokee. It was easier than trying to explain what a Melungeon is."

A tire bumped into a pothole, and the front end of the vehicle dropped to the left. Tom gunned the engine and bounced in his seat when the Explorer lurched back onto solid pavement.

Brandon had braced himself with both hands on the dashboard. "Don't get me killed. Debbie'll be even madder at you than she already is."

"Why's Debbie mad at me?" Tom asked.

"We were supposed to see the preacher after I finished my shift and settle some wedding stuff, but I kind of told her you were making me work overtime. Better she's mad at you than me, right?"

Tom laughed. "Great. Thanks a lot." The truth was, Brandon had begged to come along because he didn't want to miss out on any part of the investigation. Tom didn't know the boy well, but he recognized that go-getter attitude as an asset.

Brandon tapped his window. "This it?"

A silver mailbox to their right had TURNER painted on it in big black letters.

Tom swung the Explorer into the snow-covered yard and parked behind a ten-year-old Chevrolet. The house windows glowed with interior light. Tom imagined Mrs. Turner going about her business, maybe cooking supper, unaware that two cops sat outside, preparing to deliver the worst possible news. She must have known deep-down for years that Pauline was dead. But knowing something in the abstract wasn't the same as being told her daughter's bones had been found.

Brandon retrieved their hats from the back seat and held out Tom's.

Tom took a deep breath. "Let's get it over with."

They mounted steps to a covered porch and Tom, finding the screen door latched, rapped on its frame.

When a young woman opened the main door, Tom had the eerie sensation that one of Pauline's photos had sprung to life before him. But the girl, slim and delicate with long black hair around a heart-shaped face, was eighteen or nineteen at most.

Two mongrels pressed their noses to the screen to get the visitors' scents. "Hey," the girl drawled. She tugged a pink cardigan closer over her pink tee shirt. "Can I help y'all?"

Her gaze flitted over Tom's uniform, lingered on his holster and gun before shifting to Brandon. She seemed to find Brandon's face more intriguing than his weapon. He stared back as if mesmerized.

"We're looking for Mrs. Sarelda Turner," Tom said. "Is this the right house?"

"It sure is." She whispered, "My grandma in trouble with the law?"

Tom smiled. "No, not all. I need to talk to her, though."

"Okay, come on in."

Escorted by the dogs, they walked into a small, tidy living room with walls, curtains, and rug in various shades of blue. Fragrant hickory logs crackled in the grate, and country music drifted from a radio in another room. Two intertwined cats in an easy chair opened their eyes, assessed Tom and Brandon, and went back to sleep.

"Grandma, somebody's come to see you," the girl called toward the back of the house.

The woman who appeared a moment later was another version of Pauline, as she might have looked if she'd lived into her seventies. The woman had a trim figure, but sagging lids hooded her blue eyes and her hair looked like it had been dyed black with shoe polish. Wiping her knobby, arthritic fingers on a dish towel, she skimmed the two men with a bolder gaze than her granddaughter's, but without special attention to Brandon's charms.

Tom introduced himself and Brandon. "We've got some news for you."

Her face registered no alarm or curiosity. "I'm busy in the kitchen. Y'all come on through, and we can talk while I finish up."

Tom wanted her to sit on the couch and give him her full attention, but she was already leaving the room.

Away from the firewood's powerful scent, the kitchen offered the aromas of vanilla and chocolate. Tom's mouth watered, but when he swallowed he tasted the greasy burger he'd eaten earlier. Mrs. Turner moved to a flour-dusted wooden table laden with bowls and cookie sheets. The girl slipped into the room and stood next to Brandon near the door. Tom saw them exchange glances, and caught sight of her little smile and flushed cheeks before she averted her face.

Mrs. Turner gestured with a plastic stirring spoon. "Cut off the radio, would you?"

Tom found the radio on top of the refrigerator and silenced Dolly Parton in mid-lament. The big, new-looking fridge dominated the kitchen. The range also looked new. How could Mrs. Turner, a widow living on the edge of poverty, afford these things?

"I always get a bakin' spell on me when it rains or snows," she said. "When the weather's bad outside, I like the smell of sweet things in the oven."

Tom watched her drop spoonfuls of dough, bristling with chocolate chips and pecans, onto a cookie sheet. Why didn't she ask him what news he'd brought? She probably guessed it was bad and wanted to delay hearing it. "My mother always baked in bad weather too," he said with a smile. "My brother and I loved snow and rain—"

He broke off, stopped cold by the expression on Mrs. Turner's face. Her piercing scrutiny felt like a too-familiar touch and made him pull back.

"You're just like your daddy," she said.

"So people tell me."

"He was a good man. He never forgot where he come from." She scooped up dough for another cookie. "It was a real shame, him and the rest of the family dyin' so sudden." She slid a sidelong look at Tom. "All except you and that little boy of your brother's."

She caught him off guard, and without warning he was immersed in the memory of the worst night of his life. It all came back in a flash—harsh overhead lights burning his eyes, a dagger of pain in his ribs every time he took a breath, his nephew in the next ER cubicle, screaming for his mommy and daddy.

He shoved his memories into a dark corner of his mind and pulled himself back to the present. What the hell was this old woman's game? The dig had been deliberate, calculated to sting and put him off balance. But why would this stranger want to take a jab at him? His father couldn't have meant anything to her. John Bridger had simply been the officer who investigated her daughter's disappearance.

In blunt words he delivered the news he'd brought. "We found human bones today on Indian Mountain. We believe they're your daughter Pauline's remains."

He braced for an outburst. But she inserted the loaded cookie sheet into the oven and set a timer before she spoke. "What makes you think that?"

"We used her dental records for comparison."

Mrs. Turner seemed to consider this for a moment, her shuttered face giving nothing away. At last she nodded.

"Can you tell what Aunt Pauline died of?" the girl put in.

"Hush now, Holly," Mrs. Turner said.

Tom answered the girl. "We believe she was murdered."

Her face lively with fascination, Holly advanced into the room. "How? Did she get shot, or—"

"Holly!" Mrs. Turner snapped. "You stop runnin' your mouth or go to your room."

Holly flinched as if slapped.

Watching the girl retreat like a beaten puppy to her place by the door, Tom wanted to make the old woman feel some of the pain she was dishing out so freely. "We think Pauline was hit on the head with an ax."

"Oh, my gosh," Holly murmured.

Mrs. Turner showed no emotion. She plunged a hand into a Pillsbury bag and brought out a fistful of flour. When she scattered it on the table a cloud of white dust flew up, and a substantial portion of it came to rest on Tom's jacket. He ignored it.

"I guess it's too late to be startin' up the investigation again."

Was he imagining the hopeful note in her voice? Why wouldn't she want her daughter's murder solved? "There's no statute of limitations on murder. The case won't be closed until we make an arrest."

Mrs. Turner upended a bowl, dumped a ball of yellow dough onto the floured surface, and brought a rolling pin down with a *thwump*. "Your daddy never got anywhere with it."

"I plan to have better luck. We found parts of two skeletons on the mountain today. Do you have any idea who the other person was?"

The rolling pin dropped from her fingers and clattered to the floor. "Danged arthritis. Can't hold onto a thing." She retrieved the rolling pin and turned to the sink to wash it, hiding her face from Tom. "How would I know who it is?"

She sure as hell knew something. "Mrs. Turner," Tom said, "we need to sit down and talk about the people in your daughter's life."

Drying the rolling pin with a towel, Mrs. Turner returned to the table. "I told your daddy everything. He wrote it in his notebook."

"We might find something that didn't come out the first time."

"You gonna round up all the suspects?" Holly asked.

Tom almost smiled, at the question and Holly's quick recovery from her grandmother's bullying. "We might have trouble locating some of them after all this time." He said to Mrs. Turner, "Maybe you can help us. The two handymen who worked at Pauline's house—"

"Troy Shackleford and Rudy O'Dell," Holly said.

"Right." Tom eyed the girl with interest. "You know them?"

She looked about to answer, but her grandmother didn't give her a chance. "Holly don't know nothin' about it. She wasn't but a young'un when it happened."

Holly's face screwed up with vexation, and she opened her mouth as if to protest. A sharp glance from Mrs. Turner kept her silent.

"Do you know where I can find Shackleford and O'Dell?" Tom asked Mrs. Turner.

"Couldn't tell you."

"Does Holly's mother live here with you?" he asked. He wanted to talk to both of Pauline's sisters.

"Jeannie?" Mrs. Turner said. "Lord no, she's been gone a long time." Before he could ask, she added, "Ain't got the least idea where she is."

Again Holly started to speak, but a look passed between her and Mrs. Turner and the girl changed her mind. Tom would have to get Holly alone sometime soon and find out what she was so eager to tell him. What her grandmother didn't want her to tell him.

"Where can I reach Pauline's daughter? I have to notify her as quickly as possible."

"Mary Lee don't keep in touch with her poor relations. We're not good enough for her." Mrs. Turner said this in a matter-of-fact tone.

"Maybe the McClure family can tell me where she's living now."

"Yeah, they probably keep track of her so they'll know how much McClure money she's spendin'. Or wastin', is how they see it. That bunch would skin a flea for its hide. And they hated my daughter. You talk about suspects, well, there's your suspects. Go ask them your questions." After this deluge of words escaped, Mrs. Turner clamped her lips together in a thin line. Her hand shook as she jabbed the rolled dough with a cookie cutter.

Tom doubted he could get anything useful from her today. He didn't believe her obstinacy had anything to do with grief. Maybe, he thought wryly, he was seeing the fabled Melungeon penchant for intrigue. More likely, this family had real secrets its matriarch didn't want the cops to discover. He was about to tell her he would come back another time when a large gray goose walked into the kitchen.

Brandon gave a startled laugh. The bird waddled to Holly and honked, and the girl scooped it into her arms.

"Holly," Mrs. Turner said, "you know she's not supposed to come in the kitchen." She spoke with the exasperation of someone who has repeated a reprimand too many times with too little effect. "You need to scold her when she does, so she'll mind."

"I don't want to scold her," Holly said. "You don't like to be scolded, do you, Penny?" The goose wiggled contentedly in her arms.

"Go put her on the porch."

Holly carried the goose to the back door, which Brandon rushed to open for her. She flashed a quick smile before she took the goose onto an enclosed porch.

Mrs. Turner said, "I don't know why the girl can't be happy with cats and dogs."

Tom joined Brandon at the door and watched Holly fill a bowl with chicken feed. She spoke softly to the goose, and the bird tucked into its meal. Four homemade wire cages, all empty except for straw bedding in one, occupied the porch.

"You enjoy looking after animals?" Tom asked. "Do you take in orphaned babies?"

"It's not against the law, is it?"

"No, don't worry about it." Technically, she was breaking state law if she didn't have a rehab license, but she probably wasn't doing any harm. "Just don't let yourself get bitten."

"I raised a litter of baby coons after their mama got hit by a car." Holly added with a brilliant smile, "I let 'em go, but they come back to see me sometimes."

Brandon grinned as if her smile had been meant for him. "You ever thought about studying to be an animal doctor?"

Holly burst out laughing. "I can think about it, but I sure couldn't pay for it."

"Do you have a job?" Tom asked.

She shrugged. "I work afternoons at Rose's place. You know it? The diner on Crow's Nest Road?"

Tom exchanged a glance with Brandon. The diner was a drug market, the center of illegal dealing in Mason County. Tom had trouble seeing this girl in a place like that. He was about to suggest she call Mountainview Animal Hospital about a job, but he didn't want to raise her hopes. Better check with Rachel Goddard first. "It was nice meeting you, Holly. What's your last name, by the way?"

"Turner, like my grandma."

So the girl's mother and father hadn't been married.

Behind Tom, Mrs. Turner said, "Anything else I can help y'all with?"

"Not today. But we'll be talking again."

"Next time, call first."

Tom and Brandon headed for the front door, trailed by Mrs. Turner. Tom had the feeling she was making sure they left, rather than politely seeing them out. "I'm sorry about your daughter," he said.

She didn't answer, didn't meet his eyes. He and Brandon barely cleared the door before she shut it.

Tom was unlocking the Explorer when the front door of the house flew open and Holly darted out. She hurried down the front steps and trotted across the yard, as light and surefooted as a fox in the snow. Pressing a folded piece of paper into Tom's hand, the girl said, "She's livin' in McLean. Her name's Scott now, and she—"

"Holly!" Mrs. Turner yelled from the porch. "Get yourself in here!"

The girl dashed back to the house, disappeared inside. Mrs. Turner slammed the door.

Tom assumed Holly had written down a number or address where he could reach her mother. In the vehicle, he unfolded the paper, which turned out to be an envelope. It was addressed to Mrs. Turner and postmarked a month earlier.

In the upper corner was the return address of Pauline's daughter, Mary Lee, the granddaughter Mrs. Turner claimed she never heard from.

Chapter Four

"Dr. Goddard! Help!"

Rachel heard the girl's cries even with her office door closed. She charged down the back hallway, her athletic shoes squeaking on the tile floor, and followed the screams to the kennel room at the rear of the animal hospital.

"Dr. Goddard!" The plea rose to a panicked wail.

Rachel slammed open the kennel door to find Daphne, a young assistant, cowering against a wall. Tom Bridger's bulldog sat in front of the girl, panting and slobbering and grunting.

"What?" Rachel brushed back the hair that had fallen into her eyes during her mad dash. With unobstructed vision, she still didn't see the problem. "What's wrong? I thought you were hurt."

Daphne, a freckled blond, spread her arms against the wall as if bracing for assault. A leash dangled from one hand. "He tried to bite me!"

The brown fireplug of a dog tilted his head to show Rachel an expression of pure innocence. Saliva dripped from one corner of his mouth. "Daphne, Billy Bob doesn't have a mean bone in his body."

"Then you walk him!" The girl hurled the leash to the floor.

Rachel debated whether to reprimand her. This wasn't the first incident of its kind. What sort of person took a job in a veterinary clinic and revealed her terror of dogs only after she started working?

The sort who desperately needed a job and couldn't find one anywhere else. Rachel sighed and scooped up the leash. Phobias couldn't be reasoned or scolded away. Her psychologist mother had taught her that. "Help Shannon finish up on the desk, then you can go home. I'll take charge of this vicious beast."

The girl edged along the wall, never taking her eyes off the dog until she shot through the door.

Billy Bob planted his feet on Rachel's shoes and snorted.

"Yeah, I know, sugar. It's a bum rap. Not a word of truth to it." She crouched to scratch his ears. Why hadn't Tom picked him up yet? Maybe she should drop the dog off at the Sheriff's Department when she left work. "I could steal you and take you home with me. Would you like that?"

Billy Bob hoisted his feet to her knees and swiped his tongue across her cheek. When she averted her face, he got her on the other side. Rachel yelped and laughed. "Oh, you are a sweetheart, aren't you?"

In a fit of pleasure the dog bounced his muscular body up and down, back and forth like a teenager on a dance floor. Rachel grabbed his paws and swayed with him, singing to the accompaniment of snorts and grunts, "Jeremiah was a bulldog…"

The sound of clapping made her swing around. Tom Bridger leaned in the doorway, grinning. Rachel lost her balance and plopped onto her butt. Scrambling to her feet, she tried to hide her embarrassment with a laugh. "Clients are not supposed to know how silly I can get when I'm alone with an animal."

"If I was a real jerk, I could say you're cute when you're surprised."

Rachel straightened her lab coat. "And if I were the kind of feminist who resorts to violence, you'd get clobbered for a line like that." *Listen to yourself. He probably thinks you're flirting with him.*

Tom strode over, lanky and loose-limbed in his brown uniform, and dropped to one knee to greet the dog. "Hey, pal. Did you think I wasn't going to show? Let me see your choppers."

He pulled back Billy Bob's lip to examine the teeth that had been cleaned, then reduced the dog to rapture by vigorously scratching his neck and dewlaps.

Rachel watched Tom's face, fascinated as she always was by his striking features. If she weren't afraid he'd catch her staring, she could study him endlessly, identifying the different blood-lines that had converged to produce such an intriguing result. She'd read that Melungeons believed they were descended from shipwrecked Portuguese or Turkish explorers of the sixteenth century who settled in the mountains and took Native American wives. Rachel could see a Mediterranean heritage in Tom's olive complexion and black hair. But Indian blood must have given him those high cheekbones and near-black eyes and that strong blade of a nose.

Why on earth did this attractive man keep asking her out, knowing she would turn him down? He must have women throwing themselves at him.

He gave the dog a last pat on the back and stood. Rachel shifted her gaze.

"Sorry I didn't keep my appointment," Tom said. "Something came up at work."

"I've been hearing rumors about that all day. What's going on?"

"We found some human bones up on Indian Mountain."

"Oh, my God. Do you know who it is? Was?"

"We think it's a local woman who's been missing for ten years. You might have heard of her—Pauline McClure."

"Yeah," Rachel said, her interest piqued. "The poor girl who married a rich banker, then vanished without a trace. The stuff of local legend."

"The marriage and the disappearance happened twenty years apart, but yeah, that's the one. From the look of the bones, it wasn't a natural death. We think she was—" Tom broke off, wincing. "You don't want to hear this stuff."

One more person tiptoeing around her fragile emotions, afraid she couldn't endure the slightest reminder that the world was a dangerous place. She told herself this had nothing to do with her and forced herself to ask, "You think she was shot? Murdered?"

"Not shot, but— I'd rather not talk about it, okay?"

Smiling to soften her words, she said, "You know, every friend I've made here tries to protect me from bad news. I'm amazed somebody hasn't told the paper carrier to skip me when *The Herald* has a story about a crime."

"I considered that, but I decided it might be going a little too far." Tom laughed when she did, and added, "People don't want to upset you because they like you so much. And in a small community like Mason County, everybody's going to know…"

"My history," she finished. *The part that's on the record. About the rest, you have no idea.* "It's very considerate, but I hate the feeling that everybody's watching their words around me."

Tom nodded. "I can understand that. I've got the same problem when it comes to certain subjects."

His family. Of course he understood. "It keeps people at a distance, doesn't it," she said, "when they're afraid to talk freely around you."

He smiled and said, "The last thing I want to do is keep you at a distance."

Rachel was groping for a response when Tom pulled a handkerchief from his pants pocket and wiped her cheek with it. "I apologize for my dog's bad manners," he said.

The intimacy of his action startled her. Every time she was with him—and she seemed to encounter him a lot these days—Tom trespassed on her personal space in some small but crucial way that left her off-balance.

While he stuffed his handkerchief back in his pocket, he kept his gaze on her. "You have beautiful eyes, Rachel."

Oh, don't do this. She said as lightly as she could, "I'm covered in cat fur and dog drool, but I have beautiful eyes. I'll hang on to that. By the way, Billy Bob's just had a meal, so don't let him tell you different. And he might seem tired tonight from the anesthetic."

"I'm going to leave him with my nephew for the next few hours. I have to get back to headquarters and go over the case file. I've already given Pauline's mother the news."

"That couldn't have been easy." Rachel didn't know how anyone could bear a job that required him to go out in a snowstorm and tell a mother that her daughter's bones had been found.

"Tomorrow morning I have to go see her daughter. She lives in McLean. That's where you're from, right? Maybe you know her. Mary Lee Scott."

"Oh, my gosh. No, I don't know her, but I know who she is." A vague memory came to mind of a woman in a newspaper photo—young, beautiful, arriving at a White House dinner with her much older husband. "She's married to one of the major developers in the Washington area. Small world, huh?"

"Yeah. I went to elementary school with her," Tom said. His mild tone didn't match the haunted look that settled into his eyes.

"So you know the family?" Wait a minute. The dead woman had been Melungeon. That was part of the story the locals told about her. "Are you related?"

He shook his head. "No, nothing like that." He paused and stared into space, his gaze unfocused. "It was my dad's case. His biggest regret was that he never found out what happened to her."

Rachel saw the shadow pass over Tom's face when he mentioned his father, sensed the sadness his memories brought, and she had to snap up a barrier to keep it from invading her. Tom's arm brushed hers. She took a step back to put some distance between them.

"You can give them closure, at least." What a dumb thing to say. She sounded like some shallow idiot spouting feel-good psychobabble.

"I'm not so sure about that," Tom said. "We have to reopen the case. Stir up a lot of bad feeling. To tell you the truth, I…"

The uncompleted thought hung between them, and he seemed to wait for her to prompt him. Maybe he needed somebody to talk to, outside the official circle at work. But she had enough worries without taking on his. "I don't envy you your job," she said.

Billy Bob gave a deep-throated bark and tugged on the leash in her hand. "He needs to use the facilities, then he'll be ready to go."

Pushing open the door to a dog run, she let the bulldog out. He halted abruptly when he discovered snow on the ground and more falling, but after a loud snort he sallied forth with a rolling gait. Rachel and Tom stayed inside and kept an eye on him through a window in the door.

Rachel pulled a grim face. "I'm afraid he's been terrorizing my staff today."

Tom watched the dog plow through the snow in search of the ideal spot to lift a leg. "He's a menace, all right."

Laughing, Rachel said, "I've got an assistant who's afraid of him, if you can believe that. Him and dogs in general. I don't think she's too comfortable with cats either."

"You're kidding. Why do you keep somebody like that around?"

"I can't fire Daphne. Her father's out of work and the family needs her salary."

"You're too kindhearted, you know that?"

Tom was looking at her the way he often did, with an intensity that made her acutely self-conscious. Her hair was probably a mess. Running her tongue over her lips, she detected no remaining trace of her only makeup, the lipstick she'd applied that morning. She knew she was reasonably attractive, tall and slim, with good features, but Tom's admiration made her feel uncomfortable and vaguely guilty. The last man who'd looked at her that way had been Luke Campbell. Her former boss. Her former lover.

She pushed her hair off her forehead and said, "Daphne does the rest of the job reasonably well, which is more than I can say for some people I've tried out." A sigh escaped, and before she could stop herself she blurted, "Maybe moving here and buying the clinic was a mistake. I didn't realize half the staff would quit because an outsider was taking over. I'll lose my clients if I don't get this place humming again." *Why are you telling him your problems?*

"Come on, be honest," Tom said. "No matter how much trouble it is, I'll bet you love walking in here every morning and knowing it all belongs to you."

"Yeah, well, there is that." Her clinic, her business. And as hiding places went, it wasn't bad. "I just wish staffing was somebody else's worry."

"I've been spreading the word that you're hiring. In fact, I might have found a prospect for you. No training at all, and she's not what you'd call polished, but she's good with animals. I wrote down her name and number." He pulled a slip of paper from his jacket pocket. "I'm pretty sure she'd be interested."

"Great. Tell me about her."

A slight frown puckered his brow. "She's the murdered woman's niece." He gave Rachel a searching look. "Would that bother you?"

"Of course not."

"And she's Melungeon, from Rocky Branch District. How do you feel about that?"

Rachel's mouth fell open. "Is that a serious question? I realize you don't know me very well, but—"

"Okay, okay." He held up a hand to stop her. "Sorry, but I've learned you never can tell about people. Sometimes you get an unpleasant surprise."

He was right about that, unfortunately. "Let me give you a pleasant one. Her being Melungeon has nothing to do with anything. I just want somebody who's willing to work."

What had happened to Tom that made him assume people were biased until proven otherwise? Rachel had always believed the opposite, but she was lily-white, so how could she know what discrimination felt like? An awful thought occurred to her: Did Tom believe she'd turned down his invitations because his skin was darker than hers? How could she clear that up without embarrassing him? She couldn't very well say, *Oh, no, I rejected you for other reasons.*

"Tell me about her," she said.

He described a shy girl named Holly Turner who loved animals and had some experience with injured and orphaned wildlife. "She's been working at a diner that's a drug market, and I'd like to see her get out of there."

Rachel tensed, her hands curling into fists in the pockets of her lab coat.

"The diner's owned by a woman called Rose Shackleford," Tom went on, "but Rose's cousin Troy runs the drug business in this county, and he sells out of the diner. He also happens to be the prime suspect in the Pauline McClure case. Has been from the beginning."

"Is there any chance this girl's a drug user?" Rachel asked. "Or sells drugs? If there is, then I—"

"I'd never steer you toward somebody like that. Even if I didn't know what happened to you, I wouldn't do it."

She looked into his eyes until the depth of compassion she saw there became unbearable. Nodding, she said, "I know you wouldn't."

"But she might go down that road someday if she doesn't get out of there. She seems smart, but kids who start out poor don't have much chance to get ahead if they stay around here. If they've got Melungeon blood and dark skin, that's another strike against them." He raked his fingers through his hair, his eyes burning. "It's no wonder a lot of them get hooked on drugs. The dealers get them when they're young, and that's it, their lives are over. It's damned frustrating because I can't do a thing about it."

This passionate anger was a side of Tom that Rachel hadn't seen before, and one she couldn't help admiring. She'd always been a sucker for crusaders. "You can help one person at a time, which is what you're doing now. I'd be happy to talk to Holly Turner about a job. I'll call her before I go home."

Rachel held out her hand for the slip of paper, but Tom hesitated, frowning at the name and number. "Why don't I find out a little more about her first, make sure she's what she seems to be? If you've got doubts about her."

"You took care of my doubts." Rachel snatched the paper from his fingers. "You can't give me a speech like the one I just heard, then back off."

"Okay, but I have to warn you, the grandmother's a problem. She doesn't like Holly talking to strangers."

Billy Bob barked and Tom opened the door to let him in. Rachel attached the leash and handed it to Tom. "Shannon has your bill at the desk. I need to lock up for the night back here. I'll let you know if things work out with the girl."

Instead of saying goodbye and leaving, Tom got the look on his face that usually preceded an invitation. Rachel hated this, hated struggling to say no in a firm but pleasant way. It was harder every time.

But all he said was, "Can you make it home okay in the snow?"

"Oh, sure." *So much for my irresistible charms,* Rachel chided herself, but she was relieved. "My Range Rover can go anywhere. Good night, Tom."

"I'll see you again soon."

His smile brought a flush of warmth to her cheeks. The door swung shut behind him and his dog, and Rachel heard his footsteps recede up the hall.

"Don't push me," she whispered. "Please." Despite the front Tom put up, she felt his loneliness and pain when she was near him. She'd heard about the freak road accident that killed most of his family, leaving only Tom and his small nephew alive. Rachel could imagine the grief and survivor's guilt that made him quit his job as a homicide detective with the Richmond Police Department and move back home to be part of his nephew's life as the boy grew up. She'd heard that Tom left behind a fiancée who didn't want to live in the mountains.

More than once Rachel had wondered if Tom was attracted to her because he thought they were alike—two wounded people who could lean on each other. The thought made her cringe. She couldn't let herself get close to his grief when she was struggling to live with her own problems.

As she flipped the deadbolt into place on the back door, she thought about Perry Nelson plotting his revenge on her, she thought of Luke and the life she'd left behind, and she felt the familiar sinking, the descent from the light into a darker place. So much of her energy went into staying up, sailing far above the reality of her life. If she relaxed her guard for a second, she crashed like a broken kite.

Chapter Five

Rachel didn't want to wait till she got home to call Michelle and risk her sister hearing about Nelson's petition on the radio or TV. With the animal hospital closed for the day, she settled at her desk and punched in Michelle's home number in Bethesda.

"Oh, hi!" Michelle said when she heard Rachel's voice. "I was just about to call you and give you our good news. Well, Kevin's news, but of course it affects both of us."

"Oh? What's that?" Michelle sounded happy, exuberant, and Rachel grabbed the chance to put off telling her about Nelson a bit longer.

"Kevin's made partner," Michelle said. "Faster than any other associate in the firm ever has. Isn't that great?"

"That's wonderful, Mish. Give him my congratulations." Kevin Watters, Michelle's husband of two years, was a sweet, down-to-earth guy who adored her, and Rachel would always be grateful to him for helping Michelle through the awful months after their mother's death. She kept hoping they would have a child, one with Michelle's blond, blue-eyed beauty and Kevin's generous disposition, but Michelle preferred to devote her nurturing to the autistic children she worked with as a psychologist.

"We're going out to celebrate," Michelle said. "I'm sorry I don't have time to talk long. We'll catch up tomorrow, okay?"

"Mish, wait. I need to tell you something."

"What?" Michelle's voice instantly took on a wary edge. "Is something wrong?"

"I hate to bring this up and spoil your good mood." *Get it over with.* "Perry Nelson's asking the judge to let him spend time at home with his parents. Leslie Ryan's trying to block it."

Rachel waited for an eruption of anger, fear, outrage, but Michelle was silent. Rachel heard her draw a breath. When she spoke at last, she sounded icily calm. "No judge in his right mind will let that happen. But if it does—well, thank god you're not in McLean anymore. After his mother attacked you in the Safeway—"

"She didn't attack me, Mish."

"Not physically, but for heaven's sake, screaming at you in public about ruining her baby boy's life— You couldn't be sure she *wouldn't* end up assaulting you someday. And you'd never be safe for a second if he got out. You made the right decision, getting away from McLean and the Nelsons and… and everything else."

Everything else. The memories. Reminders of Mother everywhere she looked. And, of course, Michelle included Luke among the things best left behind. "To tell you the truth," Rachel said, "I'm not always sure I made the right choice. I loved spending Christmas with you and Kevin, and I've been wanting to see you again ever since. But we're so far apart."

"I miss you too. I miss you a lot, and I wish we could just drive around the Beltway and see each other anytime we want to. But you went through a traumatic experience, Perry Nelson *shot* you, and you were in a bad relationship that was just making matters worse. You needed to make a clean break and start fresh. You know that's the truth, Rachel. Regrets are to be expected, but I'm sure that most of the time you realize you did what was best for you."

Sometimes Michelle sounded so much like their mother that Rachel could hardly bear to listen to her. Bit by bit, she had perfected that *I'm always right and you have to be sensible and listen to me* routine.

"Well, anyway," Rachel said, trying to sound upbeat, "I'm sure everything's going to be fine. Leslie can handle Nelson. I'll let you go and get ready for your big celebration. Give Kevin my congratulations and a kiss for me, okay?"

She hung up, feeling absurdly bereft. Why had she believed that Michelle would need reassurance and calming? Michelle, who had once been so dependent on Rachel, no longer seemed to need anything from her, not even her presence nearby. *My little sister. My shadow.* She had a sudden image of the two of them as children, Rachel racing through the fresh snow with Michelle on her heels, slipping and sliding and squealing, and the happy memory pierced her with sadness.

Oh, stop it. Be glad she's finally grown up. She certainly took her time about it.

Resolutely turning her mind to other things, Rachel pulled the scrap of paper Tom had given her from her lab coat pocket and called Holly Turner.

The girl answered the phone. Rachel introduced herself, mentioned Tom's recommendation, and asked if Holly would like to apply for a job. This met with silence from the other end of the line.

"Well," Rachel said, "if you're not interested—"

"You offerin' me a job in town?" The girl sounded amazed.

"Come see me and we'll talk about it."

"I don't have a car," Holly said, dispirited now. "I can't drive, anyway."

"Oh." How would the girl get to work and back every day? Mason County didn't have bus service. Rachel was about to make an excuse to end the conversation when Holly spoke up.

"I really, really want to talk about the job. I could meet you at Rose's diner. I'm workin' there tomorrow, and I always go early so I can eat lunch before I start work."

The diner where drugs were sold. No. She couldn't go there. Rachel didn't even want to brush up against drugs, the people who sold them, the people who used them. Her fist closed around the paper that held Holly's name and number, crumpling it into a ball.

When Rachel didn't answer, Holly said, "I know I'm puttin' you out, askin' you to drive over here. But workin' at the animal hospital, that'd be like a dream come true. And I'm willin' to do anything that needs doin'."

Rachel remembered saying something similar to a vet when she'd begged for a part-time job at the age of sixteen. Turning down Holly without interviewing her would be heartless. She loosened the crumpled paper, spread it smooth. The diner couldn't be all that bad in broad daylight. Could it? "I can get away at lunchtime tomorrow."

"That'll be just perfect!"

Rachel jotted down directions. Holly was describing the diner when Rachel heard a woman's shrill voice in the background. "Who you talkin' to?"

"Nobody, Gran—"

"Don't lie to me! I heard you plottin' somethin'. Give me that phone."

What on earth? Rachel listened intently, trying to make sense of what was happening. A scuffle, scratchy noises. Were they fighting over the receiver?

The line went dead.

"Good grief," Rachel muttered as she hung up. The girl was a young adult, but she couldn't speak freely on the telephone. It was outrageous. Yet Holly's grandmother apparently didn't object to her working where drugs were sold. That didn't make sense to Rachel.

Would the woman try to stop Holly from keeping the interview appointment? If Holly did show up, and she wanted the job, she could have it. Tom was right. This girl needed help.

Seven-year-old Simon barreled out the front door of his grandparents' house and streaked across the lawn to the driveway. "Tom! Tom, it's snowing!"

Tom caught his nephew and swung him around. "Yeah, champ, I kinda noticed that. I guess you'll have to haul out the sled in the morning, huh?"

"You think we'll have enough?" Simon leaned back in Tom's arms. In the glow of the porch light, the boy's small face looked serious, worried. Snowflakes stuck to his spiky black hair. "Grandma says I can't go on the sled if it's just a little bit."

Tom glanced over Simon's shoulder to the front porch of the rambling Victorian house, where Darla Duncan, the boy's grandmother, stood with arms crossed. Tall and thin, with shoulder-length brown hair, she wore her usual jeans and shirt. When Tom waved she didn't respond with so much as a smile.

"Simon," she called, "come back in the house. You don't even have a coat on."

Tom set Simon down and let Billy Bob out of the cruiser. Boy and dog ran to the house together, laughing and barking.

By the time Tom walked into the house and Darla could close the door against the cold, her stern expression had deteriorated into peevishness. "You're early," she said. "Supper won't be ready for a while and Grady's not home yet."

Her husband, Grady Duncan, was a deputy and had been a friend to Tom's father. Tom tried to see his nephew at least briefly every day, but he usually came when Grady was around to act as a buffer between him and Darla.

"I can't stay for supper, I'm afraid." Tom wiped his boots thoroughly on the mud rug. God forbid he should leave tracks on Darla's shining floors.

Simon grabbed Tom's hand and wailed, "But you promised!"

"Yeah, I know." Tom stooped so they were face to face. "But I have to do something important at work. Hey, don't you see enough of me? You ought to be sick and tired of me hanging around so much."

"No!" Simon locked his arms around Tom's neck and clung to him. "I wish you and Billy Bob could come live with us."

Tom caught Darla's sour look. Yeah, she'd love that.

"Listen, champ," Tom said, gently pushing the boy away, "after I get this problem at work taken care of, you can bring your sled out to my farm and ride the biggest hill on the place. Okay?"

Simon nodded, but he was trying hard to hang onto his sulk.

"Billy Bob can stay and visit for a while." Tom glanced up at Darla. "If that's okay. I'll pick him up before you go to bed."

"Yeah!" Simon cried. He spun around and hugged Billy Bob. The dog snorted.

"Sure," Darla said with a shrug. "He's no trouble. Let him stay the night."

"Naw, he likes to be at home." The truth was, Tom hated being alone in the farmhouse where he'd grown up. The bulldog he'd inherited from his father brought a little life and noise to the place. "Don't run him ragged, okay?" he told his nephew. "Now give me another hug before I go."

Simon threw himself into Tom's arms again with the ferocity he gave to every action. His father, Tom's older brother Chris, had been that way. All out, nothing held back, wringing the last drop of sensation from every experience. Reckless, in Darla's view. Tom smoothed down Simon's hair, letting his hand rest for a second on the back of the boy's head where he could feel the bony bump at the base of the skull.

As Tom got to his feet, Darla said, "Grady called and told me about y'all finding that Melungeon woman."

In her mouth *Melungeon* sounded like a dirty word. Tom wished to God she'd try harder to hide her prejudice in front of Simon. If she had her way, the boy would never know he had Melungeon blood, but that wasn't possible in Mason County, so she would raise him to be ashamed of that part of his history.

"Right. I need to go over the case file tonight."

"You know," Darla said, nodding with satisfaction, "sometimes people really do end up exactly the way they deserve to."

He headed for the door without bothering to answer. In addition to being Melungeon, Pauline McClure had no doubt fallen short of Darla's strict standards of conduct and accountability. Just as Tom had. He could never be around her without feeling the urge to apologize.

I'm sorry I was driving that night.
I'm sorry your daughter died.
I'm sorry I lived.

Chapter Six

Tom sped past rolling hills dusted with snow and fields where horses stood hoof-deep in mud. He crossed into a neighboring county to get on the interstate to Northern Virginia.

In the Explorer's passenger seat, Brandon was uncharacteristically quiet, drumming his fingers on his knees and staring out the window. Tom used the silence to work out his approach to Mary Lee McClure Scott. Against Tom's strong objection, the sheriff had revealed every detail of the previous day's discoveries to the Mason County lawyer who still represented Mary Lee, and the attorney had passed the information to his client. Tom was left with no surprises to provoke a reaction from her, and she'd had plenty of time to compose herself for this morning's interview. He'd have to rely on close observation and hope that if she was hiding something he would sense it.

Eventually Brandon said, "What do you think the chances are Dr. Goddard'll give Holly a job?"

So the girl was still on Brandon's mind. He'd chattered non-stop about her yesterday during the drive back from Mrs. Turner's house. "Listen, Bran, I can't tell you what to do, but—for God's sake, Debbie's planning your wedding."

Glancing at Brandon, Tom saw the young deputy's cheeks redden. Brandon turned back to the window and let the advice go unanswered. Tom's misgivings about putting Rachel in touch with Holly hardened into conviction. Bringing the girl to town was a bad idea, for a lot of reasons.

Gradually the countryside gave way to the urbanized landscape of Fairfax County, across the Potomac from Maryland and Washington, D.C. Office buildings rose higher, acres of townhouse developments appeared, traffic clotted and slowed. But when they left the busy roads and drove through Mary Lee's McLean neighborhood, Tom felt as if he were back on the rural lanes of Mason County. The illusion vanished with his first glimpse of the enormous houses among the trees. Mason County had a few wealthy residents. It didn't have entire neighborhoods filled with mansions.

Rachel had grown up in McLean, maybe in one of these houses. For the first time, Tom wondered if the differences between them might be too great to overcome.

The Scott property was identified only by brass numbers affixed to the roadside mailbox. Tom followed the long driveway around a curve before the house came into view. Constructed of soft pink brick, designed like an overgrown French manor house complete with a tower, it sprawled in every direction. Enough space, Tom thought, to shelter twenty families.

Brandon whistled.

"Yeah," Tom said. "Nice place."

"Not the house. *That.*" Brandon hooked a thumb toward a sleek red Jaguar in the parking circle.

Tom was more attracted to the shiny green SUV next to the sports car. By comparison, the old Explorer looked pitiful.

As they climbed out, the front door of the house opened and a woman dressed in slacks and a sweater emerged with two small children who were bundled up against the cold. With her delicate figure, her long black hair and olive complexion, the woman had the unmistakable look of a Turner.

She halted on the steps when she caught sight of the deputies, and in a move that looked instinctive, pulled the children to her as if protecting them from a threat.

"Good morning," Tom called. When he reached the bottom of the steps and saw her up close, he realized Mary Lee wasn't as beautiful as her mother had been. Still, he doubted many men could pass her without sneaking a second glance. "I'm Tom Bridger. We talked on the phone. This is Deputy Connelly."

Tom smiled at the children, and they rewarded his attention with gap-toothed grins. The boy and girl looked the same age, around four. Twins, probably. The Turner traits showed through strongly in yet another generation—black hair, blue eyes, and attractive, fine-boned faces that bore an unmistakable resemblance to Mary Lee.

"I'll be with you in a minute," she said, her voice toneless. "Mark and Lisa are just leaving for a friend's birthday party."

"Pizza for lunch!" the boy announced. When Tom laughed, both children giggled.

The door opened again and a Hispanic woman rushed out, tugging on a coat over jeans and a sweater. Mary Lee pulled a ring of keys from a pocket and dropped them into the other woman's hand. "Make sure they're both buckled in properly. And don't let them eat too much cake."

"Yes, ma'am. I take best care." The woman steered the kids toward the SUV.

"Please come in," Mary Lee said to Tom and Brandon.

They trailed her across an expansive foyer, their boots slapping the black and gold marble floor, and entered the biggest living room Tom had ever seen. A grand piano at one end, French doors leading to a patio at the other end, three formal seating areas in between—how did a family with young kids do any ordinary living in this showplace?

Mary Lee led them to two yellow sofas that faced each other in front of a carved marble fireplace. Tom and Brandon waited for an invitation to sit, but none came. Turning her wedding ring around and around on her finger, Mary Lee stared into space as if she were not quite present, not fully aware of the two men in the room.

"Are you all right?" Tom asked.

She started and drew a deep breath. "I'm sorry. I'm not functioning very well today. Please make yourselves comfortable. I'll bring in some coffee."

"Thank you, but—"

"I'll only be a minute," she said on her way out.

Tom figured this would be his only chance to snoop, so he'd better take advantage of it while it lasted. He headed across the oriental carpet toward a table covered with photos in silver frames. No pictures of Mary Lee's parents. Her children appeared in candid snapshots, but the largest photo was a formal portrait of Mary Lee, her son and daughter, and a man Tom assumed was her husband. From his weathered face and gray-streaked dark hair, Tom estimated he was at least twenty years Mary Lee's senior.

Brandon came up beside Tom. "She married an older guy, like her mom did."

Tom heard Mary Lee's footsteps in the foyer. "Shh."

A second later she appeared, carrying a silver tray. Her gaze flicked from the deputies to the photos they'd been examining, but she said nothing.

Tom and Brandon sat on one sofa while Mary Lee sat across from them. She insisted they remove their wool uniform jackets, offered to light a fire, dispensed coffee according to their preferences, but she never allowed her eyes to meet theirs.

Tom sipped and swallowed before he asked, "Is your husband at home?"

"No. He's out of town on business. I'd rather wait till he gets back to make arrangements." Tears came to her eyes, and she blinked rapidly. Her blue irises were ringed with dark gray.

"You have plenty of time. I'm afraid your mother's remains won't be released for a while yet."

"How are you going to investigate something that happened so long ago?" Mary Lee twisted her wedding ring and frowned at some point beyond Tom's head. "Doesn't it get more difficult as time goes by?"

"Difficult, but not impossible." Tom placed his cup on the tray and pulled a notebook and pen from his shirt pocket. "You've had a long time to think about what might have happened to your mother—"

"I don't think about it." Instantly she seemed to regret her harsh tone. Squeezing her eyes shut, she drew a shuddering breath. Tom waited. When she spoke again her voice was quiet. "I *try* not to think about it. It's always there, in the back of my mind, but I've made a new life, I have a husband and children. I can't dwell on the past."

"You want us to catch your mother's killer, don't you?"

"Of course." She struggled to keep her composure, but tears welled in her eyes and spilled down her cheeks. With a trembling hand, she batted them away. "Oh, God. This is going to blow up out of control. When the papers and TV find out that my mother's skeleton— They'll jump right on it, because of who my husband is. They'll pry and probe—" Her voice fell to a whisper. "He's going to hate it."

Jesus Christ, was all this emotion generated by a fear of embarrassing her husband? Tom glanced at Brandon, who didn't try to hide his disgust. "The press can be pretty unpleasant sometimes," Tom said, hoping he was doing a better job of concealing his own reaction. "But we have to reopen the case, not only for your mother, but also for the other victim."

Mary Lee's gaze met his, darted away. "How do you know there's even a connection between my mother and the other... person?"

"We don't know for sure. But when we find two skeletons close together in a spot that's inaccessible except by foot, common sense tells us to look for a connection. Was anybody visiting your mother around that time?"

"I don't think so. I can't imagine who it could be."

"Where were you at the time your mother disappeared?" Late the night before, Tom had read summations of his father's talks with Mary Lee, but he wanted to hear the answer in her own words.

"I'd already left for college in California."

"Did you spend the summer at home?"

"No. I was with a tour in Europe. I went home for a few days before I left again."

"You didn't spend much time with your mother, did you?"

"It didn't matter. We were close. We talked on the phone all the time." Tears sprang up in her eyes again. "I loved her very much."

"How did you feel about being sent to boarding school in Connecticut after your father died? You were, what, twelve?"

Tom expected at least a spark of anger, but she seemed to take his inference in stride. "I didn't have any simmering resentment toward my mother. She sent me away to protect me."

"From what?"

"From—" She caught herself, seemed to pull back from a perilous subject. After a second she went on, "Life at home wasn't exactly peaceful after my father died."

"How so?"

"I'm sure you know my father's will was challenged." Her voice betrayed a slight edge of impatience.

Tom wrote *Fight over will* on his notepad. "After your mother disappeared, the McClures tried to keep you from inheriting, right?"

"No one inherited anything for seven years, until she was declared dead. I had a trust fund left by my father, so I would have been very well-off even if I hadn't inherited from my mother."

If she was trying to convince him she had no motive to kill her mother, Tom wasn't impressed. Plenty of people who had money would kill to get more.

"Do you think any of the McClures hated your mother enough to want her dead?"

A slight tremor ran through her body. "Please don't ask me to accuse someone of murder."

"But would you say the McClures hated your mother?"

"Not all of them. Robert was the one who tried to break my father's will. Ed—my father's youngest brother—was very good to my mother. He…" She seemed to search for the right words. "…befriended her."

"Oh? Was your mother friendly with Ed McClure's wife, too?"

Mary Lee's gaze jumped to his for a second, then fastened on the silver coffee pot between them. She moistened her lips before answering. "All I know is that my mother and Ed McClure were friends. They had things in common."

"Such as?"

"A love of nature. A way of looking at the world. I can't tell you anything more."

Tom scribbled *P affair w/ Ed Mc?* in his notebook, then moved on. "What kind of work did Troy Shackleford and Rudy O'Dell do for your mother?"

"Mr. O'Dell did yard work and little chores. Mr. Shackleford did electrical work and plumbing. They weren't full-time employees."

"Did she ever quarrel with either of them?"

"I'll tell you the same thing I told your father. I can't imagine any reason why they'd harm her."

Tom wrote in his notebook: *Background P/Sh/O'D—how personal?* He moved on to another subject. "Will you be coming to Mason County anytime soon?"

"Why would I?"

The cool question stopped him for a second. "To see your grandmother. Your other relatives. They've all suffered a loss."

"I doubt I could be any comfort to them."

"Do you keep in touch?"

She shrugged. "I send Christmas cards. If they ever need anything, all they have to do is let me know."

Sometime recently, he'd bet, Mrs. Turner had let Mary Lee know she needed the big new refrigerator and range that looked so out of place in her tiny kitchen. "Why would your grand-mother tell me she never sees you or hears from you?"

Mary Lee showed no surprise at the question. "It's true she doesn't see me. I haven't been back to Mason County since my mother disappeared."

"She told me she didn't even know where you were living."

A faint humorless smile touched her lips, disappeared. "My grandmother believes the less she shares with outsiders, the better. She takes being Melungeon very seriously, and she thinks it makes us vulnerable. But of course it means nothing in today's world."

"Maybe not in the world outside the mountains. Believe me, it still means something in Mason County."

This brought a sharp look from her, full of defiant anger and outraged superiority. "Thank you for correcting me," she said, her voice as cold as the winter day.

Tom didn't believe for a minute that Mary Lee was blissfully ignorant of the bias against Melungeons that still existed in Mason County. But, being rich and half McClure and well out of it, she could afford to look down on her poor relations. He couldn't stop himself from goading her. "Aren't you interested in your heritage?"

Her expression was a cross between amusement and a sneer. "What heritage? Melungeons don't have a language or folklore. Nobody even knows where the original Melungeons came from. All those people who make a big production of being Melungeon, starting web sites and holding meetings—they're very sad, in my opinion. They should be happy to blend in, instead of trying to set themselves apart."

"Is it a bad thing for people—especially young people, like your cousin Holly—to be proud of their history instead of ashamed of it?"

Her blue eyes sparked with fury. "I know you have Melungeon blood. I shouldn't have to remind you that Melungeons used to be classified as colored. They couldn't vote, they couldn't testify in court, they couldn't go to school with white children, they couldn't marry whites and pollute the Caucasian bloodlines. What part of that do you take pride in?"

Now she was making Tom mad, but he tried to keep his tone mild. "For somebody who's not interested, you know a lot about Melungeon history."

"I've made my opinion clear. I don't want to discuss it anymore." To Tom's surprise, her expression shifted, became uncertain, almost wary. "You mentioned Holly. Have you been talking to her?"

"I met her last night, but I didn't have much chance to talk to her. I'll get to that sometime soon."

"Why? She was only a child when my mother disappeared. I wish you wouldn't bother her."

Mary Lee sounded a little too insistent, and Tom's antennae popped up. This was the second member of the family who didn't want him asking Holly questions. "I'll do whatever I have to," he said. "This is a murder investigation."

Mary Lee drew a deep breath. "Is there anything else I can help you with?"

"Yeah, I've been wondering why you keep your mother's house in Mason County, if you never visit."

"I'll sell it someday, I suppose, but I haven't been able to bring myself to do it yet. My mother loved it so much, because she grew up with so little."

He could accept that. Tom kept his parents' property even though he'd be better off if he sold it and bought a smaller house closer to town. Owning land had been his father's proudest achievement.

"I'd like to go inside the house," Tom said. "Does your lawyer in Mountainview have the keys?"

Mary Lee frowned, but said, "I suppose that'll be all right. I'll make sure you get the keys."

"Thanks." He wrote *keys* in his notebook. "That's all for now. I'm sure I'll have more questions later on."

"Will you keep me up to date on what's happening?"

"I'll let you know about any important developments."

"Thank you." She almost smiled. "Your father was very good about calling me. Even after everybody else lost interest in trying to find my mother."

"You kept in touch with my father?"

"He called me every few months, even if he didn't have any news. The last time I heard from him was the week the court declared my mother legally dead. The same week he died."

Tom hadn't known his father was talking to Pauline's daughter regularly. But a cop staying in contact with a victim's family wasn't unusual while a case remained unsolved. Why did he feel so shaken by the thought? What did it matter?

He stared down at his notebook, with its list of unanswered questions to follow up on. Without realizing he was doing it, he'd added one word to the end of the list: *Dad?*

Chapter Seven

Rachel rounded a curve and the Wild Mountain Rose Diner appeared through the rain and mist, an oblong wooden building crouched against a mountain. She hadn't seen another structure for the last two miles. She approached uneasily, Tom's words blaring in her head. Drug dealers, a possible killer—he'd made all of Rocky Branch District, and this little diner in particular, sound alien and dangerous.

A strip of pavement in front served for parking. Trucks and cars had churned unplowed snow into filthy slush, and the rain that had started an hour before was washing the whole mess into a drainage ditch. Rachel pulled into one of the few remaining spots.

Outside the diner's door, a girl with long black hair huddled in the shelter of the overhanging roof. Rachel popped open her umbrella and jogged to the entrance. "Hi, are you Holly?"

"I sure am. You Dr. Goddard?"

"Yes. I'm sorry I'm late. I had an emergency." The girl wore a shabby brown coat with faded jeans and sneakers, but she was gorgeous, a flower blooming in a trash heap. What a smile, and those cornflower blue eyes were astonishing with her dark hair and olive complexion. Rachel shook rain off her umbrella and folded it. "Why didn't you wait inside? You must be freezing."

"Oh, I don't mind." Holly cast a nervous glance at the door.

"Let's get out of the rain."

"Well, uh, maybe we oughta talk out here. So nobody'll interrupt us, you know?"

Why had she asked Rachel to come here if she didn't want to take her inside? Maybe, Rachel thought, she should get this over with right now, let the girl down as gently as she could. Then Holly shivered and wrapped her arms around her body.

"You need to warm up," Rachel said. "Come on." She pushed the door open and walked in, leaving Holly no choice but to follow.

The odor of over-spiced chili hit Rachel in the face and made her throat close up with nausea. A haze of cigarette smoke burned her eyes and nose, and "Take This Job and Shove It" roared out of the jukebox at a volume that made her ears ring.

Aside from the fat middle-aged woman behind the counter—Rose?—Rachel and Holly were the only females in the place. Heads turned as they passed a dozen men on stools. One called out, "Hey, Holly, ain't you gonna introduce us to your friend?"

Holly kept her chin high and her eyes straight ahead. Rachel tried to ignore the men, but they set off a twinge of fear inside her. They'd been drinking a while, if the number of empty beer bottles on the counter was an indication.

Holly and Rachel slid into a booth in the rear corner, next to the plate glass window. As they wriggled free of their coats, the jukebox nearly drowned out Holly's whisper. "Those guys're all out of work, and they don't have nothin' better to do than hang out here and pester people."

"They don't bother me," Rachel lied. With the edge of one hand, she brushed crumbs into a small pile on the tabletop, then shoved them toward a patch of dried catsup. The general reek and dirty feel of the place reminded her of a restaurant in Mexico where she and Luke had eaten. Mice had run across their feet to get to the garbage can.

The woman who'd been working behind the counter plodded over. An enormous green tent of a dress draped her short body from neck to ankles. Straight black hair, chopped off at ear level, emphasized puffy cheeks and protruding eyes. The image of a huge toad crossed Rachel's mind, and she chided herself for the uncharitable comparison.

"Hey, Rose," Holly mumbled. She looked stiff with tension, as if she were waiting for something awful to happen.

Rose turned slitted eyes on Rachel. "Ain't seen you in here before."

"No. First time." And the last. Every man in the place was staring at her. Strangers seldom ventured into the diner, she gathered, and when they did they weren't welcome. She smiled at Rose, hoping to ingratiate herself, but the woman's cold, flat eyes didn't warm up.

"Dr. Goddard," Holly said, "you ought to try one of Rose's chili cheeseburgers. That's what I'm havin'. They're out of this world."

If they were made with the stuff she was smelling, Rachel would give them a pass. And asking for a salad was probably pointless. "I'm really not hungry. Just coffee, please. Black."

From Rose's sour expression, Rachel knew the woman correctly read criticism into her lack of appetite. "All right then." Instead of leaving, Rose continued to examine Rachel suspiciously. "You a doctor?"

"A veterinarian. I'm the new owner of Mountainview Animal Hospital."

"Hunh," Rose grunted. She threw Holly a look that seemed freighted with meaning and walked off, her bulk rolling from leg to leg.

Holly leaned an elbow on the table, propped her chin in her hand, and said, "You've got the most perfect job. You get to help animals, and you make a livin' at it, too." As she spoke, her gaze shifted toward the men at the counter.

What on earth did Holly expect the men at the counter to do? Rachel told herself to relax, stay cool, but she felt the muscles in the back of her neck tightening. "Captain Bridger told me you're very good with animals."

"Well, I guess I like animals a lot better'n people." As soon as the words were out, Holly grimaced. "Grandma tells me I oughtn't to say stuff like that. People'll think I'm weird."

Rachel smiled. "I feel the same way most of the time. You always know where you stand with animals."

"That's exactly right." For a second Holly lost her watchful expression and regarded Rachel with the wonderment of someone who'd found a soulmate. "Grandma thinks so too, but she wouldn't ever say it out loud. She fusses about her old dogs and cats like they're babies."

"She must be happy you're thinking about working in an animal hospital."

Holly's face slammed shut like a door. When she spoke, her voice was so low Rachel barely heard. "I haven't figured out how to tell her yet."

Rachel remembered the shrill, demanding voice that had ended their phone conversation. "Well. Tell me about yourself. You're out of school, aren't you? Did you graduate?"

"Yes, ma'am, last June." Holly rushed on, "I'm a real hard worker, and I learn fast. I'll do anything. I mean, if you decide to give me the job."

What a change she was from the sulky young applicants Rachel had interviewed during the past few months. "You'd have to hold animals when they're being treated, walk the dogs, do some cleaning. I'm afraid the pay would only be minimum wage to start."

"Gosh, any kind of real pay sounds great to me. I just work for tips here. I'm lucky if I make twenty dollars a week."

Rachel's mouth dropped open. Good grief. Hadn't slavery been outlawed?

Before Rachel could say anything, Rose returned, placed Holly's meal on the table, then plopped a mug in front of Rachel with enough force to splatter coffee onto the table. Without a word, she turned and left.

"Thanks a lot," Rachel muttered, mopping up the spilled coffee with a paper napkin.

Holly bit into the cheeseburger. Chili leaked onto her fingers, but she didn't seem to notice. She stuffed two french fries into her mouth and gulped cola through a straw.

Watching, bemused, Rachel recalled Tom's warning about Holly's lack of polish. The girl had plenty of enthusiasm, though, and Rachel would take that over social graces any day.

The jukebox fell silent, and as if on cue, men rose from stools and shuffled toward the exit. When the door opened, a draft of cold air brushed the back of Rachel's neck.

She dared to look around, hoping the source of Holly's uneasiness had departed. A handsome, long-limbed young man with black hair remained at the counter, deep in muted conversation with Rose. As they talked, both of them stared at Rachel and Holly. The man caught Rachel's eye and flashed a wolfish grin.

She snapped her head around. "Who is he?" she whispered to Holly.

Holly answered quietly, "My cousin. Buddy Shackleford. His daddy and mine's brothers. I didn't think he'd be here this early. He must've come in to meet a… a customer."

Shackleford. Another member of the drug-dealing family. But Holly wasn't a Shackleford. "I thought your last name was Turner."

"It is. My daddy never married my mama." Blushing at this admission, Holly dragged a french fry through catsup and pushed the result into her mouth. She said while she chewed, "Captain Bridger's lookin' for my daddy. He worked for my Aunt Pauline. The police've always thought he killed her."

Oh, dear God. Holly's father was Troy Shackleford. Did Tom know? Rachel didn't believe his overdeveloped protective instincts would allow him to suggest that she hire the daughter of a murder suspect and drug boss. What was she going to do? She couldn't walk out on Holly, tell her the job wasn't available after all. The girl was sweet and eager to please, and she wanted the job so much.

"Hey, ladies."

The voice made Rachel jump. Buddy Shackleford ambled to their booth and grinned down at them. "Holly, you gonna introduce me to your pretty friend?"

Holly wiped chili from her hands with a paper napkin and didn't acknowledge him. He slid into the booth beside her, bumped her hip and forced her to move over. "Holly's downright rude, don't you think?" he asked Rachel. "I'm Buddy. What's your name?"

His gaze crawled over her and left her feeling slimy. She would not surrender so much as a scrap of herself to him. "Mary," she answered. She caught Holly's surprised look and quick smile before they vanished behind an expressionless mask.

Buddy chuckled, a nasty little sound. "Is that right? You got a last name?"

"Smith."

His eyes narrowed. "And where'd you come from, Mary Smith?"

"Somewhere else."

"Mary, Mary, quite contrary," he said in a mocking singsong. "I got to look out for my little cousin, you know? What do you want with Holly?"

"That's between her and me."

"Leave us alone, Buddy!" Holly pleaded.

He turned a murderous scowl on her. "Shut your fuckin' mouth till I say you can open it again."

Holly scooted into the corner of the booth, arms wrapped around her waist, head lowered.

Watching Holly cringe made Rachel want to hit him. This guy was in a league with Perry Nelson. Where did scum like that think they got the right to push other people around? "Look," she said, her hands curling into fists on the table, "we're not bothering you. And we didn't invite you to sit down."

Cold eyes bored into her. "I'm gonna ask you one more time. What do you want with Holly?"

"I've already answered you. That's between her and me."

A long moment passed. Rachel held his stare. When Buddy spoke, his voice was soft. "Well, Mary Mary from somewhere else, I think you just wore out your welcome. You're leavin' now." He slid from the booth and stood over her.

Holly sat rigid, her eyes huge.

Rachel looked up at him without wavering. "Holly and I haven't finished our conversation."

Buddy leaned one hand on the table, one on the back of the booth, and brought his face within inches of Rachel's. She got a blast of his beery breath when he said, "It's finished."

Before she could answer, he grabbed her arm and hauled her out of the booth and onto her feet. "Get your hands off me!" she cried.

He tossed her belongings at her and as she fumbled to catch her coat and purse, her umbrella clattered to the floor. Under his baleful gaze, she snatched it up and almost gave in to the impulse to bash him in the face with it. Only the sight of Holly, with both hands over her mouth and her eyes wide with terror, stopped her.

Buddy gripped Rachel's arm, spun her around and pushed. She tried to pull free, but he was bigger and stronger and he propelled her out the door. He shoved her into the rain, gave her one last malicious look, and stalked back inside.

"Damn it, damn it, damn it," she swore, dripping wet and furious that she'd let herself be manhandled, furious that he'd gotten the better of her, furious that a creepy thug and drug dealer like Buddy could decide what Holly did with her life. Feeling like an abject failure, she climbed into her Range Rover, slammed the door and locked it. Her shaking hand took forever to maneuver the key into the ignition.

A knock on the window made her gasp. But Holly stood there, not Buddy. He was nowhere in sight.

"Dr. Goddard, I'm sorry!" Holly called through the closed window. Rain plastered her black hair to her head and ran in rivulets down her cheeks and neck.

Rachel lowered the window halfway.

"I'm so sorry," Holly said. "I'm not like him. Really I'm not."

"I can see that, Holly. What's his problem? He doesn't even know me."

"That's just it. He don't like strangers comin' around." Holly gripped the top of the window glass with both hands. "Dr. Goddard, all I want in the world is to get away from here. You callin' me, it was like God answerin' my prayers. Please give me a chance, I'm beggin' you. Please let me work for you."

Rachel squeezed her eyes shut against sudden tears. Her head hurt. Her heart ached. She wanted nothing more than to whisk this girl away to a better life, free her from this dive and these people and everything they represented. But how could she make it work?

"Listen," she said. "I'll check around and find a place for you to live in town. Then it won't matter that you can't drive."

Holly nodded, but murmured, "My grandma's not gonna like that one bit."

"Do you want me to talk to her?"

"No!" The word burst out loud and urgent. Holly shot a glance at the diner before she said, "No, ma'am, please don't. I'll handle it. When do you want me to start work?"

"Whenever you're ready and I've found a place for you to live."

With the rain pouring down on her, Holly chewed her lip, her forehead creased by doubt. Rachel knew exactly what the girl was feeling, the hope and frustration swirling together, the fear that she wasn't strong enough to stand up for what she wanted. Rachel had spent most of her own young adulthood trying not to let that mix of emotions paralyze her as she tried to assert herself against an iron-willed mother.

"Look," she said, digging in her shoulder bag for a memo pad and pen, "I'll give you my numbers at work and at home. Call me when you're ready. I'll pick you up."

Holly nodded, her smile tentative, her eyes conveying more anxiety than excitement.

Rachel was about to hand the scrap of paper to Holly when Buddy Shackleford opened the door of the diner and stepped out. "He's watching," Rachel said. "Don't let him see you take this." Out of his sight, she folded the paper into her palm. She placed her hand over Holly's and they managed to transfer the note without exposing it.

"Thank you," Holly whispered. She hustled back to the diner.

Buddy made an elaborate show of sweeping open the door for Holly, but he didn't follow her. He strode to a black SUV nearby and climbed in. When Rachel started her Range Rover and backed out, he pulled onto the road behind her.

Her grip tightened on the steering wheel. All those miles of lonely road before she reached Mountainview. Isolated stretches where he could do anything without being seen.

Get hold of yourself, for pity's sake. She was being ridiculous, letting her imagination run away with her. He was mad at her, yes, but why on earth would he want to hurt her, risk getting in trouble with the police?

But she couldn't relax because he stayed right behind her, close enough that even in the rain she could make out his face in her rearview mirror. What the hell did he want? Was he so damned macho that he couldn't let a woman get away with talking back to him?

She kept trying to reach 911 on her cell phone, although she knew she would sound absurd when she reported that a man was driving behind her. She didn't get the chance, because the hills blocked the signal from the county's only cell tower near Mountainview.

Buddy was never more than a few yards behind her. When houses appeared along the road, widely spaced at first, then closely grouped to form neighborhoods, Rachel told herself she was safe now. The tension drained from her body and hot anger flooded back. She didn't have a speck of doubt that she'd be doing the right thing if she rescued Holly from her bullying cousin and that grandmother who sounded like a jailer.

He stayed behind her all the way into town, but stopped short of following her into the animal hospital's parking lot. As she stepped from the Range Rover into the rain, Buddy braked his vehicle on the street, powered down the passenger window, and leaned over so she could see him clearly. Rachel thought he was going to speak, but instead he fixed her with a threatening stare she would have found laughably melodramatic if it hadn't made her so damned mad.

She did something she'd never done before in her life. She threw up a hand and gave him the finger.

Chapter Eight

Tom rattled the nearly bare fax sheet and told the sheriff, "I was hoping they'd give us a little more than this."

Sheriff Willingham relaxed in his office chair, lacing his fingers over his belt buckle. "You know the lab's always backed up. We're damned lucky we got that much the same day we sent them the bones. Sit down, will you? You put me in mind of my wife's cat, the way you prowl around a room."

Tom dropped into a chair facing Willingham's desk and skimmed the brief report again. The first skull they'd found had officially been identified through dental records as Pauline McClure's. The wound to the parietal region could have been inflicted by the ax head found with the bones or by a similar object. On cursory examination, the other skull also appeared to be a woman's, and like Pauline's bones, it might have lain out in the open for years. The back of it was crushed, the probable cause of death. The report contained not a word about her age or ethnicity, the two pieces of information Tom most needed. Had she been Melungeon too? So much of the skull was missing that they couldn't check for an Anatolian bump.

"We could have a facial reconstruction done of the second woman," Tom said. "Then release a picture and see if anybody recognizes her."

"We don't have the budget for that kind of thing," Willingham said. "Let's ask the neighboring counties to check their old missing persons reports."

"If she died in Mason County, the chances are she lived here. Maybe nobody reported her disappearance because nobody realizes she's missing. She could've had a falling out with her family, or left her husband, and they think she's living a new life somewhere else. We should ask the public to call in if they know of anybody who hasn't been heard from since she left."

The sheriff nodded. "But don't tell them it has to be somebody who went missing ten years ago. Remember, we don't know if this second woman's body was put on the mountain the same time as Pauline's. Hell, we don't know she was *put* there at all. She could've wandered up there by herself, got lost, and died of exposure. Maybe a tree limb fell on her head. Maybe a bear did the damage."

Tom wanted to keep an open mind, but he was convinced they were looking at a double murder. The second woman's identity might give him a clue that would lead to the killer. But the logical thing to do was start with the known facts, the date Pauline disappeared and the way she died, and work from there.

He stood. "The rain's getting rid of most of the snow for us, so the State Police cadets should be able to search up there tomorrow." He was at the door, on his way out, when he paused. "By the way, how well did my dad know the McClures?"

Willingham shrugged. "About as well as anybody does, I guess. They seem to think pretty much everybody's beneath 'em. They never have been chummy with people like sheriff's deputies. Or sheriffs."

"How well did he know Pauline? He spent a lot of his time looking for her."

Willingham frowned at him. "They were in high school at the same time. That was about it, I guess. But you know what your dad was like. He wouldn't have stopped looking even if she'd been a perfect stranger."

Tom nodded. His father had never been able to put a case aside unfinished. He had to close them all. But had he ever dreamed how high a price he would pay in the end for his dedication to the job?

‹›‹›‹›

After faxing the bulletin and calling the newspaper, Tom walked down the hall from his office to the combination conference/interrogation/lunch room. Billy Bob, who'd spent the day in the doting care of Janet, the young dispatcher, was back at Tom's side.

The original case files had been in such chaos the night before that Tom hadn't learned much. He'd assigned Brandon to put them in order.

"Here's the interviews with Pauline's relatives, including her daughter," Brandon said, tapping a folder with his fingertips. He moved down the long table, pointing. "The McClures, Shackleford and O'Dell, the housekeeper, Pauline's neighbors and other acquaintances. Your dad's case notes are in this folder, reports on the physical evidence in this one."

"Good work. Let's get to it." Tom had already seen his nephew, Simon, that day—picked him up at school and drove him home—and he planned to spend the evening immersed in the records.

He turned his attention first to the bulging case notes folder. The stack of loose yellow sheets torn from legal pads was at least six inches thick. Page after page was covered with his father's familiar, angular handwriting, and the sight of it stirred a memory that had been buried for years in the back of Tom's mind.

He saw his mother, Anne, in the doorway of his dad's den at home. *The turkey's on the table, John. We need you to carve.* Her voice carried only the gentlest hint of reproach. His father's reply had sounded distracted, impatient. *I have to finish these notes. Y'all go on and eat. I'll be out shortly.* Tom's older brother Chris had ended up carving the Thanksgiving turkey, and the assembled relatives—mostly McGrails, from his mother's side—had poured on the false cheer, never mentioning the host's absence. Later, past midnight, Tom awoke to sounds he'd never heard before: his parents arguing in their bedroom across the hall. Not the kind of mild, bantering disagreement they sometimes had. Shouts and accusations. John was obsessed with Pauline McClure's disappearance, he was shutting out his family. Anne didn't understand his work, she wanted him to put minor things ahead of a woman's life and safety.

"Boss?" Brandon's voice interrupted Tom's thoughts. "Where do you want me to start?"

For a moment Tom remained caught up in the mixture of sadness and alarm he'd felt years before when he'd overheard his parents' quarrel. He shook off the memory. "Look at the physical evidence. See if anything was found at the house. We'll go see the place in the morning."

Tom began reading his father's notes.

Pauline McClure's part-time housekeeper, Lila Barker, had been the first to suspect something was wrong. After finding the house empty at a time when Pauline should have been there, and noting that Pauline's car was in the garage, Mrs. Barker reported her employer missing. Sheriff Willingham refused to authorize an investigation until forty-eight hours had passed. He cited the housekeeper's own statements as evidence that nothing criminal had occurred—she had found no damage or disturbance in the house, and Pauline's jewelry and cash were untouched.

At first John Bridger suspected kidnapping, but no ransom demand came. While waiting for the go-ahead to launch a full missing person investigation, John had called Pauline's nearest neighbors, a mile away on each side. They never visited her and couldn't remember the last time they'd seen her drive past. John also called Pauline's family and the McClures, none of whom had seen or heard from her.

A rap on the door broke Tom's concentration. Dennis Murray stepped in. "Hey, Tommy, somebody's out front asking for you." Dennis' brown eyebrows rose meaningfully above the wire rims of his glasses. "It's Shackleford."

"Well, what do you know." Tom closed the file and scraped back his chair. "I thought I'd have to hunt him down."

Three minutes later, Tom sat behind his office desk. Dennis ushered in a swarthy man dressed in jeans and a suede jacket.

When the man reached across the desk to shake hands, beads of rain dropped off the suede onto the legal pad in front of Tom. "Troy Shackleford. I figured you'd want to talk to me, so I thought I'd come on by."

"I appreciate it."

Shackleford settled in a chair, crossed an ankle over a knee, unzipped his jacket. Strands of gray streaked his wavy black hair, but his broad-shouldered body looked as fit and powerful as a much younger man's. He gestured at Billy Bob, who sat next to Tom's desk. "That your dad's old dog? He must be pretty long in the tooth."

"This is Billy Bob," Tom said. "You're probably thinking about Fang, my father's first bulldog."

Shackleford chuckled and nodded. "Fang. Yeah, that was his name. Everybody swore that dog could tell when somebody was up to no good. You couldn't tell a lie if Fang was in the room. Mean little devil. This one looks friendlier."

He leaned over and extended a hand to Billy Bob. The dog scrambled to his feet, growling. Shackleford jerked his hand back.

"Sit," Tom ordered, trying to hide his astonishment at Billy Bob's sudden vehemence. Noting how shaken up Shackleford looked, Tom decided to give Billy Bob an extra dog biscuit later.

This was the first time Tom had seen Shackleford, but he'd heard rumors about him for years. Shackleford drifted in and out of the county, had a Miami residence, and was the courier and ringleader of his family's drug business. Although Rose's diner was well-known as Mason County's drug bazaar, Sheriff Willingham argued that shutting it down might lead the Shacklefords to bring their business into the streets of Mountainview.

"So you've heard we found Mrs. McClure's remains," Tom said.

"Yeah. Poor Pauline." Shackleford made a clucking sound. If he felt the slightest nervousness about this interview, he didn't betray it in his posture or expression. "It's hard to think about her ending up that way."

"What did you imagine had happened to her?"

Shackleford shrugged. "I was hopin' she was alive some-where."

"Why would she leave without telling anybody, without taking her car or any clothes or money?"

"I never knew what to think. But I always figured the cops would find her, and darned if you didn't." One side of Shackleford's mouth lifted in a grin. "Even if it did take ten years."

Tom ripped the water-spotted top page from the legal pad, dropped it in the waste basket under the desk, and picked up a pen. "I need your address and phone number."

Shackleford gave information for a Miami residence. "I've got a little business of my own down there in the sunshine. Electrical work."

Yeah, right. "You knew Pauline all her life, didn't you?"

"I sure did."

"Did you date her when you were teenagers?"

Shackleford let loose a full-throated guffaw that went on a little too long. When his laugh subsided, he said, "I wasn't her type and she wasn't mine. I was wild, I liked girls who'd give me what I wanted, if you know what I mean. Pauline didn't let boys get away with anything. She knew what she was worth and she held herself back."

"What she was worth? You mean a rich husband?"

With amusement crinkling his eyes, Shackleford ran his tongue around in his cheek and slid his gaze along the wall behind Tom before he answered. "Yeah, when it comes down to it, I guess that is what I mean. She sure wasn't gonna settle for a boy from Rocky Branch District. She knew she could do better."

"So she married Adam McClure for his money?"

Shackleford raised his hands, palms out. "Oh, now, don't put words in my mouth. I don't know what went on between Pauline and her husband. I don't think I ever seen 'em together, 'cause he was always at work when I was there. She coulda been crazy about him for all I know."

"The McClures didn't welcome her into their family," Tom said.

"Can't help you there either. I wouldn't know how she got along with her in-laws."

Lies probably slithered off this man's tongue more naturally than the truth, and Tom wondered why Shackleford didn't try to divert suspicion from himself with embroidered tales about the McClures. On the other hand, Shackleford seemed savvy enough to realize that accusing others might make him look guilty. "Were you ever more than friendly with Pauline?"

"Nope. Just did my work and took my pay."

"You and Rudy O'Dell worked out there together a lot, didn't you? What kind of relationship did O'Dell have with Pauline?"

"Lord, that boy was plain crazy about her. He was just a kid, you know, and he thought she was a queen."

"Did he ever make a move on her?" If she'd rejected O'Dell's advances, that might have set off a murderous rage.

Shackleford shrugged. "If he did, I never heard about it."

"Where is O'Dell now?"

"Still livin' with his mama, last I heard. I never see him. Got no reason to." Shackleford sat forward with elbows on the chair arms, locked his fingers together and produced a look of frowning earnestness that was so phony it almost made Tom laugh. "Pauline disappearin' the way she did, it knocked Rudy for a loop. I don't think he's ever got over it."

"He sounds like a sensitive soul."

Shackleford laughed. "You know, Captain, the way you said that, kind of dry-like, you sounded just like your dad. You remind me of him a lot."

"You're not the first to say that."

"No, I don't imagine I am." In the next instant, Shackleford was on his feet and heading for a wall where half a dozen framed photos hung. Billy Bob growled again, and Shackleford gave the dog a wide berth.

"Look at the three of you. Father and sons, no mistakin' it." Shackleford tapped a picture of Tom in his Richmond PD uniform and his brother, Chris, and their father in deputies' uniforms.

Tom's mother had taken that picture seven years before, when he'd been a cop for a few months. He remembered the warm April day, the fallen blossoms of dogwoods and cherries dotting his parents' lawn. It seemed a lifetime ago.

Without looking around, Shackleford added, "I was real sorry to hear about your tragedy."

Yeah, I'll bet. Probably thought you were home free when Dad died. Tom said nothing. The sound of rain pelting the windows filled the silence.

Shackleford threw a glance over his shoulder. "Must be hard to live with, you comin' through okay and that little boy losin' his mama and daddy both. Especially since you happened to be behind the wheel."

Cheap shot, and an obvious attempt to get under Tom's skin. He was beginning to think he would come up against a lot of that in this investigation. His voice cool, Tom said, "My father always thought you had some reason to want Mrs. McClure dead."

Shackleford sauntered to his chair, avoiding Billy Bob. Instead of sitting, he gripped the back of the chair. "I was a suspect because I was around her. And your father couldn't find any evidence against nobody else. But I didn't have no reason to hurt her. Hell, after she went missin', I lost work. I had to relocate to make a livin'."

Tom looked down at the legal pad and darkened the dot on each *i* in Miami. "I'll need to talk to you again. Probably more than once. So stick around."

"Sure. I'm stayin' at my mother's house." Shackleford paused, then added, "Say, can I ask you a favor? You won't drag my daughter into all this, will you? She was just a little kid when it happened, no point gettin' her upset."

"Your daughter?" Tom said.

"Holly. Lives with her Grandma Turner."

"You're Holly's father?"

"Yeah. You didn't know that? Her mama's Jean—Pauline's baby sister. Anyway, I'd appreciate it if you didn't get Holly involved. No way she could know anything that'd help you. Well, if that's it, I'll take off. Get in touch if you need to."

When Shackleford was gone, Tom snapped his pencil in half and flung the pieces at the door. God damn it, why hadn't he trusted his own second thoughts about Holly? He had to stop Rachel before she brought his prime suspect's daughter into her business and her life.

Chapter Nine

Rachel stopped at the entrance to the McKendrick horse farm to collect her mail from one of the roadside boxes, then drove through the open gate and up the lane. The rain had stopped, and wisps of fog crept over the pavement. On the left, security flood lights illuminated Joanna McKendrick's two-story brick colonial, but the house's windows were dark. Joanna had gone to Kentucky to deliver one of her American Saddlebred horses to a buyer, and Rachel was surprised at how lonely she felt in her new friend's absence.

She drove past three more houses, where the farm manager and other employees lived. Warm lights in the windows and glimpsed movements of parents and children brought a stab of longing for the ordinary lives other people shared.

When she'd come to Mason County six months before, after the all-consuming business of prosecuting Perry Nelson had reached its devastating end, Rachel had craved solitude. She'd wanted to be left alone so she could sit all evening staring at the wall if she couldn't bring herself to do anything more. Cry if she needed to, without Luke hovering solicitously. But lately privacy had begun to feel like a prison of isolation, and what she craved was life, activity, the noise of other people.

Her rented cottage was a mile down the farm lane, beyond the stable and paddocks. When she pulled into her driveway, the downstairs lights were blazing because she always left them on when she went to work in the morning. She'd rather pay a bigger electricity bill than come back to a dark house at night.

She opened the door to a greeting from Frank, a black short-haired cat with blotchy white markings and one and a half ears. Her African gray parrot, Cicero, squawked, "Hello, Rachel! Hello, Rachel!" and flapped from atop his big cage in a corner to land on her shoulder. She petted Frank, let Cicero kiss her with his beak, and felt some of the loneliness ebb away.

Half an hour later, she was heating a small pot of vegetable soup on the stove when the telephone rang.

With the care that had become automatic to her, she checked her Caller ID monitor. The number on the display made her groan, not because it was unfamiliar but because she knew it all too well. Luke, calling from his townhouse, the house she'd shared with him for more than two years.

Torn between longing and dread, she let the phone ring four times. In the middle of the fifth ring, when voice mail was about to cut in, she snatched up the receiver. "Hello, Luke."

"Hey," he said. "How're you doing?" He sounded worried, as if he expected to find her in an emotional crisis.

Squeezing her eyes shut, Rachel clamped down on the riot of contradictory feelings he always stirred up in her. She pictured his blue eyes clouded with concern, his sandy hair messy because he'd raked his fingers through it. A squeak in the background told her he was in his home office, his lanky frame folded into the desk chair, swiveling back and forth the way he always did when he was nervous or distracted. That chair had been squeaking as long as Rachel could remember, but he was oblivious to it.

"I guess you've heard the news about Perry Nelson," she said.

"Just a minute ago, on the TV news. This is the craziest thing I've ever heard of. He tries to kill you and gets away with it, he spends a few months in a hospital, and now the doctors want to let him out? I'm worried about you. I couldn't stand it if that nutcase hurt you again."

The distress in his voice brought an answering rush of emotion and made Rachel want to reassure him even though she could barely reassure herself. "He won't get to me. I hope he isn't released because he doesn't deserve it, but if it happens, he'll just be going to his parents' house for weekends."

"And he could take off any time he wanted to, go anywhere. You're way out there in the country where you don't know anybody, you don't have anybody to call on for help."

"But I know a lot of people here, including the sheriff's deputies. Most of them bring their pets to me." The sizzle and burnt smell of boiling-over soup jerked her attention back to the stove. She grabbed the pot's handle, pulled it off the burner, and snapped off the heat. "I'm all right, Luke, please don't worry."

"I always will, you know that. I want you to come home. Please. I'll never feel like you're safe unless you're here with me and I can look after you."

She turned on the cold water to soothe her scorched fingers while she groped for something to say that wouldn't provoke yet another dissection of their relationship. Why couldn't she make a clean break with him? Why did she let him go on calling her, trying to talk her into coming back? Was it because some part of her believed that moving out here had been a mistake? "I don't think going back where his family lives would make me any safer."

"We'll buy a house in Vienna or Arlington. And you don't have to work for me in McLean. Look, I heard about this guy who wants to open a new clinic in Alexandria, specializing in cats. He needs a partner who can put up some of the money. If you sold the place you've got now, you'd be able to swing it. I've got his phone number—"

"*Luke.*" At one time, she would have been outraged, but she'd long ago grown used to him deciding what was best for her and simply informing her of it. "I have to deal with this in my own way."

"It's the perfect solution," Luke said. "We'll move out of McLean, but I'll still work here and you'll still have a clinic of your own."

"I'm not going to uproot myself again." She twisted the faucet off and shook water from her fingers.

"Rachel, come on, be honest with yourself. You left because Michelle pushed you into it. She was determined to separate us, and she used the whole Nelson thing to scare you into running away."

Rachel felt anger bubbling up in her and forced herself to keep it in check. "Do you really believe I let my sister make major decisions for me?"

"She sure as hell knows how to push your buttons. She's an expert manipulator, just like that woman who called herself your mother."

Rachel sighed. "Do you have any idea how it makes me feel when you talk about my sister that way? She's the only family I have, and it took me a long time to get close to her again after Mother died. I never got any help from you."

"And Michelle doesn't get any of the blame?" Luke said. "How do you think I feel about the way she treated me? Accusing me of trying to turn you against your family, as if I'm responsible for everything that happened, when we all know the truth about the whole damn mess."

"Luke, *stop it*." Rachel pressed a hand to her mouth, swallowed down bitter nausea.

"I'm sorry," he said instantly. "I shouldn't have brought that up. I'm just so damned worried about you, I miss you so much— Look, I know you love your sister. And we both love you. That's one thing we've always had in common. I give you my word, if you come back home I'll learn to get along with her."

"You've made that promise before and you've never been able to keep it," Rachel said wearily. "And Michelle can't do it either. The two of you make me feel like the rope in a tug of war."

"Rachel." His voice softened to a quiet plea. "I'll do whatever you want. I love you, and I can't believe you've just turned off your feelings and stopped loving me."

A wave of yearning shook her, weakened her resolve. She wanted to pour out her loneliness, tell him about all the nights when she'd lain awake, wishing he were beside her. But no. However much she loved him, she couldn't live with him. That door was closed, and if she reopened it she would walk back into the maelstrom of emotion that had driven her away in the first place.

"I can't talk about this anymore," she told him. "I love you and I don't want to hurt you, but I just can't do this anymore. Please don't worry about me." Rachel hung up before he could answer, and she switched off the ringer so she wouldn't hear it if he called back.

Too agitated to think about eating, her mind still on Luke, she absently shuffled through her mail on the counter, separating junk and bills. It was easy to pretend that the Perry Nelson ordeal was the reason she'd left McLean, but he was only one of several forces that had driven her away, and perhaps not the most important. Even before Nelson attacked her, she'd felt smothered by Luke's knowledge of her past. He knew what her life had been like as Judith Goddard's daughter, what she'd gone through to learn the truth about her family. Every day, in some way, he reminded her of the most painful part of her life, and his protectiveness, added to the implacable enmity between him and her sister, made it impossible for any of them to put the past to rest.

She started to toss a plain envelope with no return address into the recycling bin under the sink, but paused when she noticed the Richmond postmark. A friend from vet school lived in Richmond and occasionally sent her articles.

She slit open the envelope with a paring knife and pulled out a single sheet of white paper. Two sentences were laser-printed on it: *I know where you live. Want me to pay you a visit some night?*

She gasped and threw the paper onto the counter. Perry Nelson. It couldn't have come from anyone else. He was doing it again, he'd found out where she was and he was invading her life again. Nelson was locked up in the state hospital in Petersburg, south of Richmond, but he'd gotten the letter out somehow. He'd found somebody to do his dirty work, the same way he had when he was in jail awaiting trial.

Rachel paced the kitchen without taking her eyes off the letter. *Calm down,* she told herself. *This could be a good thing.* Nelson had violated a restraining order. However alarmed she might be that he'd found her, she had to hope this contact would give the prosecutor a solid case for keeping him locked up. But only if the note could be tied to him. Was he stupid enough to leave his fingerprints on it? Could the police even lift prints from a piece of paper? She didn't know, but it was worth a try.

Her hands shaking, Rachel grabbed tongs from a drawer, used them to fold the paper. Tomorrow morning she would express mail it to Leslie Ryan. Stuffing the note back into its envelope, Rachel made the decision to attend Nelson's hearing and insist on speaking. "I can stop him in the courtroom," she muttered, "or I can stop him at my door. That seems to be my choice."

Her appetite had vanished, but she knew from experience that she'd make herself ill if she started skipping meals. She switched the gas back on under the vegetable soup and put together a grilled cheese sandwich.

On the kitchen's wooden table a stack of computer printouts waited to occupy her while she ate. The night before, she'd found plenty of information about Melungeons online, and hadn't yet been able to read through everything she'd printed. She wanted to learn more about the heritage Tom Bridger and Holly Turner shared.

Cicero perched on the back of a chair opposite hers and preened his red tail feathers. Frank, on another chair, uttered a demanding meow, and Rachel tore off a bit of her cheese sandwich for him.

Determined not to think about Perry Nelson or Luke or Michelle, she began reading about the history of the Melungeon people, a centuries-long tale of poverty and legalized discrimination. She could hardly believe that Tom, so strong and confident, was descended from people who had been driven off their land by encroaching white settlers, denied basic rights under the law, and shunned by their mountain neighbors. Even the name Melungeon had been a product of racial hatred. It could have

come from the French word *mélange,* which meant mixture, but
Rachel was inclined to believe the theory that it came from the
Turkish phrase *melun jinn*—cursed souls. Small wonder that
some Melungeons had always refused the name. Tom seemed
to accept it, but he certainly wasn't indifferent to the lingering
prejudice against mixed race people.

A sound outside made her break off reading and jerk her head
up. A vehicle was approaching the cottage. The car stopped, the
engine died. Who would come to her house at night without
calling first?

A door slammed. She reminded herself that the person she
feared most was locked in a mental institution on the other
side of the state. But she'd made a new enemy that day. Maybe
Holly's cousin Buddy had decided to follow up with a visit, in
case he hadn't made his point at lunchtime.

Sweat broke out on her body but her skin felt icy. She jumped
up, took three quick strides and grabbed the telephone, ready
to punch in 911.

Footsteps sounded on the front porch. She didn't have time
to call. She dropped the receiver, yanked open a drawer and
scrabbled among the knives, nicking a finger painfully. She
pulled out a meat cleaver.

The visitor rapped on the door. "Rachel? It's Tom."

Oh, for God's sake. She leaned against the counter and swiped
perspiration from her upper lip. *Scare me half to death, why don't
you?* What on earth was Tom doing here?

"Just a minute," she called. Feeling a little foolish, she shut
the knife drawer, caught the telephone receiver and dropped it
back on the hook. By the time she swung the front door wide
she wore a smile.

Tom's grim expression instantly told her he'd brought bad
news.

"Sorry to bother you," he said. "I need to talk to you and I
didn't want to do it on the phone."

As she let him in, she clicked through all the possible reasons
for his appearance at her door and hit on one that made her

heart lurch. "Has something happened to Joanna? Did she have an accident?"

"Oh, God, no. I didn't mean to scare you."

"Then what is it? You look like—"

"Hello, hello!" Cicero, who had followed Rachel from the kitchen, swooped onto Tom's shoulder.

Tom's dour expression dissolved. Laughing, he reached up to scratch under the bird's neck feathers. "Hey, pal. What's your name?"

"Cicero," the parrot answered.

"Great bird," Tom said. "Does he talk a lot?"

"Oh, yeah, a blue streak. So what brings you out? What's wrong?"

Again Tom's features shifted, settling back into an ominous seriousness that alarmed her all over again. "Could we sit down?" he said.

"Sure. Want some coffee?"

Rachel hoped he would say no and get to the point, but he accepted the offer. With the parrot still perched on his shoulder, he followed her to the kitchen. Rachel quickly flipped over the top printout on the table so he wouldn't see what she'd been reading. He might assume she was learning more about Melungeon history out of personal interest in him.

She filled a mug and turned to find him sitting at the table, reading the page she'd tried to hide. He had the courtesy to look abashed at being caught. "Sorry," he said with a grin. "I've been a professional snoop for so long I don't have any manners left."

She couldn't be annoyed with him when he flashed that grin, and she had a feeling he knew it. With one hand she pushed the letter from Nelson out of sight under a dish towel, with the other she offered Tom the mug. "You take it black, right?"

His smile widened. "You remembered."

How had this happened, him in her kitchen in the evening, flirting with her and making her feel like a flustered teenager? "Cicero," she said to the parrot, "go back."

"He can stay," Tom said. "Makes me feel like a pirate. I like it."

"He won't seem so charming if you end up with bird droppings on your uniform." Rachel picked up the squawking bird and set him on the back of Frank's chair. He shook out his feathers with an air of indignation.

"If you're interested in Melungeon history," Tom said, "I'll lend you some of my father's books. He probably collected everything that's ever been published on the subject. He was kind of an expert, I guess."

Tom couldn't have anything urgent to tell her, if he was willing to engage in chitchat. Rachel sat opposite him. "What about you? How well do you know the history?"

"I know enough. Most of it's pretty grim. I'd rather live in the present."

"We all have to do that, whether we want to or not," Rachel said.

"Hungry," Cicero said. "Feed me."

Rachel gave him the rest of her cheese sandwich, and hoped it would keep him quiet for a few minutes. He held it in his claws and began to nibble.

"So," Tom said, "is this interest in Melungeons because of Holly Turner? Did you call her?"

"Not only did I call her, I interviewed her and offered her a job."

He sighed. "Damn. I was afraid of that."

"You're not still having doubts about recommending her, are you?"

"I've been wishing all day that I'd held back on it." Tom sat forward with his hands clasped around his mug. "If I'd known yesterday who she really is—"

"Troy Shackleford's illegitimate daughter?"

He lifted a black eyebrow. "She told you?"

"Yes, but it doesn't matter. I'm hiring Holly, not her family."

"Did you interview her on the phone or in person?"

Okay, here we go. Prepare for a lecture. "I saw her at the diner where she works."

"Jesus Christ, Rachel. After what I told you, you went to that place by yourself?"

"And survived." She spread her arms and smiled, hoping she seemed more casual about it than she felt. The memory of Buddy Shackleford's hand gripping her arm brought back a shiver of fear and outrage. "Remarkable, isn't it?"

"This isn't a joke, Rachel. Those people are dangerous. All the Shacklefords are involved in criminal activity, and I doubt they like strangers showing up on their turf."

You don't know the half of it. She wasn't about to describe her run-in with Buddy and her unwilling exit from the Wild Mountain Rose. "Holly's not involved in their drug business."

"You don't know the girl."

"Neither did you when you recommended her for a job."

"You have to hold off on hiring her."

That sounded like an order. "I beg your pardon?"

"Just till we get this case squared away."

"Holly hasn't done anything wrong. You're the one who wanted to get her out of that environment."

"And I still do. This isn't about Holly. I'm trying to protect you, Rachel. I can't even tell you from what. I've just got a bad feeling about it. I think the Shacklefords are capable of anything. You don't want to get mixed up with them."

"Do you think Holly's father killed Mrs. McClure?"

Tom pushed fingers through his thick hair. "My father thought so, but I'm just getting started, and I can't jump to conclusions. At the very least, though, Shackleford's hiding something."

"He could be innocent," Rachel said. "Of murder, anyway." She was surprised at how much she already cared about Holly, how much she wanted the girl to escape the burden of having a killer for a father.

"Don't count on it."

"I don't care what her family's like. I will not break that girl's heart by taking back my offer." Rachel saw his earnestness turning to exasperation, but she couldn't give him what he wanted.

"When does she start?" he asked.

"We haven't decided that yet. But soon."

"Will you at least do me one favor? Don't go into Rocky Branch District by yourself again."

"I'm afraid I can't promise that either," Rachel said, remembering her commitment to pick up Holly when she was ready.

"You're a damned stubborn woman, you know that?" He threw up his hands in surrender. "All right. Well, I have to get back to headquarters." He rose and Rachel followed him to the front door. "I hope that girl doesn't come trailing trouble behind her. Call me if you need me. For anything, anytime."

He touched her cheek with his fingertips, so lightly she couldn't protest, but the feel of his skin on hers brought a flush of heat that dismayed her.

She shut the door behind him, locked it, slid the bolts into place. Listening to his car drive away, she wondered if Tom was exaggerating about the Shacklefords because it was his job to consider the worst-case scenario. Or was he speaking the simple truth?

Back in the kitchen, she placed the dishes in the sink, poured soap and ran hot water. She stared absently at her ghostlike reflection in the window above the sink, her mind focused on the coldly menacing look on Buddy Shackleford's face after he'd followed her back to the animal hospital. She had seen that look before, in Perry Nelson's eyes, and knew it existed independent of her, that she'd done nothing to deserve it but would always have to fear it.

Something moved outside. Rachel snapped to attention. Somebody was out there in the dark, watching her. She yanked the curtains shut and took a step back.

A crash outside jolted her. Metal, something falling, rolling. Then she realized what it must be. She slumped against the sink in relief. The possum that lived under the cottage. Of course. It was getting into the trash again. *Get hold of yourself.*

She breathed slowly, deeply, and felt her heart slow down. She ran a glass of water and drank it straight down, washing the cottony dryness from her mouth and throat.

Then she froze, the empty glass halfway between her mouth and the sink. She could have sworn she heard another noise. Only her imagination, she told herself. But it had sounded like a car engine starting up somewhere among the trees behind her house. She listened intently, but heard nothing more.

The silence of the winter night settled around her again.

Chapter Ten

At nine in the morning Tom, accompanied by Brandon, pulled into the swath of mud, snow, and iced-over puddles that served as the O'Dells' front yard. They lived near Mrs. Turner but appeared to be several steps farther down the economic ladder. Bare clapboard showed through where the green paint had peeled off, and a downspout leaned away from the gutter, shimmying in the wind.

In answer to Tom's knock, a woman cracked the door a few inches to peer at him and Brandon. A tangled mass of dull red hair surrounded a face so lean that her cheekbones threatened to slice through papery skin.

"Mrs. O'Dell?" Tom asked.

"Who wants to know?"

He introduced himself and Brandon. "We need to talk to Rudy."

She stared at Tom for a moment, her watery blue eyes taking in his uniform before shifting to examine his face. "You John Bridger's boy?"

"Yes, ma'am, my father investigated Mrs. McClure's disappearance. Now I'm investigating her murder."

"So you come straight here to blame my Rudy."

"We just need to ask him some questions, then we'll be on our way."

Tom watched the play of emotions in her eyes and realized she was as likely to slam the door as to invite them in. He placed a palm on the door to keep her from shutting it without warning.

He was disappointed, though, when she stepped back and opened the door wider. If her son was in the house, she wouldn't be letting them in. Rudy had probably fled out the back when he saw the police car pull up.

"Take a look." She gestured. "See for yourself he ain't here."

Followed by Brandon, Tom entered a stuffy, overheated living room. The fireplace was unused, but hot dry air rattled from a baseboard vent.

Mrs. O'Dell stationed herself next to a battered tweed couch, pulled her sweater closed, folded her arms. She was trying hard to be defiant, but she looked scared to death, maybe for herself, more likely for her son. Tom thought of Pauline McClure's skull, laid open by an ax. This frightened little woman might be shielding a murderer.

"Where is he?" Tom asked.

"You already made up your mind it was Rudy, and you want to put him on Death Row. Well, I ain't helpin' you kill my boy." Her voice wavered on the words.

"I haven't made up my mind about anything. I want to hear his side of the story."

"Your daddy never cared about Rudy's side. He accused him without a bit of proof." She shook her head. "I wish to God my boy never went to work for that woman. Uppity trash, that's all she was. Thought she was so fine, catchin' a rich husband. Well, she was still colored, and no better'n any of you."

She glared at Tom as if daring him to take offense. The middle class and the moneyed class had their streak of prejudice, but it always seemed to Tom that it ran deepest and most bitter in people at the bottom of the heap.

"If it makes you feel better to look down on me," he said, "go right ahead. But I've got a job to do, and I intend to find your son."

He glanced around at the worn furniture, the open *National Enquirer* on the coffee table, the knitting needles and yarn on the arm of the easy chair. If any man lived with the widow O'Dell, he hadn't left an impression. "Troy Shackleford told me Rudy was living here."

Her mulish toughness vanished the second she heard Shackleford's name. She stiffened and pulled in a breath. "Why're you talkin' to him about me? I ain't got nothin' to do with none of the Shacklefords. I steer clear."

"Has Troy threatened you?" Tom asked.

"I didn't say that! I didn't say nothin' against him. You can't claim I did." She trembled, her bony shoulders vibrating. She might be afraid of the police, but she was downright terrified of Shackleford.

"We won't repeat anything you tell us," Tom said.

"You listen to me. I got to live here. If it gets around I was talkin' to deputies about the Shacklefords—" She broke off, stalked to the front door, yanked it open. "You want to come back, you come with a warrant."

Tom wanted to shake her till the truth fell out, but the loathing and fright on her face told him she was done talking.

The second he and Brandon cleared the door, it slammed behind them. Almost as warm a goodbye, Tom thought, as Mrs. Turner had given them.

He opened the door of the cruiser, but closed it again without getting in. "Where would O'Dell hide if he saw a police car drive up?"

"The wood shed?" Brandon suggested.

"We can't look in it without a warrant." Tom scanned the hillside behind the house. Near the top, almost hidden among the trees, he thought he saw a curl of smoke. Hard to tell with the winter sun hanging directly above the ridge and shining in his eyes. He squinted. Yeah, that was a cabin up there. "Come on, let's take a hike."

They rounded the house, crushing a path through tall weeds. Catbriars caught at the wool of Tom's pants. Out back, he and

Brandon surveyed the mud and snow in the yard and on the steps. No fresh footprints, no sign they'd flushed O'Dell from the house.

They set off up the steep incline through the bare-limbed oaks and maples. Halfway to the cabin, they stopped to rest, and Tom looked down at the house. Mrs. O'Dell stood on the back porch, moving a mirror back and forth to make sunlight flash off the glass.

"Damn it." Tom swung around to look above them. "He's going to take off."

They scrambled up the mountain, their boots slipping on mud and matted leaves. They'd gone ten yards when Tom heard the crack of a rifle shot, and a split second later a bullet slammed into an oak two feet from his head.

"Take cover!" Tom yelled. Brandon threw himself behind a tree trunk. Tom pressed his back to a maple and plucked his radio off his belt. He keyed it with shaking fingers. "Come in, come in." Static. "Shit! We're out of radio range."

Another shot rang out. "Jesus Christ," Tom muttered. He felt like tossing the useless radio into the nearest ravine. If he lived long enough, he might.

Brandon looked over at him with wide, scared eyes. "We can't get any backup?"

"We're on our own." Tom tried to swallow the hard, dry lump in his throat. A trickle of cold sweat crawled down his spine. "If we start down, he could shoot us in the back. We can flank him, try to take him. You game?"

"Yes, sir, I'm up for it." Brandon bounced on his toes and looked ready to jump out of his skin.

"Draw your weapon, and try to stay covered." *Do it. Go.* Gun in hand and his heart banging against his ribs, Tom spun away from the tree and ran in a half-crouch to the right. Brandon took off to the left.

Rifle fire split the air again and again and bullets sprayed the ground and trees.

Keep moving, don't give him a target. Tom saw the cabin clearly now. Log walls, one window in front, chopped wood piled outside the door, smoke twisting from the stone chimney.

Where the hell was O'Dell firing from? Inside, outside? A bullet whistled by Tom's head, glanced off a tree and sent shredded bark flying. He kept going, heard bullets hit farther away, aimed at Brandon. Through the trees Tom saw Brandon weaving his way upward. He was just a kid. If he got hurt, if he got killed— Tom shoved away thoughts of Brandon's family, his girlfriend. *Keep moving.*

Tom zig-zagged up the mountain from tree to tree. A couple of minutes passed before he realized the shooting had stopped. He paused and leaned against a tree to catch his breath. Every gasp of icy air made his lungs ache.

He's just waiting for us. O'Dell wanted them to get closer so he wouldn't miss next time. With the right kind of rifle, he could blow their heads apart.

Tom approached the cabin from the right and Brandon closed in on the left. When they reached the edge of the small clearing, twenty feet from the cabin, Tom took cover behind a tree and gave Brandon a hand signal to stop. "Police!" Tom shouted. "Drop your weapon and come out with your hands up!"

No answer. All Tom heard was his own hoarse breathing.

"O'Dell! You're surrounded. Come out now and you won't get hurt."

Silence from the cabin.

How long since O'Dell had fired a shot? Five minutes?

Tom waited another minute but no response came. He swung away from the tree and sprinted across the clearing to the cabin. He flattened his back against the wall next to the door. Brandon dashed forward, dropped into a crouch below the window. Tom rattled the door with his fist. "O'Dell! Come out now if you want to get out of this alive."

Not a sound from inside. Tom's bare fingers, wrapped around his pistol, felt like sticks of ice. Across from him, Brandon's face twitched with excitement underlay by pure terror.

Tom banged on the door again. "Don't make things worse for yourself."

Long seconds, endless minutes passed.

"You think he's even in there?" Brandon asked.

"He could've been outside when he saw his mother's signal." Tom scanned the woods. "He might be watching us right now. Come on, let's go in, but take it slow."

Tom reached sideways, turned the knob, pushed the door open. *God help us,* he thought. *God help us all.*

Gripping his gun in both hands, he pivoted away from the wall to face the doorway. He heard the crack of a shot, but when the bullet hit, he was more surprised than anything, as if somebody had come up from behind and punched him hard on the arm. He staggered over the threshold and dropped to his knees inside the cabin.

"Captain!" Brandon rushed in and knelt beside him. "You're hit. You're bleeding— Your arm—"

A splinter from the plank floor pierced Tom's knee, then he became aware of a greater pain, burning and throbbing at once, in his upper left arm. "Close the door, for God's sake."

Brandon scrambled to his feet and slammed the door.

His head buzzing, Tom holstered his pistol and examined his arm. Blood had already seeped through a ragged hole in the front of his jacket sleeve and saturated the wool fabric. The stain spread as he watched, fascinated and horrified. He'd never been shot before. He felt around and located a neater hole in the back of the sleeve. He stuck a finger in it, trying to judge the size of the entry wound. Deer rifle, maybe. *Damned lucky to be alive.* Pain pulsed outward until his entire upper body throbbed.

He glanced around the cabin's single small room, hoping against reason to find a telephone he could use to call for backup. A kerosene lantern hooked to a ceiling beam cast a feeble light that feathered to darkness in the corners. On the iron bed, quilts and blankets formed a rumpled mound, topped by a potato chip bag. Heat radiated from a wood stove, and a jumble of food jars and boxes on a wooden table gave off a sour odor. No phone anywhere.

How the hell could they get out of here? What possessed him to charge up the mountain, Brandon in tow, after O'Dell started shooting? They should have retreated, gone for reinforcements. But, he reminded himself, they would have risked being shot in the back and O'Dell would have disappeared.

Brandon, on his knees, peeked left and right out the window. "Hey!" he yelled. "There he is! There he is!" Then Brandon was up and out the door.

"Come back here!" Cursing, Tom pushed to his feet and ran outside.

Brandon dashed around the cabin to the rear. Tom chased after him. Far ahead of them, a man with long red hair and beard jogged upward through the trees. Blue jays screamed alarm as the man passed, and a great horned owl, startled from sleep, glided away. Tom and Brandon lagged a hundred feet behind him when O'Dell vanished over the ridge. By the time they reached the top, O'Dell was nowhere in sight.

"God damn it." Tom bent over, hands on his knees, struggling to catch his breath. His leg muscles burned. The pain in his arm spiked with each beat of his heart. "We don't have a chance in hell of catching him."

Brandon leaned against a tree and gasped, "He's probably running straight to some kinfolk who'll hide him."

"Or help him get out of the county." If O'Dell wasn't guilty of murdering Pauline McClure, he'd picked an unconvincing way to protest his innocence. "We've got to start a search before it's too late. The damned car radio won't work out here. We need a phone, but something tells me Mrs. O'Dell won't let us use hers."

"Mrs. Turner's right down the road. But, hey, we gotta get you to the hospital. You're bleeding like crazy."

Tom looked down. Blood soaked his jacket sleeve to the wrist. "It looks worse than it is." He hoped. "We're calling headquarters before we do anything else. Keep an eye out. O'Dell could've circled around to ambush us."

All the way down the mountain Tom kept his pistol raised, at the ready. The woods had gone dead quiet, the birds shocked into silence by the ruckus. He smelled his own blood, mixed with the mold of decaying leaves underfoot, and the rank odor made him queasy.

Every few seconds he glanced behind him, searching for a glint of metal, a movement. A rustling noise made him spin around, gun up, finger on the trigger. He stared into the eyes of a gray squirrel that had leapt onto a nearby branch. Tom drew a deep breath, tried to make his heart slow down. The squirrel followed them, sailing from branch to branch overhead, as if it were escorting Tom and Brandon out of the woods.

They skidded the last few feet of the muddy incline into Mrs. O'Dell's yard.

She stood on the back porch, her body a rigid column. "You shoot my boy?"

"No," Tom said. "He got away."

She relaxed. Angling her head, she studied Tom's bloody sleeve. When her eyes shifted to meet his, her lips twisted in a nasty smile. "Next time, his aim'll be better."

⟨⟩⟨⟩⟨⟩

Tom clamped a handkerchief against his arm but couldn't stanch the bleeding. By the time Brandon parked the cruiser in Mrs. Turner's yard, blood saturated the handkerchief and colored Tom's hand red.

"Oh, man," Brandon said. "I'll call. You'd better wait in the car."

"No." Tom yanked on the door handle with blood-sticky fingers. "Maybe Mrs. Turner can give me something to make a pressure bandage."

When he climbed out he swayed and had to steady himself against the car door. Damn it, he hadn't lost enough blood to make him feel this bad. It was nothing but a flesh wound. It wouldn't kill him and it wasn't going to get the better of him.

But his damaged arm screamed for mercy and his head felt like a balloon bobbing on a string.

"Guess she's got company," Brandon said. He nodded toward a dark blue pickup parked behind Mrs. Turner's old Chevy. "We're just gonna have to be rude and interrupt."

Mrs. Turner answered Brandon's knock. When she saw the deputies on her porch, her expression soured. "I ain't got nothin' else to tell you."

"We need to use your phone," Tom said. "It's an emergency."

"What kind of—" Mrs. Turner broke off when she caught sight of the blood. "Oh, my lord, what happened to you?"

"He's been shot," Brandon said.

"It's not serious," Tom said. "But we have to use your phone."

"Get on in here and let me tend to that arm." Mrs. Turner ushered them into the living room. Her two dogs danced around Tom, sniffing, excited by the smell of blood. She shooed them away, and they whined in frustration.

"Phone's in the kitchen, where we're headin'," Mrs. Turner said.

"I'll call," Brandon said. He headed for the kitchen and almost collided with a man and woman in the doorway. He edged past them.

Tom had a quick impression of the man as middle-aged, stocky, dark-haired. But the woman caught his attention and made him forget his pain for a second. She was another version of Sarelda Turner, of Pauline, of Holly. Small and delicate-boned, with black hair and blue eyes, she might have been something special even in middle age if she didn't have deep worry lines etched into her face.

"Bonnie, my middle daughter," Mrs. Turner said in introduction, "and her husband Jack."

"Jack Watford." The man extended a hand, but changed his mind when he saw Tom's bloody fingers.

Tom nodded, but he'd already turned his attention back to the woman. Bonnie Watford. Pauline's younger sister. He had to question her, had to ask her about—

"Let us by, for heaven's sake," Mrs. Turner said. Her daughter and son-in-law stepped aside and she steered Tom into the kitchen.

Brandon was on the phone, accenting his rapid-fire words with broad gestures.

"Sit." Mrs. Turner pushed Tom into a wooden chair. Bonnie and Jack Watford watched from the doorway, while the two dogs tried to squeeze past their legs.

Tom let Mrs. Turner remove his jacket, cut away his shirt sleeve above the wound, swab off blood. Her efficient but gentle nursing made him think of his mother's attention to childhood cuts and bruises.

"You're real lucky your arm didn't get tore up worse than this," Mrs. Turner said.

The bullet had gouged open the skin and muscle but missed the bone.

"Go get me the alcohol and a Kotex out of the bathroom," Mrs. Turner told Bonnie. Without questioning the order, her daughter disappeared.

Kotex? Tom couldn't process the strange request.

Mrs. Turner ripped a clean white dish cloth into strips. "Jack, run some water in the kettle and put it on the burner."

Watford obeyed. The dogs took advantage of the unguarded doorway to rush at Tom, but Mrs. Turner scolded them and they retreated. Bonnie reappeared with a sanitary pad and a bottle. Cold liquid doused Tom's skin, and the fumes of alcohol brought tears to his eyes. A second later a fiery sting made him yelp and wrench his arm free.

"Now hush, it's nothin' but a little red pepper," Mrs. Turner said. "It's good for bleedin'. The burnin' won't last but a minute."

She was right. Already the sensation was fading. Tom let her get back to work. Mrs. Turner pressed the sanitary napkin to his arm, and her daughter helped her secure the makeshift pressure bandage with a cloth strip.

"All right now," Mrs. Turner said. "That oughta hold you till you get to the hospital. I'm gonna give you somethin' hot to drink before you leave. You look kinda like you're goin' into shock."

"No, I'm fine. I'll be okay."

"Men," Mrs. Turner scoffed as she turned to the stove, and Tom was again reminded of his mother. Placing a mug in his hand, Mrs. Turner said, "Drink."

He recoiled from the bitter odor steaming off the liquid. "What is it?"

"Herb tea. It's good for you." She guided the cup to his lips.

Tom swallowed and coughed. Revolting, but probably harmless enough, and the liquid felt good in his dry mouth. He choked down the rest. When Mrs. Turner took the empty mug, his blood-covered fingers stuck to it and she had to pry it loose.

With a wet cloth she began wiping his hand. "Who done this to you?"

"Rudy O'Dell."

"Oh, dear lord!" Bonnie exclaimed.

Mrs. Turner dropped the cloth in Tom's lap and took a step backward.

"Why'd he shoot you?" Watford asked.

Tom stifled a groan. God, he was tired. He didn't want to answer questions. "We were on our way up to his cabin to talk to him, and he opened fire on us." Tom closed his eyes, and for a second he was back on the mountain, his heart pounding as he dashed from tree to tree, dodging death.

"The State Police are on their way out now," Brandon said. "They'll get him."

"Oh, God," Bonnie whimpered. Her husband placed an arm around her shoulders and leaned to whisper something Tom couldn't hear. "You don't know that," she answered. "He's crazy, he's—"

"Hush now," Watford said. "Don't get yourself all worked up."

A strangled sob escaped Bonnie. Mrs. Turner grasped her arm. "Be quiet, girl. Get ahold of yourself."

Bonnie stuck a knuckle in her mouth and bit down on it.

Rising slowly to prevent dizziness, Tom spoke to Bonnie, who didn't seem to be getting any reassurance from her husband or her mother. "I don't think you have to be afraid of him. He'll be in custody before long."

Bonnie cried out and spun away from her husband's embrace. Watford caught up with her in the living room. Through the doorway, Tom watched their quiet exchange but heard none of it. Watford grabbed a jacket and coat from the sofa and called, "We're goin' on home." They walked out into the cold without taking time to pull on their coats.

Mrs. Turner's shoulders slumped. "I hate to think what Rudy'll do if he's scared." Her voice fell to a murmur. "We're all at his mercy now."

Chapter Eleven

"Hi, Dr. Goddard," Holly said on the phone. "You told me to call you when I was ready and you'd pick me up."

"Yes, of course." Rachel dropped into her office chair, glad to sit for a minute. She'd been on her feet all morning, performing neuterings on four cats, a beagle, and an Irish wolfhound. "But I'm afraid I'm still trying to find a place for you to live. Something should turn up soon."

"Oh. I was hopin'—" Holly paused, and in the background Rachel heard the sounds of country music, voices, and clattering dishes. The diner. "Okay. I understand. It's just, if I don't leave today, I might not be able—" Holly broke off, and for a moment all Rachel heard were muffled sniffs and gulps and the noises of the diner.

Rachel sat upright in her chair. "Are you all right?"

"I'm sorry I bothered you. I'm bein' way too much trouble."

The girl's voice had gone flat with despair, and Rachel couldn't stand it. To hell with details. She'd work them out later. "Wait, Holly. I'll come today. Give me directions."

◇◇◇

Rachel drove out to the Turner house in the hope she might sit down with Holly's grandmother and work out a plan to suit everybody. But the ferocious little woman wouldn't let Rachel past the door, much less discuss options.

.

Mrs. Turner stood on the porch, her arms crossed and two muddy dogs flanking her. Rachel advanced only as far as the bottom step. On the top step Holly hovered like a weak buffer between her grandmother and Rachel.

"She's not interested," Mrs. Turner said.

"I think she'd enjoy the work very much," Rachel said.

"Go back where you come from."

In the second Rachel needed to rein in her anger and form a civil response, Holly startled her by swinging around to face her grandmother. "I want this job!" she cried.

Mrs. Turner stepped forward, a hand raised. Rachel moved closer. If the woman dared to touch the girl—

Mrs. Turner flicked a look at Rachel and lowered her arm. "I'm not gettin' any younger. I'll be sick and helpless before you know it, and I'll be here by myself."

"I'll take care of you when you need me to," Holly said. "But right now, you can get along fine without me."

The dynamic between these two was something Rachel understood all too well: guilt plus pressure equaled obedience. Thank God Holly was breaking free.

"Where you gonna live?" Mrs. Turner asked.

Holly looked at Rachel. Mrs. Turner looked at Rachel.

"I wanted to talk to you about that," she said. "If Holly had a ride to and from work every day, she wouldn't have to move."

Mrs. Turner sniffed. "I'm not spendin' money on gas—"

"Then I'll live in town," Holly said.

"Where?"

In the silence following Mrs. Turner's question, Rachel wondered why on earth she'd walked so willingly into this situation. The plea on Holly's face was answer enough. Something about this girl and her plight touched Rachel so deeply she couldn't turn away. "She can stay with me till she finds a place of her own."

"You're just some stranger to us," Mrs. Turner said. "Why would I let you take my granddaughter?"

The woman had changed her argument again, and she would keep coming up with new objections, an endless stream of them, as long as this conversation dragged on. In a way, Rachel could sympathize. Mrs. Turner didn't want to lose her young companion and be left alone without so much as a neighbor's house in sight. But Rachel had chosen the side she was fighting for, and she had to harden her heart against Mrs. Turner.

"Are you ready to go?" she asked Holly.

Holly threw a fearful glance at her grandmother, but said, "I got my stuff all packed up. Is it all right if I bring my goose? She's my pet, and I hate to leave her."

A goose?

"Let her stay here," Mrs. Turner said. "I'll have a nice dinner of roasted goose tomorrow night."

"Grandma, you can't eat Penny!"

"Okay," Rachel said quickly. "Bring the goose."

"I'll be back in a minute." Holly moved past her grandmother cautiously as if expecting to be grabbed. When she opened the door the two dogs dashed inside ahead of her.

Stepping to the edge of the porch, Mrs. Turner glared down at Rachel. "You little fool. You'll find out what you're takin' on and you'll be bringin' that child back here soon enough, glad to get rid of her."

The woman's words and fierce expression sent a chill through Rachel.

Before she could answer Mrs. Turner, Holly reappeared, wearing her coat and struggling to balance a cardboard box under one arm and a big gray goose under the other.

Rachel relieved Holly of the box. It seemed so small and light, apparently containing everything Holly thought was worth taking with her. Everything except the goose, which honked as Holly shifted it and wrapped both arms around it.

Mrs. Turner grabbed the girl's shoulder. "Your daddy's ain't gonna like this."

"It's none of his business!" Holly twisted free, scooted down the steps, and ran to Rachel's Range Rover.

"Sit in the back," Rachel said, "and hold her tight." All she needed was a terrified goose flying at her while she was driving.

"You'll be sorry!" Mrs. Turner yelled.

Rachel didn't know which of them she was addressing.

◇◇◇

On the trip to Mrs. Turner's house, the bad roads and unfamiliar territory had forced Rachel to drive at a speed just north of a creep, but on the way back she moved as fast as she dared in the growing darkness. Judging by the sounds from the back seat, Holly was having a tough time keeping the frantic, honking goose under control.

The girl stayed silent during the drive. Rachel could easily imagine the mix of anxiety and excitement Holly must feel, at leaving home, breaking away from her controlling grandmother.

When Rachel drove through the gate to the horse farm and up the lane past Joanna's brick colonial, Holly exclaimed, "What a beautiful house! Who lives in it?"

"Joanna McKendrick. She owns the farm." Illuminated by security flood lamps, the house must look like a palace to Holly in comparison to her grandmother's place. At the thought of Mrs. Turner, Rachel said, "You know, I didn't give your grandmother my address and phone number. I'd better call her."

"No!" Holly cried. "If she knows where you live, she'll come after me."

Rachel was a lot more worried about Holly's bullying cousin Buddy than she was about a little old lady, but she let it drop for the moment. After a while, both Holly and her grandmother might view the situation more rationally.

A mile down the farm lane, past the darkened stable, barn and paddocks, Rachel pulled up to her cottage. Seeing it through Holly's eyes, she realized it wasn't all that different from Mrs. Turner's place—in better repair, but just as small and isolated. Rachel hoped Holly wouldn't be disappointed in the cottage after getting a look at Joanna's house.

As soon as they walked in, Cicero screeched, "Hello! Hello!"

Startled, Holly almost dropped the goose but managed to keep her arms around the squirming Penny and prevent her from opening her wings.

Cicero glided across the room and landed on Holly's shoulder, drawing a delighted laugh from her. Leaning close to the goose, Cicero inquired, "Bird?" The goose honked in his face. Cicero jerked back, almost lost his balance, and flapped his wings to right himself. The alarmed goose let out a string of honks and paddled the air with her webbed feet. Frank, the cat, watched from the safety of a chair.

"Cicero," Rachel said, "go back."

Cicero kneaded the wool of Holly's coat, uttering the little noises Rachel called his *I-don't-wanna* whine.

"Oh, you silly thing." Rachel held out her arm. "Come to me, sweetie."

Cicero stepped onto her wrist and marched up her arm to her shoulder. He leaned forward to touch his beak to her lips. "I love you," he said.

"I love you too. And I'll love you even more if you don't upset the goose." She returned him to the top of his cage.

She didn't have a chance at conversation with Holly until after they installed the goose on the enclosed back porch and deposited the girl's belongings in the spare room. In the kitchen, while they chopped onions and tomatoes for marinara sauce, Holly peppered Rachel with questions about the animal hospital, the other people who worked there, the daily routine. She was clearly disappointed to learn she would be wearing a tee shirt and pants instead of a white coat at work, but accepted the idea that only doctors should dress in white.

While Holly set the kitchen table, Rachel checked on the boiling spaghetti and gave the sauce another stir. "By the way," she said, "if your mother calls, your grandmother will tell her where you're working, won't she?"

Holly shifted a plate on the table, looked at it, moved it another inch to the left. "My mama's not gonna call. She never has."

"What? Do you mean you haven't talked to her since she left?"

Holly ignored this and said, "Captain Bridger's nice. Real handsome, too."

Questions about Holly's missing mother troubled Rachel, but she could see the subject was off-limits. She said, "Tom Bridger's a little old for you, don't you think?"

Holly laughed and blushed. "I'm not interested in him or anything." She threw a sly glance at Rachel. "Is he your boyfriend?"

"Good heavens, no. Tom's just a friend." Maybe not even that, after their disagreement over Holly. "He brings his nephew out here to ride a lot."

Tom was wonderful with little Simon, patient and gentle, but watching them together opened an aching space inside her. Luke loved kids too. He was great with them. He'd wanted to get married and start a family with Rachel.

Stop it. Don't think about it.

She swiped a finger over the stirring spoon and tasted the sauce. "Everything's done. Let's eat."

While Rachel poured the sauce into a bowl, Holly came up beside her. "Dr. Goddard? The way my grandma carried on… You're not sorry you let me come, are you?"

"Of course not. Your grandmother will get over it."

"No, she won't. And she might be right about you bein' sorry."

A prickle of apprehension made Rachel frown. "Why would I be?"

Holly hung her head. "She says I'm more trouble than I'm worth."

Oh, for pity's sake. "Well, you're no trouble at all to me."

She couldn't let the old woman's melodramatic warning bother her. Mrs. Turner was an over-possessive grandmother who didn't want to let go of Holly, yet had obviously abused her psychologically and perhaps physically. She had convinced the girl no one would want to be her friend. But Rachel was determined that before long Holly would be enjoying her freedom and her new life.

〈〉〈〉

A scream shocked Rachel awake. She struggled upright in bed. Another scream tore through the house. Downstairs, Cicero squawked. Holly screamed again.

Rachel sprang from the bed, ran down the darkened hallway, and flung open the door to the guest room.

When she flipped the light switch, she found Holly thrashing in her bed, flailing at the covers twisted around her body. "Don't hurt her!" Holly shouted. "Leave her alone!"

Rachel hurried to her, grabbed her by the shoulders, shook her. "Holly! Wake up!"

"Mama!" Holly wailed. She flung out a fist and connected with Rachel's cheek.

Rachel recoiled but held onto the girl's shoulders. "Wake up, Holly!"

Holly's eyes popped open. Her body rigid, she stared wildly at Rachel.

"It's me," Rachel said. "You're in my house. Remember?"

Holly went limp with a long exhalation of breath. Rachel let go of her shoulders.

Sinking back against the pillow, Holly hid her face beneath folded arms and burst into tears. "I'm sorry. I'm so sorry."

"Don't be silly." Rachel probed her stinging cheek. She could almost feel a bruise forming. "You just had a bad dream."

Holly curled on her side and buried her face in the pillow.

Rachel placed a hand on Holly's shoulder and felt the tremor in the girl's thin body. Holly was a young adult, yet Rachel experienced a rush of tenderness she might have felt for a frightened child. A flash of memory took Rachel back to those long-ago nights when Michelle would wake from bad dreams and crawl into bed with Rachel for comfort. "Talking about it might help," she told Holly. "What were you dreaming about?"

Holly shook her head. "I can't tell you," she said, her voice muffled by the pillow. "Grandma says people'll think I'm crazy if—" She broke off and pulled her body into a tighter ball, her breath coming in little gasps.

The grandmother from hell had really done a number on this girl. "A nightmare doesn't make you crazy, Holly. Everybody has them sometimes. I do."

Slowly Holly's body uncurled, and she peered skeptically at Rachel. "Do you?"

"Yes." *If you only knew the things I dream about.*

Sniffling, Holly dragged the back of her hand across her cheeks and nose. Rachel grabbed tissues from a box on the bedside table and pressed them into Holly's fingers. The clock on the table said 2:17. "Do you want to stay up a while? We can go down and have some milk and crackers."

"That'd be real nice." Holly blew her nose.

When she climbed out of bed, her faded pajamas draped her small body like a baggy clown's costume. To Rachel's question about a robe and slippers, Holly blushed and said she didn't have any. Rachel had extras, and she retrieved them from her closet and offered them to the protesting girl. "I don't want you to be chilled," Rachel said. "You might get sick, and I need you too much at the hospital."

"Oh." After a moment's consideration Holly added, "Okay then." She pulled on the robe, which fell to her ankles, and stuck her feet into the too-big slippers.

They sat at the kitchen table and ate graham crackers and drank milk, while Frank lapped up his own portion of milk from a saucer between them on the table. Rachel's mind hummed with questions, but Holly seemed lost in some sad and private world. Rachel was afraid that pressing her to talk would stir up another whirlwind of emotion.

When they returned to bed, Holly seemed exhausted and ready to sleep again. For a long time Rachel lay awake, alert for sounds of distress from the guest room, wondering about Holly's life and about the dream that had terrified her. Had it been only a phantom of the night, or was it, like Rachel's own nightmares, all too real a memory?

Chapter Twelve

Three reporters, their shoulders hunched against the cold wind, waited outside headquarters when Tom arrived at eight a.m. They surrounded him as he stepped out of his truck. One took pictures of Tom holding the door for Billy Bob to hop down.

Figuring they must be desperate for material if they thought his dog was worth attention, Tom took pity on them and answered a few questions about the shooting. He assured them his arm, now in a sling, had suffered no permanent damage and Rudy O'Dell would soon be in custody.

He called a halt when Darla Duncan pulled into the parking lot with her husband, Deputy Grady Duncan, and their grandson, Simon, in the car. "You've got your answers," Tom told the reporters. "Now back off, okay?"

Simon jumped out of the car and barreled toward Tom before Grady got his door open. Tom stooped and caught the boy with his free arm.

"You got shot!" Simon wailed, clinging fiercely to Tom. "I thought you were gonna die!"

"Hey, now, don't talk that way." Tom pulled back to look into his nephew's face. The boy's eyes, puffy from crying, held a deep terror that Tom hadn't seen since the months after Simon lost his parents and his Bridger grandparents. "It takes more than a little nick on the arm to bring me down. You know that, don't you? Huh? You believe me?"

Simon's mouth screwed up and tears dribbled down his cheeks, but he bobbed his head. "Please don't get shot again," he said in a tremulous whisper.

"I won't, champ. I won't." Tom hugged the boy and hoped to God he could keep that promise. Looking over Simon's head, he saw Darla staring at him from the car, her pitiless expression obvious even through the tinted glass.

Grady walked up, touched Simon's head briefly, then laid a hand on Tom's shoulder. "Glad you're okay, son."

Tom didn't think he could speak without blubbering. He swallowed hard and nodded. When he saw one of the reporters lift a camera, he shot the man a look that was enough to make him change his mind.

"Uh, listen, Tom," Grady said. "Darla was thinking, since school's out Monday and Tuesday because of the teachers' meeting, maybe she'd take Simon to her sister's place in Charlottesville. That okay with you?"

As if he had any say in the matter. But he appreciated Grady asking—and he understood why Darla wanted to get Simon out of the county. She was afraid Tom's bad luck would slop over onto his family and Simon would be hurt. The same thought had occurred to Tom. "That's a good idea."

"I want to stay with you." Simon clung to Tom's hand.

"Hey, you always have a good time with your cousins in Charlottesville, don't you? When you get back, maybe I won't be so busy and we can go over to Mrs. McKendrick's place and ride the horses. Okay?"

"All right now," Grady said to Simon. "Say goodbye to Tom and Billy Bob, then you go on to school and work hard today, make us proud of you."

Persuading Simon to let go of Tom and get back in the car with Darla took a few tearful minutes. When Darla drove out of the lot, Simon pressed his face to the window, his eyes on Tom until the car turned a corner.

"The State Police have been helping us look for O'Dell since yesterday," Grady said on their way into headquarters, "but he's just vanished, like a goddamn rabbit down a hole. How can a man that's half-crazy, and looks it and acts it, just disappear into thin air?"

"He can't. I doubt he's got money or transportation. And his relatives can't protect him forever. We'll get him." Tom shifted his wounded arm in its sling, trying to find a more comfortable position, but only succeeded in ratcheting up the pain. He felt groggy from a big dose of medication the night before, and he'd had a hell of a time getting into his uniform and driving his truck to town.

In the squad room, Dennis Murray and the Blackwood twins hit him with good-natured jibes about guys who use Kotex. The sheriff's bellow from his office doorway cut them off. "What the hell are you doing here? I told you to stay home today."

"I can't sit at home and do nothing," Tom said.

"Stubborn as a damned mule. Just like your dad." Despite the gruff words, Willingham's lips twitched in a barely suppressed grin. "Well, come on. Since you're here, let's talk about this."

In his office, Willingham leaned on the windowsill and stared out as if he hoped to locate O'Dell in the parking lot. "Our guys went around to all of his relatives, and they'll keep going back till they get a lead." Turning, Willingham pointed a finger. "If you're bound and determined to work, you're not gonna waste your energy running after O'Dell. Interviewing people, that's the best use of your time. Whether it's us or the State Police, somebody'll bring O'Dell in. And the son of a bitch is looking at attempted murder for what he did to you, on top of two murder charges."

"We don't have any evidence tying him to those women's deaths."

"An innocent man wouldn't shoot a cop."

"Unless he's gone a little nuts from living like a hermit for too many years," Tom said. "Whether he killed those women or not, Pauline's relatives are scared to death of him. And he's out there with a gun he's not afraid to use. I want him caught before he shoots somebody else."

<><><>

Rachel had brought Holly to work an hour before opening time so she could show the girl around and teach her a few routine tasks, but she felt as if she were operating on autopilot while worry over Tom claimed her mind. The newspaper story said the wound was minor. Why couldn't she stop thinking about him?

After a tour of the building they returned to the reception desk, where Rachel showed Holly how to enter information in the big appointment book. Rachel didn't trust the hospital's aging computer system enough to use it exclusively for keeping records.

"I can't wait to get started," Holly said. "I'm gonna do the best job I can for you."

"I have no doubt about that." Rachel looked forward to proving Tom wrong about Holly.

At the thought of Tom, anxiety gripped Rachel again. *He's perfectly fine,* she told herself. *Stop worrying about him.*

She picked up a manila envelope with a small square bulge in the middle. Somebody had put it through the mail slot, and she'd found it on the floor when she came in. No postmark. On the front was written *Dr. Goddard—this belongs to you.* She couldn't think of anything she'd lost.

Puzzled, she ripped tape from the envelope's flap, reached in and pulled out a little white box. The lid was taped on.

"Somebody send you a present?" Holly asked.

"I don't know what it is." Rachel slit the tape with a fingernail.

She lifted the lid and a black spider crawled out onto her fingers. She yelped and shook her hand wildly. The box and lid went flying and the spider landed on the appointment book.

"It's a black widow," Holly said, pronouncing the word *widder.*

"Good grief," Rachel gasped, her pulse thundering in her head. She stared down at the creature. It moved sluggishly across the open appointment book, stopped, changed directions, slowly crawled another couple of inches and stopped again. The thing was hideous and awakened a deep, primal fear in her. Spiders were the only animals she found truly revolting.

Wide-eyed, Holly looked at Rachel. "Why would somebody send you a black widow spider?"

Rachel pressed a hand to her chest and tried to catch her breath. "Keep your eye on it while I find something to put it in."

The first thing she spotted when she looked around was a glass vase that held a pink hothouse rose Shannon had brought in the day before. Rachel grabbed the vase, dumped water and flower in the wastebasket under the desk, and clamped the vase over the spider.

The glossy black creature was still for a moment, as if surprised. Then it stirred, tentatively touched long legs to the glass, rearing up so the bright red spot on its globular abdomen was visible. Either the damp glass wouldn't give it purchase or it was too weak to climb. It fell back and lay motionless.

Had Perry Nelson sent it, hoping she'd be bitten? No. It was hand-delivered. Rachel doubted he could get anybody to do that for him.

This little gift had come from someone right here in Mason County.

⟨⟩⟨⟩⟨⟩

Tom was about to enter Mason County Bank & Trust when he stopped in his tracks on the sidewalk to watch the scene playing out in the bank president's ground floor office. Through the slats of the blinds, Tom saw Pauline McClure's brothers-in-law, Robert and Ed McClure, stalk back and forth and fling out their arms in angry gestures. He couldn't hear a thing, but he knew they were yelling at each other. Ed's wife, Natalie, sat in a chair facing the desk, head lowered and sleek blonde hair falling forward to hide most of her face.

Meeting with Tom was Robert's idea—"Let's get it over with, then you won't have to bother us again," the banker had said when he called to set it up—and Tom had doubted anything illuminating would come of talking to all of them at once. Now he had more hope. He pushed open the bank's mahogany door, eager to get inside before the brothers cooled down and started watching their words.

When Tom entered Robert's office, Ed still looked flustered and pink-cheeked, riding the crest of his anger, but he summoned the composure to shake Tom's hand. "How are you? Have you met my wife, Natalie?"

Tom had met her at a charity event, but he didn't expect her to remember him, and apparently she didn't. Without rising, Natalie McClure extended a pale hand.

He walked over to her, but the brief, limp touch of her fingers hardly seemed worth the trip. Her little smile disappeared as she shifted position and faced forward. She was still cheerleader-pretty, with golden hair and blue eyes, but she was over fifty now and Tom doubted she maintained her drum-taut skin without a surgeon's help.

"All right, ask your questions and be done with it," Robert McClure said as he crossed the room to his desk. He made Tom think of a rooster, with his beaky nose and shock of reddish brown hair that bobbed like a cockscomb when he moved. Some genetic quirk had denied the middle McClure brother the boyish good looks bestowed on Adam, the oldest, and Ed, the youngest.

Robert stood straight and stiff behind the desk, his fingertips pressed to the blotter. A handshake wouldn't be forthcoming.

Refusing to be hurried, Tom said, "This must be a rough time for you folks."

He took a seat next to Natalie. The wooden chair's knobby spindles dug into his back. Maybe McClure had chosen the seating deliberately to make supplicants miserable. The rest of his office was equally uninviting, with brown tweed industrial carpeting, beige vinyl wallpaper, and beige draperies flanking the window Tom had looked through a few minutes before. Only framed citations from civic organizations hung on the walls.

Robert sat down and clasped his hands on the blotter. "This doesn't involve me or interest me. Frankly, I couldn't care less that you've found her."

"For God's sake, Robert," Ed muttered. He moved to the window and stared out at the street.

Tom studied Ed's tall, youthful figure, the thick dark hair with no trace of gray. Mary Lee had said that Ed and Pauline were friends, they'd had things in common. But Pauline had been a beautiful widow and Ed a married man. Tom glanced at Natalie and found her watching him without expression. When their eyes met, she looked away.

To Robert, Tom said, "Pauline was a member of your family."

"Technically."

Jesus Christ, the man was cold. "She was murdered, Mr. McClure. And I'm afraid the investigation does involve you—all of you—and everyone else who knew her."

"We'll cooperate any way we can," Ed said, turning from the window. "We want her killer punished."

"Of course we do," Natalie said. "I didn't know Pauline very well, we weren't what you'd call friends, but..." Her voice trailed off.

No, I don't imagine you were, Tom thought.

Robert's knuckles had turned white. When Tom looked at them, Robert seemed to realize he was betraying a reaction and hid his hands under the desk. An unpleasant smile lifted the corners of his mouth. "The paper said you identified her with dental records. I'm glad her dental work's finally served a useful purpose. God knows it cost enough."

"You didn't approve of her having her teeth fixed?" Amazing, the petty grudges people held onto for years, decades.

Robert sniffed. "Thousands of dollars of my family's money were poured into that woman's mouth. So she could have a perfect smile. But it couldn't disguise what she was."

"Robert, please." Ed looked disgusted. "Think about what you're saying."

Afraid Robert might have an attack of civility and yield to his brother's plea, Tom goaded, "And what, exactly, was she?"

Robert's right hand reappeared and plucked a Bic pen from the desktop. Tapping the pen against the blotter, he said, "She married Adam for his money, and—"

"She loved him," Ed said.

"And she spent it like there was no tomorrow," Robert continued, raising his voice a decibel. "She went to work at the bank with every intention of ending up as Adam's wife. She had him completely fooled, and he gave her anything she wanted."

"Damn it, Robert," Ed said, "it was his money. And Pauline was his wife. I don't complain when you let Christina—"

"Don't you dare compare my wife to that—"

"I won't stand here while you slander a kindhearted woman who always made our brother happy."

"Oh, I'm sure she made Adam *happy*, in one way at least."

"Stop this!" Natalie jumped up, her blonde hair swinging as she looked from her husband to her brother-in-law. "Don't you realize what kind of impression you're giving?"

Tom wanted to wrestle her back into her chair and tape her mouth shut. He cursed silently when he saw that Ed was pulling himself together, damping down his anger.

"Was money the only reason you didn't like Pauline?" Tom asked Robert. "Did she do something to you personally?"

"I don't have to explain anything to you."

"No, you don't," Tom said, "but I think you'd be wise to try. You've expressed a strong animosity toward Pauline. You had a reason to want her dead and out of the way."

Robert's mouth fell open and a flush stained his cheeks a blotchy red. "You can't come in here and accuse me of murder."

"Answer my questions and this'll be easier on both of us."

Rigid in his chair, Robert expelled air through his nostrils in short bursts, like a bull revving up. For a moment he said nothing, then he blurted, "Pauline Turner was Melungeon trash, and she dragged my brother down with her."

"Good God, Robert," Ed exclaimed, "remember who you're talking to."

"It's nothing I haven't heard before," Tom said, and he was surprised at how calmly he reacted to Robert's ugly words. "I figure everybody needs somebody to look down on. For some, it's Melungeons. For others, it's bankers."

Robert drew back defensively. "I wasn't talking about people like you and your father, who try to make something of themselves."

"That's generous of you."

Tom's tone was mild, but the sarcasm wasn't lost on Robert, and his jaw set in a hard line. After a moment of silence, though, he seemed to abandon the idea of counterattack. "I was talking about parasites like the Turners."

"Let's go, Natalie," Ed said. "I'm not listening to this."

"I want you to stay," Tom said. "I need to talk to you."

But Ed grabbed their coats from the brass rack and pulled the door open for his wife. "Come out to our house anytime," he told Tom.

Then they were gone.

Damn it. He wasn't likely to get the two brothers together again and mad enough to air the family's dirty linen in front of a cop.

But Robert was willing to keep talking. When the door closed, he went on, "She turned my grandparents' fine old house into a pigsty. The yard was full of dog turds. You couldn't walk through the door without gagging on the smell of cat piss. She was always dragging strays home with her. It got to the point where people were leaving boxes full of kittens and puppies on the doorstep."

Tom thought of Holly, Pauline's niece, who obviously shared her aunt's love of animals. "So you think Adam was forced to lower his standards?"

"He certainly wasn't raised to live that way. Our mother was appalled."

"She didn't like Pauline either?"

Robert's mouth worked as if he were shifting around something too sour to swallow. "Not at first."

"Oh? You mean your mother changed her mind?"

The words came out as a grudging admission. "She learned to tolerate the woman because of the child."

"Pauline and Adam's daughter?"

Robert's short laugh held bitterness and derision. "Well, she was Pauline's daughter, anyway."

Tom frowned. "What do you mean?"

"Draw your own conclusions."

"Consider me dense, Mr. McClure. You'll have to spell it out."

"My mother accepted Mary Lee as her granddaughter, but I never believed she was Adam's child. And no, I don't have any proof, if you're about to ask. Maybe you should be looking for Mary Lee's real father. There's probably quite a tale to be told about Pauline's secret life. You might find her killer if you take the trouble to find out what kind of woman she really was."

"Did you tell my father you believed Adam wasn't Mary Lee's father?"

"Of course I did."

Tom couldn't have overlooked or forgotten something as explosive as Robert McClure's allegation. The information simply wasn't in the case records. Why would his father leave it out? Whom had he been protecting?

Chapter Thirteen

If anybody knew the truth about Pauline's daughter, Reed Durham would.

After leaving the bank, Tom turned left and walked up Main Street through swirling snow flurries to the law office of Durham & McCullough. Durham had been Pauline's attorney and confidant and he still represented Mary Lee in a limited way.

He had also been a good friend to Tom's father and was Tom's boss for a few weeks, ten years before. During the last summer of Pauline McClure's life, Tom was a University of Virginia student between his sophomore and junior years, undecided about his future. Law seemed the most attractive possibility, and he'd taken a job with Durham & McCullough to learn more about the profession. Never before or since had he endured such unrelieved tedium. When he headed back to school in early September, his biggest worry had been the choice of a career alternative. His father, at the same time, was falling into the grip of an obsession with Pauline's disappearance.

Hoping the exercise would clear the painkiller fog from his head, Tom passed up the office building's ancient elevator in favor of four flights of stairs.

When he walked in, the three female employees greeted him with a chorus of concern. Tom held up his free hand to silence them. "I'm okay, I'm fine." He turned to Debbie Schiller, the pretty receptionist with long wheat-colored hair. She was Brandon's fiancée. "I'm glad Brandon wasn't hurt."

To Tom's dismay, her blue eyes filled with tears and her lower lip quivered. "Me too. When he told me about it, I nearly fainted." Forcing a smile, she added, "I guess I have to grow some backbone if I'm going to be a policeman's wife."

Tom was trying to come up with something reassuring to say when Reed Durham threw open his office door. "Hey, Tommy. Come on in, son." Despite the early hour, he already looked a mess. The tail of his blue shirt ballooned from his waistband and emphasized a spreading middle, his sleeves were rolled to the elbow, and his gray-streaked brown hair spilled across his forehead. "How're you feeling? You caught the bastard yet?"

"Not yet. But we will."

Durham ushered him into a room that looked more like a sportsman's den than an office. Durham's grandest trophy, a mounted marlin his wife wouldn't allow in their home, took up most of one wall. Smaller mounted fish swam across the opposite wall, next to framed degrees and the same sort of civic association awards Robert McClure displayed. Among the family photos on the credenza behind the desk was an eight-by-ten shot of Durham and Tom's father, grinning with fake pride as they held up two tiny bass.

"Here you go." Durham snagged a set of keys from his cluttered desktop and tossed them to Tom. "I'll leave it to you to figure out which key fits which lock. The house has been broken into a couple of times, and I've had enough extra locks installed to keep out squatters. I hope and pray Mary Lee will finally sell it now. I never thought I'd still be looking after the place at this late date."

Tom jingled the ring of keys. Eight or nine, at least. He stashed them in his pants pocket.

Durham scooped a handful of darts from a drawer, walked around the desk and took aim at the target on the inside of his door. He scored a bull's-eye.

Tom took a few darts from Durham. His own shot landed outside the center of the target. "You're better at this than I'll ever be."

"Ah, but you're a better marksman. I wish I could handle a gun the way you do." As soon as the words were out, Durham grimaced. "Oops. Sorry."

Tom laughed. "I wish I could say you oughta see the other guy, but I never got a shot off." He unbuttoned his uniform jacket to lessen the pressure on his throbbing wound. The jacket, which he'd dug out of a storage box, had originally belonged to his brother and was a little tight around Tom's more muscular shoulders and upper arms.

Durham hit the bull's-eye again. Tom's second dart landed closer, on the center ring but not inside it. Durham collected all the darts from the board and offered half to Tom.

"I had an interesting talk with Robert McClure before I came here," Tom said.

"Oh, man. I can imagine." This time Durham's aim was off, and his shot landed in one of the outer rings. "I don't get the stink of bile coming off you, so I guess you managed to duck when he started spewing it out."

"He told me Mary Lee isn't Adam's daughter."

Durham grunted. "Singing his favorite refrain."

Tom struck the bull's-eye with his dart, and laughed in surprise. "Do you believe she's Adam's daughter?"

"Of course she is." Durham's next shot missed the board and the dart struck the door with a *thunk*. "Well, damn," he muttered. "Robert thought a woman like Pauline, from her background, well, she *had* to be the kind who'd run around on her husband. It was all lies. Robert was trying to get something he wasn't entitled to."

Tom tended to believe Durham, but he needed more information before making up his mind about the kind of woman Pauline was. "Adam never had any doubt that Mary Lee was his daughter?"

"No. He was crazy about her, called her his little princess. The child made his mother ecstatic. Adam was her favorite son, and before Pauline came along she'd just about despaired of him ever settling down and having kids. Too bad she died so soon after Adam did. The two of them kept Robert in check. With her gone, Robert went after Pauline like a cat after a bird."

"Tell me about the challenge to Adam's will."

"It was the worst thing I've ever been through as a lawyer. I'm not cut out for nasty court fights." Durham turned away from the dart board and moved to his desk. He plopped into his capacious chair, the black leather squeaking under his weight.

Leaning against an oak file cabinet, Tom asked, "How did Ed feel about what Robert was doing?"

"Totally against it."

"How close were Ed and Pauline?"

Durham's jaw tensed and his gaze shifted to the sky beyond the window. "They were friendly."

The same uninformative statement Tom had heard from Mary Lee, with the same undercurrent of something unspoken. He debated whether to pursue the subject and decided to save his questions about a possible affair for Ed McClure. He wandered to the big marlin on the wall and gazed into one of its glass eyes. "Robert became president of the bank when Adam died, right?"

"Yeah, but he wasn't satisfied. He wanted everything—the money and land their parents left to Adam, the very house Pauline lived in."

Tom turned away from the fish. "What made him think he could keep Pauline from inheriting her husband's estate?"

"Robert claimed she was drugging Adam right from the start, so he wasn't responsible for his actions when he married her or when he wrote his will."

"What?" Tom said with a startled laugh. "Are you serious?"

"Oh, yeah. Robert even suggested, never came right out and said it, but suggested real strongly that she might've killed Adam."

Tom's amusement faded. None of this was in the case record either. He stepped over to the window and watched snowflakes blow against the glass and melt into rivulets. What else had his father left out of the file? And why? He looked back at Durham. "How was she supposed to have killed him?"

"Oh…" Durham waggled his hands. "Some poison that could cause a heart attack, but no test could detect it. It was crazy. Adam had a plain old garden-variety coronary, like his father before him. They both died fairly young." He laughed. "With any luck, Robert will too."

Tom sat in a burgundy leather chair facing the desk. "Robert says Pauline was Melungeon trash, and she dragged Adam down to her level. He claims their house was a pigsty, with all those animals in it."

"The goddamn son of a—" The rest of Durham's words strangled in his throat. He drew a deep breath before he spoke again. "Pauline was the sweetest, most softhearted girl I ever met. And Robert's a fussy little old lady. Pauline's house was always clean. She had her housekeeper in to do the place top to bottom three times a week."

"Do you think Robert could've killed Pauline?" Tom asked, putting aside the mystery of the unidentified second victim for the moment. "Is he capable of it?"

With a wry smile, Durham said, "I can't see him getting his hands dirty. I doubt he takes out his own garbage."

"He could have hired somebody."

"Like O'Dell, you mean?" Durham shrugged. "It's a thought."

"Her killing looks like something personal." Tom absently rubbed his aching arm. "The house wasn't robbed. I don't see how anybody benefited financially except Mary Lee, and she had to wait seven years to inherit. The other skull we found makes me think there's some angle nobody's even considered."

"You'll have a hell of a job running it down after all this time." Durham shook his head and hair spilled across his brow again.

"I'd better get going." Tom rose. "I told Brandon to pick me up out front right about now. Pauline's housekeeper's meeting us at the house."

"Lila Barker? Oh, lord." Durham frowned and laughed at the same time. "I doubt you'll get anything useful out of her."

"She probably spent more time with Pauline than anybody else. She might remember something she didn't tell my dad."

"Yeah, maybe, but…" Durham rubbed his face with both hands as if fighting sudden exhaustion. "Just don't believe everything you hear."

"Somebody else told me the same thing. I still don't know what I'm being warned about."

"Just be careful, Tom. You never know what'll jump up and bite you on the ass if you turn over the wrong rock."

Chapter Fourteen

The little brown and white mutt trembled on the steel examining table. Rachel stroked his head and murmured, "It's okay, Teddy, it's okay."

He seemed oblivious to her reassuring touch. He looked neither at Rachel nor at Holly by her side, but fixed his eyes on his owner, an elderly man named Johnson.

"He pees all over the house," Johnson said. "Since my wife died, he won't mind me at all."

At the sound of his master's angry voice, the dog shuddered under Rachel's hand and curled his tail between his legs.

A faint whimper escaped Holly. When Rachel glanced at her, the girl's eyes were filled with tears. *Oh, no.* Holly had done well all morning, observing silently, getting a feel for the work, helping in little ways when Rachel gave half a dozen cats and dogs routine exams and vaccines. But maybe exposing her to an animal in trouble was too much for her first day.

The dog's problem was obvious, but if Rachel stated it baldly the man would take offense. "He's an old animal," she said, "and he spent his entire life as your wife's pet. I'm sure in his own way he misses her as much as you do." Rachel imagined dog and man in an all-too-quiet house, each isolated in his grief.

"She called him her baby." Johnson's voice thickened, and his eyes grew moist behind his glasses.

"Are you disciplining him?"

"I give him a little tap so he'll know he's done something wrong."

"You hit him?" Holly asked in a horrified voice. "No wonder he's scared to death of you."

Johnson's face went red with outrage.

"Anybody who'd hit a little animal—"

"Holly," Rachel said, "please go wait for me in my office."

Holly clapped a hand over her mouth, threw Rachel a teary apologetic look, and fled from the room.

"I'm just trying to make him behave," Johnson protested.

His harsh tone brought on wild tremors in the dog. Rachel pulled the animal against her, hoping the gentle contact would help. "He doesn't understand why you're punishing him. All he knows is that the person he loved all his life has disappeared. He has no one but you now, and he probably thinks you hate him."

Johnson's expression shifted from indignation to confusion. He reached out to the dog. The animal pressed against Rachel and issued a string of frantic whines. "My lord," Johnson said.

Rachel suppressed a sigh and began her education of the dog's owner. Johnson's resistance melted and he began to listen to her. When he left she was satisfied the dog's life would be better from now on.

Glad to have the busy morning behind her, Rachel went looking for Holly. She found the girl in the office, standing at the window and watching Johnson cross the parking lot with his dog tucked under his arm. Holly turned reluctantly. Like the little mutt, she seemed to cringe in anticipation of a blow. "Are you gonna fire me?"

"Of course not."

Holly's shoulders slumped with relief. This job, and all it represented, meant so much to her. Rachel would find a way to help her thrive here, even if it meant giving her lessons in courtesy and self-restraint.

"The dog's going to be all right," Rachel said. "But what would have happened to him if we'd made the owner mad enough to walk out without listening to me?"

"I'm sorry, Dr. Goddard." Holly's fingers plucked at the green polo shirt that was part of her employee uniform. "I couldn't help myself. I can't stand to see somebody hurtin' a little animal."

"I understand." Rachel leaned against her desk. "When I was a kid, I'd ring the neighbors' doorbells and lecture them about keeping their cats indoors so they wouldn't be killed by cars."

Holly's laugh came out in a delighted gust. "I did stuff like that, too. But my grandma said—" Her face sobered. "She made me stop."

"My mother made me stop too," Rachel said, smiling although the memory was a bitter one. "You've got the right instincts, but I've learned there are better ways to make people listen than by accusing them."

Holly nodded. "I won't do anything like that again, I promise."

"Don't worry about it." Rachel pushed away from the desk. "Will you clean the exam table so it'll be ready when—"

Raised voices from the outer office interrupted her. Shannon, at the front desk, said, "Sir, please, you'll have to wait till—"

"Get out of my way!" a man shouted. "I'll find her myself."

Rachel froze. Fear hit her like a punch, took away her breath. She'd heard those same words so many times in her memory, in her nightmares, that for a moment she was thrown back into the past, where a wild-eyed young man with a pistol had come looking for her.

"It's Uncle Jack!" Holly cried, backing against a wall.

Rachel forced her mind to the present and clenched her hands to stop their shaking. It was just another of Holly's crazy relatives. She could deal with this. She could.

Shannon cried, "Dr. Goddard!"

Rachel raced out to the reception area. Shannon stood next to the desk, both hands raised to stop the stocky man who leaned menacingly over her.

"Can I help you, sir?" Rachel asked.

He faced her, his hands curling into fists. He was probably in his fifties, with sun-weathered skin and graying black hair, but he looked fit enough to do some damage.

"I come to get Holly and take her home," he said. "This girl says she's in the office. Where is it?"

"What's your name, please?"

Shannon scooted back behind the desk.

"Jack Watford. Holly's uncle. Her grandma wants Holly back home right now."

What on earth was wrong with these people? Why were they so determined to hold on to Holly? "She's an adult, Mr. Watford. She can make her own choices, and she's chosen to work here."

"I'm takin' her home. Now where's the office?" Rachel was about to answer when Watford threw back his head and bellowed, "Holly! You come out here right now!"

"Call the police," Rachel told Shannon, "and tell them we have an intruder causing a disturbance." The Mountainview City Police had only one officer, Lloyd Jarrett, on duty during weekdays, and he was probably nodding off at his desk right now.

"You don't have to call the police," Holly said from the office doorway. "I don't want to cause any trouble."

Oh, God. Why didn't Holly have the sense to stay out of sight?

"Come on," Watford said, "let's go home. I'll come back and pick up your stuff."

Holly shuffled forward, arms wrapping her waist, her head down.

Behind the desk, Shannon spoke into the phone, summoning help.

"Holly," Rachel said, "do you want to stay here or do you want to go back to your grandmother's house? Tell me the truth."

When Holly raised her head, her cheeks were wet with tears. "You know I want to stay here. But—"

"Then it's settled." She had to make Holly believe that her own wishes mattered, that she didn't have to wait meekly for other people to decide her fate. Rachel told Watford, "You have your answer. I want you to leave."

"This ain't none of your business," he said. "Come on, Holly."

Rachel held up a hand to stop Holly in her tracks. She asked Watford, "Why do you want to drag her back home against her will? Why can't her family be happy she has a job and she's starting a life for herself?"

Watford leaned closer and spoke in a low growl. "You leave our family alone, you hear me?"

The beer and tobacco stink of his breath made her queasy and she had to swallow hard before she could speak. "Get out of my clinic right now, or I'll have the police throw you out." She envisioned Lloyd Jarrett, short and skinny and probably incapable of throwing anybody out of any place. She prayed that his gun and uniform would make an impression.

"Holly," Watford said, "come on now."

"No."

The single defiant little word made Rachel want to shout with joy. *Stand up to him. You can do it.*

"What did you say to me, girl?" Watford demanded.

Don't let him bully you.

"I said no." Holly's voice gathered strength. "I'm stayin' here."

"The hell you are." Watford bumped Rachel aside, and she stumbled against the reception desk. Holly yelped when his hand closed around her wrist.

Her blood roaring in her ears, Rachel lunged at him. She grabbed his free arm and wrenched it backward, at the same time planting a foot behind his knee and pushing hard. His legs went out from under him, he let go of Holly and tumbled to the floor.

The front door opened with a jingle of the bell, and Officer Lloyd Jarrett stepped in. "Well, now." He looked from Rachel to Watford. "What seems to be the trouble?"

Chapter Fifteen

Tom kept an eye out for potholes as Brandon maneuvered the cruiser up the long driveway to Pauline McClure's house. Brandon's wild driving on the way out had jolted the pain in Tom's arm up to full strength, and he didn't need any more shocks. He blew out a breath of relief when they cleared the last crater and Brandon slammed on the brakes.

The gray stone mansion and a detached four-car garage sat in a clearing circled by five acres of woods.

As they got out, Tom said, "A full-scale massacre could have happened out here and nobody would've seen or heard a thing."

Brandon stared open-mouthed at the house. "Oh, man. I think I saw this place in some horror movie."

Boarded-up windows and dead vines spider-webbing the walls gave the house an atmosphere of forbidding isolation, emphasized by a gray sky and swirling snow flurries. In the front yard garden, mounds of fallen leaves rotted around blackened coneflower stalks, but Tom could imagine the plot as a spectacular swath of summer color when Pauline had been alive to tend it.

They took the flagstone walk through the garden to the covered porch. Mounting the steps ahead of Brandon, Tom pulled out the keys Durham had given him. In addition to its original lock, the oak door had two deadbolts, installed after Pauline's disappearance to keep out vandals and squatters. Tom began the trial and error process of finding the right key for each lock.

A couple of toots from a car horn made Tom and Brandon turn. A twenty-year-old Plymouth Reliant, painted neon yellow, bounced up the driveway without missing a single pothole and shuddered to a stop behind the cruiser.

A tall, angular black woman in a red coat unfolded herself from the car. "Good day, gentlemen," she called. "I trust I'm not tardy." She slung the strap of a purse onto her shoulder and strode up the walk.

The housekeeper? Not exactly what Tom had expected.

When she reached them, Tom realized his first impression of a young, energetic woman had been wrong, at least as far as age went. The braids coiled on her head were as much gray as black, and the skin around her luminous dark eyes formed soft pouches, with wrinkles at the corners.

"Mrs. Barker?"

"I am." She sucked in a breath and released it. "I vowed I would never set foot in this house again. But when I heard your voice on the telephone, I felt as if your father was speaking to me through you. I knew in my heart I had to help you find the monster who murdered that gentle lady." She added with no change in tone, "I can sense it even now."

"Sense what?" Tom asked.

Her eyes met his. "Evil. Can't you feel it? The very air we're breathing is drenched with evil."

Jesus Christ, Tom thought, one of those. Next she'd be claiming she had "the sight" and wasn't bound by the natural world. Brandon gaped at her as if she'd brought the horror movie set to life.

"Thanks for coming out," Tom said. "Let me get the door open and we'll go in." So far he'd managed to open only the top lock.

Mrs. Barker's icy hand on his stopped him. "Allow me." She rotated her open palm above the keys, then touched two with a fingertip. "This silver one is for the middle lock. This blue one fits the bottom."

Tom tried them. The bolts slid back. He turned the knob and pushed the door open. He answered Brandon's astonished expression with a shrug. Maybe Mrs. Barker was an amateur locksmith.

Tom gestured for the woman to enter the house, but she stood with her eyes shut and her head thrown back. "The moment I turned into the driveway that morning, a terrible foreboding swept through me. It grew stronger and stronger as I approached the house. I wanted to flee, but something told me I had to go inside. I rang the bell, but there was no answer. I knocked, and there was no answer. Something made me try the door, and I discovered it was unlocked."

"Was that unusual?" Tom asked.

Her eyes opened. "It was unprecedented. Mrs. McClure believed a woman living alone in the country must take precautions."

Tom studied Mrs. Barker, wondering what this articulate, intelligent woman's personal story was. He vaguely recalled hearing about her popularity as a fortune teller for rich and poor alike. Why had she been cleaning Pauline's house for a living? He pulled his mind back on track. "What did you do when you found the door unlocked?"

"I entered the house." Spine stiff and chin up, Mrs. Barker marched past Tom and Brandon into the foyer.

Tom flipped a switch next to the door and the brass chandelier lit up. The foyer was larger than the living rooms of more modest houses. Peacocks fanned gaudy tails across the wallpaper. The silence seemed a physical sensation, a heaviness in the air. Motes swirled in the light, and dust invaded Tom's nostrils.

"I stood here," Mrs. Barker said. "I called Mrs. McClure's name, but she didn't answer. Two of the cats ran down the stairs and rubbed against my legs."

When she glanced down, Tom did too, half-expecting to see the cats.

"I looked in the living room." Mrs. Barker stepped through the doorway to the right.

The living room had no ceiling light, and in the gloom Tom saw only a large empty space, wall color indiscernible, the outlines of boarded-up Palladian windows faintly visible. His imagination supplied fine furniture and carpet, elaborate draperies, gold-framed paintings.

"The lamps were on," Mrs. Barker said. "One of the dogs was sleeping on the rug. One of the cats was in the front window. Mrs. McClure wasn't here. I went to the dining room next."

She turned, the folds of her red coat swishing around her body, and crossed the foyer. Tom and Brandon followed. With both hands, Mrs. Barker slid open oak doors to reveal another empty room. Tom felt for a light switch and brought a crystal chandelier to life. Thirty people could have been seated comfortably in the dining room. A sad picture came to mind of the widowed Pauline, alone after sending her daughter to boarding school, sitting at an enormous table to eat her meals.

"I began to fear she was ill or injured," Mrs. Barker said. "I rushed through the rest of the house, searching for her."

She led Tom and Brandon across the foyer and down a hallway past a library, a den, a powder room. At the end of the hall, Mrs. Barker stopped short of the last closed door. Her eyes clouded with an emotion Tom would have called fear if he'd seen any reason for her to be afraid.

"What's wrong?" he asked.

She licked her lips, her gaze fixed on the door. "I would prefer not to go into the kitchen."

"Why?"

She shook her head. "I can't."

More bad vibes, probably. Tom felt them, too, crawling like millipede legs up his spine, but he told himself his reaction was normal in a house where a murder—maybe two—had been committed. "Did you see something out of the ordinary in the kitchen?"

"It's not only what I saw or didn't see. It's what I felt. I feel it now. A terrible anger. And hatred. Evil, consuming hatred."

Brandon backed against the wall and gaped at the kitchen door. *Jesus Christ,* Tom thought, *am I the only sane one here?* "What did you see in the kitchen?"

"The cats and dogs hadn't been fed. I knew for certain something was terribly wrong. Mrs. McClure would never have neglected them."

"Did you see any signs of a struggle, anything broken or out of place?"

She shook her head. "No. But the animals refused to follow me into the kitchen."

Tom trusted the animals' instincts a lot more than Mrs. Barker's emotional sensors. Pauline might not have been killed in the kitchen, but something sure as hell happened there. "I want to take a look, but you can wait here. Brandon, you coming?"

Startled, Brandon lurched away from the wall, hitched up his gun belt, squared his shoulders. "Yes, sir."

Tom nudged open the swinging door, aware that his father's hand had probably performed the same motion ten years before, that he was retracing his father's invisible footsteps.

Tom circled the kitchen while Brandon hung back at the door. If the windows hadn't been boarded up, the kitchen might feel cozy and cheerful, with its strawberry vine wallpaper, light oak cabinets, and breakfast nook. Maybe Pauline had eaten her solitary meals here instead of the cavernous dining room.

After Pauline's disappearance, the State Police crime scene techs had found no blood in the kitchen—or anywhere else in the house. But something about this room disturbed Tom. His heartbeat quickened.

Jesus Christ. He shook his head to clear it. He was letting Mrs. Barker spook him.

"What?" Brandon said. "What's wrong?"

"Nothing, nothing." Tom searched for keys to fit the three locks on the back door. When he finally swung it open, he looked out onto a flagstone patio, a lawn, and another garden. Pauline might have been killed outside. Probably was, if an ax was the weapon. He imagined her struggling with her assailant in the kitchen, breaking free and frantically throwing open the back door, escaping into the night. He saw her killer pursuing her, grabbing an ax that leaned against a stack of firewood outside the door, running after Pauline with the weapon raised and ready to strike. Maybe she had tripped, fallen—

If she'd bled on the ground, the killer could have shoveled up the evidence and hauled it away. But the crime scene report didn't mention disturbed soil in the yard.

A gust of freezing air struck Tom on its way into the house. He saw three possibilities: Pauline was murdered somewhere else; the killer had expertly covered his tracks and concealed the spot where Pauline died; or the investigation was so slipshod that vital evidence on her property was overlooked. Tom didn't want to think about the third scenario, or what it would say about his father as the cop in charge.

"Mind if I take a look around outside?" Brandon asked.

"Go ahead." Brandon probably wanted to get out of the house because it was giving him the creeps. Tom locked the back door after Brandon and returned to the hallway.

Mrs. Barker wasn't there. He found her deep in the shadows of the living room, standing at the fireplace with her dark hands spread on the white marble mantel.

She spoke without looking around. "I feel her presence so strongly. On a snowy winter's day like this, she would curl up in her big chair by the fire, with her animals around her, and knit or read. She said she found peace in this room."

The shadows near the fireplace seemed to float before Tom's eyes, shifting into an image of a small woman nestled in a massive wing chair. *Get a grip, Bridger.* He unhooked his flashlight from his belt and switched it on, and the apparition vanished. He cleared his throat. "What did you do after checking the kitchen that morning?"

"I looked upstairs. I looked in the garage, and her car was there. Then I called Mr. Durham."

Durham wasn't mentioned in the initial report. "You didn't call the police first?"

"Mrs. McClure told me to notify Mr. Durham if anything ever happened to her, if she was in an accident or incapacitated, and he would see to everything." Mrs. Barker paused, and when she spoke again her voice quavered. "She said he was her rock, the one person she could depend on."

"Didn't he tell you to call the police?"

"Not right then. He told me to wait for him. I fed the animals while I waited. I had to put their food in the dining room to persuade them to eat. Mr. Durham arrived and we went through the house together. We talked about the possibility that she had been kidnapped for ransom. Then he told me to call your father."

Why didn't Durham call? Tom would rather hear the explanation from Reed Durham than Mrs. Barker.

He asked, "Had Shackleford and O'Dell been working here the day before?"

"I don't know. I wasn't here."

"How would you describe her relationships with them?"

Mrs. Barker frowned at a spot Tom couldn't see on the mantel and rubbed it with her fingertips. "Cordial, from all appearances. But I didn't care for Shackleford. I had a strong sense of corruption—immorality, criminality. It surrounded him like a black aura."

"Why did Pauline have scum like him working for her?"

Mrs. Barker abandoned her cleaning effort and faced Tom. "It was a way to make certain the child was provided for."

"What child?"

"Her sister Jean's little girl. Holly. Troy Shackleford is her father, but I'm sure you know that. Mrs. McClure had an arrangement with Shackleford. Most of what she paid him was passed on to Jean for the child's support."

Interesting. Maybe Pauline didn't have much contact with her family, but she'd cared enough to find an indirect way to help her sister and niece.

Before Tom could pursue this line of thought, Mrs. Barker went on, "But I was always uneasy about having him around. He's the one I would have predicted would do something like this—"

When she reached toward his wounded arm, Tom took an unthinking step backward, out of her range. His flashlight beam bounced with his movement, illuminating her faint, brief smile. She lowered her hand.

"I have to admit I'm quite surprised that Rudy O'Dell shot you," she said, "and people don't surprise me very often. He was so shy and tongue-tied I rarely heard him utter a sensible word. Harmless as a baby rabbit. Something has driven him to this extreme. Something… wicked."

Tom's arm throbbed and his mouth went dry at the memory of the bullet gouging his flesh. Wicked, all right. "Did you ever hear Mrs. McClure argue with either of them? About money, or anything else?"

"In my hearing, not a single contentious word ever passed among them."

Terrific. The person who'd spent the most time with Pauline was turning out to be useless as a witness. "Do you remember any women who visited her around the time she disappeared?"

"Let's see." She pursed her generous lips as she thought. "Both of her sisters came to see her that week—came together, I mean. Her niece, Amy, was here on a couple of occasions."

"Really? I thought Pauline didn't have much to do with her family."

"I couldn't tell you anything about her relationships with her family." Mrs. Barker drifted around the room, her hands moving as if she were mentally replacing each missing piece of furniture. "It was a private matter. It didn't concern me."

Tom doubted she was ignorant on the subject, but he was sure she didn't intend to tell him anything. He'd get back to it. For now, he took another tack. "Aside from Reed Durham, did she have any male friends?"

Mrs. Barker stepped closer, willing to face him again. "Ed McClure was a friend."

"How often was Ed here?"

"Two or three times a week."

That sounded like a hell of a lot more than friendship. Tom would have to ask Natalie McClure how she'd felt about her husband's attentions to his beautiful sister-in-law. "Did you hear what they talked about?"

"Plants," Mrs. Barker said. "You know he's a botanist? He teaches at the college in Blacksburg and he hybridizes fruit trees."

Tom nodded.

"Mrs. McClure enjoyed working with plants herself." Now Mrs. Barker seemed relaxed and expansive, maybe because she considered this topic safe. "She had her flower garden in front, and she grew herbs out back. She was a great believer in herbal cures for all manner of conditions. Learned it from her mother."

For a second Tom tasted again the bitter brew Mrs. Turner had urged on him after she'd bandaged his arm. "Did Pauline ever try any of these herbal cures on her husband?"

She tensed like a line jerked taut. "I doubt it. He wouldn't even drink herbal tea." Her eyes narrowed. "Mrs. McClure didn't poison her husband, if that's what you're getting at."

Tom's knowledge of herbs was limited to the parsley sprigs on restaurant plates. He'd have to learn more before he pursued the idea of Pauline as a poisoner. "Did her friendship with Ed McClure continue up to the time she disappeared?"

"Almost," Mrs. Barker said. "He'd fallen out of favor shortly before. She told me never to admit him to this house again. I don't know why."

A scorned lover? "Did you tell my father all this after Pauline disappeared?"

"Well, no, I don't think I ever discussed it with him."

"Why not?"

Her brow creased. "Why would he have to be told something he already knew? She talked to your father all the time about her husband's family. I wasn't eavesdropping, but I heard enough to know she confided in him."

"What—what are—"

For a long moment Mrs. Barker held his gaze. "I was certain you knew they were close," she said at last, grimacing as if the mistake pained her.

"Are you saying—" Good God. His respectable, dependable father, the upstanding citizen, the good husband, the church-goer—

"I'm only saying he came to see her. Had a cup of coffee and talked a while. He was being nice to an old friend who was widowed and didn't have many people to depend on. They were both interested in their Melungeon heritage. Your father knew all the history, and she had many questions for him. What a shame that she never lived to see the creation of the Melungeon Heritage Association and witness the surge of interest in—"

"An old friend?" Tom broke in.

She eyed Tom warily. "I believe they had known each other for many years. I could be completely wrong."

"How long did it go on?" Tom asked, his voice a croak.

"You're jumping to conclusions. I never said—"

"When did my father start coming here?"

She twisted her hands together. "Two, three years before she—well, I suppose I ought to say before she died."

Two or three years. Tom dragged in a deep breath to combat sudden light-headedness. "When was the last time he came?"

"As far as I know, a few days before she went missing."

The front door opened, letting in a cold draft, then slammed shut. A second later Brandon appeared in the living room.

"Thanks for your help," Tom said to Mrs. Barker, his voice more brusque than he intended. The sickening knot in his gut wasn't her fault. She'd only been the messenger. But he had to get away from her and her knowledge of his father's secret life.

Tom brushed past Brandon and headed for the front door. Mrs. Barker and Brandon followed. On the porch, Mrs. Barker stood by silently, offering no help, while Tom searched through the keys to find the right three for the door's locks.

When the house was secured, Tom turned and found her watching him with a penetrating gaze.

"I wish you'd never found her." Mrs. Barker's voice was low and fierce. "I wish she'd been left to rest where she was. You mark my words, young man, no good will come from disturbing the dead."

Chapter Sixteen

During the drive back to Mountainview, Tom tried to keep up with Brandon's string of theories about the murders while another part of his mind struggled to understand what he'd learned from Mrs. Barker about his father and Pauline McClure.

"How about the lawyer? Durham?" Brandon asked. "Suppose he was stealing from Pauline, defrauding her somehow, and she found out and threatened to bring charges?"

"I'll talk to him." No way around it. The notion of Reed Durham killing a woman with an ax was ludicrous, but his behavior after Pauline disappeared—assuming Mrs. Barker had described it accurately—was peculiar at best. Still, Tom didn't know where he would find the words to phrase the questions. How the hell did he ask an old family friend whether he'd stolen from a client and committed murder?

"Or maybe he was, like, involved with Pauline," Brandon said, "and Pauline started making noises about telling his wife? Or maybe he found out she was sleeping with somebody else at the same time and he flipped out."

The two old friends, John Bridger and Reed Durham, competing for the same woman—or sharing her? The thought sickened Tom, and it went against everything he knew about both men. What he *thought* he knew.

He'd have to ask Reed Durham outright if he'd had an affair with Pauline. That confrontation promised to be a lot less painful than tearing apart his lifelong image of his father and replacing it with that of a lying cheat.

Static burst from the police radio. Janet, the young 911 dispatcher, spoke up in her singsong voice. "Unit two, come in. Over."

Tom grabbed the mike and answered.

"Sergeant Murray wanted you to know there was an intruder causing a disturbance at Mountainview Animal Hospital a while ago and it might be connected to the case you're working on?" Janet said with a questioning lilt. "I sent the city police. Over."

Rachel. "Is anybody hurt? Over."

"I don't have any details, sir, but I heard Dr. Goddard used karate on the guy. The intruder, I mean. Over."

Rachel knew karate? Tom signed off and dropped the mike onto its hook. "Speed up," he told Brandon.

<><><>

Rachel decided the best way to calm Holly down was to keep the girl busy and avoid further mention of her uncle. They ate bagged lunches in the tiny staff lounge and used the rest of the hour to continue Holly's on-the-job training. She learned quickly and didn't have to be told anything twice.

They were behind the front desk, and Rachel was giving Holly a lesson in the use of a three-line telephone, when Tom charged in with Brandon Connelly. They halted on the big welcome mat and swept the place with wide eyes as if they'd expected to find a riot in progress. Rachel's stomach flip-flopped at the sight of Tom's left arm in a sling. But he was in uniform, working. He must be all right.

"Everything okay here?" Tom asked.

He must have heard about Jack Watford's visit. "Just fine," Rachel said, determined not to let him use the incident as proof that Holly was trouble.

"Good," Tom said, but while he wiped his boots on the mat he examined the reception area again as though he might detect lingering evidence.

Brandon gave his own boots a couple of swipes, then headed for the desk. He leaned on the counter and grinned at Holly. "Hey. Remember me?"

"Sure I do. Hi." Holly smiled, her cheeks flushed.

Rachel rounded the desk and walked over to Tom. Up close, she saw the bulge of a bandage under his jacket sleeve. "The newspaper story about the shooting made it sound like nothing but a scratch. I hope that was the truth."

"Yeah," he said. "It's a minor flesh wound."

Pure dumb luck, Rachel thought. A few inches over, and the bullet could have hit his heart, an artery, his spine— She slammed her mind shut on the horrifying possibilities. Just as well that she'd kept Tom at arm's length. Even a country cop could be shot—could be killed—in the line of duty. She didn't want that uncertainty and dread in her life.

"I'm glad you're okay," she said.

"I heard you had some excitement a while ago."

Glancing at Holly, Rachel said, "Let's talk in my office."

Holly and Brandon seemed too engrossed in conversation to notice when Rachel and Tom walked past them and down the short hallway. The young deputy's obvious interest in Holly worried Rachel. Wasn't he engaged? She was sure she'd seen an announcement in the newspaper.

In her office she settled in the chair behind her desk. The conscious effort to underscore her authority here probably didn't impress a cop, but it made Rachel feel more in control. "It was Holly's uncle. He claimed her grandmother sent him to take Holly home. She didn't want to go, so I told him to get lost."

Tom, still standing, shook his head. "I hate to keep harping on this, but you don't know what kind of people you're dealing with."

She didn't like the emotions on Tom's face—consternation, anger, and the frustration of someone whose good advice has been ignored. He looked tired and edgy and was probably in pain. Rachel hated to add to his stress with an argument, but she wouldn't back away from her commitment to Holly.

"Sit down, please." She waited until Tom sat in the visitor's chair facing the desk. "Holly loves being here. She doesn't want to go back to living with her grandmother and working for nothing at that filthy diner."

"What did Jack Watford do that made you call the police?"

Rachel started to fold her arms but realized that would look confrontational. She clasped her hands on the desktop. "He seemed to think he had the right to drag Holly out of here. We called the police, but I had everything under control by the time Lloyd Jarrett arrived."

A grin sneaked through Tom's stern expression. "Did you really use karate on him?"

Rachel laughed, mostly out of relief that Tom hadn't launched into a lecture about her foolhardiness in hiring Holly. "I wouldn't glorify it by calling it karate. But he ended up on the floor. I'm probably lucky he didn't file an assault charge, but he seemed awfully eager to get out of here when a cop showed up."

Tom frowned and leaned forward, examining her face. "What the hell— Did Watford do that?"

Rachel touched the bruise on her right cheekbone. "This? No. I had a stupid little accident last night." She had no intention of telling Tom or anyone else that Holly had socked her in a nightmare frenzy.

He looked doubtful about her explanation, but he let it pass. "Where's Holly living?"

"With me, for now."

"Jesus Christ, Rachel. What if Watford shows up at your house?"

The same fear had hunkered down inside her and was making a fine meal of her nerves. "He won't get inside," she said, trying to reassure herself as much as Tom. "I have grilles on my windows and bolts on my doors."

"You're not always locked inside your house. I don't like it. You need to find somewhere else for her to live."

Rachel rolled her chair back, stood and moved to the window. Fat snowflakes coated the parking lot. "If Holly rented a room somewhere, her family could get to her at any time, and she wouldn't have anybody to back her up."

Tom joined her at the window and laid a hand on her shoulder. Rachel tensed under his touch and avoided looking at him because she expected to see disapproval on his face.

But when he spoke his voice was gentle. "What is it about this girl that gets to you? Why are you going to so much trouble for her?"

"I've been wondering about that too." Rachel faced him. "You know what I came up with? She reminds me of myself."

Tom burst out laughing. "You're joking, right?"

"No, I'm serious. I spent most of my life letting my mother tell me what to do, what to think, how to feel. She even tried to choose my profession for me—she wanted me to be a medical doctor. To her dying day, she never forgave me for 'wasting' my ability on cats and dogs. When I see Holly's family trying to control her, I feel like screaming. She wants a life of her own. I have to help her."

"You need to put yourself first, Rachel."

So much for persuading him with personal confidences. But Tom's opinion was beside the point. "Holly's here and she's staying."

Tom raised his eyes heavenward as if pleading with a higher power for patience with this woman. Rachel hated it when men did things like that, but she stifled her irritation.

"Well," Tom said, "I have to talk to Holly. Can I do that in here?"

"Please don't. She's not responsible for her uncle's behavior."

"It's not about that," he said. "It has to do with the case."

Rachel sighed. "All right, but keep in mind that she's had a rough morning. It wouldn't take much to upset her again. And I've got an arthritic German shepherd coming in for an acupuncture treatment in—" She consulted her watch. "—twenty minutes. I'll need Holly's help."

Rachel went to the door and poked her head out. Shannon had returned from lunch, and she and Holly were laughing at some tale Brandon was unreeling.

"Sorry to break this up, kids," Rachel said. "Holly, please come here for a minute. Captain Bridger would like to ask you something."

Holly hesitated, her eyes darting left and right as if seeking an escape route, before she walked slowly to the office.

Rachel placed an arm around Holly's shoulders and said, "I'll stay with you, okay?"

"Me, too," Brandon said. "And I promise the captain won't bite."

Rachel stationed herself inside the office door and gave Tom a look to tell him she wasn't going anywhere. Brandon stood beside her, his gaze following Holly.

Tom settled on the edge of the desk and gestured for Holly to take the visitor's chair. She sat with her shoulders rigid and her hands squeezed together in her lap. Absolutely terrified, Rachel thought.

"How do you like your new job?" Tom asked.

Holly's gaze flicked to Rachel, back to Tom. "I like it a lot. I hope I can stay on."

"No reason why you wouldn't," Rachel said. She smiled, but Holly remained tense.

"I was hoping you could tell me where your mother's living now," he said, "so I can give her a call."

Holly's hands separated and formed fists, her fingernails digging into her palms. Rachel winced, sure Holly was about to draw blood, and she wished she could grab the girl's hands and uncurl her fingers.

"I don't know where Mama is," Holly said. "She always sent Grandma money when I was in school, for clothes and stuff, but she never has been good about callin' or writin'. She always sends a Christmas card, though." Her voice fell. "Just one for both of us."

The childlike bewilderment on Holly's face was painful for Rachel to look at.

"Do you have an envelope with her return address on it?"

Holly stared at her hands in her lap. "Grandma burns the envelopes before I get a chance to see them. She's always been afraid if I knew where my mama was, I'd run away and try to get to her." She added in a whisper, "I guess I would."

That selfish old witch, Rachel thought. But was the runaway mother any better?

"Do you think your father would know where your mother is?" Tom asked.

Holly gave a bitter little laugh. "Not hardly. She wouldn't want him to know. I think she left in the first place to—" She broke off and bit her bottom lip.

"To get away from Shackleford?" Tom prompted. "Was she afraid of him?"

"I don't know. Grandma says I don't recall things right because I wasn't but eight."

Rachel added mind control to the list of Mrs. Turner's sins. One more form of manipulation that Rachel knew entirely too much about. What was the old woman so determined to erase from Holly's memory?

"Regardless of what your grandmother told you," Tom said, "I'd like to hear anything you remember from around that time. It could help us solve your aunt's murder. Were your father and Rudy O'Dell—"

Holly shot to her feet, making her chair rock behind her. Rachel moved toward the girl, but Tom stopped her with a look. Brandon shifted as if he could barely hold himself back.

"I don't remember anything," Holly said. "I swear I don't."

Tom stood. "It's okay. Anytime you want to talk to me, give me a call. I really would appreciate your help."

Holly bolted for the door, and Rachel and Brandon stood aside to let her leave. But when her hand was on the knob, Holly turned back to Tom. "My daddy was at my grandma's house the evenin' after you came out to tell us about Aunt Pauline."

"What did he want?"

"I don't know. Him and Grandma went out in the yard to talk so I couldn't hear." Holly faltered for a second, then blurted, "She's dead scared of him, Captain Bridger. I can't stand to think about him hurtin' her."

"Why is she afraid of him? What do you think he might do?"

"I don't— I can't— My grandma would be real mad if she found out I was talkin' to the law—to anybody—about our family." Holly yanked the door open and fled.

Brandon hurried after her, but Rachel blocked the doorway when Tom tried to follow. "Leave her alone! She's been through enough for now."

"Rachel—"

"Do I have throw you on the floor too to make you behave?"

Tom flashed a grin. "Go ahead and try it. I'd like to see you in action."

"Don't tempt me, pal." *Stop flirting with him.* "Look. I get the same feeling you do—Holly's been frightened into keeping her mouth shut about something. But I think you scare her too, with your uniform and your badge and your gun. She might open up to me, though, without you around."

Tom cocked his head and eyed Rachel. "You're already closer to this investigation than I want you to be. Now you want to question Holly for me?"

"I'm not saying I'll grill her for information. But she's more likely to talk to me than to you. I want this over with—for her sake and mine." She had to tell him about that damned spider and then he'd probably launch into another speech. "I need to show you something."

She opened a cabinet and took out an alcohol-filled vial. The spider floated in it. "Somebody put this through the mail slot here at the hospital. It came in this package—" She retrieved the manila envelope and box from a shelf. "—and you can see how it was addressed. The spider was alive when I opened the box. It crawled out onto my hand."

Tom stared at the creature in the vial. He looked more than alarmed. He looked horrified.

"Maybe it's somebody's notion of a sick joke," Rachel said, not believing it for an instant.

"This isn't a joke," Tom said. "Whoever sent it was trying to hurt you. Maybe kill you."

"Black widow bites aren't fatal to healthy adults."

"But most people think they are. Somebody went to the trouble of finding this thing in the middle of winter because they thought it might bite you. And I don't believe it's a coincidence that Holly's just moved in with you over her family's objections."

"Nobody could have counted on it biting me. Maybe somebody just wants to scare me and make me kick her out, but I'm not going to." Rachel released a shaky breath. "Do you think you'll get any fingerprints off the packaging?"

"Probably not, if the person who sent it was careful, but I'll try. And I want you to be on your guard. There's somebody out there who needs to keep Holly quiet about what she knows. If they think she's talking to you, they'll be determined to get rid of you too."

Chapter Seventeen

"Let me handle him," Tom warned Brandon as they approached the Watford house. "I need to question Bonnie before we jump all over Jack."

"The son of a bitch," Brandon muttered. His grip on the steering wheel tightened until his knuckles went white. "Trying to drag Holly off, like she hasn't got a say in her own life."

He swung the cruiser into the driveway and the tires slid on wet gravel before gaining traction. The Watfords lived up the road from Sarelda Turner, in a clapboard bungalow painted pearl gray. Smoke twisted from the brick chimney and danced in the wind before whirling away with the snow flurries. The most striking thing about the house, to Tom's eyes, was the presence of immaculate white shutters at every window. Most people out this way didn't bother with routine maintenance, much less decorative touches like shutters.

Watford opened the front door before Tom and Brandon reached it. "Hey. What can I do for you?"

Tom almost smiled at the mental image of Rachel bringing down this sturdy, barrel-chested guy. He'd give anything to have seen it. "We just need to ask you a few questions."

"Yeah, sure." Watford stepped out on the porch and spoke quietly. "My wife, she's got bad nerves, and she's havin' a hard time dealin' with all this. I'm takin' time off so I can stay home and help her. Go easy, will you?" He stepped back to let them pass.

Bonnie stood by the fireplace, winding a dishtowel around her hands. She bobbed her head in answer to their greetings. "How's your arm feelin'?"

"Better," Tom said. "I appreciate y'all helping me out yesterday."

The furniture in the small room was plain but looked new, and it might look that way forever if the clear plastic covers stayed on. Watford and his wife sat on the green sofa, Tom and Brandon took matching easy chairs facing the couple, and for a moment the only sound was the crinkle of plastic under everybody's weight.

"I know you've probably expected the worst about Pauline all along," Tom said to Bonnie, "but it must be a shock to have it confirmed."

Up close, he saw that her husband hadn't exaggerated her emotional state. She had the exhausted, puffy-faced look of someone who'd been crying off and on for days. Her eyelashes stuck together in wet clumps. "It's been awful," she answered in a near-whisper.

"I'm sure it has. Were you and Pauline very close?"

"Not after she got married."

"We moved to Pittsburgh," Watford said. "Lived up there for a few years, so we wasn't even here for a long time. Her husband didn't want nothin' to do with Pauline's family anyway. We never got invited for supper, if you know what I mean."

"She was doin' what she needed to," Bonnie said, "so she could keep hold of what she had."

"Her husband died six years before she disappeared," Tom pointed out. "Didn't his death change anything?"

Neither answered. Watford watched the fire in the grate, Bonnie studied the terrycloth dishtowel in her hands. Tom imagined they'd been envious of Pauline's luck in snagging a McClure, and resentful because she lived in a mansion while they lived in the county's poorest district. "Maybe she was afraid her family would ask her for money."

Watford shot to his feet. "We never went beggin' to her for money. I work for what I've got, always have." When Tom didn't respond, Watford seemed driven to fill the silence. "I had a good job in a steel mill in Pittsburgh, and ever since we come back here I've been deliverin' furnace oil. I don't ask nobody for nothin'."

On the sofa, Bonnie had begun to weep. "I just wanted to see her now and then," she murmured. "But Pauline treated me like poison."

Watford sat down and gathered her into his arms. He threw a resentful look at Tom, clearly blaming him for the tears.

Tom waited for Bonnie to cry herself out. What was she mourning? A lost sister who wanted nothing to do with her, lost opportunities for a close family? When she was composed and had pulled away from her husband, Tom asked, "Why did you and your sister Jean go see Pauline the week she disappeared?"

"Mama wasn't feelin' too well," Bonnie said, "and we were tryin' to get Pauline to pay her a visit."

"Did she?"

Bonnie shook her head and ran a thumb along a stripe in the dishtowel.

Maybe bluntness would prod these two into speaking more openly. "Pauline sounds like a selfish woman who didn't care about anything but money and her big house."

Tom wasn't sure what he'd expected, but he got silence and a total absence of visible reaction. He pushed it farther. "I've heard she slept with a lot of men, and her husband might not have been the real father of her daughter."

They both winced. "Her new life meant too much to her," Bonnie said. "She wouldn't take a chance on losin' it all by runnin' around on her husband." She paused and bit her lip. "But Pauline always did like the company of men better'n women, so I'm sure she had her men friends after her husband died."

A ripple of apprehension ran through Tom. He forced himself to ask, "Do you know of anybody in particular she was involved with?"

"I couldn't name any names."

Her glance touched him briefly, and a glint of something in her eyes, at once mocking and pitying, turned him cold inside. Tom recalled the sly look Mrs. Turner had given him when she'd mentioned his father. These people knew about his father's relationship with Pauline. The thought brought a sour taste to his throat.

He rose and took half a dozen steps to the fireplace, where he gave studious attention to the line of photos on the mantel. Four young men and a young woman. They looked like teenagers, and the photos appeared to be bland studio portraits made on picture day at school. "Are these your children?"

"Yeah," Watford said. "When they was in high school."

"I like to be reminded of when we had them all at home," Bonnie said.

With a little laugh, Watford said, "She would've kept them babies if she could've."

His teasing didn't go down well with his wife, Tom noticed. Tears pooled in Bonnie's eyes again and she dabbed at them with the dishtowel.

"Do they live around here?" Tom asked.

"No," Watford said with a note of regret. "They're all over the country. California, Wisconsin, Texas."

"Were your sons living here when Pauline disappeared?"

Watford stiffened and his eyes turned wary. "No. They was grown up and gone by then. I hope you're not thinkin' one of them had somethin' to do with—"

"I'm only trying to get everybody straight in my mind." Tom did some quick calculations, based on what he'd read about Bonnie in the case notes. She'd been in her thirties when Pauline disappeared. If her sons were adults by then, she'd started having babies when she was sixteen or seventeen at the latest. A baby a year, probably. No wonder she looked so worn out. She'd probably been worn out by the time she was twenty.

He picked up the photo of their daughter as a teenager. Although heavy makeup coated her face like a mask, the Turner family resemblance was unmistakable in her features and the long black hair. She looked familiar in another way too, as if he'd known her or seen her in the past. They'd probably been in high school at the same time. "This is Amy? Where is she now?"

The couple exchanged glances. A moment passed before Watford answered Tom with a grudging, "South Carolina."

"Where in South Carolina? I'd like to talk to her."

"Listen," Watford said. "We want to help, but we're not tellin' you how to get in touch with Amy. Not if you're gonna talk to her the way you been talkin' to us. Her husband's in bad shape from a car wreck, and Amy's run ragged lookin' after him and the kids too, and tryin' to get their insurance to pay up. We didn't even tell her yet about Pauline bein' found. She was real fond of Pauline. She don't need you upsettin' her when she's got enough to worry about."

Tom returned to his chair. "I've been told Amy visited Pauline right before Pauline disappeared," Tom said. "Your daughter might have seen or heard something that'll help in the investigation. I won't know till I talk to her."

Watford shook his head. "She's never mentioned anything. She was confounded like the rest of us about what happened. You leave her alone."

Bonnie touched her husband's hand and said tentatively, "Maybe if we broke the news to her first—"

"That's fine with me," Tom said. "Let me know when she's ready to talk to me."

Bonnie nodded. Her husband's stubborn expression didn't change. Tom was betting on Watford to win the inevitable argument after he and Brandon left.

"Where is Holly's mother now?" Tom asked Bonnie.

"Oh, I couldn't tell you where Jeannie is. She moves around."

"Why didn't she take Holly with her when she left home?" Brandon asked. "What kind of a mother leaves her little kid for somebody else to raise?"

Tom was startled by Brandon's vehemence, but intrigued by the reaction it provoked in Bonnie. Her tears spilled over again and drenched her cheeks. "A bad mother, that's what kind." She pressed a hand to her mouth to hold back sobs.

"Honey, come on now." Watford patted her shoulder and threw a baleful look at Brandon and Tom. "Holly's been better off with her grandma. Jeannie would've dragged her all over creation."

"Jean left before the Sheriff's Department had a chance to question her about Pauline's disappearance," Tom said. "Was she running away from the police?"

Bonnie blotted her tear-streaked face with the dishtowel. "What are you accusin' my little sister of?"

Tom doubted Jean Turner had killed Pauline and the nameless victim—this didn't look like a female crime to him, and he didn't see how a small woman could have carried two bodies to the mountaintop—but she might have been involved somehow. Especially if her lover, Shackleford, had done the killing. "We're looking at every possibility."

"It oughta be clear enough by now that Rudy O'Dell done it," Watford said. "He damned near killed you too, didn't he?"

"O'Dell's a suspect," Tom said, "but he's not the only one. How well do you know him?"

Watford gave a sneering laugh. "A hell of a lot better'n I want to. He's a sneaky little bastard. I caught him outside here one night, lookin' in the window at Bonnie. He, uh—" Watford cleared his throat. "He had his pants down, if you know what I mean."

Bonnie averted her face, her cheeks flaming.

Evidently O'Dell wasn't a hermit after all. "When was this?" Tom asked.

"Late last summer."

"Did you report it?"

Watford shook his head. "Naw. I hauled his ass out to the road and told him if I caught him on my property again, I'd put a bullet in him."

He would shoot O'Dell for peeking in a window and masturbating, but hadn't acted on his belief that O'Dell murdered Pauline? "Did he ever do anything, say anything to make you think he killed Pauline?"

"He was wild about her," Bonnie said. "He went around tellin' people she loved him and she was gonna ask him to come live with her. It was pure craziness. Pauline never would've... you know... with somebody like him."

Watford nodded. "We figure he went too far with her, and she put him in his place, and he went over the edge."

That made sense to Tom. O'Dell's attack on him and Brandon reinforced the appearance of guilt. But where did Shackleford fit in? Tom's instincts were screaming that the man was in this up to his neck. "You don't think Troy Shackleford could have done it?"

"She wasn't robbed," Watford said. "Troy don't do nothin' except for money."

"Rudy O'Dell killed my sister," Bonnie said. "You got to find him and put him behind bars. I'm afraid he's gonna go after little Holly, 'cause she looks so much like Pauline. He's already been botherin' her."

"What?" Brandon said. He was on the edge of his seat. "What's he been doing to Holly?"

"Snoopin'," Watford said. "I went by my mother-in-law's house a couple weeks back, and I spotted him in the trees across the road. He had his old binoculars, and he was watchin' Holly. She was playin' with the dogs in the front yard. He claimed he was lookin' at birds, but he was watchin' Holly."

"Son of a bitch," Brandon muttered. He scrubbed his palms on his pants legs.

Tom made a mental note to have another talk with Brandon about Holly. "Then it's a good thing Holly's moved. O'Dell won't be able to find her. Unless somebody tells him where she is. And by the way, I don't want you causing another uproar at the animal hospital."

Watford jumped up and stalked over to the fireplace. He poked at the logs, sending a shower of sparks up the chimney, but his gaze slid back toward Tom as if he were trying to gauge how much Tom knew. Watford seemed the kind of man who wouldn't forgive a woman for getting the better of him in a physical contest and couldn't stand having other men know about it.

"Are we clear?" Tom asked.

Watford coughed. "I think she—the vet, I guess she was—made too much of it. I wasn't doin' nothin' except tellin' Holly her grandma wanted her back home."

"Holly wants to stay where she is."

Watford stabbed a log with the poker and the wood popped and blazed. "The girl's got obligations to her family."

Suddenly Brandon was on his feet and in the man's face. "She's got a right to live her own life, and you don't have anything to say about it."

"Who the hell do you think—"

Brandon grabbed the front of Watford's shirt. "You stay away from her!"

"Stop it," Tom said. He tugged on Brandon's arm. Brandon and Watford stared into each other's eyes, refusing to give ground. Tom was afraid Watford wouldn't need much more provocation to use the poker he held. Tom shoved himself between them, and they stumbled apart. The effort brought the pain in Tom's arm roaring back.

Watford dropped the poker on the hearth, where it landed with a clank. He stuffed his rucked-up shirt back into his waistband.

"Mrs. Watford," Tom said, turning to Bonnie, "I'll expect a call after you've talked to your daughter." He pulled a Sheriff's Department business card from his jacket's inside pocket and offered it.

She hesitated a second before accepting the card.

Tom waited till they were in the cruiser before speaking to Brandon. "Look, I can't stop you from throwing away your relationship with Debbie, if you're determined to. But you're not going to let this crush—"

"It's not a crush. I really care what happens to Holly."

"Be quiet and listen to me. You're not going to let it interfere with your work. You either act like a professional or I'm taking you off this case."

"Yes, sir." Brandon gripped the steering wheel and stared straight ahead. A second passed, then he burst out, "We gotta find O'Dell. We can't let him hurt her."

Chapter Eighteen

Rudy O'Dell had been missing for more than twenty-four hours and neither the State Police vehicle stops nor the county deputies' rounds of his relatives had turned up a trace of him.

When the deputies gathered in the conference room in mid-afternoon, Tom told them, "I think O'Dell's holed up somewhere in the county. He's stayed close to home all these years, and I doubt he'll strike out on his own now."

"His mother's real proud of her boy for what he did to you," Dennis Murray said. The sergeant, on Tom's left, nudged his wire-rimmed glasses up the bridge of his nose with a fingertip. "But she's worried about Troy Shackleford getting to Rudy. She said Rudy'll be fine as long as he can steer clear of Troy."

Sheriff Willingham, on Tom's right, grunted and said, "Everybody seems to feel that way about Shackleford."

"But Pauline's sister Bonnie and her husband say they don't think Shackleford had anything to do with Pauline's death," Tom said. "They want me to believe O'Dell did it. The whole family acts as if they're scared O'Dell might come after one of them now." He shook his head. "We'll get answers when we find him. Start searching sheds, barns, abandoned houses. Ask permission before you go on anybody's property. Quit at sundown, then start again in the morning. This guy's likely to shoot at anybody he sees coming, and I don't want y'all going into a dangerous situation in the dark."

Willingham cleared his throat. "I got a call this morning from the guy that owns the Indian Mountain property. He wants his construction crew to get back to work clearing the land. He wants the foundation for the house in by March."

"It's a crime scene," Tom said.

"Well, now, he's got a point," Willingham said. "It's not like there was a murder up there yesterday and we're finding a lot of fresh evidence."

"The search team's still finding human bones." Tom made an effort to keep his voice level. "I'm not letting anybody destroy those women's remains or bury them forever."

"Tom—" Willingham broke off and heaved a loud sigh. "Yeah, you're right. I'll let him know. He's not gonna be happy."

"He'll survive." Tom pushed his chair back and stood. Every movement intensified the ache in his arm, but the pain was losing its edge, which he took to mean healing had set in. "Sorry about the overtime, guys."

"You're working as hard as the rest of us," Grady Duncan said. He grinned as he stood. "Anybody but a Bridger would be in bed with a gunshot wound. Go on home and change your Kotex and get some rest."

Laughing, most of the deputies filed out. Brandon hung back.

Tom didn't want anyone else to hear what he had to say to the sheriff. "Would you go call the lab for me?" he asked Brandon. "They promised this morning they'd put a rush on the bones, and I want to make sure they're following through."

"Yes, sir," Brandon barked, the words sounding like a salute. "I'll get right on it." Tom could see him fighting to hold back an ear-to-ear grin. Giving orders to the crime lab was a responsibility that hadn't come his way before.

"Don't be too rough on them," Tom said to his back. When Brandon was gone, Tom turned to Willingham. "Shackleford and O'Dell look pretty good as suspects, but I'm not going after them blindly and risk overlooking other people who had motives. Her own relatives, and the McClures—"

"The McClures? Good lord. I grant you they're snobs and Pauline had her problems with them, but kill her? I doubt it."

"I'm not ruling anybody out, and I don't think my dad did either. He must have put together a lot of very personal information about all these people. But what's happened to it? Why am I finding big gaps in the case file?"

Willingham drew back, his jaw forming a rigid line, his eyes wary. He'd snapped into fight or flight mode and seemed to be leaning toward flight. If he tried to walk out without answering, Tom was ready to block the way. The old man was hiding something Tom needed to know, and Tom wanted to find out *why* even more than *what*.

In the end, Willingham chose to stand his ground and bluster his way through. "I don't know what you're talking about. What gaps? How can you tell something's missing if you don't know what it is?"

"I do know. Some of it, anyway. Why can't I find a single word in the records about Robert McClure claiming Mary Lee isn't Adam's child?"

"Oh, God almighty." Willingham sighed. "It's got nothing to do with the case—"

"The hell it doesn't," Tom said. "It gives more than one person a motive. And I don't see anything in the file about Pauline's relationships with other men. Ed McClure, for example." He couldn't bring himself to mention his father, and that made him feel as weak as the sheriff.

"Nothing but nasty gossip," Willingham protested.

"No," Tom said. "It's what we call a lead in a homicide investigation."

Willingham's face darkened to a dangerous shade of red. "You'd better let me hear a little more respect in your voice. I'm your superior officer, and don't you forget it."

Tom choked back an angry reply. This wasn't the way to get what he wanted. "If I'm going to solve Pauline's murder, if I'm going to find out who the second woman was, I need to know everything. How much is missing from the file and what happened to it?"

Willingham turned away, rubbing a hand across his mouth and jaw. From experience Tom knew the sheriff wanted to pull his thoughts together, formulate an answer. It drove Tom crazy, but all he could do was wait out the process and hope he'd get the truth.

At last Willingham spoke, without looking at Tom. "I did it myself. After your dad died."

"What?" Tom stepped around to face the sheriff. "Why?"

Willingham wouldn't meet his eyes. "I didn't want sensitive stuff laying around."

"It's a criminal case file. It's supposed to contain sensitive information. Why would you—" Tom searched for a word. "—*cull* it? You can't erase what happened, what people said, by destroying a few pieces of paper."

"I'm not going to argue with you about it." Willingham made for the door.

In three quick strides Tom got between the sheriff and the doorway. "What did you take out?"

Willingham threw up his hands in surrender. "You already guessed it. Robert McClure thinking Mary Lee wasn't Adam's daughter."

"A lot of people already know Robert believes that. What harm does it do to have it in the case file?"

The sheriff looked back at him in stubborn silence.

"Tell me, for God's sake! Don't you want those murders solved? What the hell are you holding back?"

Willingham took a long moment to answer. "Robert's right. She's not Adam's daughter."

"Then who— How did— What—" The words fell over each other as they tumbled out of Tom's mouth.

Willingham raised a hand to stop him. "I don't know who her real father is—or was. All I know is what your dad wrote in his notes, and I didn't read them till after he died."

"What else was in his notes that I haven't seen?" *Do I really want to know?* Yes. He had to know.

"He said Robert was right but didn't have the proof."
Willingham's eyes held a weary sadness. "Your dad always wanted
to protect the girl from Robert, but I didn't understand till I read
the file how much damage the s.o.b. could do to her. I'm not hand-
ing him any ammunition. That's all I can tell you, I swear."

Tom stepped away, turned his back on the sheriff. Through
the window he saw starlings swoop across the pewter sky, the
massive flock expanding and contracting like an airborne school
of fish. Why had his father cared so much about Mary Lee? Was
she more to him than simply the daughter of a woman he...
Tom stopped short of forming the words for what Pauline had
been to his father. Mrs. Barker had said John Bridger visited
Pauline during the last two or three years of her life. But had
their relationship actually begun a long time before?

Tom drove through the close-in neighborhoods south of
Mountainview and into a landscape of pure country, fields and
woods and occasional farmhouses set far back from the road.
Ravens picked at the remains of a cornfield that would soon be
buried under snow. He drove this route every day, from home
to work and back, and he'd let Sheriff Willingham and Brandon
believe he was headed home now. But he planned a detour to
see Ed McClure. According to the maid he'd spoken to on the
phone, "the missus" was at a Junior League committee meeting,
but "the doctor" was at home, working with his plants.

Ed and Natalie McClure's property wasn't far from Tom's, but
he lived on a ten-acre sheep farm and they owned a hundred acres
of riverside land. Most of it was planted with the apple trees Ed
used in his hybridizing projects. Pauline's house was about five
miles from Ed and Natalie's place. Her body had ended up on
a mountaintop at the opposite end of the county.

A long driveway wound toward the McClure house. In
summer, the oaks lining the drive would create an oasis of shade,
but today leafless branches arched against a deep gray sky. Tom
pulled into a brick-paved parking area that circled a fountain,

now drained for winter and collecting snow. The spacious house was a classic plantation manor, built of white brick with columns along a low porch.

At the front door the McClures' maid, a middle-aged woman in a ridiculous blue uniform with frilly cuffs and collar, gave Tom directions to the orchard.

He retrieved his hat from the cruiser to keep the increasingly heavy snow off his head. Pulling up his jacket collar against the wind, he walked around the house, passed a patio and a covered swimming pool, and struck off down a flagstone path through a screen of evergreens. He skirted a tennis court and a stable. These people, he was beginning to think, had too much money and too much leisure time. Beyond the stable loomed a massive greenhouse. Snow coated the roof, and the walls were so steamed-up Tom couldn't see the plants inside.

He found Ed McClure at the near end of the apple orchard, squinting at a thermometer mounted on a tree trunk. Beneath the tree sat a square, waist-high object swaddled in a blue blanket. More of these objects, all wrapped, were evenly spaced along the rows of trees. Bee hives? They looked the right shape and size. Tom had honeybees on his farm and he'd never noticed them needing blankets to survive winter.

"Dr. McClure," he said as he approached.

Ed spun around. "My God," he said, "I guess you really do have Indian blood. I didn't even hear you." He could have been mistaken for a local farmer, in his old wool coat, tweed cap, and scuffed boots.

Tom pulled off a glove and stuck out his hand. "How're you doing?"

In response, he got a gloved hand and an indifferent grip.

"Your bees coming through okay?"

"I hope so. I depend on them." Ed cast a distracted glance at the nearest hive.

"I'm hoping you can clear up a few things about your relationship with Pauline."

He expected a pretense of ignorance about his meaning, but Ed said, "I've been wondering when you'd show up."

Without altering his conversational tone, Tom asked, "Did you two have an affair?"

No surprise at the question. "Our relationship ended long before she... went missing." Ed's sigh caused an eddy in the downward stream of snow. "I still want to think of it that way—she simply disappeared. I can't believe she was murdered. And in such a vicious way."

If he was acting, he was good at it. "Murder's always vicious," Tom said. "No matter what the method is."

Ed nodded and stared into the distance, where the river flowed dark and wide. "This has been the saddest week of my life."

Cold numbed Tom's cheeks and earlobes but he didn't want to break Ed's mournful, reminiscent mood by suggesting they take shelter. "Were you in love with her?"

"Yes." The word carried a heavy burden of grief and loneliness.

"When did you fall in love with her?"

Ed didn't answer for a long moment. The silence around them was complete. Snow fell on a darkening world without birdsong or the noises of human activity. At last Ed said, "I was in love with her the instant I first saw her. When she started working at the bank."

"Were you married then?"

"Less than a year. Natalie was pregnant with our first son."

"And Pauline married your brother," Tom said. "But your feelings for her never changed?"

"No."

"You were a married man with two children." *And so was my father.*

"You don't have to remind me of my obligations," Ed said.

"Was she in love with you?"

"At one time I thought so, but— No. In the end she made it very clear that she didn't feel the same way I did."

"You were hurt. Did you want to hurt her too?"

Ed's face went hard with anger. "I didn't kill Pauline."

"If a person's pushed far enough—"

"I would never have harmed her in any way," Ed said, his voice rising. "I'm not capable of it."

Tom stepped closer, hoping to see Ed's face more clearly in the dusky light. "I know Mary Lee isn't Adam's daughter. Are you her father?"

Ed took a step back.

"A simple yes or no, Dr. McClure."

"None of that matters now," Ed said. "Why are you bringing it up?"

"I think it might matter a lot. We've got something we didn't have when Mary Lee was a child—DNA testing. We could prove conclusively whether she's your daughter. Whether she's a McClure at all."

In the bad light, Tom couldn't read any emotion on Ed's face. "Are you planning to do tests?" Ed asked.

"Would you be willing to give a blood sample?"

"For God's sake, leave Mary Lee alone! She doesn't deserve to have this ugly mess dragged up again. I don't give a damn about myself, but I won't let you ruin her life. It's a family matter. I'm telling you to let it be. Do you understand me?"

He sounded like his obnoxious brother Robert now, spouting orders to a cop. Tom opened his mouth to fire back, but he swallowed the angry words before they escaped. He didn't want Ed to shut down yet.

Keeping his voice level, he changed tack. "Robert hated Pauline. He thought she conned Adam into marrying her, then had another man's baby but ended up with all of Adam's money. Maybe Robert hated her enough to kill her."

Ed's laugh sounded bitter, scornful. "Robert's a weakling. He makes a lot of noise, but he lets lawyers do his dirty work. He wouldn't have killed Pauline because he'd be too afraid of getting caught."

Although Robert's hatred of Pauline seemed to make him a solid suspect, Tom tended to agree with Ed. Robert didn't have the guts to commit murder. Tom asked, "How did your wife feel about your affair with Pauline? She knew about it, didn't she?"

Ed paced several feet to the right and for a second Tom thought he was walking off. Tom followed and almost bumped into him when Ed turned.

"Yes, Natalie knew. What are you getting at?"

"I can understand how she might have felt. If you fathered Pauline's child, then continued the affair for years— How much can a wife take, after all?"

"This is utterly absurd," Ed spat out. "You've seen my wife. Do you think she could— could—" He stuttered to a stop.

"Split Pauline's head open with an ax?"

Groaning, Ed stumbled away.

"Yeah, she could have done it," Tom said. "Or hired somebody."

"I have nothing more to say to you."

"If you're withholding information—"

"I want you to leave." Ed strode up the path, shouting back to Tom, "Get off my property."

Tom dogged his footsteps all the way to the house, but Ed didn't speak another word before he entered through the patio door and slammed it in Tom's face.

Chapter Nineteen

One second Holly was standing outside the paddock, watching the chestnut mare, and the next she hoisted herself onto the fence and dropped to the other side.

"Hey!" Rachel yelled. "What are you doing?" She made a grab for Holly, but the girl eluded her.

"I'm okay." Holly fixed her attention on the horse twenty feet away.

The mare, Marcella, snorted and stamped in the snow.

"She'll be all right," Joanna McKendrick said. Windblown tendrils of strawberry-blonde hair hugged her cheeks. "Just wait and see."

"Marcella has the nastiest disposition of any animal I've ever encountered," Rachel said. "And Holly's never been near a horse in her life."

Joanna poked her with an elbow. "Look at that."

Rachel watched the little drama in the paddock with amazement and a twinge of envy. Marcella had already abandoned her effort to terrorize Holly into retreat. Rachel could see that Holly was speaking as she approached the mare but couldn't hear what she said. Three feet from the horse, she pulled off a mitten and extended her hand. Rachel held her breath, waiting for Marcella to chomp off those vulnerable fingers. Marcella snuffled, a curious rather than angry sound. Holly stroked the white blaze on the horse's forehead.

"Unbelievable," Rachel said.

"This girl has got the magic. She ought to be working with horses." Joanna turned to Rachel with mischief in her blue eyes. "I could offer her more money."

"What kind of friend are you, stealing my staff?"

Joanna laughed. "Yeah, I know how shorthanded you are. But I'm going to teach her horse care. Maybe she'll work for me part-time. I could give her a permanent place to live too—I've got plenty of room, and I'd enjoy her company. I wouldn't even mind having a goose in the house, with a few restrictions."

At their feet Holly's goose, Penny, brushed aside snow with her beak to get at the grass underneath. Joanna's beloved flock of gray geese browsed nearby, but Penny seemed to want nothing to do with them.

"I don't think the goose would be your biggest worry if Holly lived with you," Rachel said. "She's got some serious problems."

"What kind of problems?" Frowning, Joanna edged closer and lowered her voice, even though Holly couldn't possibly hear her over the cawing of crows in a nearby pecan tree. "Emotional?"

"Both nights she's been with me, she's had awful nightmares. She wakes up screaming. And she talks in her sleep."

"About what?"

"Something to do with her mother." The night before, Holly's agitated cries had again drawn Rachel to the door of the girl's room. She'd stood in the hallway listening. *Leave my mama alone! You're hurtin' her! Stop it!* Unable to bear the panic in Holly's voice, Rachel had gone in to wake her.

"Well, if her mother abandoned her when she was little," Joanna said, "I guess it would leave a mark. But nightmares about it at this late date—"

"It's more than that. I haven't told you everything. Tom Bridger thinks Holly knows something about her aunt's murder. I promised I'd try to find out what she remembers."

"For heaven's sake, that's not fair. Tell Tom to do his own work."

Rachel shook her head. "No, I'm glad he's not trying to force anything out of her. She's too fragile. And I doubt she was an eyewitness to the murder." She watched Holly stroke Marcella's neck. "Not her aunt's murder, anyway."

Joanna grasped Rachel's arm. "What are you saying?"

"I'm afraid the second skull the police found might belong to Holly's mother. And Holly's father might have killed her."

The stale air in his parents' bedroom reminded Tom of Pauline's boarded-up house. His footsteps on the braided rug raised a swirl of dust motes. He wasn't much of a housekeeper even in the rooms he used, and since he never used this one he always left it for his aunts to dust when they showed up for their periodic cleaning blitzes.

If any evidence existed that his father had an affair with Pauline, Tom didn't think he'd find it here in the room John Bridger had shared with his wife. He'd come to collect his father's keys, which might get him into more likely hiding places.

He wouldn't take sly looks and innuendoes from people like the Turners and Mrs. Barker as proof of anything. The notion that they'd gotten together to decide on a strategy was too far-fetched to take seriously, but they were all holding something back, possibly trying to set him off on a personal mission so he'd be diverted from the murder investigation.

Wasn't that exactly what was happening? Here he was, letting questions about his dad's past eat away at him. If his father had been involved with Pauline— If Mary Lee wasn't Adam McClure's daughter—

Get on with it.

He unlocked a window, shoved it up, let the cold, clean air sweep in.

His former fiancée, Sheila, had stood in this spot when she told him she was not going to marry him. *"I can't live in this place. I'd go out of my mind."* Tom had watched her resistance grow as he drove her around the county, seen the dismay in her eyes when she examined the old farmhouse, but he hadn't wanted to acknowledge what was happening. He'd been rattling on about knocking down a wall and turning his parents' bedroom into a master suite when she stopped him and told him she wouldn't marry him if he insisted on moving back to Mason County.

Remembered hurt and anger rose in him again, but with them came a new emotion: relief. He realized now that he and Sheila were so different they would have been miserable together even if he'd stayed in Richmond.

He smiled, thinking about Rachel Goddard, her gentleness, her warm, husky laugh, that amazing auburn hair that he itched to get his fingers into. For a while he'd been seeing an old girlfriend who now lived in Roanoke, but that had ended when Rachel moved to Mason County. She was the only one he wanted, and he would wait as long as it took for her to let him into her life.

His smile faded as he turned away from the window. On his right, one of his mother's beautiful quilts covered the bed in white, gold, and blue. The top of his mother's maple dresser, on his left, was bare.

He stepped across the room to his father's highboy chest and swung the doors open to expose a shelf and four drawers. The drawers were empty. While Tom was hospitalized after the accident, his grandmother and aunts had removed all his parents' clothes, except for his father's uniforms, and given them to a charity.

The shelf above the drawers held his parents' keys, wallets, and watches. Tom's grandmother had retrieved them from the hospital after the accident.

He pocketed his father's keys. One of them would open the steel box where his father had stashed his pistol every night when he came home. If John Bridger had hidden anything, it would be in that box.

As Tom started to close the doors of the chest, his father's wallet made him pause. His mother would never have dreamed of going through her husband's wallet. His father could have kept anything in there without fear of her finding it.

Tom had to call his left hand into service when he looked through the wallet, but he tried not to jostle his injured arm in its sling. The dry, stiff cowhide wallet made a faint creaking sound when he pulled it open. Inside he found only the usual things: driver's license, credit and insurance cards, organ donor card.

He fingered the donor card and his mind filled with the racket of the emergency room, the controlled panic, the flurry of motion and the squeak of rubber soles on the floor. A doctor leaning over him. *I know this is a difficult time... need to act quickly... Will you sign? Will you give consent?* In a daze, Tom had signed the forms, and organs had been taken from his parents and brother. Bits and pieces of his family lived on in the bodies of strangers.

He shook off the memory and tossed the wallet back onto the shelf.

He turned to leave the bedroom, go downstairs to the study and get that box open, but the bookcase in one corner caught his attention. The shelves held the mysteries his mother had devoured and the biographies his father had favored, but on the bottom were six slender high school annuals, three for each of his parents.

He squatted, pulled out the yearbook with the latest date and dropped it onto the floor. Gretchen Lauter had said that Pauline attended Mason County's only high school at the same time as his father. Flipping the pages, he searched for names, faces.

He stopped on the pages that pictured his father and his mother, Anne McGrail. Both in the same grade. In their senior photos, they had hairstyles that must have been outdated already—hers flipped up on the ends and his only slightly longer than a crew cut. The late-sixties revolution might have raged around them, but Tom's parents had never been hip.

Farther on in the seniors section, he found a young, cocky Troy Shackleford. He'd looked like trouble even then. Shackleford had probably been in classes with both of Tom's parents.

Pauline had been a sophomore, two years younger than Tom's father. Her picture jumped out at him as soon as he turned the page. Tom wanted to see a witch, her cunning and selfishness plain on her face, but instead he saw a beauty that made his breath catch in his throat. A fall of shining black hair, a heart-shaped face, long-lashed eyes, full lips that curved in an innocent smile. But nothing about her had been innocent. She knew the value of what nature had given her, and she didn't sell it cheap. She'd set her sights on the richest man in the county, and she'd snagged him, despite an age difference of nearly twenty years.

Had Tom's father become part of her life as early as high school? Wouldn't he have been attracted to her? Not only was she beautiful, she was Melungeon. Maybe some deep ethnic connection had drawn John Bridger to Pauline.

But Tom had always heard that his parents never so much as dated anyone else. His father served in Vietnam, and his mother attended nursing school while she waited for him. Soon after John Bridger came home, they were married.

When Mary Lee was born, John Bridger was already a father. Pauline had been married to Adam McClure for several years. Why hadn't she produced a child earlier, to cement Adam's ties to her?

Tom summoned a mental picture of Mary Lee, sitting across from him in her living room a few days ago. He'd registered her lack of resemblance to the McClures. But she didn't look like a Bridger either. She was all Turner.

The school yearbook told him nothing he didn't already know. Tom tossed it aside and went downstairs.

His computer and printer sat on the big oak desk, but he hadn't changed anything else in the room that had been his father's study. With its walls covered in photos of family and friends, its deep easy chair, the room felt inviting and comfortable, and Tom understood why his father had retreated from the household hubbub to read in this quiet spot. Every time Tom came in here, he imagined he could smell his father's English Leather aftershave.

The metal box was where it had always been, on a closet shelf. Standing on a footstool he'd brought from the kitchen,

Tom stared at the box, his throat tightening, and wondered if he really wanted to do this. What did he want to find? Nothing. He didn't want to find anything that would tie his father to Pauline. Disgusted with his reluctance to face the very truth he was searching for, he slid the box forward on the shelf. He couldn't lift anything this heavy with one arm. He maneuvered his left arm free, gritting his teeth against the pain, pulled the sling over his head and tossed it behind him.

When he had the box out of the closet and on the desk, he found the right key and coaxed the old lock to click open. An odd mixture of relief and disappointment washed through him when he saw only his father's pistol and holster inside the box. The gun was the property of the Sheriff's Department. He ought to return it. He lifted out the pistol and holster. Then he spotted the envelopes in the bottom of the box.

His heart kicked into a gallop. He set the gun and holster aside and scrabbled in the box, gathering all the envelopes, at least half a dozen.

His hands shook as he opened them. Birthday cards. Christmas cards. The same signature on every one. *With love, P.* Tom suddenly imagined his mother finding these things, here in the house she'd shared with her husband, and his stomach clenched with fury. What the hell was wrong with his father, bringing his cheap affair into their home?

How far did the cards go back? They hadn't been mailed, the envelopes had no dates stamped on them. Each was addressed simply *John Bridger.* Someone had delivered them personally. Pauline's housekeeper? Tom shuffled through them. Three birthday cards. Three Christmas cards. Mrs. Barker had been telling the truth about his father and Pauline toward the end of her life. That didn't mean they'd been involved as far back as when Mary Lee was conceived.

A last envelope, this one letter-sized, lay in the bottom of the box. Tom slid a folded sheet of blue note paper from the envelope and stared at it. Jesus Christ, was this a love letter from Pauline to his father?

Feeling sick, he opened it.

> *J—*
> *Ed has been following you, spying on you. I could strangle him! He's threatening to tell Anne we're having an affair. And he says he's going to tell everybody the truth about ML. Dear God, I was out of my mind to confide in him! I don't know if I can get through to him, but I've got to try. That silly wife of his was here, making accusations about Ed and me. She doesn't know about ML, but I'm so afraid everything will come out in the open if I don't get Ed calmed down, and ML and your wife are the ones who will be hurt.*
> *It breaks my heart to say this, but you have to stay away. We can't risk him seeing you here again. I don't know what he might do.*
> *I love you, my dearest friend.*
> > *P.*

Chapter Twenty

Holly poked her head out of the store's dressing room. "You ready?"

"Come on," Rachel said, laughing. "Let me see."

Holly crept out. She straightened the hem of the pale blue sweater and picked a stray thread from the black slacks, then stood with her arms stiff at her sides and her face screwed up as if she expected the worst. "How do I look?"

"Absolutely beautiful."

The compliment made Holly blush but didn't erase her doubtful expression. She seemed to have no idea how pretty she was.

"I'll pay you back every penny," she said for at least the tenth time. "I promise."

"I know that. You don't have to keep telling me."

Holly wasn't easy to do a favor for, and she wouldn't accept gifts. Rachel had spent the better part of an hour persuading her to come into Mountainview and pick out some new clothes at All Dressed Up. Once there, they'd wrangled over how much Holly needed. They would leave with more than Holly thought was necessary and a lot less than Rachel wanted to buy. But the shopping expedition was a great success. Holly already looked more like a modern young woman and less like a waif from a hollow.

"Let's have lunch at the Mountaineer and celebrate," Rachel said. "Wear what you have on. The clerk can take the tags off at the desk."

"What are we celebratin'?"

"Your new job, of course." Even as Rachel spoke, worry nagged at her. Tom had called last night and repeated a story about Rudy O'Dell spying on Holly with binoculars. Tom hadn't sounded convinced that the story was true, since it came from Jack Watford, but he'd asked Rachel to keep an eye on Holly until the police caught O'Dell. Maybe they shouldn't have come to town today. But surely they were safe in a moving vehicle and here on Main Street. Besides, O'Dell had more important things than Holly to think about—such as evading capture. She dismissed the thought of the fugitive. She and Holly were both going to enjoy this day.

Holly retrieved her old shirt and jeans from the dressing room and pulled on her coat. The ratty brown garment looked about twenty years old, but after Holly had seen the prices of new coats, she'd refused to let Rachel buy one for her. Next time, Rachel hoped.

The clerk snipped the tags off Holly's sweater and slacks and handed her a big white bag filled with her other purchases. When Rachel finished the credit card transaction and turned to go, Holly was nowhere in sight.

Rachel looked around. "Holly? Where are you?"

Don't let her wander off anywhere by herself. Tom's warning echoed in Rachel's head.

"She stepped outside, hon," the sixtyish clerk said.

Rachel shoved the door open and felt a momentary relief when she spotted Holly in front of the hardware store next door. Then she registered the full scene. Holly was backed up against the store's display window and two tall men loomed over her. One was her creepy drug-dealing cousin, Buddy.

Rachel's mouth went dry. She strode quickly toward them, braced for another skirmish with Buddy and determined to win this one.

With the white shopping bag clutched to her chest like a shield, her head bowed and shoulders hunched, Holly seemed

to be expecting a blow. Rachel came up beside her and threw
the men a challenging look. "What's going on here?"

The two men were a lot alike—tall, handsome, dark-haired.
The second, though, was middle-aged.

"Well, hey there, Mary Mary," Buddy drawled. His taunting
grin and cold eyes told her he hadn't forgotten a thing about
their first encounter. "Didn't I say I'd be seein' you again real
soon? I bet you—"

The older man silenced him with a touch on the shoulder.
Buddy's grin collapsed like a popped balloon.

"You must be Dr. Goddard," the man drawled.

His lips formed a slow smile that was enough like Buddy's
smirk to send a spasm of revulsion through Rachel. Father and
son? Or uncle and nephew? Could this be—?

"This is my daddy," Holly mumbled.

"Mr. Shackleford," Rachel said, struggling to keep her voice
even. "I've heard a lot about you."

Amusement crinkled his hooded dark eyes. "Call me Troy."
He leaned toward Rachel and she willed herself not to recoil,
but she broke out in a sweat and she knew he could see it. In a
confidential tone, Shackleford added, "Don't believe everything
folks tell you. I doubt I could live up to it all."

"Oh, I'm sure you can." *Watch it, watch it.* Troy Shackleford
was too dangerous to mess around with. She had to think about
Holly now, not just herself.

Shackleford stroked his chin and gazed down at Rachel
through half-closed eyes. His large, strong hands bore scars across
the knuckles that made her imagine barroom brawls and fights
in parking lots. "How's my little girl doin' on the job?"

"Great. I'm lucky to have her." A gust of wind chilled Rachel's
face and neck and made her shiver.

Shackleford reached out, caught the collar of her coat and
tugged it up around her throat. She flinched, and Buddy laughed,
a low, derisive snicker.

"You're cold," Shackleford said. "You ought to get indoors."

"Let's go," Rachel said to Holly. If the girl bit down any harder on her lower lip she would draw blood.

"Yeah, let's go." Holly edged away from her father and cousin and struck off down the sidewalk at a near-run.

Rachel hurried after her. She prayed the two men would give up and go away, but she didn't believe for a second they would.

"Hey, hold on, Sugar," Troy Shackleford called after Holly. With long strides he caught up to her. Grabbing her arm, he pulled her to a stop. "We've got a lot to talk about."

Despite the cold air, sweat beaded on Holly's upper lip. "I'm busy," she squeaked.

Stay calm, Rachel told herself, trying to make her racing heart slow down. Across the street several men and women had stopped to watch them. Shackleford couldn't get away with anything out here in plain view. Could he?

"You got time to eat, don't you, baby?" Shackleford smiled at Holly, but it was a coldly calculated expression with no affection in it. "Let's drive on out to Rose's place for a bite. She's been missin' you."

His grip on Holly's arm tightened, and when the girl whimpered in pain Rachel couldn't hold herself back anymore. "Let go of her," she told Shackleford. "Right now."

Shackleford regarded Rachel with mock reproach. "Are you tryin' to keep me away from my daughter? That's not nice, Dr. Goddard."

All right, you son of a bitch, enough of this. She pawed through her shoulderbag and dredged out her cell phone. "Let go of Holly or I'll call the police."

Shackleford laughed. "What are you gonna tell 'em I'm doin'? I'm invitin' my daughter to have lunch with me, and you're interferin'. You're the one in the wrong."

"She doesn't want to go anywhere with you."

Holly squirmed and tried to free her arm, but Shackleford held on. "I need to talk to you." His voice lost its oily smoothness. "Now stop bein' contrary and come on with me. We got things to straighten out."

He twisted Holly's arm. The bag slid from her grasp and plopped onto the sidewalk. "No!" Holly cried. "I don't want to!"

"I'll call the Sheriff's Department," Rachel said. "They're right around the corner." Thank God for speed dial. Even 911 might be more than her trembling fingers could manage.

Buddy stepped forward and leaned his face into hers. "Stay out of this, bitch."

With an effort of will Rachel stood her ground and ignored Buddy. She said to Shackleford, "You're trying to kidnap Holly off a public street in front of witnesses. Do you think the cops will be on your side?"

He barked a laugh. "Girl, you've got a bad habit of stickin' your pretty little nose where it don't belong."

But he released Holly, and she backed away from him.

"We're leaving," Rachel said. She bent to retrieve the shopping bag, but Buddy scooped it up and, grinning, held it beyond her grasp. An explosion of fury shook her and she needed every ounce of self-control to keep her voice down to a growl. "Give me the goddamned bag and get out of our way."

To her amazement, Shackleford said, "Let her have it, Bud."

"Aw, shit, Troy," Buddy whined. When his uncle threw him a pointed look, he shoved the bag at Rachel. A sullen little boy, reprimanded and not liking it a bit.

"Come on," Rachel told Holly, "let's go."

They'd walked twenty feet when Shackleford called out, "Hey, Rachel."

She froze for a second. Then she slowly looked back at him.

He was grinning. "You be real careful now, you hear? You never know what might happen."

Inside the Mountaineer, Rachel chose a booth in a rear corner, away from the hubbub of customers coming and going. She tossed her coat into the booth and slid in after it, then sat for a moment breathing deeply and trying to calm down. She had to get some answers from Holly before she talked to Tom again, and although she felt guilty for taking advantage of the girl's emotional turmoil, she knew this was a perfect time to pry.

Holly sat opposite Rachel with her arms wrapped around her waist, her gaze vacant and her thoughts obviously still on the street with her father and cousin.

"This is a nice place, isn't it?" Rachel said.

Holly gazed around as if seeing the restaurant for the first time since they'd entered. Rachel hoped she was comparing it to Rose's diner. Bright and clean, The Mountaineer had green vinyl booths, pine tables, framed nature photos on the walls and two wagon wheels suspended from the ceiling as lighting fixtures.

"Are you okay?" Rachel asked.

Holly regarded her with bleak eyes. "Now he's gonna hurt you because of me."

"He can't do anything to me," Rachel said with a confidence she didn't feel.

"You don't know what he's like. He'll find a way."

"He's not going to hurt either of us. I won't let him. The police won't let him. You have a lot of people on your side, Holly."

"Then he'll take it out on my grandma. Maybe I oughta go back home."

"No, you can't let him—"

The waitress' arrival cut Rachel off. After the young woman took their order and left, Holly leaned over the table and burst out in a fierce whisper, "I *hate* him! I'd have growed up with a mother if it wasn't for him."

Rachel laid a hand on Holly's. She was aware of other customers looking their way. *To hell with them.*

"How is he responsible for your mother being gone?" Rachel felt as if she were coaxing answers from a child, not an eighteen-year-old.

"He— He—" Holly gulped. "I'm afraid to tell you."

Rachel wanted to scream in frustration. What would it take to free Holly from her family's grip? To drag her demons out into the open? "Please let me help you."

"You have already," Holly said. "You gave me a job, you let me move into your house. You went and got me, and you didn't let Grandma stop you from takin' me."

"Why won't they let you go? Do you know something they don't want you to tell anybody?"

"I can't—" Holly shook her head.

"Why are you afraid of your father? Has he ever hit you or—or anything else?"

Holly bit her lip and didn't speak.

The son of a bitch. "Please tell me what he did. I'm your friend, I want to understand."

Holly stared into space for a long moment before answering. "The last night I ever saw Mama, they were yellin' at each other. I was so scared, I got under my bed. I covered up my ears, but I could hear them yellin'."

"What were they fighting about?"

"I don't know. She said she wasn't gonna help him, she wasn't gonna let him get away with something, I don't know what. He called her awful names. And he said—" Holly fought back a sob. "He said he'd kill her if she went against him."

Rachel's chest felt so tight that she had to force each breath in and out. "What happened then, Holly?"

"He beat her up. He beat her so bad—" Holly squeezed her eyes shut. "Her face was all bloody, her nose and mouth. Her arm was hurt because he shoved her and she fell down and hit a table. He said he'd kill her if she called the law on him. Then he walked out and left her like that."

"Did he come back later?"

Holly shook her head. "She put me to bed and pulled up the covers and—" Her hand rose to stroke her hair. "She touched me like that. She called me her darlin' little girl and told me not to worry. And I went to sleep. I thought it was gonna be all right. But when I woke up, Mama was gone. I never saw her again. She didn't even say goodbye."

"Were her clothes gone?"

"Yeah. But she left me behind."

Rachel squeezed Holly's hands. "What did your grandmother say about your mother leaving?"

"She said Mama needed to go somewhere and find a job, and she'd come back for me. But she never did. She left because she was scared of him, and she was scared to come back." Holly sniffled, yanked a tissue from her coat pocket and dabbed her runny nose. "But don't you think she could've took me with her? If she really loved me."

"Oh, Holly. I'm sure it broke your mother's heart to leave you. There must be a good explanation."

Rachel had no salve for wounds so deep. As long as Holly lived, she would always be a girl waking up to find her mother gone. If she learned her mother had been dead all these years, her body lying on a mountaintop a few miles away, would that final blow shatter her heart?

The waitress brought the food, glanced at Holly's flushed face and puffy eyes, and served them quickly and silently. Rachel watched Holly drag a spoon back and forth through her soup. *Let her eat. Leave her alone for now.* But Holly would have to tell her story to Tom before long.

During the drive to the horse farm, Rachel's gaze drifted every few seconds to the Range Rover's rearview mirror, but for a long time the only vehicles she saw on the narrow country road were cars and trucks passing in the other lane. Then an enormous SUV seemed to appear out of nowhere, bearing down on them from behind. It was dark—blue? black?—but Rachel couldn't tell if it was the same one Buddy had been driving when he'd followed her before. Her fingers squeezed the steering wheel and she held her breath as she stomped down on the gas pedal and sent her Range Rover flying over potholes and bumps. The SUV kept pace. *Good God, he's going to ram us.* Rachel held on tight, determined to control her vehicle if he tried to force it off the road.

The blare of a horn jolted her, then the SUV swung hard to the left and sped by. As it passed Rachel got a look at the driver and saw the features of a stranger. "Idiot!" she muttered at him. "Grow up!" Her heart hammered wildly and she gulped air.

Beside her, Holly stayed silent, her face blank. She seemed immersed in her thoughts and oblivious to everything that had just happened. As soon as they reached the cottage, Rachel would call Tom. He had to be told that Troy Shackleford had beaten and threatened Holly's mother before the woman disappeared. And Holly had to be protected from her father.

Where had Troy and Buddy Shackleford gone? While Rachel and Holly were in the restaurant, the two men had plenty of time to get to the farm, find their way to Rachel's cottage, scout for a place where they could lie in wait.

Stop it. The Shacklefords were dangerous but not stupid. They wouldn't try anything now, so soon after witnesses had seen them harassing her and Holly on the street. Besides, the farmhands would spot anybody skulking around in broad daylight. The farm was the safest place to be. And they were almost there. When Rachel saw the rail fence coming up on the left, she released a long breath and allowed herself to relax.

Along the right side of the road stretched acres of evergreens, planted in thick rows for harvest as Christmas trees. The winter sun cast a deceptively warm glow over the snow-covered landscape. Rachel slowed for the turn through the farm gate.

From the corner of her eye she caught a movement in the evergreens and the glint of sunlight off—what? She looked directly at the trees and saw it. A rifle barrel. Leveled at them.

"Holly!" she yelled. "Get down! Get down!"

Holly's window exploded and she screamed and threw up her hands as glass showered into the Range Rover. A shard sliced Rachel's cheek. Her window blew out. The shock of it made her let go of the steering wheel and the vehicle veered toward the ditch.

Another shot slammed into Holly's door. Rachel grabbed the steering wheel and floored the gas. A third shot pierced the rear window.

Chapter Twenty-one

Tom raised the ax above his head and brought it down on the oak log. Not easy to do with one arm in a sling. The blow landed at the edge and shaved off a strip of bark.

"God damn it." He tossed the strip onto the back porch in the direction of the kindling pile, and Billy Bob rose from his resting spot and shuffled over to sniff it.

Tom lifted the ax again, trying to ignore the dull throb in his other arm. God, he was sick of hurting and struggling to get the simplest things done. Sick of hanging around the house thinking about his father and Pauline McClure. The sheriff had ordered him to take the weekend off, but Tom thought it was crazy to be off duty at a time like this.

He slammed the ax down on the log and stared at the blade buried six inches in the wood. Had Pauline been running when her killer caught up and split open her skull? Did she know her life was about to end? Did she know why? The reason for many murders could be found in the victim's own life. What had Pauline done to make her killer decide it was time for her to die?

Remembering Pauline's note to his father, Tom tried to imagine Ed McClure sinking an ax into the head of the woman he loved. *I'm not capable of it,* Ed had said the day before. Of course he was. If he'd been driven crazy by jealousy, he might have had the strongest motive of any of the suspects.

Pauline's blood relatives made likely suspects in theory, and they were the oddest and most secretive bunch Tom had ever come across, but he couldn't figure out what motive any of them had to kill her. No one except Mary Lee had benefited from Pauline's death, and she had to wait seven years to cash in on Pauline's six-million-dollar estate. That much money would have been worth waiting for, though. What Tom needed was solid evidence that Mary Lee, comfortable with her own trust fund, had been willing to kill her mother to get a fortune that she would have inherited eventually anyway.

As for Shackleford and O'Dell, Tom's father had suspected both but never came up with a scrap of evidence tying them to Pauline's disappearance. The case stood exactly where Tom's father had left it: plenty of suspects and motives, but no proof against anybody.

Tom turned away from the chopping block and started up the steps. He would change into his uniform and get back to work. Five days into a murder investigation, he had no business wasting time at home. Whatever he felt toward Pauline McClure, his job was to find her killer.

As he crossed the porch to the door, he heard the faint tinny ring of the kitchen telephone. Inside, he used his teeth to remove his right-hand glove before he snatched the receiver from the wall hook. "Yeah! Hello," he barked as he started struggling out of his leather jacket.

"Tom, it's Joanna McKendrick. You need to get out here."

She sounded frantic. In the background Tom heard someone crying and caught snatches of words. ...*kill me...come after me...* He went completely still, his jacket half off. A clutch of dread squeezed his chest. "What's happened?"

"Somebody shot at Rachel and Holly—"

"What?" *Rachel. Good God.* He lunged for the door, panic compelling him to move, to go to her, but the short phone line stopped him. "Are they—"

"They're all right. Rachel's got a little cut on her face, but— Just listen, okay?"

Staying silent was the hardest thing he'd ever done. His mind raced, gruesome scenes of carnage flashed before him. *She's not hurt,* he told himself. *She's all right.*

"They went to town," Joanna was saying, "and on the way back somebody shot at them from my Christmas tree farm across the road. I've called 911, but I want you here."

"I'm on my way," Tom said, and dropped the receiver onto the hook.

He wrenched off the sling and flung it into the trash can. "Let's go, Billy Bob."

He needed his good arm for driving, and trying to hold the radio mike and join in the chatter was hopeless. All the right things were getting done, from the sound of it—deputies converging on the shooting site, State Police jumping in to provide support.

Why had Rachel and Holly left the farm after Tom warned Rachel to be careful? *My own damned fault.* He hadn't specifically told her not to leave home, because he wasn't convinced that Bonnie and Jack Watford were right—or truthful—about O'Dell being a danger to Holly. But somebody was after Rachel too, and that black widow spider, sent in a package carefully wiped free of fingerprints, was the proof. Why the hell hadn't he been firmer? Because he hadn't wanted Rachel to think he was giving her orders. He should have put her safety and Holly's first instead of worrying about whether she'd think he was too bossy. And Rachel should have had more sense than to take chances.

Damn it, why couldn't he get a handle on this case? Everybody he talked to seemed to be hiding something, and the truth about Pauline's death lay beneath a web of lies that he hadn't been able to penetrate. How much more violence would erupt in the present before he uncovered the truth about the past?

Near the farm gate, he passed two unoccupied cruisers on the main road. Orange traffic cones and flares protected a scattering of glass on the pavement. When Tom roared up the farm lane to Joanna's house, he saw another cruiser in the driveway behind Joanna's Jeep Cherokee and Rachel's Range Rover.

Tom parked in front of the house, and with Billy Bob beside him he strode across the snow-covered lawn to the Range Rover. Yellow crime scene tape wrapped the vehicle. A maze of cracks forked out around a bullet hole in the rear windshield. Ragged outlines of glass hung in the two front seat windows. He found a hole in the passenger door two inches below the window. Pushing the yellow tape up out of the way, he opened the door for a look inside. No exit hole. The bullet was in the door.

From the pattern of glass shards on the seats and floor, Tom guessed that one bullet had gone straight through and out the driver's side, taking part of the window with it. The shot had probably missed Rachel's head by inches. If she'd been sitting forward, if the car had been in a slightly different position—*Jesus Christ.* Fighting a wave of nausea, he slammed the car door and headed for the house.

Brandon, white-faced and wide-eyed, answered the bell. "Hey, Boss. Sergeant Murray and the Blackwoods are searching the shooting site. I checked around over here and didn't see any sign the shooter'd crossed the road, so—"

Brandon rattled on, but Tom didn't listen. He needed to find Rachel. He followed the murmur of voices into the living room on the left. The drawn draperies, the blazing fire, the soft glow of lamps made the room seem smaller than it ever did in the blaze of sunlight. Rachel sat on the brown leather couch with Holly. When she rose and came toward him Tom felt the first moment of peace he'd known all day.

He wanted to put his arms around her, but when he took her by the shoulders to pull her close he felt her resist and realized he was in serious danger of making a fool of himself. He touched her cheek. The bandage there was too damned close to her eye for comfort. "How bad is that?" he asked.

When she leaned to pet Billy Bob her hand trembled, but she spoke calmly. "Just a scratch. I'm fine. I think he was trying to hit Holly. Thank God he didn't."

"Are you sure it was a man?"

Rachel frowned. "No, now that I think about it. I don't believe I saw anybody. Just a rifle barrel, sticking out from a tree at the edge of the road."

"Did you get any idea of height? How high up was the gun held?"

She ran both hands through her hair, pushing it back from her face. Her flushed skin and her quick, short breaths betrayed the turmoil she was trying to hide. "I can't even guess. It happened so fast."

"The shooter must have been waiting for you to come back. Which means he knew you'd gone out."

"Right." Rachel glanced at Holly, who sat on the sofa with Brandon, and lowered her voice. "Could we talk in the hall?"

Out of Holly's hearing, Rachel told him about their encounter with Troy Shackleford and his nephew Buddy. "They would've dragged her into a car and taken her away if I hadn't stopped them."

Tom listened with mounting exasperation. "What were you doing in town anyway? I asked you last night to be careful."

Anger flared in her eyes. "Holly needed some new clothes, and I thought we'd be okay if—"

"Clothes? You almost got killed because you went *shopping*?"

"You told me to be careful, you didn't say we had to hole up at home in fear for our lives. But if you're determined to blame me for this, go ahead. I blame myself, okay? Mea culpa!" She struck her breast with her fist. "Satisfied?"

She was ready to crack, but Tom couldn't summon the words to calm her. Aware that he was making matters worse, he said, "None of this would be happening if you hadn't brought Holly home with you."

"Don't you dare throw that in my face! I did the right thing for her, and you'll never make me regret it."

"Hey!" Joanna called from the kitchen doorway. "What's the matter with you two?" She marched toward them with a tray of cups filled with steaming tea.

Rachel glared at Tom, he glared at her, she turned her back on him.

"Here," Joanna said, holding the tray out to Rachel. "You need something hot and sweet."

Rachel took a cup of tea, and Joanna shot a reproving look at Tom. "You leave her alone. She's been through enough. You ought to thank God she's standing here alive."

He did. When he thought of Rachel dying at the hands of some nutcase, an icy fist closed around his heart. But he didn't answer Joanna, and she moved on to the living room.

One gulp of the hot liquid made Rachel gasp and wince.

"It's too hot to drink that fast," Tom said.

"Thank you for pointing that out." Rachel set her cup on the hall table next to the phone. "If you're finished trying to make me feel guilty, will you listen for a second?"

"Is it important? I've got a lot to do."

"You might find it relevant to your work." Folding her arms, she launched into a story about Shackleford beating up Holly's mother, Jean Turner, the night Jean left. "I think he killed her. I think that second skeleton you found is Holly's mother."

Tom shook his head. "I don't, for one simple reason. The teeth in the skull are too healthy-looking. Pauline's mouth was full of bridges and caps, so I wouldn't expect her sister to have nearly perfect teeth."

"Bridges and caps don't mean Pauline had bad teeth. Maybe she didn't like the way they looked. Have you checked Jean Turner's dental records?"

"No. I haven't seen any reason to."

"Well, maybe you should, because Holly has beautiful teeth. Somebody taught her to take care of them. Maybe that somebody was her mother."

"Everybody in the family says Jean is alive."

"Has anybody produced proof? Holly never hears from her. If she doesn't keep in touch with her own daughter, how can you be sure she's not dead?"

The Turners all talked about Jean as if she were alive. He'd accepted what they said at face value. What the hell was wrong with him?

"I think Holly's ready to talk about her family," Rachel was saying. "When she's recovered a little, you might be able to get some honest answers from her."

"I'll talk to her right now." Tom turned and started into the living room.

"Tom!" Rachel quick-stepped past him and got to Holly before he did. Sitting on the arm of the couch with one hand on Holly's shoulder, she gave him a look that warned he would upset the girl at his own peril. Joanna, standing behind the couch, wore the same expression.

Tom unzipped his leather jacket and sat on the coffee table. For a second the sight of Holly's delicate face, with its frame of lustrous hair, robbed him of words. Her resemblance to the young Pauline was more than striking. It was eerie. This was the face his father had seen when he passed Pauline in the halls at school. If Holly had style and a certainty of her own worth, she would be what Pauline had been: spellbinding. And no man who encountered her would be immune.

"Hey, Holly, how are you feeling?"

She gripped her tea cup with white-knuckled fingers. Without raising her eyes, she said, "I'm okay."

"Do you have any idea who could have done this?"

Holly nodded. "My daddy."

"Why would your father want to hurt you?"

"He's probably afraid I'm gonna tell people things that'll get him arrested."

Excitement prickled the skin on the back of Tom's neck. She did know something. She was going to give him a memory, an overheard conversation, some vital detail. "What things?"

Holly pulled in a deep breath. "About his drug business." She met Tom's gaze with the terrified boldness of someone exposing a closely held secret.

He tried not to let his disappointment show. If she believed this was the worst she could tell the police about her father, she must not know anything that would connect Shackleford to Pauline's death or that of the unidentified victim. Still, her inside information might be useful if he decided to take a whack at shutting down the Shackleford family's illegal business. "Your father deals drugs?"

Holly bobbed her head. "Him and his mama and Buddy and Rose. They're all in it. My daddy brings a lot of the drugs up from Miami, and they've got somebody around here makin' meth for them. They sell anything anybody wants. Oxy pills and meth and crack and tons of pot."

"You've witnessed this?" Tom said. "You've actually seen it?"

"All the time. Most of the customers come in the evenin', and Saturday night's the busiest, but Rose sells drugs durin' the day too."

"How often are Troy and Buddy there?"

"Buddy's there every night. My daddy's there if he's not in Miami."

"Thanks, Holly. I appreciate this information."

She leaned forward eagerly. "You gonna bust 'em? Put 'em in jail?"

"I'll have to discuss it with the sheriff."

Holly's face crumpled. "If you don't put 'em where they can't hurt me—"

"Nobody's going to hurt you," Brandon and Rachel said at the same time.

Tom hoped neither of them was unrealistic enough to believe the shooter wouldn't try again. Whoever fired those shots didn't want to scare Holly. He wanted to kill her.

"We can't assume it was your father or cousin who shot at you," Tom told the girl. "Your aunt and uncle seem to think Rudy O'Dell's a danger to you because you look so much like your Aunt Pauline. They said O'Dell was hanging around your grandmother's house not long ago, watching you. Is that true?"

"Yeah. He was in the woods across the road. I didn't even notice him till my uncle came by and saw him." She screwed up her face in disgust. "He was so weird-lookin', with this big bushy beard and long hair. It made me feel dirty, knowin' he'd been spyin' on me like that. With binoculars, too, so he could see me real close. That's… crazy."

So Bonnie and Jack Watford had told the truth about the incident. Maybe their instincts about O'Dell had some validity.

"You think he coulda shot at us?" Holly asked.

"I don't know what to think right now," Tom admitted. "I have to wonder how O'Dell could have found you. How many people know you've moved?"

"If Rose told people at the diner, it'd get around pretty fast. There's some O'Dells that go there a lot. They might've told Rudy."

"Yeah, maybe." But why would O'Dell's relatives help him find an innocent girl for the sole purpose of harming her? That didn't make much sense. Neither did anything else that was happening. "I'd better go see what our guys have turned up across the road. Brandon, I want you to stay here for the time being."

He expected an argument from Brandon, who loved nothing more than prowling around a crime scene, but the young deputy accepted the order with a crisp, "Yes, sir."

Holly had a hold on him, all right, if he'd rather play bodyguard to her than be in the thick of the investigation.

Tom rose to leave, but asked Holly one last question. "Do you know which dentist your mother went to?"

She frowned up at him. "Dentist? Why?" Before he could answer, realization flooded her face. "That's how y'all identify a dead person. You think that other skull you found is my mama's, don't you? It's not! She's not dead!"

Holly leapt to her feet, fists balled in front of her as if she meant to hit him. Rachel and Brandon got to her quickly and caught her arms to restrain her. The look Rachel threw at Tom mixed incredulity and outrage.

What the hell did she want from him? She was the one who thought the second skull was Jean Turner's, and she'd urged him in a none-too-gentle fashion to check Jean's dental records. He might be able to pry information out of Holly's grandmother, but getting it from Holly was simpler and faster.

"No," Tom told Holly, "I don't really believe it's your mother, but we need to rule it out. If we can find her dental records, we'll be able to tell you for sure it's not her."

That seemed to mollify the girl. "Okay. That'll be good. She went to the county clinic. She took me there too."

"I'll let you know what we find out." He zipped his jacket, preparing to leave. "You two stay indoors and out of sight."

Joanna spoke up. "I want you girls to move in here with me till this is over. You're sitting ducks in that cottage at night, way out there by yourselves. I'll go get your animals and whatever personal things you need."

"Good idea," Tom said.

Rachel agreed.

"How about I stay here at night?" Brandon said. "I can sleep on the couch. Anybody breaks in, they'll have to deal with me."

Tom imagined Brandon, half-awake, facing Shackleford in the dark. "No, I'd better be the one to sleep here."

Brandon looked crestfallen, but to Tom's surprise Rachel said, "Thanks. We'll all feel safer with you here." Then she sat on the couch and gave her attention to Holly.

Tom turned to leave. He hated walking out without trying to make Rachel understand why he was on edge, why he'd blown up at her. But he knew he couldn't blame his foul mood entirely on concern for her safety and Holly's. The poison of the past was leaking into the present and he didn't seem able to hold it back.

Get a grip, Bridger. Nothing in his own life, the here and now, had changed. He was a big boy. He could take the truth about his father. Then why did he feel as if he'd stepped off firm ground into a black, empty hole? In a thousand tiny ways, his clear perception of the past, his happy childhood, happy family, had blurred and transformed into a lie that he could never believe again.

Just do your job.

Joanna caught up with him at the front door. "I want to talk to you privately," she said. "Right now. In my office."

Tom trailed her down the hall, feeling like a naughty student about to get a tongue-lashing from the principal. He could claim he was too busy for this, but as a rule people didn't say no to Joanna McKendrick without rapidly coming to regret it.

In her pine-paneled office, she folded her arms across her chest and fixed him with a stern look. "Don't you have any idea how shaken up she is?"

"I know Holly's upset, but I need—"

"Not Holly, you nitwit. My lord, the human male is the densest creature that ever walked the earth. I'm talking about Rachel. Somebody fired a gun at her and Holly. A bullet came within inches of her head. You, of all people—" Joanna gestured at his wounded, aching arm, which he'd been absentmindedly rubbing. "—ought to understand what that would do to her. But maybe you're too damned macho to be upset by a little thing like narrowly escaping death. That still doesn't give you an excuse to come in here and blame her for bringing it on."

"That's not fair," Tom protested. Or was it?

"What happened today could make anybody fall apart, but this is someone who was shot by a madman less than two years ago. You know that, don't you?"

"Yes, I—"

"And she lost her mother not long before that. She's had a rough time." Joanna's blue eyes filled with tears and her outrage melted away. She felt behind her for the desk chair and sank into it. "I haven't known Rachel very long, but I already love her as if she's my own daughter. Every time I think about her getting shot, what kind of memories she must have—"

"Will you tell me about it?" Tom sat in the leather visitor's chair next to the desk. "I want to know exactly what happened." He'd learned a lot about Rachel's life, but he didn't know much beyond the surface facts. Some part of her, the part that was willing to love and be loved, was locked away with her memories, out of Tom's reach.

Joanna snatched a tissue from the box on her desk and blotted her tears before they could spill over. "Rachel had a client who kept bringing his dog in with different kinds of injuries, and he was always asking for painkillers to give the dog some relief."

"He was hurting the dog himself?" Tom asked.

"That's what Rachel thought. She'd already made up her mind to report him when she got a call from a pharmacist. He said she'd written a painkiller prescription and forgot to put her DEA number on. But she didn't write it. The guy with the dog somehow got hold of a prescription pad when he was at the animal hospital."

Tears came to Joanna's eyes again, and she rubbed them away before she went on. "She turned him in, he was arrested, he got out on bail, and the next thing she knew he was barging into the hospital with a gun, ready to kill her for ruining his life. She set off the silent alarm as soon as she saw him and when the guy heard the police siren, he ran out. But he'd already shot her. The bullet went through one of her lungs and out her back. It just missed her heart and her spine."

Images flooded Tom's mind as Joanna spoke. How many times, as a cop in Richmond, had he walked into the aftermath of gang shootings or robberies gone bad and looked down at blood-soaked bodies? He'd consciously hardened himself to it, put aside all thought of the cataclysmic shock waves that violence sent through the lives of witnesses and survivors. He'd tried to keep the reality of violence in Rachel's life at a safe distance, too, and because he was falling in love with her he'd told himself she would eventually be ready to trust again. But now the enormity of what had happened, what it had done to her, hit him with a visceral punch.

"After all she's been through," Joanna said, "it must be terrifying to have somebody shoot at her. She knows it's because of Holly, but she's so determined to help that child, she won't even think about turning her out. When somebody puts herself on the line like that for another person, you have to respect what she's doing. You don't berate her and tell her it's her own fault if she gets hurt."

"No," Tom said, his throat constricted with guilt over his stupid argument with Rachel. "But I'm sure as hell not going to stand by and let her get killed."

〈〉〈〉〈〉

Dennis Murray and the Blackwood twins were stringing crime scene tape around evergreens across the road from the horse farm.

"Is somebody taping off the perimeter?" Tom asked Dennis. The Christmas trees covered ten acres, bordered by roads on two sides. They'd have to search every inch, and they didn't need any curious onlookers getting in the way.

"Yeah, our guys are doing it. I figure we're blowing the whole year's budget for tape." Dennis knotted yellow plastic tape around a fir branch. "The State Police are sending cadets to help with the search. Right here's where our shooter fired from."

Boot prints marched across the snow and beneath the droopy branches of a ten-foot spruce. The tree stood within yards of the road but would easily conceal a man from passing motorists. Like a spider waiting patiently for a fly, the son of a bitch had hidden here until Rachel and Holly rode into view and the Range Rover slowed for the turn into the farm lane. "Did he leave us anything?"

"Gum wrappers," Dennis said. "We might get a fingerprint if we're lucky. But that's not all. These look familiar?" From his jacket pocket he pulled a plastic sandwich bag containing three brass shell casings.

"Thirty-aught-six." Same caliber fired by O'Dell's rifle.

Chapter Twenty-two

The diner's plate glass window was the only spot of light in the blackness enveloping the hills. From his truck at the edge of the parking lot, Tom had a slantwise view of the crowd inside. The dull throb of country music escaped every time the diner's door opened.

All the warmth built up in his truck's cab on the drive to the diner had leaked away and the frigid night air had seeped in. The only good thing about the cold was that it seemed to tamp down the ache in his arm. He'd always heard people felt little pain when they were freezing to death.

He rubbed his gloved hands together but decided against starting the engine so he could run the heater. He didn't want to attract attention. After sitting here for almost an hour, he was wondering if somebody had already spotted him and warned off the Shacklefords. He consulted the luminous dial of his watch: 9:02. Troy and his nephew Buddy should have shown up by now.

Tom had left Brandon at the horse farm with the women while he came out here to have a word with Troy. If he'd miscalculated and Shackleford decided to pay his daughter a visit this evening—

Headlights strobed his truck and a massive black SUV swung into the space marked RESERVED outside the diner's door. Tom craned his neck to see over the tops of vehicles. The SUV's lights died, Troy Shackleford and his nephew Buddy hopped out and slammed the doors. Buddy carried a gym bag, but Tom doubted it held workout clothes.

Okay, give them a little time. Let them settle into a routine evening. Tom wasn't dreading this encounter, but inside his gloves his palms felt sweaty.

Through the plate glass window, he watched the crowd surround the Shacklefords. Mostly men. Two skanky women. Everybody looked young. Buddy hoisted the gym bag over the bar to Rose.

This family had operated a drug ring in Mason County for as long as Tom could remember. Whenever he talked about putting a stop to it, the sheriff groused that shutting down the Shacklefords would be a pointless exercise. Somebody else, maybe somebody worse, would fill the gap in an instant. As long as they weren't selling the stuff on street corners in Mountainview or in schoolyards, the sheriff didn't seem concerned about what the Shacklefords did. But Tom knew how much the drug trade in the county had troubled his father, especially because it was dragging down the young people of Rocky Branch District, who already had too many strikes against them. Tom and his brother Chris had grown up hearing the lectures: Steer clear of the kids who use dope, keep your mind clear and your body clean.

Ten years ago, Troy Shackleford's father had been the local drug boss. Troy was a courier, but he'd also worked at legitimate jobs. Pauline McClure, one of his employers, might have stumbled onto something that would help John Bridger nail the Shacklefords. A long shot, but it would have given Troy a motive for killing her. And O'Dell? A younger, weaker man pushed into the role of accomplice?

In the diner, Rose gestured to the crowd and they formed a ragged line leading to the bar. She passed something to each customer, received something in return.

Tom pulled his binoculars from the glove compartment. Through the powerful lenses, he got a good look at the small plastic bags Rose dispensed and the cash she accepted. Jesus

Christ. Right out in the open. And why not? The Shacklefords had been given a pass by the cops for so long they probably felt invincible. Tom watched, with simmering fury and disgust, until most of the customers had been served. He'd seen enough to justify a warrant for a future raid, and by God, he was going to follow through no matter how loudly the sheriff squawked. He'd be damned if he'd let these people go on selling dope like it was candy.

He stashed the binoculars in the glove compartment and climbed out of his truck. Hunching his shoulders against the wind, he headed for the door.

Inside, he paused, his ears ringing from the noise, his nose and throat burning from the smoke that floated in the air like a cirrus cloud. Some of the smoke probably came from tobacco, but the sickly sweet odor of marijuana was what Tom smelled.

Gradually all heads turned his way. He wasn't in uniform, but everybody seemed to know who he was. People leaned together and exchanged whispers. Conversation died. Joints disappeared under tabletops. Rose Shackleford's bulging eyes peered at him from her bloated face, and her mouth twisted in a sneer. Thunderous jukebox music made the floorboards vibrate under Tom's feet.

Troy Shackleford grinned at Tom. He had to raise his voice to be heard above the Clint Black song when he said, "Hey there, Captain. Come on in and have a seat." He yelled toward the back of the room, "Somebody shut that thing off."

A second later the music died and the place was quiet as a cave.

Aware of his audience, Tom took time to strip off his gloves and stuff them into his pockets before he ambled to the bar and claimed the stool next to Shackleford. Half a dozen other men at the bar apparently decided they'd be more comfortable in booths, and they shuffled across the aisle. Tom could see through an open door into the small back room, where Shackleford's nephew lurked, a scowl on his face. Buddy's gaze connected with Tom's, swerved away.

"What'll you have, Captain?" Troy Shackleford asked. "Rose, get the man a drink."

The bulky woman lumbered over to stand across from Tom. Her eyes looked hard as marbles.

"A beer," he said. "Whatever you've got on tap." He reached into his back pocket for his wallet.

"Hey, forget it," Shackleford said. "It's on me."

Since Tom didn't intend to drink the beer, he shoved his wallet back into his pocket and let the question of payment go. Rose plopped a green glass mug in front of him and some of the beer foam cascaded down the side. Tom smiled. "Thanks."

Rose grunted and moved away.

"So what brings you to our little patch of the world?" Shackleford asked. "You workin' undercover?" He grinned. "Or gettin' in touch with your roots?"

Out of the corner of his eye, Tom saw Rose ten feet away, quietly but quickly scooping up plastic bags from the counter behind the bar and stowing them in the gym bag. When she realized he was watching she went stiff as a statue.

Tom shifted toward Shackleford. "I'd like to know where you were around one-thirty this afternoon. You and your nephew both."

Shackleford paused with his mug halfway to his mouth. He set it down. "If you're askin' me if one of us took a shot at the lady vet's car, you're way off base."

"How do you know about it?"

"Aw, you know how word gets around. Especially about a shootin'."

"Where were you?" Tom asked.

"One-thirty? My mother's house. Both of us. Go ask her."

"Yeah, well, I'm pretty sure she'd back you up, so I think it'd be a wasted trip."

A grin snaked across Shackleford's face. "You callin' my mama a liar, Captain?"

"Was anybody else there? Besides relatives. Did any of the neighbors see you? You speak to any of them, wave at them when you drove by?"

"Well now, let me see." Shackleford wrinkled his brow in mock concentration. "By golly, I don't believe I saw another soul." He grew serious again. "But I didn't shoot at a car that had my daughter in it, I can promise you that. Whoever did it was personally insultin' me, and when I find out—"

"What were you up to on Main Street today?" Tom glanced toward the back room and saw Buddy straighten his shoulders defiantly. Tough guy, in his black leather jacket, black shirt, black jeans. He was good-looking enough to have a bunch of girls running after him, and Tom could imagine how he treated them.

Troy Shackleford lifted his beer and swallowed half of it. When he set the mug down, he answered, "Just tryin' to get a little time with my daughter. I don't see her nearly enough these days."

"What accounts for this sudden interest in Holly?"

"Nothin' sudden about it. She's been my daughter all her life."

"And you've ignored her all her life. What's so important that you had to talk to her today? Are you trying to shut her up about something?"

Shackleford ran his tongue around the inside of his lower lip. "I don't know what you're talkin' about."

"Stay away from her. She doesn't want anything to do with you."

Assuming a sorrowful expression, Shackleford shook his head. "It's a downright shame when folks try to turn a child against her own flesh and blood."

"I want you to steer clear of Mrs. Turner, too." Shackleford opened his mouth, but Tom went on before he could speak. "When was the last time you saw Rudy O'Dell?"

Shackleford sipped his beer again. Everybody in the room was silent, watching and listening. "He's not come to me for help, if that's what you want to know. I'd be flat-out amazed if he did."

"You got any idea where he could be?"

"Not a clue. Try turnin' over some big rocks, you might find him that way."

Giggles burst from the two women in a nearby booth. Their male companions growled orders to shut up.

"You know any reason why O'Dell would try to kill Holly?" Tom asked.

Shackleford swiveled to face Tom. "You sayin' it was Rudy that shot at her?"

The man's surprise seemed genuine, which could mean a couple of things. Tom decided to feed Shackleford a little information to see what reaction it provoked. "The bullets could have come from his rifle. Of course, plenty of rifles fire the same calibre. We'll know more when we get the ballistics report."

Shackleford didn't seem to hear the qualifiers. "Well, I'll be damned," he murmured, rubbing his chin and staring into space. "Now, Rudy doin' that is somethin' I don't understand in the least."

Although Shackleford was a good bluffer, Tom didn't think he was acting now. That meant Shackleford himself had nothing to do with the attack. Tom went on, "I hear O'Dell's got some kind of fixation on Holly. Because she looks so much like Pauline."

Shackleford came out of his reverie. "Hmmph. Well, you know more than I do. I don't keep up with him and his fixations."

"I'd think you'd want to keep close tabs on O'Dell," Tom said.

"And why would I want to do that?"

"In case he decided to reminisce about the past."

Shackleford shot a sideways glance at Tom, and for a fleeting moment Tom saw confusion and apprehension in his face. "He's got nothin' to say that's gonna bother me."

"I think he knows what happened to Pauline," Tom said.

"Really." Shackleford held up his mug, signalling Rose for a refill. She took the empty glass and put a full one in his hand.

Tom let the silence drag out. Shackleford flexed his fingers and scrubbed them on his jeans legs, wiping off the beer they'd picked up from the sides of his mug. He drank. He cleared his throat. "You think Rudy killed Pauline? That's what your daddy thought."

"No, my father thought Rudy and *you* killed her."

"Well, your daddy was wrong. He was tryin' to pin it on the easiest targets. You oughta be askin' yourself why."

Tom felt the pressure expand inside him, and his muscles tensed with the urge to strike out. He forced himself to relax. Or at least appear relaxed. "I think O'Dell was involved somehow but probably wasn't the killer."

"I'm sure he'll be real relieved to hear that."

"Oh, he's going to jail, one way or another. But not for sinking an ax into Pauline's brain."

Shackleford winced, the briefest betrayal of revulsion.

Leaning closer, Tom said, "I wonder how it feels to have a memory like that in your head."

Shackleford pulled away from him.

"I've got my own bad memories," Tom went on softly, "and they're tough enough to live with. I can't imagine what it would be like to have that picture in the back of my mind all the time. Pauline's head split open, her brains spilling out, her blood—"

"Shut up!" Shackleford spun off his stool, his face red and knotted with fury.

A rustle of startled movement swept through the onlookers.

"I guess it's not real pleasant to think about," Tom said. "Too bad her bones were found and it's all been dredged up again."

Tom could hear Shackleford's rapid, shallow breaths. Finally an ugly little smile took shape on the man's face. His voice came out low and insinuating. "You know what I think happened to Pauline? I think your sainted daddy killed her."

Tom sprang to his feet, grabbed the front of Shackleford's jacket. The movement sent a jolt of pain through Tom's wounded arm. "If I ever hear you say that again, you're going to be riding in a wheelchair. Do you understand me?"

Shackleford's grin widened. "He went to see her one day and found Ed McClure in her bed, and they had a real knockdown drag-out, like two dogs fightin' over a bitch. Maybe that kind of thing happened one time too many and your daddy couldn't take it any more."

Tom's fingers tightened on Shackleford's jacket. "Are you telling me you saw that fight?"

"Rudy saw it. He told me about it. If you don't believe me, ask him. Oh, wait a minute. You can't find Rudy, can you? Well, you're in luck, 'cause that nigger housekeeper saw it too. Go ask her."

Tom shoved Shackleford and sent him stumbling backward across the aisle. He thudded into a table, windmilled his arms in a losing fight for balance, and dropped to the floor.

With two strides, Tom stood over him. "Enjoy this little business you've got, because you're not going to have it much longer. Enjoy your freedom, because you won't have that much longer either. And if you go anywhere near Rachel Goddard or Holly again, I'll bury you."

Tom turned away, his blood pounding in his temples. Behind him, Shackleford said, "Oooh, I'm scared, Deputy Dawg."

Tom whirled and landed a kick in Shackleford's stomach. That shut him up.

Chapter Twenty-three

By three in the morning, Holly's screaming nightmares had awakened the household twice, and Rachel's own dreams made her afraid to close her eyes again. She went down to the kitchen and found Tom leaning against a counter and tossing a pill into his mouth.

After he'd all but accused her of getting Holly and herself shot at, Rachel had decided to stay cool and aloof with him, but her resolve collapsed the instant she saw him. "Are you all right? Are you taking something for pain?"

Tom followed the pill with a gulp of water. The fluorescent bulb over the sink, the only light on in the room, gave his olive complexion a sallow tinge. "Yeah. It seems to bother me most when I'm not busy. Just lying there trying to sleep."

Rachel was torn between wanting him to get relief from the pain and wishing he would stay clearheaded in case something happened.

As if reading her mind, he said, "I only took half a pill. That'll help, but any more would make me loopy."

Dressed in jeans and a wrinkled shirt, he looked the way he always did when out of uniform, as if he'd shed his natural skin and donned a disguise. Rachel was acutely aware of her own attire, a loose robe over a nightgown, as well as her disheveled hair. She pushed strands off her face, then clicked on the ceiling light and crossed to the cabinet next to the sink. "You need plenty of rest to heal properly."

"Don't stand too close to the sink," he said. "Somebody outside could see you."

She jumped back, staring at the thin curtains drawn across the window behind the sink. Anyone in the yard could have seen the outline of her body. She ran her tongue over dry lips as she remembered the noises outside her house the other night, her certainty someone had been spying on her. "I'm going to make hot chocolate," she said, and heard the strain in her voice. "You want some? It might help you sleep."

"That and some earplugs. But yeah, thanks, I'll take a cup."

Tom leaned against the counter and watched her measure cocoa, sugar and milk into a saucepan. Her hands shook and his scrutiny made the tremor worse.

"Are you okay?" he asked.

"Well, I have to admit it's a little stressful to have somebody trying to kill Holly and me, on top of—" She broke off, annoyed that she'd almost told him about the threatening letter from Perry Nelson. Turning away from him, she placed the saucepan on the range.

"On top of what?" Tom asked.

"Nothing. I'm as okay as I can be under the circumstances. I wish I could say the same for Holly."

"Is she having nightmares about the shooting?"

"No. She's dreaming about her mother. She's terrified her mother might be dead." Rachel blamed herself for Holly's emotional state. If she hadn't goaded Tom about the possibility of the second skull being Jean's, he wouldn't have talked to Holly about it and the girl wouldn't be battling an onslaught of nightmares about her mother's skeleton rising before her eyes. "I hope you aren't going to tell me again that I never should have gotten involved with her."

"I apologize for that. I realize how much it means to you to help her."

"Well, hallelujah."

He shrugged, but only with his right shoulder, on the uninjured side. "I'm hardheaded, not hopeless."

"Oh, there's definitely hope for you." Rachel felt him watching her as she stirred the chocolate. When it was just short of boiling, she poured it into mugs. "Here you go."

"Thanks. Come sit in the living room with me. I've still got the fire going."

Rachel hesitated, but the thought of returning to her bedroom and her bad dreams was a lot less appealing than sitting before a fire with Tom. They walked up the hall together. At the foot of the stairs she stopped to listen for sounds from Holly's room, but she heard nothing.

Tom scooped his blanket and pillow off the leather couch and Rachel sat at one end, figuring he wouldn't crowd her if she left most of the space for him. After dropping the bedding onto a chair, he prowled the room, checking the drapes, making sure no potential shooter could get a peek at the human targets inside. Billy Bob, dozing on the hearth before the fire, would have made for a cozy scene if Tom's big black pistol hadn't been lying on the coffee table in Rachel's line of vision. The shadowy room seemed to emphasize their isolation.

She'd believed that having an armed deputy here overnight would make her feel safer. Even with the deputy in the same room, though, she felt shockingly vulnerable. God, it was so easy for one person to kill another. Give someone a motive and a will to commit murder and he could do it anywhere, anytime.

No one in Mason County had a personal motive to kill her, but somebody wanted Holly out of the way. The same somebody probably believed that whatever Holly knew, Rachel would also know before long. And that was exactly what she was after. Somewhere in Holly's head was hidden a secret worth killing to keep, and Rachel wanted to pry that deadly information out of the girl.

Tom sat on the couch at a distance she found comfortable, and they drank their chocolate in silence for a minute, the crackle of the fire the only sound in the room. Then he asked again, "On top of what? Has something else happened that I don't know about?"

Rachel hesitated, tugged in one direction by the need to protect her privacy, keep Tom out of her life, but wondering if that might be foolish in the long run. "I guess the police here should be forewarned, just in case."

"Hey, now you're worrying me. What are you talking about?"

"The guy who shot me—did you know he was sent to a mental hospital instead of prison where he belongs?"

"Yeah," Tom said. "Jurors can be idiots sometimes."

"He hates me because I turned him in for forging my name on a narcotic prescription. Then I did my best to get him convicted of attempted murder. The way he sees it, all his problems are *my* fault. If I hadn't turned him in, he wouldn't have gone through the trauma of being arrested and the agony of withdrawal. He wouldn't have lost his job and his girlfriend. He wouldn't have been so miserable that he just had to come after me with a gun to get even. If I got shot in the process, well, that was my own fault too."

Her throat tightened and a spasm of fury shook her when she thought about the night Perry Nelson had burst into her little world and blasted it to bits. Tom set down his mug, slid closer and placed a hand on her shoulder.

"They had to remove him from the courtroom a couple of times while I was testifying because he kept shouting at me," Rachel said. "He even tried to get at me once."

"Jesus Christ." Tom squeezed her shoulder.

His touch felt comforting and she didn't pull away. "Then when the verdict came in, not guilty by reason of insanity, he looked around at me and laughed and gave me the finger. And he told me that when he got out of the hospital he'd come after me and finish what he started. I guess I thought I could hide in the country and be safe forever. But he knows where I am. I got a letter from him a few days ago. It wasn't signed, and it didn't have his fingerprints on it, but I know it came from him."

"He's locked up, right?" Tom said. "He won't be out anytime soon."

"He's already trying to get unsupervised weekends outside the hospital, and his doctors are supporting him."

"Oh, for God's sake," Tom said. "Just proves my theory that psychiatrists are the craziest people on the planet. But the court can stop it, Rachel. In cases like that, the doctors can't act on their own."

She nodded. "He has a hearing on his petition in a couple of weeks. I'm going to be there to testify if the judge will allow it. I can't let him get out."

"Listen," Tom said. "Tomorrow I want you to write down all the information I need to keep tabs on this s.o.b." He rubbed her back gently. "I won't let him get anywhere near you."

"Thank you." She forced a smile.

He withdrew his hand and Rachel felt a ridiculous stab of loss.

Determined to steer the conversation away from herself, she said, "Right now, my main concern is Holly. She has nightmares every night. I think she knows what happened to her mother and she's dreaming about it. Maybe one of these nights she'll trust me enough to tell me everything."

"I need to know what she remembers," Tom said, "but I don't want you going without sleep night after night to find out."

"You're the one who really needs sleep, but you're sitting here awake too." Rachel examined his face more closely, saw the shadows under his eyes. "You look as if you haven't slept since all this started."

"Ah, this case is driving me a little crazy." He picked up his mug but set it down again without drinking. "I wish to God we'd never found those bones."

"Well, I have to admit both our lives would be easier right now if you hadn't. But I don't think Holly's life would be better in the long run. And the killer would go free."

"Yeah, but…" Tom's eyes had a bleak, faraway look. "It's turned out be more…personal than I expected. I've found out some things—" He shook his head. "Never mind. It's not important."

"If it's keeping you awake at night, it's important. Talking about it might help."

Tom rose abruptly and moved around checking the drapes, although they were as snugly drawn as they'd been ten minutes before. *Don't push him,* Rachel told herself.

He sat on the couch again and leaned forward with his hands clasped between his knees. "I don't want to burden you with my problems."

Let it go. But instead of taking the opening he'd offered, she said, "Go ahead and burden me. I'm a masochist. If I weren't, I wouldn't be in this situation in the first place."

He smiled at that, then jumped up again, grabbed the poker and reached behind the fireplace screen to jab at the oak logs. Billy Bob snorted and rolled over.

Why hadn't she left well enough alone? Something serious was preying on Tom's mind, and she wasn't sure she could handle the closeness that more revelations might bring.

Tom hung the poker back on its hook and stared into the flames. "I always looked up to my father. I thought he was the best example of what a man should be. With his family and his work. It sounds trite, but I really did put him on a pedestal."

Oh no. Had he discovered that his father bungled the original investigation? Took a bribe, destroyed evidence? Rachel knew little about police work or about John Bridger, and she doubted she could say anything to make Tom feel better.

He faced her. "I've found proof that my father was having an affair with Pauline McClure before she disappeared."

For a moment Rachel was too startled to speak. "Oh, Tom," she finally managed. "My God."

"She was probably sleeping with other men too. It puts a hell of a different spin on everything."

"Do you think your father—"

"Had something to do with her murder? No. But at this point, I don't believe I really knew him, so how do I know what he was capable of?"

Rachel moved to Tom's side. "You're feeling betrayed. But that doesn't mean his whole life was an act."

Tom stuffed his fists in his pockets and shifted away. "So I'm supposed to forget about it?"

"What your father meant to you, the role he played in your life, that hasn't changed. This was between him and your mother. It doesn't affect you."

"Yes, it does. I didn't know about the affair till now, but it changed my whole life. The night of the accident— Earlier that day, Pauline was declared legally dead. She'd been missing for seven years. It was eating my father up, but I thought it was because he'd never solved the case. I got the brilliant idea that going out to the fish camp for dinner with the family might cheer him up. Me, home for a visit, my mom, my brother and his wife and Simon."

Tom paced in front of the fireplace, a powerful inner turmoil visible on his face. When he spoke again he seemed to be dragging the words out of himself against great resistance.

"But all during dinner, my dad kept snapping at my mom. I'd never seen him treat her that way. I was afraid they'd get into an argument in public, so I insisted on leaving. The thunderstorm was blowing up, but I practically pushed them out the door to the van. I made them go out on the road in that storm."

"The accident wasn't your fault. You hit some pooled water and lost control, didn't you? It could happen to anybody."

"It *was* my fault, damn it!"

Rachel stepped back, frightened by his anger.

"I'm sorry," he said. "I didn't mean to— Rachel, I'll never get past it if I don't accept the truth."

Her eyes filled with helpless tears at the sight of him in so much torment. "I understand that. Believe me, I understand it better than you can imagine."

He marched toward the window, stopped, turned and strode back. "But I'm not the only one to blame. That damned woman was messing with our family right up to the minute they died. Now I'm supposed to solve the bitch's murder, get justice for her."

"You have to do your job. You won't respect yourself if you don't."

"My job," he said with a scoffing laugh. "I had a *real* job in Richmond. In my first year as a detective, I had a better clearance rate than some of the veterans. Then the accident happened and I felt like I had to come back home. I took Simon's parents away from him and I had to be here for him. And the other day when we found those bones, I thought I'd be able to do something for my dad too, I could wrap up this case for him. Now I find out he was a liar and a cheat and—"

"Stop it!" Rachel grabbed Tom's good arm and made him stand still and look at her. "Don't let go of your good memories. They're all you have left to hold on to. If you let them get buried under a lot of anger and pain, you'll have nothing—"

Her voice broke and she lurched away from him, a hand clapped over her mouth to stifle a sob. In trying to banish Tom's demons, she'd let her own out of their cage. The image of her mother drenched in blood filled Rachel's mind. *Stop it, get hold of yourself.* She swiped at the tears that flooded her cheeks.

Tom stepped in front of her and drew her against him. She stiffened for a second, but she wanted him to hold her. It had been so long since anyone had held her.

"I'm sorry," he murmured. "I shouldn't have dumped all this on you after the day you've had."

Her arms circled his body and tears leaked from her eyes and dampened the front of his shirt where she pressed her face. His strong hand stroked her back. Luke used to massage her back and shoulders when she was tense, work the knots out of her neck and leave her relaxed, calm. But Tom was not Luke. She pulled away from him.

He took a handkerchief from his back pocket and gave it to her.

"God, I'm a mess." She dried her tears and blew her nose.

"I think you're wonderful," Tom said. "Don't you know that yet? Don't keep shutting me out. I want to be part of your life."

He brushed hair off her damp face, kissed her forehead, her cheek. She tried to resist, but the touch of his lips was gentle and undemanding. She let him draw her closer, tilt her chin and kiss her.

When his arms tightened a chill moved through her. She thought of Luke, waiting for her to come back to him, and she thought of the secrets she couldn't share with Tom. She stepped back, wrapped her arms around her chest to warm herself, to hold herself together. "I'm sorry. It's not you, Tom. I'm just not ready for this."

"I won't force myself on you, Rachel. Just give me a chance."

She didn't have an answer for him. All she could say was, "We both need sleep."

Before he could say anything else she ran out, back to the safe loneliness of her bedroom.

Chapter Twenty-four

Lila Barker might not be up this early on a Sunday morning, but Tom couldn't wait any longer. He set off before dawn. Sooty clouds clotted the sky and as the sun came up drifting fog smudged the outlines of trees and hills. Tom could smell more snow in the air.

Pauline's former housekeeper lived on a dirt road in the far southeast corner of the county, an area that was mostly woods and weed-choked fields and rocky hills. Her white clapboard bungalow looked as old as the massive trees surrounding it.

Tom pulled into the gravel driveway and parked his truck behind Mrs. Barker's yellow Plymouth. She stood in the yard amid a forest of birdfeeders perched on poles and hanging from tree limbs. Fat-soled athletic shoes added another two inches to her already impressive height. The rest of her ensemble included purple sweat pants and a puffy red down jacket with a chickadee sitting on the right shoulder.

"I've been expecting you," she said as Tom got out of his car. Cardinals, titmice, and blue jays fluttered around her on their way to and from the feeders. The chickadee flew off when Tom approached. "I awakened this morning feeling certain you would be along soon. I embarked a bit earlier than usual on my morning constitutional so that I would be back when you arrived."

Christ, not this mumbo-jumbo again. "Can we go inside and talk?"

"Of course," Mrs. Barker said. "I'll answer your questions honestly and fully."

She led him up the steps to the front porch. "How are you?" she asked as she unlocked the door. "Is your arm healing?"

"It's a lot better, thanks."

She raised a skeptical eyebrow, as if she knew it hurt like hell.

A kitchen timer began chirping as they stepped into her living room. The fragrance of something warm and sweet made Tom's mouth water and reminded him that he hadn't eaten breakfast.

Mrs. Barker disappeared down a narrow hall, and in seconds the timer was silenced.

Tom unzipped his jacket as he circled the living room. The furniture was old and mismatched, but wooden surfaces gleamed and a multicolored afghan of geometric design draped the couch. Bookshelves, crammed full, covered two walls from floor to ceiling. On one shelf, in front of the books, stood a row of framed photos, most of black people, but two featuring Pauline: a formal portrait with her husband and small daughter, and a casual outdoor shot of her with a teenage Mary Lee.

With a start Tom realized that the two cat statuettes on another shelf were living animals, both solid black, sitting motionless and watching him.

Mrs. Barker returned, sailing regally into the room despite her sweat shirt and pants. "Take off your coat and make yourself comfortable." She'd already removed her jacket. "Will you share coffee and blueberry muffins with me?"

"That sounds great, thanks." Tom wrestled out of his jacket, trying not to show the pain it cost him, and dropped it onto a chair. "Is your husband at home?"

"I don't have a husband, Captain." Mrs. Barker's lips twitched with a tiny smile. "I've never been married."

"Then why—"

"Do I call myself Mrs.?" Her smile broadened. "I've found that I am accorded greater respect if I use that title. In a community where people of color are looked down on, I have to engender respect in any way I can."

"Why do you stay here if you don't feel comfortable?"

"I didn't say I'm uncomfortable. This is my home."

Tom considered the books on her shelves: biography, history, social and political commentary, many volumes on birds and other wildlife. "You're an intelligent woman. You could have had a career, a better life."

Her smile turned indulgent. "I hope you're not always this quick to reach conclusions about people. That doesn't bode well for your work."

"I'm sorry. I—"

"Don't worry about me and my life. I've always done what I pleased, said yes or no to any offer of employment according to my own desires. Now I don't work at all. I spend my time pursuing my passion—reading. On occasion I assist those who need answers about the future or about the people in their lives."

"You tell fortunes," Tom said. That round table in the corner, with its lacy cloth, was probably where she sat for those sessions. He wondered if she used a crystal ball.

"I give life readings, Captain. I know you're a skeptic. You are allowed your beliefs. And I am allowed mine." She gave a little laugh. "Incidentally, I'm not running a business without a license. I don't charge a fee. If someone wants to leave a small cash gift, that's entirely up to them."

"And I'm sure it always comes as a surprise to you." Tom couldn't help grinning any more than he could help liking this unusual woman.

"Generosity never fails to surprise me," she said. "I'll make our coffee now."

Tom followed her to the kitchen and lingered in the doorway while she placed a kettle on a burner and spooned ground coffee into the cone on a glass pot. A pan of muffins sat cooling on the counter.

He asked, "Who's Mary Lee's real father?"

A tremor in Mrs. Barker's wrist caused tiny brown granules to spill from the measuring spoon and scatter on the counter. She recovered quickly and finished her task before she faced Tom. "Adam McClure was Mary Lee's father. If you'll look at her birth certificate, I'm certain you'll find verification of that fact."

"You said you were going to be honest with me. I know Adam wasn't her father. But I'm betting you know who was. Who is."

"I don't know any such thing." Her expression was complicated, mixing wariness, resistance, sadness. "Why are you doing this?"

"I'm trying to solve Pauline's murder. And maybe a second murder. The truth about Mary Lee's real father might lead me to the killer."

"If you let people know the police don't believe Adam was her father, you'll give Robert McClure an opening to go after everything Mary Lee has. The man is merciless."

"Why do you care so much about Mary Lee? You don't really know her, do you? She hasn't lived in Mason County since she was twelve years old."

"Of course I know her. She came home from school for vacations and holidays. And we keep in touch."

"Oh, really?"

"I'm not implying that we're close friends, Captain. I receive Christmas cards from her, and—" Mrs. Barker hesitated, wet her lips with the tip of her tongue. "She provides me with a modest pension. In recognition of my years of service to her mother."

Mary Lee hadn't struck Tom as the sort who would give a second thought to her mother's former housekeeper. "Is that all she pays you for? Or is she paying you to keep quiet? Does she know she's not Adam's daughter?"

Mrs. Barker opened a cabinet above the counter and removed a tin tray, cups, and small plates. Without looking at Tom, she said, "I can't tell you what Mary Lee knows or doesn't know."

"Is Ed McClure her father?"

Mrs. Barker gave him a slant-eyed glance. "You're implying that Pauline was unfaithful to her husband with his own brother quite early in their marriage."

"Not all that early. They were married, what, four or five years before Pauline had the baby? You were working for her then, weren't you?"

"Yes." Mrs. Barker lifted the whistling kettle and doused the grounds in the pot's cone. Coffee streamed into the pot and the rich aroma filled the kitchen. "I had no reason to believe she was ever unfaithful while her husband was alive."

"But Mary Lee isn't Adam's child."

Mrs. Barker plucked two muffins from their pan and placed them on the plates. "So you say."

Tom wanted to grab her and shake her, and he was horrified at how strong the urge was. He jammed his fists into his pockets. He'd allowed Shackleford to get under his skin the night before, he'd lost control and done something he was ashamed of. Mrs. Barker was a woman, a damned infuriating one but a woman nevertheless, and he wouldn't let himself touch her.

He changed tack and asked the question that had brought him here. "Do you remember a fight between Ed McClure and my father?"

She frowned. "A fistfight?"

"Yes." He tasted sourness in the back of his throat. "I heard you witnessed it."

A slow smile of understanding broke across her face. "Ah. And I can guess who told you. I'm afraid the report you heard was exaggerated. I never witnessed a fistfight. I did overhear a few angry words between those two gentlemen."

Tom felt absurdly relieved. Why had he accepted Shackleford's word? But still, Ed and his father had argued—at Pauline's house. "What did you hear?" He steeled himself for Mrs. Barker's answer.

"Pauline had asked her brother-in-law to stop visiting. He persisted, although she never admitted him to the house again. She called your father one day when Ed appeared and began banging on the door. Your father told him he was trespassing. Ed responded that he had a right to be there, because he cared about Pauline. Because he loved her."

"And what did my father say?"

"He vowed to arrest Ed for trespassing if he ever set foot on Pauline's property again. That was all I heard. I was in the house, and she had opened the front door. After she closed it and went out into the yard, I heard no more."

"When was all this in relation to Pauline's disappearance?"

"Several weeks earlier." Mrs. Barker lifted the cone from the coffee pot and disposed of the paper filter in a trash can under the sink. Popping the lid onto the pot, she said, "Shall we go into the living room?"

The two black cats dropped without a sound from the bookshelves and padded over to join them at the round table. The animals leapt onto the table and sat side by side, their green eyes fixed on Tom. He admired cats, but he found these two unnerving. Like their owner, they seemed to know secrets he couldn't even guess at.

"Ed McClure's wife couldn't have been happy about her husband's attentions to Pauline," Tom said. How much had his mother known about his father and Pauline? "Did you ever see Natalie McClure at Pauline's house?"

"Unfortunately, yes." Mrs. Barker broke off bits of her muffin and placed them before the cats. "Queenie, Sadie, each of you eat your own and don't squabble." The cats sniffed the treats, then mouthed and swallowed them.

"So Natalie came to the house," Tom said, trying to get her back on track. "What happened between her and Pauline?"

"Natalie came several times. The first time, I answered the door to her and she screamed at me, *Where is my husband?* He came out of the living room looking white as a ghost. *Natalie, what are you doing here?* She shoved me aside and marched right in and screamed the same question back at him. Pauline came into the foyer and Natalie proceeded to curse a blue streak at her."

"How did it end?"

"With Ed dragging his wife outside by the arm and forcing her into her car. Then they both drove off."

"When did that happen?"

"Oh, months before Pauline disappeared." Mrs. Barker bit into her muffin.

"But he went on seeing Pauline even after his wife made an issue of it?"

Mrs. Barker chewed and swallowed. "Yes. As if it had never happened. However, Ed eventually became angry with Pauline for some reason. I heard them arguing one day. I didn't catch all the words, but I did hear her say that she would not allow him to run her life, and she didn't want to see him again. I believe I told you the other day, she instructed me not to let him into the house."

That could have been the point when Ed had found out about Pauline and John Bridger. Tom picked up his muffin, discovered he didn't have an appetite anymore, and set it back on the plate. "But Ed kept coming?"

"He stopped visiting for a while, but not long before Pauline disappeared, he began coming around again, begging for forgiveness. He would stand on the front porch and talk to the closed door, pleading with her to let him in."

"Was that when Pauline asked my father to put a stop to it?"

"Yes. But Ed continued his visits, even after your father spoke to him. Natalie McClure must have been aware of what he was doing, because she showed up again. Twice. She accused Pauline of going after her husband, when the exact opposite was true."

"Did this go on right up to the time Pauline disappeared?"

Mrs. Barker rubbed her eyes with fingers and thumb. "The last time—and the worst—was several days before she disappeared. Her sisters were at the house, then all the McClures descended, one after the other. It was utter madness."

"Tell me. From the beginning. And don't leave anything out."

She sipped her coffee and seemed to gather her thoughts. "Pauline's niece, Amy Watford, had been at the house all that morning. Pauline was very fond of Amy. With Mary Lee away so much, I think Amy filled a gap in Pauline's life. She gave Amy clothes, instructed her on the proper use of makeup, and—"

"Who showed up next?"

"That afternoon, Pauline's sisters arrived. Jean Turner and Bonnie Watford, Amy's mother. Jean's little girl, Holly, was with them. Pauline made a great fuss over Holly. Bonnie told Jean to be careful, or Pauline would take her child away from her too."

"What did she mean by that?"

"Bonnie resented Pauline's attentions to Amy. Or perhaps I should say she resented Amy's adulation of Pauline. She felt Pauline was stealing her daughter."

Not exactly the same story Bonnie had given Tom. "Why were they there?"

"My assumption has always been that Bonnie wanted to put a stop to Amy and Pauline's friendship."

"I've been told that Mrs. Turner was sick, and Pauline's sisters wanted her to visit their mother, but she refused."

Mrs. Barker drew back as if offended. "You were misinformed. She would never have refused to visit when her mother was ill. She did so on a number of occasions. She would have paid for a doctor if Mrs. Turner had been willing to see one. But Mrs. Turner preferred to treat herself with herbal remedies."

So Bonnie Watford had lied. What had been behind that visit, what was it that Bonnie didn't want him to find out? "Tell me everything you saw or heard," he told Mrs. Barker. "Even a scrap of conversation."

"I heard nothing after the first few minutes. Pauline told me to keep Holly occupied in the garden. The others stayed in the house, with the windows and doors closed." Mrs. Barker poured more coffee into Tom's cup. "But I could see them through the living room windows, having a furious argument. At one point Bonnie slapped Pauline, and Jean and Amy had to restrain her."

"But you couldn't hear what they were arguing about?"

"Not a word. But the oddest thing happened after the others pulled Bonnie away from Pauline. Pauline went to Bonnie and embraced her, and the two of them cried in one another's arms."

Tom drank his coffee and considered this. He would probably never get the straight story from Bonnie. He had to locate Amy. Who else could have witnessed the argument? "Where was Mary Lee?"

"She didn't return from her grand tour of Europe until the next day."

Damn. "All right, you said the McClures showed up too."

"Oh, yes. Ed arrived first. He'd been drinking. He pounded on the door, but Pauline wouldn't open it. He threw stones at the windows, shouting all the while. Poor little Holly was outside with me, as I said, and the child was terrified. This had been going on for fifteen or twenty minutes when his wife and brother arrived."

"Together?" Tom asked.

"In Robert McClure's Lincoln Town Car," Mrs. Barker said. "They leapt from the car and ran to Ed." The flowing motion of her hands described their actions. "Natalie screamed at her husband. Invective such as I have never heard before or since. Robert seized Ed and attempted to maneuver him into the Lincoln, but Ed fought him wildly. Pauline came out of the house, with her sisters and Amy. The sight of all of them seemed to enrage Robert McClure."

"Enrage is a strong word."

"Oh, he was already quite worked up. When he saw Pauline and her sisters and niece, he… what's that expression young people use? Went ballistic." Her faint smile showed her pleasure in the sound of the slang. "That describes his reaction perfectly."

"What did Robert do?"

"He advanced on them. His face was almost purple. I was sincerely concerned that the man would keel over with a coronary in the front garden."

"He advanced on them, and—?"

"He said it made him sick to see Melungeon trash in his grandfather's house. He said he was going to set things right no matter what he had to do, and if they thought they were going to live high on McClure money for the rest of their lives, they had another think coming."

A real threat, or more of Robert's bluster? "How did Pauline react to that?"

"She looked him in the eye and said, *Robert, if you weren't so funny, I'd feel sorry for you. Take your brother home and leave me alone.*"

"What happened then?"

"Natalie continued to carry on at a remarkable decibel level. Robert told her to drive Ed's car home. Ed would ride with him. Natalie finally got into her husband's car, but before she left, she rolled down the window and yelled at Pauline that if she didn't leave Ed alone she, Natalie, would… would…"

Tom sat forward. "Would what?"

The words came out in a whisper. "Kill her."

Tom took a moment to imagine Natalie McClure in the role of cold-blooded killer. She had a motive, the strongest motive in the world. In a rage, she could have swung an ax at Pauline's head. But she couldn't have taken Pauline's body up that mountain.

Maybe Natalie engineered Pauline's murder but hadn't done it herself. If the motive was Natalie's jealousy, Tom couldn't explain—yet—where the second, unidentified victim fit in, but he could easily imagine Natalie hiring somebody to get rid of Pauline. Something Jack Watford had said a couple of days before popped into Tom's head. When he'd suggested that Troy Shackleford was Pauline's killer, Watford had answered, *She wasn't robbed. Troy don't do nothin' except for money.*

Tom asked Mrs. Barker, "Do you know whether Natalie McClure ever met Troy Shackleford?"

"Met him? Of course. He's an electrician, you know, and he did an extensive rewiring job at Ed and Natalie McClure's house. She saw quite a bit of Shackleford, I would think."

Chapter Twenty-five

Rachel had barely slept the rest of the night. Lying in the dark, she was awash in guilt. How could she feel so drawn to Tom when she still ached for Luke? How could she even think of bringing her troubled past into Tom's life, when he had such a heavy burden of his own?

She didn't want Tom, or any other man, to ever know her the way Luke did. She'd loved him, still loved him, but he would always see her as damaged, fragile, and that had made her feel dependent and frustrated. Tom was already over-protective of her, and if he knew her story he'd probably be as smothering as Luke had been.

She had hoped to start a new life here in Mason County. But she hadn't realized how lonely that life might be. She couldn't let loneliness push her into a relationship with Tom that she wasn't ready for, might never be ready for.

At dawn she rose and dressed. With her cat Frank at her side, she crept past the room where Holly was asleep at last.

In the kitchen she found a bleary-eyed Joanna having coffee with Brandon. Billy Bob sprawled on the floor beside Joanna's golden retriever, Nan. "Where's Tom?" Rachel asked.

"He's gone to see Pauline's housekeeper," Brandon said, frowning into his coffee mug. "I hope he'll be able to drive okay."

"Yeah," Rachel said, both disappointed and relieved that Tom wasn't there. She opened a can of food for Frank, who had jumped onto a counter when he saw the dogs in the kitchen, then she grabbed a coffee mug and dropped into a chair. "I'd love some coffee, but I don't think I have enough energy to lift the pot. I might have blown it all on feeding Frank."

"Allow me." Brandon reached across the table and filled Rachel's cup. He wasn't exactly a picture of perkiness himself, Rachel thought. His fresh-faced look was lost to fatigue and his short sandy hair was headed in the direction of punk rocker spikes. "Man, you guys had a rough night from the sound of it. Is Holly asleep now?"

"Yeah. I wish I were." Rachel sipped the strong brew. That should help. Joanna refused to have decaf in her house, claiming coffee wasn't coffee if it didn't jolt you wide awake. "I haven't had a full night's rest since she moved in with me."

"You're not gonna throw her out or anything, are you?" Brandon asked.

"Absolutely not. She needs friends to help her stand up to her nutty relatives."

"I'm glad she's got somebody like you on her side," Brandon said. "I'm gonna be right there for her too, anytime she needs me." His cheeks flushed when he added, "She's a great girl, isn't she?"

"You seem to be taking more than a friendly interest in Holly."

"I thought you and Debbie were planning a spring wedding," Joanna said.

Brandon's blush deepened and he gave a short embarrassed laugh. "I've kinda been rethinking all that."

Uh-oh. "Well," Rachel said, "you're a terrific guy and any girl who got you would be lucky. But I don't want Holly hurt. She can't take any more."

"I wouldn't hurt her for anything in the world," Brandon said, somber and earnest. "You gotta believe that."

"You know what you sound like, Rachel?" Joanna smiled across the table. "A mother."

"What? No. Just a friend." For a moment Joanna's words flustered her, and she automatically rejected the idea. But she didn't need much time to get used to it. Why shouldn't she be a mother figure to Holly? Maybe the girl was a young adult, but she was such a lost little kid in so many ways, and she needed help and guidance. Rachel couldn't say no to that need.

Brandon wouldn't hear of Rachel going back to the cottage to get more clothes for herself and Holly. He relented only after another deputy dropped by and agreed to stay with Holly while Brandon accompanied Rachel.

As they drove down the farm lane, heavy mist blanketed the paddocks and meadows on either side. Dark clouds hung low over the hills, but lights shone in the stable and barn. At the barn door a farmhand loaded bales of hay and bags of grain onto a pickup for the short drive across the road to the horses' quarters. Through the open stable door, Rachel saw two men walking down the long aisle, giving each of the two dozen horses a morning check for overt signs of illness. Up ahead, shrouded in mist at the end of the lane, sat Rachel's cottage. The world seemed so normal, so ordinary, that the shooting yesterday seemed a bizarre incident in another dimension.

Brandon pulled the car to the side of the road before they reached the cottage. "Let me have your keys," he said. "You stay here till I go in and make sure everything's okay."

Rachel thought he was being over-cautious, but she'd noticed that arguing with a cop seldom got her anywhere, so she pulled her keys out of her coat pocket and handed them to him. She watched Brandon trot to the cottage.

He started up the short flight of steps, then stopped as if he'd hit a wall. He seemed to be staring at the porch floor. In the car, Rachel leaned forward, trying to see what Brandon saw. She was too far away, and she couldn't make out much through the mist.

She hopped out of the cruiser and jogged toward the cottage. "What's wrong?" she called.

Brandon whipped around.

"Sorry," Rachel said. "I didn't mean to startle you. What's the matter?"

Brandon gestured and moved aside so she could see.

A gray goose sprawled on the porch, its wings stretched to their full span, its head and neck twisted to one side, its eyes half-closed and glazed. An iron stake pierced its body, pinning it to the floorboards.

"Oh, my God," Rachel whispered. "Penny?"

"No," Brandon said. "It couldn't be. I saw Holly's goose at the house this morning."

"It's one of Joanna's," Rachel said. The sight of the bird sent a wave of angry, helpless pity crashing through her. "They're practically pets, they're so trusting. Who would do this?"

"Somebody that wants to scare Holly out of her mind. And you." Brandon pointed.

Rachel tore her gaze from the dead bird and followed Brandon's gesture. What she saw made her gasp. Painted in red on the front door of her home were four words.

YOUR DEAD DOCTER BITCH

<><><>

They're just trying to scare me into abandoning Holly, Rachel told herself as she paced Joanna's living room, waiting for Tom to show up again. Whoever *they* were, they'd succeeded in scaring her. But she'd be damned if she'd throw Holly's life away to protect herself.

When she heard a car door slam outside in late morning, she peeked through the drapes. Tom, at last. She ran to let him in. He'd changed into his uniform, and he crossed the lawn from the driveway with the confident stride of a man who was sure of his strength and authority. The very sight of him made Rachel feel safer.

As soon as Tom came in, Billy Bob charged up the hall, followed by Brandon. Tom looked at Rachel while he stooped to pat and scratch his dog. "The barn door was standing open this morning when the farmhands showed up, but I couldn't see any sign that your house was broken into. A crime scene tech's over there now. He might turn up something useful." Tom stood and touched her shoulder. "Nobody got to you and Holly last night. That's the important thing."

Rachel drew a deep breath and let it out. "Right. But we haven't told Holly about this, and I'd rather you didn't either, okay?"

"Sure. I need to talk to her about something else, though."

"Can I be with her?"

"Me too?" Brandon said.

Tom grinned and shook his head. "I don't know what you two think I'm going to do to the girl, but okay, you can be there to protect her from me."

Rachel led him and Brandon down the hall and through the kitchen to the enclosed porch, where Joanna was using strands of twine attached to a board to teach Holly how to make fancy braids in a horse's mane. Penny, the goose, had settled in a corner, her eyes half-closed as Cicero groomed her neck feathers.

Joanna glanced from one deputy to the other and excused herself.

"Hi, Holly," Tom said. "I need to ask you a few more questions."

Holly continued braiding twine, her fingers moving in intricate patterns, and didn't look at him.

"Do you remember going to your Aunt Pauline's house the week before she disappeared?" he asked. "With your mother and Aunt Bonnie?"

Holly's hands stilled and she frowned. "I haven't thought about that in a long time. Amy was there."

"Right," Tom said. "And the McClures showed up too—Ed and Robert and Ed's wife, Natalie. Do you remember anything Natalie said to Pauline?"

"I don't know if I remember it right." Holly looked so distressed that Rachel moved closer and placed a hand on her shoulder. "Grandma says I get a lot of stuff wrong, I claim stuff happened and it really didn't."

"Just tell Tom what you remember," Rachel said. That old woman had really done a number on Holly, and Rachel had begun to think the motive behind the brainwashing was much deeper and darker than fear of losing a companion. "I'm sure your memory is just as accurate as anyone else's."

"I'll get in trouble." Holly's voice edged toward panic. "Sayin' things about rich people."

"Don't worry about that," Tom said. "The McClures can't hurt you."

Holly picked up the strands of twine, dropped them again. Rachel squeezed Holly's shoulder reassuringly, wishing she could make her believe in the truth of her own memory and emotions.

"What did you hear?" Tom asked.

Holly looked directly at him for the first time and spoke in a rush. "Everybody was mad. Yellin' and callin' each other names. The pretty woman with the blonde hair, she said... she said she was gonna kill Aunt Pauline."

Good God. Rachel had to wonder what else was lurking in Holly's memory, but she hoped the worst of it was out now. Holly had seen and heard more violence and threats as a little girl than any child should ever have to.

The hard glint in Tom's eyes made Rachel fear he would press Holly until she broke down. But Tom moved on. "Thank you. That's what I needed to know. Maybe you can help me with something else too. I need to get in touch with your cousin Amy."

"Oh." A smile of relief transformed Holly's face. "Sure. I can tell you where Amy lives. She writes to me. She was always so good to me. She used to look after me while Mama worked at the diner."

Tom drew a pad and pen from his jacket's inner pocket. "Can you remember her address offhand? And I need her married name."

"It's Wood. Her husband's name is Darrell, and they live in South Carolina." Holly gave Tom a post office box address in a town Rachel had never heard of. While he wrote it down, Holly added on a wistful note, "Will you tell her I said hello and I'd really like it if she'd call me sometime?"

They left Brandon with Holly. In the kitchen, Rachel asked Tom, "Is her word enough to prove anything? She was so young when it happened." Rachel had seen photos of Natalie McClure in the *Mountainview Gazette*'s society column, and she had trouble imagining that pristine being wielding an ax on her sister-in-law. A jury would have the same difficulty.

"I'm hoping Amy'll back up Mrs. Barker's story about the threat," Tom said. "But to make charges stick, I'll have to get a confession out of somebody."

The telephone on the kitchen wall rang, but when Rachel reached to answer it, it fell silent. Joanna must have picked up an extension elsewhere in the house.

"What about the second victim?" Rachel asked. "Why was she killed?"

Tom shrugged. "Could be as simple as wrong place, wrong time."

"When will you know for certain whether it's Holly's mother?"

"Probably by the end of the day. The director of the county clinic is giving up his Sunday to go through old records and find Jean Turner's dental chart. I'll be back tonight. You'll be all right with Brandon here."

"We'll be fine." Rachel folded her arms tightly and lowered her head, unable to look at him when she added, "It's you I'm worried about."

"Me?" His fingertips brushed her cheek and sent a tremor through her. "There's no reason to worry about me."

"You've already been shot once," she blurted. "You're out driving around, walking the streets, going to people's houses, and one of those people is a murderer." She could barely force her next words out in a whisper. "I'm terrified you're going to get killed."

He nudged her chin up to make her look at him, his face somber, his dark eyes pinning her with an intensity that made heat rise to her skin. Gently he unfolded her arms and pulled her to him. She leaned into his warmth and wished desperately that she could keep him here, solid and real and alive.

"I promise you I won't let that happen," he said, his breath warm against her forehead. "I've got too much to live for."

A movement at the doorway made her break away from him. Joanna stood just inside the room, looking from Rachel to Tom, her mouth open in astonishment. Rachel knew she was blushing, and she turned her back to Joanna, feeling like a teenager caught making out. When Tom chuckled, she wanted to kick him.

Joanna cleared her throat. "Tom, Dennis Murray's on the phone. They've found Rudy O'Dell. Somebody shot him."

Chapter Twenty-six

Half a dozen Sheriff's Department cruisers sat in the old motel's crumbling parking lot when Tom arrived. The place had been closed, its rooms boarded up, as long as he could remember. It looked like the Bates Motel, with less charm.

He ducked under crime scene tape and fought through shoulder-high weeds to reach the shed out back.

Six deputies stood around the shed, in a patch of weeds flattened by their footsteps. Two were smoking. "Let's not trample the physical evidence, guys," Tom said. "And put out your cigarettes—but not here. Wait in the parking lot."

Four deputies departed, two looking embarrassed and two red-faced with anger at the rebuke. The Blackwood twins, Kevin and Keith, stayed in their guard positions at the shed's door. Both wore latex gloves, a precaution none of the other men had bothered with. "We're the ones that found him," Kevin told Tom.

"Good work. You can't even see this shed from the road."

The twins smiled, and Keith said, "We're intrepid."

"That you are." Tom replaced his leather gloves with the latex pair he carried in his jacket pocket. "Okay, let's take a look."

Kevin pushed the door open. It creaked on rusty hinges. A stench billowed out, a warm fetid fog on the cold air.

Tom took the flashlight Keith handed him, pinched his nostrils to shut out the odor, and moved inside the dilapidated structure. O'Dell lay on his back, arms and legs straight. His head touched one side wall and his boot-clad feet came within inches of the other. A milky blue haze covered his staring eyes. Long red hair formed a tangled halo around his head, and a bushy beard covered bloated cheeks. The visible part of his face had turned the mottled green-black of corroded copper, but his fingertips were a bloodless white. His heavy wool jacket lay open in front, exposing three bullet holes over his heart.

When Tom lifted the left shoulder, he found no blood on the floor except for smears from O'Dell's soaked jacket. The combined exit wounds formed a hole the size of Tom's fist in the man's back.

Tom left the body and stepped out into the crisp morning air. He paused for a cleansing breath before he spoke. "Any sign of a gun?"

The Blackwoods shook their heads in unison.

"He was killed somewhere else," Tom said, talking more to himself than the twins. "He's been dead for days. Maybe since the day he shot me."

Kevin stated the obvious. "So he couldn't have been the one that fired at Dr. Goddard and Holly Turner yesterday."

"You two stay here," Tom said. "I'll be back in a minute."

He waded through the weeds again to reach the deputies in the parking lot. "I've got a job for you. Two teams, two men each. Go look for Troy Shackleford and deliver him to me at headquarters. Don't tell him we found O'Dell's body. Say I want to question him. If I'm not back yet, make him wait."

<>‹›‹›

The door opened a crack and the bony, suspicious face of Rudy O'Dell's mother appeared. Before Tom could say anything, she barked, "He ain't here and I don't know where he is. Leave me alone."

Tom placed a hand on the door to keep her from slamming it. "We found Rudy a while ago."

Her face crumpled. "I guess you went and throwed him in jail already."

"No. I'm afraid I have some bad news for you."

Mrs. O'Dell gasped and staggered back from the door, horror distorting her face. "You killed him. You killed my boy."

"No, ma'am." Tom entered the house and closed the door behind him. "He was dead when we found him. Somebody shot him."

She bent double and let loose a long, high-pitched wail. "My boy, my little boy. Oh, God, my baby."

Tom steeled himself against the riot of pain boiling out of the woman. The ache in his wounded arm reminded him that the baby boy she mourned had been a fugitive, possibly a killer.

"Where is he?" she sobbed.

"At the hospital. You have to go with me and identify the body, then he'll be sent to Roanoke for an autopsy."

A fresh wail tore from her. "My poor little boy, they're gonna cut him to pieces." Mrs. O'Dell stumbled around the room like a woman struck blind, lurching into furniture, careening into walls. Tears cascaded down her face and mucus bubbled from her nose.

Tom raised his voice to get through to her. "Do you have any idea who could have killed him?"

She stopped with her back to Tom and choked out the words, "If it wasn't the law, it was Troy Shackleford."

"What makes you think that?"

She rounded on him, her face blotchy with fury. "Rudy probably went to him for help and got killed instead. I told him a million times, don't trust that bastard, stay clear of him."

"What—"

A howl of misery cut him short. Mrs. O'Dell flailed her arms and whacked a lamp off a table. Tom dove for it, too late. It crashed to the floor and shattered.

He caught her by the shoulders and steered her to the couch. "Come on now, calm down. If you know anything that'll help me catch the person who killed your son, you have to tell me. Don't lie to me."

She collapsed onto the couch and lowered her head to her knees. Tom took a chair and waited until her crying subsided to shuddering gasps.

Raising her head, she looked at him with red-rimmed eyes. "I got nothin' left to lose. I don't give a damn if he comes after me. Rudy was all I had. And now he's gone." She sniffled, took the handkerchief Tom handed across, and blew her nose. "Whatever my boy done all them years ago, he done because Troy made him. I remember that night so clear. Rudy didn't come home for supper, he didn't come home till the middle of the night, and he was all broke up. Cryin', sayin' somethin' awful happened at Mrs. McClure's house."

She paused to wipe her wet cheeks with the back of one hand, and Tom struggled to control his impatience.

"Rudy told me she was dead—before word ever got out about her disappearin'. He said Troy made him do somethin' horrible. He wouldn't say what. But I don't believe for one minute that my boy helped Troy Shackleford kill anybody."

Tom leaned forward in his chair. "What else did he say? Try to remember."

"That's all. Except for what he said about the girl."

Tom stopped breathing for a second. His skin prickled. "What girl? Who?"

"I don't know who. He said, *Mama, Miz McClure's dead, and the girl is too.*"

Chapter Twenty-seven

By late afternoon, O'Dell's body was on its way to the state medical examiner in Roanoke. The deputies Tom assigned to pick up Shackleford reported that he'd apparently left the county, but Tom wasn't worried about losing him. He couldn't stay away from his source of income for long.

Tom headed out of Mountainview to Ed and Natalie McClure's estate. This might be his only stab at Natalie. The sheriff would have stopped him from interrogating one of the county's most prominent ladies, but Willingham and his wife were spending their Sunday with Mrs. Willingham's ancient mother at a Lynchburg nursing home, and for the time being Tom didn't have to ask anybody's permission to do his job.

Light snow drifted down. As he passed Dennis Murray's house, he saw Dennis' two young sons running around with their tongues stuck out to catch flakes. Smiling at their antics, Tom honked the horn. The boys jumped up and down and waved wildly.

He should have a family of his own by now. Dennis and he were the same age, but Dennis went home every night to a wife and kids while Tom rattled around in his parents' house with only his dad's bulldog for company. Thoughts like that used to stir up regret, but now he found himself wondering what his and Rachel's children would look like.

He was getting a little ahead of himself. He'd think about the future when this case was behind him. Right now he had to organize his thoughts before he faced Natalie McClure.

The scenario that played out in his imagination made perfect sense. Ed had been in love with Pauline. When he'd found out Pauline was having an affair with John Bridger, he'd pitched a fit. That led Pauline to cut him out of her life completely. Ed went a little crazy and started making a nuisance of himself. For Natalie, already wounded by her husband's obvious feelings for Pauline, Ed's out of control behavior was the last straw. Instead of leaving her husband and her comfortable life, she decided to get rid of her rival.

Shackleford and O'Dell had played some part in Pauline's death. That was a given. Maybe Shackleford had killed her for money and roped O'Dell into helping. But even if Natalie herself was the killer, Tom was betting the men had disposed of the body for her.

"Bodies," Tom corrected himself aloud. *Mama, Miz McClure's dead, and the girl is too.* What girl was O'Dell talking about when he came home that night? O'Dell wouldn't have described Jean Turner as a girl. Who, then? Not Mary Lee. Tom had seen her, alive and well. Amy? She'd been writing to Holly for years, sending regular Christmas and birthday cards and occasional short letters.

Tom had asked Dennis to find out Amy's home address and phone number. With any luck, she would not only confirm that Natalie had threatened to kill Pauline, but would also have a good idea who the dead girl was. If Amy had stayed silent all these years out of fear of the Shacklefords, Tom would have to find a way to persuade her to talk.

Every bit of this made sense. So why did he have the niggling feeling that he was overlooking something vital?

The McClures' maid answered the door promptly. Before Tom could ask for Natalie, the mistress of the manor glided into the foyer, her golden hair shimmering under the chandelier's lights.

"Hello, Captain Bridger." Natalie smiled, appearing neither surprised nor distressed that he'd shown up uninvited. "Come in out of the cold. Cora, make some coffee, please."

Tom brushed snow off the shoulders of his jacket and stepped into the foyer.

"How can I help you?" Natalie wore slim navy slacks and a pink turtleneck sweater that looked soft and costly. "I assume you're here about poor Pauline."

"Yes. I have a few questions for you." Closer to her now, Tom detected tension around Natalie's eyes and mouth.

"Let's go in the living room where there's a fire," she said, "and you can warm up. The snow is so beautiful, isn't it, but I hate to be out in it."

Tom's boots shed mud and snow on the foyer's white marble floor. Why would anybody have a white floor in the country? He was momentarily overwhelmed by the opulence of the living room, the swagged red draperies with gold fringe, red oriental carpets, huge oil paintings on cream-colored walls. He'd thought Mary Lee's house was pretentious, but this one had it beat.

"Sit near the fire," Natalie said. "You must be frozen after that long drive out."

"I'm fine, really." Did she think his vehicle was unheated? She settled in a red velvet armchair and Tom sat on a sofa covered in cream silk. He felt like a clodhopper in his brown wool uniform.

With long fingers Natalie brushed back her hair. "What can I help you with?"

"Is your husband around?"

"He's out in the greenhouse. Would you like me to—"

"No, I'm here to see you." With any luck, Ed would stay out of the way. Tom got right down to business. "You said you didn't know Pauline well. Was that your choice?"

"No, it wasn't." Natalie's expression melted into sadness. She laced her fingers together in her lap. A diamond ring sparkled on the right hand, a gold band gleamed on the left. "Heaven knows I tried. But we had nothing in common."

Except your husband. "You married brothers."

"Yes, but Pauline was… different. She preferred animals to people. I don't know how anyone can be a friend to someone like that."

"I keep hearing she had a lover," Tom said. "Maybe more than one."

"Oh, well." Natalie's little laugh sounded breathy and nervous. "She wouldn't have confided in me about that."

"But you've heard the gossip."

"I never listen to gossip. I don't mean to be uncooperative, but may I ask where these questions are leading?"

"I'm trying to find out who had a motive to kill her. A lover, a lover's wife—those would be leads I'd want to follow up on."

She bit her full lower lip and averted her eyes.

The maid bustled in, carrying a silver tray laden with cups and saucers, sugar and cream servers, a silver pot. Wordlessly the servant deposited the tray on the coffee table. As Natalie poured, Tom was again reminded of his visit to Mary Lee a few days before. Mary Lee was the first to mention Ed McClure's "friendship" with Pauline.

Tom took the coffee Natalie offered, sipped once, set the cup and saucer back on the tray. "I've received some information that's…" He paused as if searching for the right word. "…disturbing. I thought you'd want to give me your side of the story."

Color suffused her cheeks. "I don't know what you're talking about."

In all these years, Tom thought, she hadn't learned how to hide her emotions. Had she been terrified every day since Pauline's bones were found that the police would come after her? "I've heard from more than one person that your husband and Pauline were… close."

"Ed tried to be a friend to her after Adam's death. She needed a friend."

Tom held her gaze, hoping he could provoke her into filling the silence with more than she intended to say.

Her expression altered to a mixture of anger and desperation. She leaned forward. "Who's been telling you lies about my husband? I have a right to know."

"Exactly what lies do you think I've been told?"

She drew back in confusion. "I—You've implied—"

"What have I implied?"

"That my husband and Pauline—" She broke off.

"What about them?"

"Why are you doing this?" she cried.

"This is my job, Mrs. McClure."

"Well, your job is despicable."

So I've been told, more times than you can imagine. "Your husband's obsession with Pauline wasn't a secret. I've heard all about his jealousy of her other relationships. And your jealousy. I've heard about the scenes you made at her house."

Natalie grabbed her cup and gulped the hot liquid. "I suppose you're getting all this so-called information from Pauline's housekeeper. She's probably been spreading lies about my husband and me for years."

"Why don't you tell me your side of the story?" Tom said. "Did you go to Pauline's house shortly before she disappeared and threaten to kill her if she didn't leave your husband alone?"

"Oh, dear God." Natalie's hands went to her throat as if she were choking. "Are you going to believe a crazy black woman who claims to see visions? You'll take her word over mine?"

"Mrs. Barker wasn't the only person there that day."

"It's a lie, no matter who says it." Natalie stood. "I want you to leave."

Tom got to his feet. "We'll be talking again. Soon."

"Not without my lawyer present."

"That's up to you."

Without answering, Natalie turned her back on him and faced the fireplace.

Tom walked to the door. Pausing, he said, "By the way, how well do you know Troy Shackleford? I understand he did a lot of electrical work for you around the time Pauline disappeared."

Natalie bowed her head and didn't reply.

Chapter Twenty-eight

"Holly, I've got some great news for you." Rachel settled in an easy chair in the den, where Holly and Brandon were watching lemurs on PBS. Frank slept on Holly's lap and the two dogs, Joanna's and Tom's, reclined at her feet.

A smile broke across Holly's face. "It's not her, is it? The dental records don't match?"

"No, they don't. Tom called a minute ago. He doesn't know who the second victim was, but it wasn't your mother."

"I knew it!" The exclamation made the cat and dogs raise their heads to look at Holly. "I knew she wasn't dead. She couldn't be." Holly beamed at Rachel, then at Brandon, who patted her shoulder and grinned back.

But some part of Holly must have believed her mother's death was entirely possible, Rachel thought. What else could account for the previous night's marathon of nightmares? The last time Holly saw her mother, Jean Turner was preparing to flee from Shackleford after he'd beaten her.

"You said your mother wrote to your grandmother," Rachel said, "and she sent money for you. When was the last time your grandmother heard from her?"

"Oh, gosh, I'm not sure. Mama sent her a new fridge and kitchen stove last summer, though."

"Sent them to her?"

"One day a truck came with a fridge and a stove. The men said it was all paid for, and Grandma said it must be Mama who sent 'em."

Thousands of dollars for a gift of new appliances. Wherever Jean lived, she was doing well.

Brandon used the remote to mute the TV. "So your grandmother writes to your mother? I mean, how did your mom know she needed new kitchen appliances?"

"Well, yeah, I guess she told her. Mama sends money orders sometimes. Grandma goes to the post office to cash them."

"And you never see the letters or the return address on the envelopes?" Rachel asked.

"No. But I'll bet she writes to me too, and Grandma burns the letters without lettin' me see them." Holly's expression soured. "I can see why she didn't want me runnin' off to find Mama when I was a kid, but I'm old enough to go anywhere now. And she still won't tell me where my mother is."

Tom would have to get the information out of Mrs. Turner. Jean could be an important witness against Shackleford. "How did your mother get along with your Aunt Pauline?" Rachel asked.

The question seemed to startle Holly, and Rachel was afraid she would balk at answering. Holly stroked Frank's head. After a moment she said, "I'm not real sure. I mean, I was little and I didn't understand everything. But Mama and Grandma used to talk about Aunt Pauline a lot, and it seemed like they were always mad at her."

"You got any idea why?" Brandon asked.

"I think it was because of my cousin Amy. She was spendin' a lot of time at Aunt Pauline's house and gettin' all kinds of presents from her. I remember Amy comin' by one day in this beautiful white sweater. She said it was pure cashmere and Aunt Pauline gave it to her. Pauline gave her a lot of things."

"Why would that upset your mother and grandmother?" Rachel asked.

"Maybe they felt bad for Aunt Bonnie and Uncle Jack. They said Amy was startin' to act like she was too good for them, because Pauline was puttin' ideas in her head."

"I can see why that would bother them," Rachel said. It was hardly a motive for murder, though.

Holly gave her a chiding look. "You're askin' me all these questions so you can tell Captain Bridger what I say."

"I—Well—" Rachel threw a furious glance at Brandon, who was trying to suppress a laugh and wasn't helping her at all. "Okay. You caught me. But, Holly, anything you can remember might help find your aunt's killer."

"My mother didn't kill her. And my grandmother didn't either."

Rachel hoped not. "I didn't mean to say they did. But you might remember some little thing about your Aunt Pauline that doesn't seem important to you, but it could give Tom a lead."

Holly bit her lip, her expression showing doubt and resistance. "I thought Aunt Pauline was nice. When she was visitin' she always put me on her lap and told me I was pretty. But..."

Rachel wished she could pull the words out of Holly, but willed herself to be patient while the girl pondered her memories.

"I think she was probably a snob. Grandma used to get upset because Pauline never would bring her daughter to visit. Like she didn't want Mary Lee associatin' with her own blood kin. I never even met Mary Lee. But I liked Aunt Pauline anyway. I didn't know it till about a year ago, but she was helpin' Mama and me all along. At least that's what my daddy told me."

"He told you what?" Rachel moved to the couch, next to Holly.

Holly covered her mouth with her hand. "I'm not supposed to talk about it," she said, her voice muffled by her fingers. "He said if I ever did, he'd—" She broke off and squeezed her eyes shut.

"Troy Shackleford won't get anywhere near you again. You're safe now." Rachel tried to sound confident, but she could hear doubt creeping into her voice.

"I thought he'd be in jail already, after I told Captain Bridger about him sellin' drugs."

"You gotta trust the Captain to do what's right," Brandon said. "Tell us what your father said. He'll never find out you did."

Holly's face was a tableau of fear, frustration, indecision. She kneaded Frank's fur too vigorously for his taste, and he croaked a complaint and jumped off her lap. She watched him march out of the room.

After a moment, she said, "Aunt Pauline paid my daddy to work at her house, and she made him give most of it to my mama. The only reason she had him workin' for her was so she could make sure he supported me. I guess Aunt Pauline was tryin' to help us without it lookin' like charity."

Not exactly an earthshaking revelation, and Tom probably knew already. But Holly's anxiety meant the story didn't end there. "He went along with the arrangement?" Rachel asked.

Holly gathered the fabric of her jeans leg between two fingers, formed a crease, smoothed it out.

"Sometimes he'd get drunk, you know? At Rose's diner, where I used to work? And he'd start in on me, like me and my family's the cause of everything bad that ever happened to him. He'd go on and on about how I'm one more Turner b-bitch—" She stumbled on the word and her face went red. "And how the Turner women near about ruined his life."

When Holly fell silent, Rachel tried gentle prodding. "He seems to be doing okay these days. So I guess the Turners didn't ruin his life."

"Well—" Holly pulled her shoulders up in an exaggerated shrug, as if trying to loosen tense muscles. Brandon began to knead one shoulder, and she gave him a shy smile.

These two were getting too cozy too fast, in Rachel's opinion. Having them cooped up together was a bad idea.

Holly went on, the words tumbling out. "He said Aunt Pauline was always preachin' to him about his responsibilities. She said if he didn't support me, she'd pay the best lawyer she could find to help Mama take him to court and she'd sic the law on his whole family for sellin' drugs. He told me he got tired of a woman bossin' him around. He said where Pauline was now, she wasn't ever gonna bother him again. And he was

makin' fun of what Mama told him before she… went away…"
Holly's voice faded.

Brandon squeezed her shoulder. Rachel asked, "What did your mother tell him before she left?"

"What he said to me was, *Jeannie thought she could scare me. Little bitch said we'd never get away with it. But here we are, every one of us free as the birds in the air.* And he laughed like it was the funniest joke in the world."

Rachel exchanged a look with Brandon. *We? Every one of us?* How many people were involved in Pauline's death? And who were they?

"The next day, after he sobered up," Holly continued, "he told me I'd better keep my mouth shut. He said if I ever told anybody what he said, he'd kill me and Grandma too." Holly lifted her gaze to Rachel, then Brandon. "And now I've gone and told both of you."

Chapter Twenty-nine

After Rachel called to report on her talk with Holly, Tom spread the original case files on the conference room table and started rereading them, searching for some elusive piece of information that would make everything click into place. He'd been at it for half an hour when Sheriff Willingham charged in.

"What the hell do you think you're doing?" Willingham slammed the door behind him. Under his camel overcoat he wore a suit and tie, and Tom guessed he'd just returned from taking his mother-in-law to evening church service. On his coat melted snowflakes glinted like sequins.

Tom had a good idea why Willingham was so worked up, but he feigned ignorance. "I'm going through the case files again to see if I missed anything."

"You know damned well what I mean." Willingham leaned on the table and loomed over Tom. "I got home and found five messages on my answering machine from Cecil Merck. Ed and Natalie McClure hired him to get you off their backs."

"Merck called me too. Like I told him, all I did was ask the McClures a few questions."

"The hell you did. Cecil said you accused them both of murder. What kind of half-baked theory are you going on?"

Tom sat back and waited, knowing better than to interrupt the full tide of Willingham's indignation with sensible answers.

"Or maybe you don't have a theory," Willingham went on. "Sounds to me like you're going around accusing everybody in sight, whether you've got evidence or not. I told you that your dad believed Shackleford killed Pauline, and I expect you to find proof so we can put the son of a bitch away and close this case."

The reference to his father irked him, but Tom kept his voice cool. "I'm sure Shackleford was involved. The question is whether he did it for reasons of his own or for somebody else."

Willingham's brow puckered with impatience. "You want to tell me what you're talking about?"

"Witnesses heard Natalie McClure threaten to kill Pauline. I think it's possible Natalie hired Shackleford to do the killing. And based on what Rudy O'Dell's mother told me today, I believe Shackleford coerced O'Dell into helping him dump the body. Or bodies."

"I must be losing my mind," Willingham said. "I could swear I heard you accuse one of the most prominent women in this community of putting out a hit on her sister-in-law."

Tom hadn't expected the idea to be an easy sell. "It's a theory. I need evidence."

"People like Natalie McClure don't do things like that."

Tom could point to any number of murders committed or instigated by people like Natalie McClure, but he let it go. "She had a clear-cut motive. Her husband was in love with Pauline. He admitted it to me. Natalie pitched a fit about it more than once. And she threatened Pauline in front of witnesses."

Willingham responded with a sneer. "Who are these so-called witnesses?"

"Pauline's housekeeper—"

"Oh, for God's sake." Willingham threw up his hands. "You believe that nut?"

"Ed and Robert McClure were there."

Willingham's mouth fell open.

"I don't expect either of them to give evidence against Natalie," Tom said. "But both of Pauline's sisters were also there."

"Oh, well, I'm real impressed. One of 'em took off right after Pauline disappeared and the other one's a nervous wreck."

"Both of Pauline's nieces heard Natalie threaten to kill her," Tom said. "Holly was only eight at the time, but—"

"Who's gonna listen to her, talking about what happened when she was a kid?"

"But Amy Watford was in her late teens," Tom said. "Dennis is trying to locate her in South Carolina. If she confirms the threat, we'll have at least two witnesses who were adults at the time."

"This is crazy, Tom." Willingham moved to the window and Tom swung around in his chair to keep him in sight. The sheriff scowled at the snow falling on the parking lot. "Where are you planning to go with this next?"

"Wherever the evidence takes me. I haven't ruled out Pauline's relatives."

Shaking his head, Willingham muttered something unintelligible. He raised his voice and said, "That doesn't make any more sense than trying to pin it on Natalie McClure. Your father never found any evidence Pauline's family wanted her dead."

"I can't turn a blind eye to any possibility. We've got two dead women, and now O'Dell's been murdered. Rachel and Holly were almost killed—"

"That's another thing." Willingham rounded the table to face Tom. "The department can't afford to pay Brandon Connelly a salary to be a bodyguard."

Tom took a couple of deep breaths and didn't speak until he was sure he could do it without shouting. "Somebody tried to kill Holly. I'm not leaving her unprotected. I don't want to go out there and find her—and Rachel and Joanna—dead because we left them alone."

Willingham shook a finger in Tom's face. "Now you listen to me—"

"What the hell's wrong with you?" Tom jumped up and glared at Willingham. "We've got a killer out there. We've got somebody running around with a gun shooting at innocent women. What do you want me to do? Give up? Forget about it?"

"I want you to find evidence against Shackleford that'll stand up in court." In his vehemence, Willingham spit drops of saliva in Tom's face. "And that's all I want you to do."

"I'll get Shackleford, don't worry." Tom wiped his chin with the back of his hand. "But I'm not stopping there. I won't be finished till I'm sure I've got the whole story. There's too much I don't know about Pauline's life, who she slept with, who fathered her child—"

"You don't know what a can of worms you're trying to open."

"If you're talking about my father and Pauline— By the way, is Mary Lee my half-sister?"

"What the hell— You little bastard—"

"No, Mary Lee's the bastard. Was my father sleeping with Pauline before Mary Lee was born? I assume you know, since you seem to know plenty you don't want to tell me."

"You self-righteous little prick!" Willingham's flushed face took on a purple tinge. "You're not half the man your father was. He saved my life in Vietnam, and he was a better cop than you'll ever be. I'm not gonna let you smear a good man's memory to make yourself feel important."

"I intend to find out the truth. And you'll either let me do my job or explain to the citizens of this county why you don't want these murders solved. That ought to go over big at election time next year."

Sputtering oaths, Willingham raised a hand as if he meant to strike Tom, but Tom stood his ground.

Dennis Murray opened the door and stepped in, a file folder in one hand. He glanced from Tom to the sheriff. "Excuse me, I—"

Willingham stalked out, nearly knocking the much smaller Dennis off-balance when he charged past.

"I guess I interrupted something." Dennis' face was a picture of innocence.

Tom had to laugh, and when he did he felt some of the tension leaving his body. "How far up the hall could you hear us?"

Dennis grinned. "Oh, pretty much all the way to the front door."

"Thanks for showing up. What've you got? Did you find Amy?"

Dennis shook his head, his face sobering. "The mailing address is a box at one of those rental places, not the post office. I had information check phone numbers for about fifty miles in every direction, and there's no Darrell or Amy Wood listed."

Tom took his seat again and Dennis sat facing him. "How about unlisted?"

"I talked a supervisor at the phone company into checking for me, and they're not unlisted either. I contacted all the cell phone providers down there, and they don't have any customers with those names. I asked about Watford too, but no luck. Maybe they can't afford a phone."

"If they can afford to rent a postal box, they can afford a phone." Tom reached for the folder Dennis had brought and flipped it open to look at the cards and notes Holly had received through the years from her cousin Amy. He stared at the return address printed in block letters in the corner of an envelope. He was getting a bad feeling about this. "Doesn't the mailbox place have a home address or phone number for the Woods?"

"It's closed on Sunday," Dennis said, "but I'll see what they'll tell me in the morning about who rents the box. I might have to ask the local cops to talk to them."

Tom opened one of the cards. The message was written in an open, loopy script. *Happy birthday, Princess! Fifteen already! I'm thinking of you. Lots of love always, Amy.* A tiny heart dotted each *i*.

Amy Watford and Jean Turner had both left within days of Pauline's disappearance. Jean, for certain, hadn't been seen since, although her mother claimed she sent money for Holly's expenses. Jack and Bonnie Watford had given the impression they were in frequent contact with their daughter Amy. All those details about her family, her husband's accident. Maybe Amy was lying about her married name so certain people—Shackleford, for example—wouldn't be able to find her.

Or maybe the person who sent these cards and letters wasn't Amy Watford.

Chapter Thirty

At nine o'clock Rachel collapsed into bed, desperate for a few hours of oblivion. She'd feel better with Tom in the house, but at least Brandon was there, and Tom had promised to be back by eleven.

Please, God, if there is a God, let Holly get through the night without waking the whole house.

Frank hopped onto the bed and curled up next to her. In his cage in a corner, Cicero made soft muttering sounds as he tucked his head under a wing. Rachel switched off the lamp and relaxed into sleep.

Her cell phone rang.

Struggling back to consciousness, she groped on the tabletop and knocked the phone to the floor. "Oh, crap!" She got an answering croak from Frank. At last she had the lamp on and the phone to her ear. "Hello!"

"Rachel?" Tom sounded unsure who he'd reached.

"Yes, it's me."

"I've got bad news, I'm afraid."

Rachel pushed herself upright. "What's happened now?"

"The animal hospital's on fire."

"Oh my God!" Rachel fought her way free of the covers and leapt out of bed. "How? When? What— Oh, God."

"Rachel, listen. Right now we need to know if you've got any animals in the building."

"No, no. There aren't any. But we've got tanks—oxygen, anesthetic—in the storage room downstairs, they'll explode if—"

"Oh, Christ. Hold on." He shouted the information to someone. "Okay," he said to Rachel, "they know what they're dealing with now."

"How did the fire start?"

"I don't know yet. Your alarm went off about twenty minutes ago and the manager of the Mountaineer saw flames and called it in. I was about to head out to Joanna's place when the dispatcher alerted me."

Rachel sank onto the bed. Her clinic, her business, her new life, in flames. Her mind turned to the dead bird on her cottage porch, the threat written on her door, the shots fired at her and Holly yesterday. "Was it arson?"

"I don't know yet," Tom repeated, but the edge in his voice told her he suspected the same thing. "I can't talk to the chief till the fire's out."

Rachel forced herself to ask, "How bad is it? The whole building?"

"No. The fire's in the back. The front looks okay— Well, except for your big window. The firefighters broke it to get in. They were on the scene in less than two minutes. They'll get it under control soon."

She pictured men in heavy coats climbing through the hole where the big plate glass window had been, grinding glass shards under their boots as they dragged a hose through the reception area. What was happening to the patient records, the drug supply, the expensive equipment in the back rooms? She stood again. "I'll be there as soon as I can."

"No, Rachel," Tom said. "It's snowing. The roads are too bad. I don't want you having an accident and getting hurt."

"This is my business we're talking about. I'm coming."

"Rachel, you're not—"

She pressed the button to cut him off.

Dressed in jeans, a heavy sweater, and boots, Rachel ran downstairs and grabbed her coat from the hall closet. She pulled it on as she hurried toward voices in the kitchen. Joanna and Brandon sat at the table eating chocolate chip cookies and milk.

"The animal hospital's on fire," Rachel announced from the doorway.

"What?" they exclaimed in unison.

"I don't have time to talk. Joanna, can I borrow your Cherokee?"

"Now wait a minute." Brandon rose and assumed a policeman's stern demeanor, but the smear of chocolate on his lower lip spoiled the image. "I'm not letting you go anywhere by yourself."

"You can't come with me." Rachel yanked her gloves from the coat pockets. "You have to stay with Holly."

"I don't want you driving in this much snow when you're upset," Joanna told Rachel. She blotted her lips with a paper napkin and stood. "I'll take you."

"No," Brandon protested. "It's too dangerous. What if somebody—"

"Oh, hush," Joanna said. "We'll be fine. I'll take my Glock." When Brandon's face registered alarm, she added, "Honey, I was an expert shot before you were born."

Minutes later, they were on the road, the Jeep Cherokee plowing through the snow at a speed that took Rachel's breath away. More than once she shut her eyes and braced for disaster, but Joanna negotiated every twist and turn with aplomb.

The scene on Main Street was exactly what she'd imagined. Both of Mountainview's fire trucks sat in the snow outside the animal hospital. One hose snaked through the broken window and another disappeared around the side of the building. She saw only a couple of firemen, which meant the rest were inside or out back. From the rear of the hospital rose a pillar of black smoke, illuminated by leaping flames.

City police and sheriff's cars sat sideways in the street to stop traffic. Joanna pulled to the curb a block from the hospital. Rachel flung open her door and jumped out. She ran up the sidewalk through the snow.

Tom seemed to appear out of nowhere and intercepted her with both hands raised. "Stay back, Rachel. You can't do anything to help."

She tried to push past him, but he grabbed her. "Let me go!" she cried. "I have to get things out of there before—"

"No," Tom said.

Catching up with Rachel, Joanna said, "Be sensible, honey. You can't go into a burning building."

Rachel wanted to kick and scream, but she knew Tom and Joanna were right. Reluctantly she crossed the street with them to the Mountaineer, where they could wait in warmth.

The firefighters labored for another hour before they extinguished the blaze. After they marked off the burned areas with crime scene tape, Rachel thanked them all, shaking each man's sweaty hand. One of them gave her a heavy flashlight, told her to be careful where she stepped, and led her inside, with Tom and Joanna trailing. Water pooled on the floor in the reception area and chairs lay on their sides. Glass fragments crackled underfoot. Smoke clogged Rachel's nostrils with the stench of charred wood and melted plastic.

She reached over the high counter of the reception desk and grabbed the appointment book. Dry and clean, by some miracle. With so many worries beating at her mind, she latched onto the one clear action she could take: call everybody tomorrow morning, reschedule all the appointments. She tucked the book under her arm and followed the firefighter through the door leading to the heart of the hospital.

She looked into each of the four exam rooms, ran the flashlight beam over the soot-streaked walls, the dripping wet cabinets and tables. Filthy, but intact.

She continued down the hallway to the surgery and boarding rooms, and walked into a scene of ruin. The entire rear of the hospital was gone. Nothing remained of the surgery room except the plumbing and the steel tables, now almost buried under chunks of burned roof. Falling snow melted on the smoking debris.

"Oh, honey." Joanna slipped an arm around Rachel's waist. Rachel was too stunned to speak.

"I'm sorry," Tom said, his hand on her shoulder.

Rachel choked out, "I want to know if this was deliberate."

"I'll go find the fire chief and bring him back to talk to you."

Rachel and Joanna returned to the reception area. Joanna pulled a couple of chairs upright and urged Rachel to sit. Rachel waved her off and remained huddled by the broken window, keeping vigil for Tom's return. Snow drifted in and collected on her boots.

On the darkened street only the Mountaineer blazed with light. One by one the firefighters drifted away from their trucks and into the restaurant. The sight of them sipping coffee, talking, laughing while her business lay in ruins made Rachel feel unbearably lonely and bereft. She couldn't think about the future now. If she started thinking about the work ahead, her weary mind would buckle under the burden.

She watched the snow come down. White flakes swirled under the streetlamps before spiraling to the ground, like crazed butterflies caught out of season, dying in the cold.

She was shivering by the time Tom reappeared with the fire chief.

Looking like an outsized cartoon hero in his bulky coat and hard hat, the chief pulled off one glove and wiped soot from his lips before he spoke to Rachel. "Real sorry about this, Dr. Goddard. I hope we can find out who did it."

A flush of heat shot through Rachel's half-frozen body. "It was arson? You're positive?"

"Oh, yes ma'am. No doubt about it. Soon as I saw the flames, I knew it was started with an accelerant. Hell— Heck, I could smell gas. Somebody splashed it against the back of the building and lit a match."

"Why?" She looked at Tom. "Do you think it has something to do with Holly?"

"I'd be amazed if it didn't."

"Her father. The son of a bitch. If he thinks he can scare me into—You've got to put him away, before he kills somebody else. Before he kills Holly to keep her quiet."

Tom met her gaze, and in his eyes she saw an anger and determination matching her own. "I will, Rachel. I'm going to get him out of her life and out of yours."

"When? And how?"

His face looked set in stone. "As soon as I can. Any way I have to."

Chapter Thirty-one

At eight a.m., the fax in the squad room spat out two reports from the state's regional crime lab in Roanoke. Tom snatched them from the machine, praying for something useful.

No such luck with the report on O'Dell. The pathologist confirmed Tom's guess that O'Dell had died at least three days before his body was discovered. No bullet fragments were found in the corpse, so they'd never be able to prove any particular gun had killed him.

"Hey, Tommy." Dennis Murray walked in and dropped his hat on his desk. "I heard about the animal hospital getting torched last night. What a shame."

"The real shame is we don't have a thing to go on. Not even footprints outside the building, because of the firefighters tramping around and all the water—" Tom shook his head, let go of the pointless complaint, and skimmed the lab report on the unidentified bones they'd found on the mountain. "Look at this. The second victim was a young woman, probably Caucasian."

Dennis leaned in to read the report. "Did they give us a cause of death?"

"Possible blunt trauma to the head," Tom said. "But the skull's so broken up they can't be sure how much damage was done by a blow and how much by bears. That's a lot less important than identifying her. We need to make sure Amy Watford's alive."

"I'll get back to it right now."

"See if you can find Amy's dental records," Tom told him. "I'll work on the parents."

He had somebody else to see first, though. He headed out on foot for Reed Durham's law office two blocks away.

Main Street was lively for such an early hour, with the snow plow making a final pass to reach pavement, and shovel-wielding merchants yelling their usual good-natured complaints about the driver piling snow on the sidewalks they'd just cleared. The sun peeked over the mountains and cast dazzling light on snow-covered roofs. Tom would have enjoyed the scene if he hadn't been able to see the boarded-up front of Rachel's animal hospital at the far end of the street.

The door to the law offices was unlocked, but the outer office was empty. Tom knew Durham always came in by eight because he liked to get a quiet hour of work done before the staff arrived. Passing the reception desk, Tom entered Durham's inner office without knocking.

Startled, Durham looked up and pulled off his reading glasses. "Hey. What's up?"

"I need some answers, and I think you can give them to me."

Durham frowned. "I'll help you if I can. Take a seat, have some coffee."

"No, thanks." Tom stood in front of the desk and looked down at Durham. "First of all, I want to know why you didn't call the sheriff and report her disappearance. Why weren't you alarmed when her housekeeper called and said she was missing?"

"Who says I wasn't alarmed? I was scared to death. I knew Willingham wouldn't do anything about it, so I let Mrs. Barker call him and I called your dad."

Durham's explanation, so simple and sensible, left Tom feeling foolish for a moment. But he'd come here for answers to all of his questions, and he pushed on. "All right, tell me this. Who is Mary Lee's real father?"

Durham assumed an expression of sorely tested patience. "Tom, I told you—"

"You told me a lie. Now I want the truth. I know Adam McClure wasn't her father." He raised a hand when Durham started to protest. "Willingham told me. This is one of those rare times when I think I can believe him. But he wouldn't tell me who her real father is."

Durham pushed his floppy hair off his forehead. "I don't know why any of this matters. You're investigating Pauline's murder, not her daughter's paternity."

"Come off it, Reed. If Pauline was sleeping with another man while she was married to Adam, and she had a baby with him, that could have something to do with her death. Don't tell me you can't see that. And I've also got a personal reason for asking."

Durham squinted up at him. "Personal?"

Tom leaned on the desk and fixed the other man with a stare. He had Pauline's letter to his father in his shirt pocket, and it felt like a cold weight against his chest. "Is Mary Lee my father's child?"

In the space of seconds, Durham's expression ran the gamut from shocked to flustered to annoyed. Good thing he didn't have to argue criminal cases, Tom thought. He'd never put anything over on a jury.

Then Durham laughed. "Where'd you get a crazy idea like that?"

"Let's cut the crap, okay? I know something was going on between them." He forced himself to say the words. "They had a relationship."

Durham swiveled his chair and stared out the window. After a moment, he said without looking at Tom, "You think they had an affair? You really believe your father would do that to your mother?"

Covering up for him, like a good buddy should. "Don't try to make me feel guilty. Everything points to it."

Durham swung his chair back around and met Tom's gaze. "They'd been friends since high school. That was the first time John had been around any other Melungeon kids. He grew up in this part of the county, and he didn't meet anybody from Rocky Branch District till high school. He was interested in that stuff, the history, even back then. He got to know all the Melungeon kids, even Troy Shackleford."

Tom paced the room, unable to stand still. "Just how well did he get to know Pauline?"

"I'm telling you they were *friends*, Tom." Durham's voice took on an edge of exasperated anger. "Your dad and your mother were already together, they were planning to get married. Besides, Pauline wasn't interested in him that way. She had big plans for herself. She talked about going off to New York or California to have a career of some kind. Nothing ever came of it, but that's what she wanted back then."

"She did pretty well for herself, marrying the rich bachelor at the bank." Tom wasn't ready to believe Durham's story, and he wasn't ready to see Pauline as an innocent dreamer.

"She loved Adam McClure," Durham said. "Robert doesn't want to believe that, but I knew Pauline as well as anybody, and I can tell you she loved Adam."

"Yeah, right. And I guess she carried on her *friendship* with my father after she got married."

"No, actually, they didn't see each other for a long time after high school. He went off to Vietnam, came back and married your mother and took a job as a deputy. Pauline was married to Adam by then. Different worlds, you know, even in a little place like Mason County."

Tom halted and glared at Durham. "But they started seeing each other again before she disappeared. Several years before."

Durham nodded. "But don't go jumping to conclusions. She was lonely after Adam died. With her husband gone, people in the McClures' social circle wouldn't have anything to do with her. She reached out to your dad—and your mother. She had them over to her place for dinner with my wife and me—"

"My mother went to Pauline's house?"

"Yeah, but they never got close. Just too different, I guess. She had more in common with your father."

Tom slumped into a chair. "You really expect me to believe he was over at her house all the time and they were just pals, talking about Melungeon history?"

Durham sighed. "I never would have expected John's own son to think the worst of him. Tom, you grew up in the same house with the man. You knew him. But here you are, believing the gossip—"

"People gossiped about them? Everybody knew?"

"People *thought* they knew something. It doesn't take much for busybodies to start putting two people in bed together."

"And my mother had to put up with that? How could he do that to her?"

"Don't ask me what went on between your parents. All I can tell you is that your father loved your mother more than anything in the world. And you can just forget any crazy ideas you've got about him being Mary Lee's father."

Tom clutched the chair arms. Knobby upholstery tacks dug into his palms. Could he believe this story? Durham had already lied to him once. He'd been close to both Tom's father and Pauline and might go to any lengths to protect their memories. Frustrated, Tom demanded, "Then who is her father? Ed McClure?"

Durham shook his head. "He probably wishes he were. But there's no possibility of it. Even Pauline didn't know who her daughter's father was."

"What?"

"Adam was sterile," Durham said. "But his mother kept asking when he and Pauline were going to give her a grandchild. She wanted the McClure line carried on by her eldest son. She wasn't the kind of person who would've accepted an adopted child. So Pauline and Adam went to a sperm bank, somewhere up north where nobody knew them. Some anonymous sperm donor is Mary Lee's biological father."

Tom didn't have time to absorb this before Durham's phone rang. He answered, said, "Right here," and handed the receiver to Tom. "It's your sergeant."

Dennis Murray told Tom, "We've got a major new development. It's…not good. But I don't want to talk about it on the phone."

Tom jogged back to headquarters, his thoughts bouncing from Dennis' alarming words to his conversation with Durham, all the new questions it raised, the old questions it left unanswered. When he rounded the side of the courthouse, he saw a State Police car parked outside the Sheriff's Department. *What now?*

When he walked into his office with Dennis, he found two State Police cadets and the middle-aged instructor who was supervising the trainees' search of Indian Mountain. The cadets, one female and one male, looked ready to burst with excitement. A cardboard box sat on Tom's desk.

Their instructor, a solid ex-Marine named Cochran, introduced the cadets and told Tom, "The snow didn't make these two quit. They wanted to search the caves. They found a bear in one of them and had the good sense not to bother it. But in the other one—"

"Way in the back," the young woman piped up. As soon as the words escaped, she clapped a hand to her mouth.

Cochran smiled. "You can tell it, cadet."

She went on eagerly. "We crawled way in the back, where it's real narrow, to make sure we didn't miss anything. And we started finding gobs of long black hair."

A chill passed through Tom.

"And when we got all the way to the back, we found this." The girl glanced at her supervisor for permission, got a nod. She folded back the flaps of the box.

With dread rising in him like brackish water, Tom looked in.

Another skull.

Chapter Thirty-two

Rachel settled at Joanna's desk to work through the long list of people she had to call—clients with appointments, insurance agent, contractors recommended by Joanna. She'd just finished the client list when the door flew open.

Holly rushed in, slammed the door, and leaned against it as if barring invaders. "My grandma's here! With Uncle Jack. They've come to get me."

"Oh, for heaven's sake," Rachel said. "Don't these people ever give up? Tell her you don't want to go home."

"No! I can't talk to her. She'll try to make me feel like a bad person 'cause I don't want to live with her anymore. Please don't make me talk to her."

"Holly, I can't make you do anything you don't want to do, and neither can she."

"Will you tell her to go away?"

"Yes, I will. You can stay in here if you want to."

When Rachel reached the front door, Brandon was talking through the screen to Mrs. Turner, who stood on the porch. Out on the farm road, Jack Watford sat in a pickup truck. He was going to let the little old lady do the dirty work this time.

"Good morning, Mrs. Turner," Rachel said, the soul of graciousness. A blast of cold air through the doorway made her fold her arms and tuck her hands against her sides. "Can we help you with something?"

The woman's arthritic fingers, without gloves on a frigid morning, clutched her coat collar tight around her neck. "I'm lookin' for my granddaughter," she said, her voice a whine. "I need her to come home with me."

"Holly asked me to tell you she prefers to stay here," Rachel said.

Brandon added, "She's old enough to make her own choices."

Mrs. Turner stepped close to the screen door and lowered her voice to an urgent whisper. "She's got to come home. She's not gonna be safe if she don't come home."

"Are you making a threat?" Brandon said.

Rachel touched his arm to silence him. She watched Mrs. Turner's mouth quiver as a tear coursed down a wrinkled cheek. This wasn't an act. The woman was seriously frightened. Maybe if they let her come in, they could pry some information out of her. But no. It probably wouldn't work, and it would upset Holly for no good purpose. "Holly is safe here, Mrs. Turner."

"She's not safe anywhere!" Mrs. Turner gulped air and made an effort to calm herself. "I heard about her bein' shot at. Then on the radio this mornin' they said somebody set the animal hospital on fire. What if Holly'd been in it? She coulda been burnt to death. She needs to come home."

"She doesn't want to."

"She don't have a job now, with the animal hospital bein' closed. You got no reason to keep her here, and I really need her at home. I can't get by without her."

The poor-old-me act again. If Rachel hadn't seen it before, she might be swayed. "Be careful, Mrs. Turner. I'll start thinking you set my clinic on fire to get Holly back."

"You stupid girl!" The woman's face twisted into a snarl. "Why can't you stay out of our family business?"

"Now, listen here, ma'am," Brandon said. "We're trying to be polite to you—" He broke off, looking beyond Mrs. Turner.

Rachel followed his gaze. Jack Watford was out of his truck and trudging through the snow to the house.

"Stop right there!" Brandon yelled. He shoved the screen door open, forcing Mrs. Turner to scoot out of the way. With one hand on his pistol, Brandon marched across the porch to the top of the steps. "Captain Bridger told you not to come anywhere near Holly or Dr. Goddard. So get back in your truck and get out of here."

Watford stopped, hunched his shoulders and crammed his hands into his jeans pockets. "My mother-in-law asked me to drive her. She's too old to be drivin' around by herself with the roads so bad."

Mrs. Turner took advantage of the distraction to pull the screen door open again and scurry past Rachel into the front hall. "Holly!" she cried. "Honey, it's Grandma. Come on out and talk to me."

"Mrs. Turner, please stop this." Rachel caught up with her and blocked her way. The scene was entirely too much like Jack Watford's invasion of the clinic on Friday. Rachel wouldn't knock an elderly woman to the floor the way she had Watford, but she would restrain Mrs. Turner if necessary. "Holly is free to go anytime she wants to. But she doesn't want to. If you think she's in danger, you should tell the police who's trying to hurt her."

"You don't know what you're talkin' about!"

"This conversation's over." Rachel grabbed Mrs. Turner's arm and push-pulled her to the door and out onto the porch. "Leave. And don't come back."

"Get your hands off her," Jack Watford shouted. He started for the porch.

Brandon intercepted the man in the yard, caught his arms and twisted them behind his back. "You're about two seconds away from being arrested, mister. What'll it be—go home or go to jail?"

"Okay, okay." Watford stopped resisting and Brandon let him go. "Come on, Mama Turner. We're not gonna get anywhere talkin' to these people."

Mrs. Turner peered through the screen door into the house, and Rachel was afraid she'd make another dash for it. But in the end, Mrs. Turner started down the steps. Watford gripped her arm and kept her upright on the snow as they made their way to the truck.

In the house, with the door closed and locked, Rachel listened to Brandon rant for a couple of minutes. Finally he looked at her and said, "You're awfully quiet."

"Mrs. Turner said she heard on the radio that somebody set fire to the animal hospital. But Tom asked the fire chief not to spread around the fact that the fire was arson. I listened to the local radio news this morning, and they said the fire was probably caused by bad wiring. They didn't say a word about it being deliberately set."

Chapter Thirty-three

Sunlight slanted through the windows of Tom's office and fell like a spill of cream on the skull in Gretchen Lauter's hands.

"It's Jean Turner," she told Tom and Sheriff Willingham. "The teeth match Jean's dental records perfectly. It's a stroke of luck the mandible wasn't separated from the skull, since most of her fillings and extractions were in the lower jaw."

Tom raked his fingers through his hair, but a stab of pain made him wince and lower his injured arm. How was he going to tell Holly her mother had been dead for years? "Any idea how she died?"

Gretchen laid the battered skull in the box on Tom's desk as if she were handling a delicate piece of sculpture. "Since no other bones were found in the cave, I think a bear may have torn the head off the body and taken it there to gnaw on at leisure, and at least some of the damage could have been done while the animal was feeding."

The sheriff scowled at the box with its grisly contents. "God almighty, Gretchen, sometimes I think you enjoy this stuff."

She shot a sour look at Willingham, then said to Tom, "There are three fractures that don't look like animal damage to me. The pathologist can be more definite, but it's a pretty good guess that Jean Turner was beaten to death with a blunt object."

Willingham grunted and fixed an accusing glare on Tom. "Now I want you to get moving and haul Shackleford's ass in here for questioning."

"I intend to," Tom said. "But I don't have any evidence against him for the murders, and he's not going to crack and confess. He'd get up and walk out, and he'd have a right to. I need to find grounds to arrest him, so I can hold him at least overnight."

"What're you planning?"

"A raid on the diner while the Shacklefords are selling drugs. He's back in the county—one of our guys drove past his mother's house a while ago and saw Troy's SUV in the yard. He'll be at the diner tonight, and I'll have good cause for an arrest. I'll be able to hold him till he's arraigned." As an afterthought, Tom added, "If it's okay with you."

"Yeah, I guess." Willingham's permission sounded grudging.

If the sheriff had raised objections, Tom would have dropped the subject. But not his plans for the raid.

<>·<>·<>

Tom shuffled through the accumulation of paper on his desk, gathered the message slips with names of reporters who wanted to talk to him and dumped all of them into the wastebasket.

He knew he was procrastinating, delaying the trip out to the horse farm to give Holly the news. She'd grown up believing her mother was out there somewhere, loving her, thinking about her and sending money for her support. Now Tom had to rob her of that comforting fantasy. Theoretically, she should be able to take it like an adult, but as he'd recently learned, age didn't matter when you discovered a big part of your childhood had been a lie.

With the junk cleared from his desk, he pulled his notebook from a breast pocket and flipped it open to the page where he'd jotted Mary Lee's phone number. He wanted to follow up a hunch before he saw Holly.

When Mary Lee's maid had summoned her to the phone, Tom told her, "I have some news that might affect our investigation of your mother's death."

"Oh?" A faint, reluctant sound. Tom imagined a wary expression on her beautiful face. He pictured her black hair cascading to her shoulders, her slender body dressed in an impeccably made outfit that cost more than he earned in a month.

"I'm afraid your aunt, Jean Turner, is dead."

A gasp at the other end. "When? How?"

"We found her remains this morning, on the same mountain where we found your mother's. There's no doubt about her identity. We believe she was killed around the same time your mother was."

"You're sure it's her? You're sure she was murdered?"

"Yes, on both counts. How well did you know Jean?"

For a moment she didn't answer. Tom heard her two children laughing and talking in the background. "I didn't know her well," Mary Lee said. "But she was a blood relative. I'm shocked by all this. When is it going to end?"

Mary Lee was pleading with him, as if he had the power to call a halt. "We're doing our best to get to the bottom of it," he said. "I need you to answer some questions."

"I've told you, I don't know what happened. I don't really know either the Turners or the McClures."

"Holly believes her mother's been sending money to her grandmother all these years, to provide for Holly. Now we know it's not possible. Did you send the money?"

Mary Lee sighed. "Yes."

"Why did you think you had to help support Holly?"

"Because my mother did. I thought she'd want me to continue helping Holly, especially since the child's mother had left—" She faltered. "I thought— Everyone thought—"

"Did you pretend the money was coming from Jean?"

"No, I didn't. If my grandmother invented stories for Holly— I don't know, maybe she was trying to make the child feel less… abandoned."

Or did Mrs. Turner have a more selfish reason for perpetuating the idea that Jean was alive? Tom moved on to another puzzle. "Did you know your cousin Amy? Bonnie's daughter?"

"Why are you asking about her? Has something happened to her too?"

"There's a chance the second skeleton we found, the one we haven't identified yet, is Amy's."

"Oh no." The words came out on an exhalation of breath.

"Her parents claim she's living in South Carolina, and Holly gets cards and letters from her. Supposedly from her. But we haven't been able to find her."

"If her parents and Holly are in touch with Amy," Mary Lee said, "why would you think she's dead?"

He ignored the question and asked, "Did you know her? She was pretty close to your mother, wasn't she?"

A silence, then, "All I can tell you about Amy is that she was greedy. She got close to my mother because she wanted the things Mother gave her. Gifts, money."

"Can you make a guess about why we can't find Amy?"

"My guess would be worthless, as I'm sure you're well aware," Mary Lee said.

Tom rubbed his gritty eyes, wishing he'd had more sleep the night before. This was shaping up to be another endless day. "Well, thanks anyway." He added, "I hope you don't mind me saying you have a very odd family."

He heard a gust of humorless laughter, then a click and the dial tone.

<> <> <>

Rachel's heart lurched at the sight of Tom's grim face and bleak eyes. Bad news.

Closing the door, Brandon asked, "What's up, Captain?"

Tom led them into Joanna's living room before he spoke. "The searchers found a third skull. It's Holly's mother. She's probably been dead as long as Pauline."

Brandon groaned.

For a second Rachel couldn't find words or the voice to speak them. She remembered the radiant look on Holly's face the night before when she'd heard her mother's dental records didn't match the second skull. *I knew she wasn't dead. She couldn't be.* Her eyes burning with tears, Rachel said, "This will break Holly's heart."

"What will?" Holly asked from the doorway. "What are you talkin' about?"

"Come sit down." Brandon, who looked as if he wanted to cry, tried to nudge her toward the couch.

Holly stood firm and shook her head without taking her eyes off Tom.

"I'm afraid I have some bad news." Tom spoke with the kindness he might use to force an awful truth on a child. "I didn't come to you until I was absolutely sure of the facts. We've found the remains of another woman. The teeth match your mother's dental records perfectly. I'm sorry, Holly, but there's no doubt it's your mother."

Rachel slipped an arm around the girl's shoulders. "I'm so sorry."

"No!" Holly pulled free and raked them all with a furious gaze. "It's not true. It can't be. You made a mistake."

"I know this is a terrible shock." Rachel's voice trembled with pity.

When Brandon reached out, Holly spun away. She gripped the edge of the mantel and stood with her head lowered, her slight body heaving with suppressed sobs. "She sends money for me." Holly faced Tom defiantly. "Dead people don't send money orders through the mail."

For an instant Rachel felt a spark of hope. One look at Tom extinguished it.

"You said your grandmother never let you see the return address," Tom said.

"That doesn't mean—"

"Holly," Tom broke in, his voice firm now, "your cousin Mary Lee told me she sent the money. Your grandmother lied to you."

Holly crumpled, folded in on herself, her knees giving way. Rachel and Brandon caught her and helped her to the sofa. She sank against the cushions and burst into ragged sobs. Rachel could do nothing except sit with the girl and watch her grief pour out.

Holly cried for ten minutes. At last she grew quiet, wiped tears from her cheeks and blew her nose on the handkerchief Brandon offered. "Have you told Grandma?" she asked Tom.

He sat in a chair facing the sofa. "No. I'll go see her when I leave here."

"This is gonna kill her," Holly said, choking up again. "I oughta go too."

Rachel opened her mouth to protest, but thought better of it. She wasn't going to tell Holly what to do. But if Holly went over there, and her wily fox of a grandmother played on her sympathy and guilt—

"I'm afraid I can't take you with me," Tom said. "I really need to speak to your grandmother alone."

Rachel was relieved when Holly accepted Tom's decision without protest.

He leaned forward, elbows on knees. "I'm going to arrest your father, Holly."

"When?" Brandon asked, his face alight with eagerness. "Any chance I could—"

"I'll get back to you about it," Tom said. "I want to do it tonight."

A jolt of alarm shot through Rachel. Troy Shackleford was a murderer. He'd tried to shoot his own daughter. He wouldn't meekly allow himself to be arrested. "Please be careful," Rachel said, and instantly regretted it. She had to believe he knew what he was doing, trust him not to take reckless chances.

Tom didn't seem to mind her solicitousness. His eyes warmed when they met hers, and a faint smile lifted the corners of his mouth. "I will." He went on, speaking to Holly, "If we get to the point of a trial, we'll need you to testify to what he told you about your mother and Pauline. Are you willing?"

Rachel thought Tom was asking too much of Holly, pushing her to shed a lifelong terror of her father in an instant. But Holly's face, blotched and puffy with heartbreak and anger, no longer showed a trace of fear. "Yes, sir," she said, "I'll do it."

Chapter Thirty-four

Tom wiped all expression from his face before he knocked at Mrs. Turner's door. He didn't want her to see right away that he'd brought bad news. He hoped to surprise her—or, rather, find out whether Jean's death came as a surprise to her.

"Oh, it's you." Mrs. Turner had opened the main door, but not the screen. Her two dogs, flanking her, wagged their tails and seemed happier to see Tom than their mistress was. The little one gave a cheerful yip.

"I need to talk to you." Without waiting for an invitation, Tom tried to pull open the screen door, but it resisted.

For a moment Mrs. Turner regarded the latch thoughtfully, as if keeping Tom outside might be the better choice. In the end she hooked a finger under the latch and released it. Turning her back on Tom, she walked into her living room.

He followed her with the dogs romping around him. The old woman stood by the cold fireplace, whispering to her daughter Bonnie. Both shot wary looks at Tom as he advanced with his canine escorts.

"Good morning, Mrs. Watford," Tom said to Bonnie. "I'm glad you're here."

Mrs. Turner clapped her hands twice, startling Tom. At this wordless command, the dogs trotted toward the kitchen. Mrs. Turner lifted an orange cat from an easy chair and sat down with the animal in her lap. Bonnie, her doleful eyes watching Tom, sat on the arm of the chair.

He took a seat on the couch before he spoke. "Your daughter Jean is dead. We've found her remains."

Mrs. Turner received the news with a blank look, as if she couldn't grasp his meaning. Bonnie was the one who reacted, pressing both hands to her mouth, eyes staring in shock.

"Jeannie?" Mrs. Turner, her face a picture of stupefaction, looked up at Bonnie, back at Tom. "Somethin's happened to Jeannie?"

"Oh, dear lord," Bonnie cried. Tears filled her eyes. She clutched her mother's shoulders. "Oh, Mama. Jeannie!"

Apparently they'd both believed Jean was alive. But how was that possible? "She may have been killed when Pauline was," Tom said. "We found her remains in the same area as Pauline's."

Mrs. Turner shook her head and looked at Bonnie again. "Jeannie too?"

Bonnie got to her feet and stumbled away from them. Her shoulders trembled but she cried without making a sound.

Determined not to give them time to recover and formulate careful answers, Tom barreled on. "Mrs. Turner, I know Mary Lee's been sending you money. Why did you tell Holly it was coming from Jean?"

Mrs. Turner's gnarled fingers stroked the cat she held, but the action seemed automatic. Her face said she was struggling to shift her beliefs to fit a shocking new reality. "She— I— The girl needed her mother. So I let her think…" Her voice faded to a whisper as tears puddled in her eyes and overflowed. "Jeannie was my baby. I know it ain't right, but I always loved her the best."

Bonnie wheeled around to gape at her mother. She made a guttural sound, but whatever angry retort she'd had in mind died on her tongue. Erupting in fresh tears, she collapsed into an armchair and buried her face in her hands.

Far from being moved by this display, Tom felt a growing irritation. "I don't know how you could go all these years without wondering what happened to her."

"I thought she was hidin' from him," Mrs. Turner said.

"From who? Troy Shackleford?"

Mrs. Turner averted her eyes and didn't answer.

Tom was out of patience. "Look, somebody murdered two of your daughters. If you want the killer punished, you have to start being honest with me. Do you know something that can help me put Shackleford away? Has he threatened you?"

"Leave my mother alone!" Bonnie jumped up and rushed to Mrs. Turner's side. "Can't you see she's all broke up about Jeannie?"

"I'm tired of listening to you people lie to me," Tom said. "If you think he killed Pauline and Jean, why in God's name are you protecting him? What about your own daughter, Mrs. Watford? Were those Amy's bones we found on the mountain with Pauline's? Have you been trying to fool everybody into believing Amy's alive?"

"She *is* alive! My daughter's not dead."

"Then why can't we find her?"

"You stay away from her. She's got a good life and you're not gonna drag her into all this."

"If she's alive, then where is she?" Tom said. "Why can't we find Amy and Darrell Wood in South Carolina?"

"Because Wood's not their real last name," Mrs. Turner said. Calmer now, she met Tom's eyes. "It's made-up. There's people she don't want findin' her."

"I don't believe you."

"Believe what you want to." Mrs. Turner stood, gently laid the cat on the chair, and put an arm around Bonnie's shoulders. "Now we got nothin' else to tell you. Go on and let us do our grievin' in private."

"The truth is going to come out," Tom said as he rose. "If you don't want to end up in jail as accessories, you'd better make up your minds whose side you're on."

The only answer he got from the old woman was a stubborn look that mixed defiance and sorrow and fear.

Chapter Thirty-five

Tom and Brandon sat in a parked cruiser half a mile from Rose Shackleford's diner. Too tense to talk. Freezing without the heater on. Staring into the darkness and waiting.

Tom had missed having Brandon at his side, and he was glad he'd been able to free him for the raid. Grady Duncan, who had no taste for excitement, had taken over guard duty at Joanna McKendrick's house.

Tom's handheld radio crackled and Deputy Charlie Foster's voice came through, the words fading in and out as the signal made its way up the winding road. "Checkpoint Charlie to Mason One. Blackbird's flying right at you."

"Ten-four," Tom answered.

"Oh, man," Brandon said. "I am looking forward to this. This is gonna be sweet." Tom heard, but couldn't see, Brandon rubbing his gloved hands together in anticipation.

A lot could go wrong tonight. If even one person in the diner had a gun, if the crowd panicked— But the raid could go off without a hitch. Whatever happened, good or bad, was Tom's responsibility. His heavy Kevlar vest squeezed his chest with each breath he took. They'd borrowed the body armor from the State Police, and it probably felt as strange and uncomfortable to the other men as it did to him. A reminder that they might be out of their depth, trying to pull off this raid without outside help.

He keyed the radio and said, "B and B, take your positions and stand by."

The Blackwood twins were on foot, lurking on the wooded hill behind the diner. At Tom's command, they would move closer to the back door, ready to pounce if anybody fled through the rear when the raid got under way.

"Here it comes, here it comes," Brandon said.

Troy Shackleford's black Bronco was no more than a shadow pulled by streams of light when it zoomed past the concealed cruiser. Tom started the car and eased out of the brush. He didn't take to the road until the SUV disappeared around a curve. After he'd also rounded the bend, Tom tried his radio to see if the signal would carry to the two deputies waiting up the road on the far side of the diner.

"Mason Three, do you read?"

"Ten-four," came the faint reply, mixed with static.

"Blackbird's on the wing. Take it slow." The less said the better, in case Shackleford had a scanner in his vehicle.

"Ten-four."

Charlie Foster quickly caught up with Tom and Brandon in the van he was lending for transport of prisoners. When the diner came into view, Tom doused his lights and pulled to the side of the road. Charlie did the same. They had to give Troy and his nephew Buddy time to park, go inside, hand the gym bag containing drugs to Rose, who would unpack the plastic baggies and start selling. Dennis Murray, in the woods across the road from the diner, was snapping pictures with his favorite toy, a digital camera with a telephoto lens.

In the darkened vehicle, Brandon's breathing was audible, quick and shallow. Tom drew deep, calming breaths, but his heart hammered his ribs and the familiar silence of the mountain night suddenly seemed alien and threatening.

At last he keyed the radio with cold-numbed fingers. "It's time."

"Ten-four," from Charlie.

"Ten-four," from the third car.

"B and B, on alert," Tom said into his radio.

A quiet answer, "Ten-four."

Tom repeated the message to Dennis.

The two Sheriff's Department cars and the van coasted to the outer edges of the diner's parking lot. Although nobody inside could have heard them above the throbbing beat of jukebox music, the five deputies emerged from their vehicles silently. Dennis trotted across the road with his precious camera cradled against his chest. He stashed the telephoto lens in the trunk of Tom's car. He would take the camera into the diner.

Tom drew his pistol.

His mouth had gone dry and the vest seemed to be choking the breath out of him. "Let's go."

In the lead, he burst through the diner's door with his gun sweeping the room from side to side. "Hands up, everybody," he shouted. "Stay where you are and nobody'll get hurt."

Two dozen customers scrambled like cockroaches toward the exit. Deputies shoved them back at gunpoint. Buddy Shackleford vaulted the bar and crashed through a door into the storage room, headed for the rear. Tom let him go. The twins would nab him.

Troy Shackleford slid off his stool and stood motionless in the pandemonium, his malevolent gaze fixed on Tom. Behind the bar, Rose scooped up plastic bags and dumped them down the front of her dress. Her mammoth bosom swelled with new bulges.

"Get your hands up," Tom yelled at her above the racket of the jukebox and the frantic customers. "And get out here where I can see you."

Her lips twisted in a sneer, Rose slowly raised her hands and waddled out from behind the bar.

Her bulk narrowed the aisle between bar and booths. The deputies herded customers to the open space around the jukebox and started taking names and addresses before searching them for drugs. Dennis Murray had been assigned to receive and tag evidence. A deputy pulled the plug on the jukebox, and the air became thick with the mutterings and groans of people caught red-handed with no way out.

Tom returned his attention to Troy Shackleford, who hadn't moved. The guy had the cold, flat eyes and ominous stillness of a viper on the verge of striking. "You're under arrest for distribution of illegal and controlled substances," Tom said. "You have the right to—"

"You got nothin' on me," Shackleford interrupted. "Whatever goes on here is Rose's business. I'm just a customer."

A deep, furious red mottled Rose's face. Glaring at Shackleford, she opened her mouth, closed it, opened it again but couldn't find words. She looked like a hooked fish drowning in air.

Tom leaned across the bar and snagged two plastic bags of marijuana. Dangling them from one hand, he said, "Your cousin telling the truth, Rose? You're the one dealing drugs, and he just stopped in for a beer?"

She shot a poisonous look at Shackleford, then turned it on Tom and added a smirk. "All you've got in your hand's a misdemeanor charge. I'll pay a fine and be out in a day."

"I think we can upgrade the charge after we see what you dumped down the front of your dress."

Her smirk broadened to a challenging grin. "You gonna search me, big guy?" She spread her arms and her green dress billowed around her body. "Go right ahead. No, wait a minute. I think I'd rather have that pretty boy run his hands over my curves." With a flick of a pudgy finger, she indicated Brandon.

Brandon's cheeks reddened and he threw a wide-eyed, pleading look at Tom. "Boss?" he croaked.

While Tom tried to suppress a laugh, a soft *plop* made him look down. At Rose's feet lay a sandwich bag containing about a tablespoon of brownish-white chunks. Crystal meth.

Rose clutched her bosom and frantically struggled to hold onto the cargo, but a second bag escaped and landed on the floor. And a third. Rose clamped her right foot atop one bag and tried to push the others together and cover them with her left foot.

"Idiot woman," Shackleford muttered.

"Who the hell you callin' names?" she yelled. "I ain't one of your flunkies."

"Shut up, both of you," Tom said. "And move your feet." He advanced on Rose, but she didn't budge. He stooped and grabbed a corner of one bag sticking out from under her shoe. When he tugged, the plastic tore and the crystals, now crushed to powder, spilled out.

"Oh, shit," Rose cried. She stepped back, exposing all the bags, and stared at the powder on the filthy floor. "Now look what you done."

Maybe she believed she was going to get the stuff back at some point and wanted the merchandise in salable condition. "Hey, Denny," Tom called. "Bring your camera here."

When Dennis started shooting pictures, Rose tried to back away from the evidence, but the bar and three deputies boxed her in.

Tom gathered the bags and handed them to Dennis. "Find the gym bag. We'll need to have it tested for residue. Who carried it in?"

Dennis jerked a thumb at Troy Shackleford. "And I got some great pictures."

Shackleford swore under his breath.

To Rose, Tom said, "You're under arrest for possession and sale of controlled and illegal substances. Brandon, cuff her."

"No!" she shouted. "You're not—"

Brandon yanked her arms behind her back—a little roughly, to Tom's eye, although he wouldn't have been any gentler. Tom recited her rights while she spouted a stream of obscenities. He didn't know whether she would turn on her cousin in exchange for leniency, but the dawning alarm on Troy Shackleford's face told him the man didn't trust Rose's loyalty.

Tom was unhooking his handcuffs from his belt, preparing to cuff Shackleford, when a gunshot sounded outside. He raced around the bar and dashed through the storage room. When he shoved open the rear door, the streak of interior light fell on Keith and Kevin Blackwood, wrestling in the snow with Buddy Shackleford. Buddy's right arm was straight up in the air and he clutched a pistol in his hand. One of the twins leaned a knee into Buddy's stomach while the other bent his wrist back until Tom expected to hear bones snap. Buddy let out a moan of pain, his fingers opened, and the gun dropped into the snow. Tom snatched it up, shook off the snow, and stuck the pistol into his waistband.

Kevin and Keith hauled Buddy to his feet. "Man!" Kevin exclaimed, while Keith fastened cuffs around Buddy's wrists. "He took off toward the hill like a hound after a coon."

Peering around Buddy's shoulder, Keith grinned at Tom. "We tackled him, though. Our old football coach'll be proud of us when he hears about it."

"I'm not exactly ashamed of you myself," Tom said. He shook his head at Buddy. "Resisting arrest, threatening police officers with a firearm. You're not helping yourself, Buddy."

"Go to hell, motherfucker." Buddy spat and a wad of saliva landed in the snow by Tom's left boot.

What a pleasure it would be to slam a fist into Buddy's insolent face. Another time, maybe. "Lock him in one of our cars," he told the Blackwoods.

As soon as Tom emerged from the storage room into the diner, he realized Troy Shackleford was no longer there. "What the hell?" he shouted. "Where'd he go?"

The three harried deputies working the crowd of customers at one end of the room looked around in bewilderment. Rose cackled a laugh.

Brandon was gone too. Tom hustled out to the parking lot. Shackleford sat behind the wheel of his Bronco and Brandon tugged the handle of the locked door. The engine started. The headlights came on.

Shouldering Brandon aside, Tom rapped on the window with his pistol and yelled, "Cut the engine and step out, or I'll shoot."

Shackleford stared back, his defiant face painted red by the diner's fluorescent sign.

Tom leveled the pistol at the window. Shackleford gunned the engine and the Bronco shot backward out of the parking space and swung around. It crashed into a car, then lurched toward the road.

Tom jumped in front of the Bronco but Shackleford kept coming.

"Captain!" Brandon screamed. "He'll run you down!"

Tom put a bullet through one front tire, then the other. The vehicle careened out of control but Shackleford didn't brake. Tom ran after it and shot out both rear tires. The SUV bounced and swerved and crashed into a utility pole. A geyser spewed from the radiator.

Four bullets. He had plenty left. He walked up to the Bronco and pressed the gun barrel against the driver's window. "Get out. Now. Slow and easy."

For a minute Shackleford locked his eyes on Tom's and didn't move. If he had a gun in the vehicle, if he went for it, Tom would have no choice but to shoot. An icy calm spread through him. He knew what he had to do and didn't doubt he could do it. The only decision left was Shackleford's to make.

At last Shackleford raised both hands, palms out to show they were empty. He killed the engine, flipped the lock, slowly opened the door. Tom moved back, gripping his pistol, and Shackleford stepped into the snow. Brandon started to cuff him.

Shackleford shoved Brandon aside and took off toward the back of the building.

"God damn it!" Tom charged after Shackleford with Brandon close on his heels.

They caught him in the same spot where the Blackwoods had subdued Buddy. Tom grabbed Shackleford's arm and spun him around. Shackleford's fist came up and walloped Tom in the jaw. He staggered backward, slipping and sliding in the snow. Brandon, trying to keep a hold on Shackleford, looked like he was wrestling with an octopus.

Tom regained his balance, shifted his pistol to his left hand, and slammed his right fist into Shackleford's gut. The man sank to his knees.

"You got no proof against me," Shackleford gasped. "You're wastin' your time."

With both his jaw and wounded arm throbbing, Tom led the prisoner to his cruiser. They'd have no trouble making felony drug charges stick. But the murders—Tom would have to dig deep in the few hours he could hold Shackleford before bond was set. If he came up with nothing tonight, maybe a surprise encounter he was planning for tomorrow morning would shake the truth loose.

Chapter Thirty-six

"Hey, out there!" Shackleford yelled above the racket of his former customers, now his fellow inmates. "I want my phone call!"

Tom, leaning against the booking desk outside the cell block, ignored Shackleford. He peeked over Carl Madison's shoulder as the elderly night jailer typed the last booking sheet into the computer. The jailers who worked the other two shifts had come in to help take fingerprints and mug shots, but the process hit a snag when their handwritten paperwork reached Carl, who had to be the world's most inept computer user. The other jailers had gone home, and so had all the other deputies except Brandon. He'd stretched out on a hard bench and fallen asleep after Tom promised to wake him when Shackleford was questioned.

Carl whipped the final sheet from the printer and added it to the pile on the desk. Tom checked his watch. The booking process, begun late Monday night, had lasted until 2:12 a.m. Tuesday. People charged with marijuana possession had been booked first and released on their own recognizance until arraignment. Everybody else was locked up.

"I want my phone call!" Shackleford yelled again from the other side of the door.

"I think it's time for a chat with our star prisoner," Tom said. "Hey, Brandon, wake up. We'll be out with Shackleford in a minute."

Carl unlocked the door between the booking room and the cell block.

Tom had put Troy, Buddy, Rose, and three other women into individual cells and herded eleven men into the holding pen. When Tom and Carl entered the cell block, the men mobbed the door of the pen, gripping the bars or sticking their hands out in supplication.

"How long we gonna be here?"

"You can't keep us all in here together!"

"We ain't got but one toilet!"

"You brought this on yourselves, guys," Tom told them. When this bunch arrived the place had smelled of antiseptic. Now it stank of sweat and piss. "The sheriff wants you locked up till you see the judge."

Sheriff Willingham had put in a brief appearance around midnight, found the chaotic scene not to his liking, and gone home to bed. Before leaving, he'd told Tom, "You went to the trouble of arresting them, now make it count. Teach 'em a lesson."

Tom followed Carl past the cell where Buddy paced and fumed. Rose was his neighbor. She slumped on a cot, her voluminous dress spread around her, and stared glumly at the opposite wall. Earlier, Rose had been searched by Maggie Jenkins, who acted as matron when the jail had a female prisoner. Tom surmised that Maggie's no-nonsense manner and the legendary thoroughness of her body cavity search had done nothing to improve Rose's mood. The thought made him smile.

"What the hell you grinnin' about?" Troy Shackleford said when Tom reached his cell. His gray-streaked black hair flopped onto his forehead in disheveled waves and stubble darkened his cheeks. "You enjoyin' this? Well, you better get your jollies while you can, Deputy Dawg, 'cause you're gonna be damned sorry you messed with me."

"Are you threatening me, Troy?" Tom said.

"Sure sounded like a threat against a police officer," Carl said.

"You take it any way you want to. Now, I got a right to a phone call."

"Sure. No problem." Tom unhooked a pair of cuffs from his belt.

"You ain't cuffin' me again."

"You want the phone call, you wear cuffs while you're outside the cell." Tom was still cursing himself for letting Shackleford sock him at the diner, and he didn't plan to let it happen a second time. "That's the deal. Take it or leave it."

Shackleford stewed in silence for a minute. Finally he said, "All right. Let's get on with it."

"Smart choice. Make your call, then we'll talk."

Tom reached through the bars to click the cuffs around Shackleford's wrists before Carl unlocked the cell door. They escorted Shackleford to the phone at the booking desk. Brandon sat up on the bench, rubbing his eyes.

Maneuvering the phone awkwardly with his bound hands, Shackleford punched in a number and waited a full minute before he got an answer. "Mama? Yeah, I know what time it is. Rose and Buddy and me are at the jail. They arrested us. You gotta find us a—What? Some bullshit drug charges. Just listen, will you?"

The conversation lasted several minutes, with Shackleford's mother apparently shaking off sleep and launching into a tirade against her son's stupidity in getting caught. When she raised the volume, Shackleford held the receiver away from his ear and Tom had no trouble catching the gist of her complaint. Soon the son was shouting curses at the mother, but in the end they seemed to reach an understanding. After he hung up, Shackleford told Tom, "I'll have a lawyer in the mornin' by the time I see the judge."

"Actually, you won't be arraigned till Wednesday. I talked to the prosecutor a while ago, and he'll need the whole day tomorrow to process these other people. He'll take you and Rose and Buddy in for arraignment Wednesday morning. Meanwhile, you'll stay here."

Shackleford's face colored deep red. "You son of a bitch, you can't—"

"We can hold you for forty-eight hours without arraignment."

Shackleford muttered something Tom didn't catch—although he gathered it was uncomplimentary—then said, "You can hold me, but I ain't answerin' questions without a lawyer, and maybe not then either. That's my right."

"Okay, I won't ask you any questions." Tom steered Shackleford across the booking room toward the jailer's private office. Brandon followed. "I'll do the talking. You listen."

Shackleford balked at the office doorway. "I'm not goin' in some little room with two cops so you can shut the door and do what you damned well please."

"I'm disappointed that you have so little confidence in our integrity." Tom planted a hand on Shackleford's back and shoved him into the room. "Have a seat."

Each taking an arm, Tom and Brandon propelled Shackleford into a chair. Brandon sat beside him.

As Tom sank into the jailer's leather chair behind the desk, Shackleford gave him a nasty grin. "You oughta put some ice on that jaw, Captain. You're gettin' a real bad bruise."

Tom didn't acknowledge the remark. His jaw was a little sore, but he'd bet that Shackleford's gut felt a lot worse. "I suppose you heard what the searchers found on Indian Mountain this morning. Yesterday morning, I guess I should say."

Shackleford's brow creased.

"No? I'm surprised the news didn't reach you." Tom sat back and watched Shackleford. He couldn't tell whether the man was simply wary or didn't know what Tom was talking about.

Almost a minute passed in silence. Wind rattled the windowpanes.

Shackleford blurted, "Damn it, what're you gettin' at?"

So he hadn't heard. He'd be a lot cagier if he had. Tom sat forward, laced his fingers on the desktop. "The State Police cadets found Jean Turner's head."

Shackleford snapped back in his chair as if he'd been clobbered with a fist. His swarthy cheeks paled and he gasped for breath.

Tom paused to study this reaction. Looked like genuine shock. Setting aside the questions that crowded his mind, Tom kept his gaze locked on Shackleford's face and pressed the advantage. "We found her skull and her hair. All that pretty black hair, scattered

around in a cave. We haven't found the rest of her yet. Our local
M.E. thinks a bear probably tore Jean's head off and took it into
a cave and made a meal of it, brains and all."

Looking like he was about to barf, Shackleford gulped and
started to rise. Brandon pushed him down.

"All these years," Tom said, "Holly—your daughter, your
own flesh and blood—she believed her mother was alive. I wish
you could've been there to see her face when she found out her
mother's been dead all along."

Bent from the waist, Shackleford hung his head so his face
was hidden. Tom wanted to grab him by the hair and yank him
upright, make the son of a bitch look him in the eye.

"It hit Mrs. Turner pretty hard too," Tom continued. "Finding
out she's lost two daughters, not one. Her family thought Jean
took off to get away from you, but she never left the county. I
know you beat her, and I'm guessing you killed her because she
threatened to turn you in for killing Pauline."

Shackleford jerked his head up and met Tom's gaze. "No. I did
not kill Jeannie. I didn't kill nobody. Sarelda Turner knows that.
You'll never make her say I did it 'cause she knows I didn't."

"I have to admit we're stumped about who the third victim
was," Tom said. "It could have been Amy Watford. Maybe she
stumbled onto the truth. She was close to Pauline. She would've
turned you in. Her parents claim she's in South Carolina, but I
think they're so terrified of you and your family that they'll say
anything you tell them to."

Shackleford's face stiffened. Instead of folding, he seemed
to be gaining strength and resolve. "You arrested me on drug
charges. Now you're talkin' about murder. What's one thing got
to do with the other?"

"You're the only person with a motive to kill Jean."

Shackleford didn't answer.

"As for Pauline," Tom said, "a number of people had griev-
ances against her. You were one of them. I can understand why
you hated her. She pushed you to take responsibility for a child
you never wanted, threatened to take you to court if you didn't

pay support. Told you how to live your life. You might've lost your temper and killed her for that reason alone."

Shackleford shifted in his chair and the handcuffs clinked together.

"But maybe you had even more incentive. If somebody else wanted her dead, and offered you money to do it—well, why not get rid of a thorn in your side and make a nice profit at the same time?"

For a second Shackleford's eyes widened, but he quickly hid the reaction behind a shield of defiance. "You been watchin' too many cop shows on TV."

"We know all about Natalie McClure, Troy."

Shackleford's gaze darted to the windows, back to Tom, away again. His chest heaved as his breathing quickened. "The lady's got nothin' to do with me." His attempt to sound dismissive came off as nervous and furtive.

Good God, it's true. Shackleford and Natalie McClure had plotted together. "Are you going to let her get away with her part in it because she's rich and comes from an important family? You think she'll mind seeing you go to death row while she goes on living her comfortable life? Give her up, and you won't get the death penalty."

"I never killed nobody, and you can't prove I did."

"We can prove motive and opportunity, and you've been talking a little too freely about what happened to Pauline. We'll use your own words against you. People have been convicted with a lot less proof than we've got."

"I'm not sayin' another word till I've got a lawyer in the room."

"What I don't understand," Tom went on, "is how a man can kill a woman he's been close to, had a child with. Oh, I know it happens all the time. But I've never been able to understand it, how a man can go from sleeping with a woman, touching her that way, to beating the life out of her. And a woman like Jean—she was beautiful, and so small and delicate. Helpless against a man your size."

The transformation taking place on Shackleford's face made Tom fall silent and stare. The man's features contorted as if he were in pain. His mouth trembled. "God damn it. God damn it all." Then he shook his head. "I want to go back to my cell, and I want to be left alone till my lawyer gets here."

This time when Shackleford made ready to stand up, Brandon looked to Tom for direction and Tom nodded. "Take him."

As they left the room, Tom rose, stretched his aching shoulders, and walked to the window. Outside, the little town lay silent and calm. He was damned glad Shackleford was in custody and no longer a danger to Rachel and Holly, but to put Shackleford away for good he had to come up with enough evidence to charge the man with murder. When he'd called Rachel earlier to tell her about the arrest, she'd sounded relieved but very much aware that nothing was settled.

God, he wanted this case behind him so he could focus on her. Finally breaking through Rachel's defenses had felt like walking into a warm room after wandering through a cold, dark night. He couldn't lose his chance with her.

Brandon came in and closed the door. "What the heck do you make of it?"

Tom rubbed his gritty eyes and returned to his seat behind the desk. "I don't know. He acts like he didn't know Jean was dead. But if he didn't kill her, who did? And why?"

Brandon slumped into a chair. He looked as worn out as Tom felt, stubble-chinned and bleary-eyed and running on empty. "Rudy O'Dell?"

"I guess that's possible. But after what O'Dell's mother told me, I don't believe he did anything willingly. I think Shackleford coerced him into helping to get rid of the bodies—two of them, anyway—and from the sound of it, O'Dell was traumatized by the experience. Why would he kill Jean Turner? Shackleford's the one who had a reason to want her out of the way."

"Well, he sure did react when you brought up Natalie McClure. Who would have thought it? A rich, pretty woman like that, president of the Junior League and all."

"It won't be easy to make a jury believe it. We'll probably never get as far as a trial if we don't get a confession out of one of them."

"Oh, man," Brandon said with gleeful relish, "if they did plot the murders together, Mrs. McClure's gonna do a meltdown when she comes in for her interview in the morning and you put Shackleford right in her face."

Chapter Thirty-seven

At nine a.m., Tom saw Natalie McClure and her lawyer, Cecil Merck, drive into the parking lot in Merck's black Cadillac. After he parked, the two sat with their heads together, the lawyer apparently delivering last-minute instructions. Their huddle gave Tom time to send Brandon and Dennis next door to fetch Troy Shackleford. When Natalie and Merck entered the building, Tom was in the lobby, leaning on the reception desk.

"Good morning," he said. "Thanks for coming in."

Natalie didn't return the greeting. With an expression of mild revulsion, she took in the FBI Wanted posters on the walls, the worn green linoleum, the wooden bench and the sand-filled receptacle bristling with cigarette butts. Her gaze came to rest on the frizzy hair and sharp features of Maggie Jenkins, the part-time jailer who was back at her regular job on the front desk. When Maggie returned Natalie's stare with a mocking smile, Natalie drew the collar of her mink coat closer and hugged her purse to her side.

"I want to remind you," Merck said, "that Mrs. McClure is under no obligation to submit to questioning. She's here as a courtesy, to clarify matters so you'll be free to focus your efforts on pursuing the actual criminal."

Tom had never liked Merck, and his distaste for the lawyer was reinforced by the sight of him standing like a protective white-haired father next to a woman who thought she was superior to 99.9 percent of the people she encountered.

"I appreciate the help." What was taking Brandon and Dennis so long? He hoped Shackleford wasn't resisting the unexplained excursion out of the cell block. "Can I get you some coffee, Mrs. McClure?"

"No, thank you."

Wise decision. The coffee was as bad as she probably thought it was. While Tom was wondering how to keep Natalie and Merck standing out here for another minute or two, he heard the sound he'd been listening for. The lock clicked open in the side door. Dennis entered first, followed by Shackleford in handcuffs, then Brandon.

Natalie yelped and took a step backward. Merck's puzzled expression told Tom that the lawyer didn't recognize Shackleford. "Natalie?" Merck said, a solicitous hand on her shoulder.

Shackleford came to an abrupt halt when he spotted Natalie, and his startled gaze swung from her to Tom. He needed only a second to recover his composure. Pasting on a grin, he gestured at Merck with his manacled hands and asked, "You my lawyer?"

Merck looked affronted. Before he could answer, Tom said, "No, Troy, I'm afraid Mr. Merck is a little more selective about who he represents. Your mother called and said to tell you she's working on finding somebody for you, but it might take a while."

Natalie retreated to a window, her back to the men. She trembled so violently that the dark hairs on her fur coat vibrated as if stirred by a breeze.

"You two know each other, I believe," Tom said. "Mrs. McClure? Didn't you tell me that Troy used to work for you? Back when he worked for a living."

"He did a few chores for my husband and me," she said without looking around. Her voice sounded high and thin. "A long time ago."

"How you doin', Mrs. McClure?" Shackleford said. "How's Dr. McClure?"

Natalie started as if he'd poked her with a stick.

Merck demanded, "What's going on here?"

Not enough to suit Tom. "Let's all sit down and see if the two of you can fill in some gaps for me."

"This is absurd," Merck blustered. "We're leaving."

Natalie turned, and her eyes flew to Shackleford like metal to a magnet. His gaze held hers, and Tom could see in Shackleford's face a warning, a threat.

An amazing thing happened: Natalie's already fragile composure cracked like crazed glass. A faint keening sound rose from her throat.

"Natalie?" Merck said, clearly unnerved. "Let's go. I'll take you home."

But she seemed rooted to the spot, her eyes locked on Shackleford. And Shackleford was beginning to look as alarmed as Merck.

Tom stepped closer to her and said quietly, "It's been a long time, hasn't it? A long time to live with such a terrible secret."

"Leave my client alone!"

"I'm sure you've heard how Pauline was killed," Tom said to Natalie. "Her head was split open with an ax, right through to her brain."

"Oh, God," Natalie whimpered. She pressed a shaking hand to her mouth.

"Get ahold of yourself," Shackleford said. "Don't let him play this game with you."

"We're done here," Merck said. Grabbing Natalie's arm, he pulled her toward the door.

She stumbled, then her legs gave way and she folded. Tom sprang forward and he and Merck caught her and helped her to the bench. Tom pushed her head down to her knees and ordered, "Breathe. Deep and slow." He signaled Dennis and Brandon to remove Shackleford.

"I don't know what the hell you think you're doing," Merck said, "but you're way out of line. This stunt is unprofessional and unethical and—"

"I think it's time for your client to tell me the truth," Tom said.

Natalie began to sob, her face buried in the lush fur of her coat.

Dennis and Brandon shoved Shackleford through the door to the jail. He shouted back to Natalie, "You'll keep your mouth shut if you know what's good for you!"

Chapter Thirty-eight

"I don't want you saying another word," Cecil Merck told Natalie. With a hand on her elbow, he hauled her to her feet. "We're leaving."

"I think we should go in my office and talk," Tom said.

"Absolutely not. Mrs. McClure came here willing to answer questions, but after the stunt you've pulled, she's withdrawing her cooperation."

Natalie stared at the floor, her smooth golden hair draping her cheeks.

"Mrs. McClure," Tom said, "I believe you have something to tell me."

When she raised her head, she was so pale that Tom was afraid she might collapse again. Her tortured eyes seemed fixed on some inner vision.

"Mrs. McClure?" Tom said gently. "Do you really want me to get all my information from Troy Shackleford? Why don't you tell me your side of it?"

For a second he didn't think the bluff would work. Then she nodded, and Merck groaned.

In Tom's office, Natalie sat stiffly in a hard wooden chair, her mink coat drawn close around her, and stared at the whirring tape recorder on the desk. Sunlight through the windows bathed her face, giving a touch of warmth and life to bloodless cheeks. Tom watched Natalie while Merck recited the official line: Mrs. McClure didn't get along with her sister-in-law, she wasn't happy about her husband's closeness to Pauline, but she had nothing to do with Pauline's murder. Puffing himself up in his chair and looking down his nose at Tom, Merck added, "And I'm certain you have no proof that she did, regardless of what you're hearing from garbage like Shackleford."

"Pauline wasn't the only victim," Tom said. "Her sister Jean was murdered around the same time, probably because she threatened to go to the police. Another woman was also killed. We think it was Pauline's niece Amy, and she might have been killed because she knew too much. A few days ago, Shackleford's pal Rudy O'Dell was murdered, probably for the same reason. Somebody tried to kill Pauline's niece Holly and her friend, Dr. Goddard. All because, years ago, someone was angry at Pauline."

"I hope you're not suggesting," Merck said, "that my client murdered three women and is now running around the countryside hunting people down like a savage."

Natalie whimpered and brought a hand to her mouth.

Tom concentrated on her. "Here's what I think happened. Your husband had an affair with Pauline. Ed was in love with her, and he would have left you for her. Left you with two sons to raise while he went off to indulge his romantic fantasies with Pauline."

"This is cruel," Merck said. "You have no right—"

"She didn't even want him," Natalie broke in. "She didn't love him, but he wouldn't stay away from her."

"Natalie," Merck said, his voice heavy with warning.

Agitated now, Natalie blurted, "Why do men do things like that? He humiliated himself. He made a fool of me. Our sons knew about it, but he didn't care whether they respected him or not."

"You must have been very angry at him," Tom said. "And at Pauline."

"I *hated* her."

"That's enough now." Merck placed a hand on her arm.

Tom pushed on, "She was destroying your marriage. As long as Pauline was around, he'd never belong to you again."

Natalie bowed her head.

"So," Tom said, "you decided to get rid of her. And you knew somebody else who hated her because she was interfering in his life. Did you pay Troy Shackleford to kill Pauline?"

"Don't answer that," Merck told her.

Natalie was back in her private world, her eyes focused on a scene only she could see. "I was desperate. I had to get her out of our lives."

Merck shook his head. "Natalie," he said with weary resignation, "I am strongly advising you not to say anything more."

Shut up, damn it. Natalie was on the verge of spilling everything, and Tom wanted to gag Merck to keep him quiet. "People do extreme things when they're desperate," Tom said. "That's understandable."

Natalie's eyes filled with tears. "I came to my senses, though. I'd gone a little crazy, I knew it was wrong, and I told him I'd changed my mind."

"What?" Tom said.

"I told him not to kill her."

"You hired Shackleford to kill Pauline, but you changed your mind?"

"I told him the money didn't matter, he could keep the money, but I didn't want him to hurt her." Natalie's voice rose to a wail. "But he did it anyway. I told him not to, but he killed her anyway."

Chapter Thirty-nine

With half his jaw numbed by Novocaine, Sheriff Willingham made Tom think of a stroke victim, speaking indistinctly out of one side of his mouth while the other remained slack and motionless. "I can't even go to the dentis' wi'out all hell breakin' loose aroun' here." Pacing Tom's office, Willingham jammed fingers against his numb left cheek as if he could force feeling back into it. "You planned 'is, didn' you? So I wouldn' be here."

Tom, leaning against his desk, pretended surprise. "It just worked out this way."

"Like hell." Willingham dropped into the chair where Natalie McClure had sat not long before. "She won' be convicted. She had a momen' of weakness, 'a's all. Didn' follow 'hrough."

"She confessed to hiring Shackleford to do it," Tom said. "Money changed hands. And Pauline ended up dead." Willingham started to interrupt, but Tom cut him off. "She's the prosecutor's problem now. He's setting up a quick arraignment. He'll be asking for a high bail, but the McClures can manage it. She'll stay in the holding cell at the courthouse till then. I don't want her in the jail with the Shacklefords. We can't take any chances on them intimidating her."

"Rober' McClure's gonna have a fi," Willingham said.

"I don't imagine her husband's going to be too happy, either. He's teaching in Blacksburg today, but Merck's probably already let him know." Tom had wondered why Ed McClure wasn't with

Natalie when she came in for questioning. His guess was that she hadn't told Ed about it.

"Pauline never meant to hur' a soul," Willingham muttered. Sighing, he gazed into space as if he were replaying a scene from long ago in his head. "But she hur' so many people. I tried and tried to tell your dad to stay away from her—"

"I'm going to talk to Shackleford now," Tom broke in. He still wasn't sure what to believe about his father and Pauline, he hadn't had a quiet minute to think over what Durham had told him, and he'd be damned if he'd stay here and listen to Willingham talk about them. He pushed away from the desk and headed for the door, speaking without looking back. "We'll be in the conference room if you want to sit in."

‹›‹›‹›

Shackleford seemed subdued, perhaps humbled by a night in jail and the knowledge that Natalie McClure had been arrested and charged and had already signed a statement. He took a chair facing Tom across the conference table. Under the merciless fluorescent light, every line in Shackleford's face looked like an etching in stone and the stubble on his face was more gray than black.

Willingham sat at one end of the table, out of Shackleford's direct sight. Tom hoped the sheriff would stay quiet.

When Brandon placed a Styrofoam cup of coffee—lukewarm, on Tom's orders—before Shackleford, he lifted it with his cuffed hands, brought it to his mouth for a sip, set it down with a grimace. Brandon, standing guard behind the prisoner, grinned at Tom.

"Where's my lawyer?" Shackleford demanded.

"I'm afraid you'll have to wait for the court to appoint one," Tom said. "Unless you want a public defender."

"I've got money to pay a good lawyer. My mother's had time to find one by now."

"Your mother says she's called everybody, and nobody's willing to take your case. You see, they all know the court wouldn't allow them to keep your money because it's proceeds from illegal activity. Besides, the prosecutor's asking the court to freeze your assets, and Buddy's and Rose's. So you don't have a cent to pay an attorney."

"Shit." Anger and frustration stewed in Shackleford's face.

"Like I said, we can get one of the public defenders to represent you. I don't think either of them's ever handled a murder case, so they'll probably be fighting for the chance to get the experience."

"I don't want no snot-nosed little kid straight out of some backwater law school." Shackleford shoved his cup away. Coffee sloshed onto the table.

"All right then," Tom said, "you'll have to wait till tomorrow. Meanwhile, I think it'll be in your best interests to answer a few questions."

Shackleford glowered at him with the helpless hostility of a cornered animal.

"I've heard Natalie McClure's side of the story," Tom said. "She says she paid you to kill Pauline, then decided not to follow through. But you went ahead. You took money from Natalie to commit a murder, and you did, in fact, murder Pauline."

"I never killed nobody. You can't prove I did."

"Now, come on, Troy. If a jury compares your story to Natalie's, who do you think they'll believe? Why would a woman like Natalie McClure, with everything in the world to lose, confess to hiring a hit man if she didn't do it?"

"I'm not a hit man, damn it!" Shackleford half-rose, but at the touch of Brandon's hands on his shoulders he dropped back into the chair.

"Did you take money from Natalie McClure to kill Pauline?" Tom persisted. "Did she tell you she wanted Pauline dead?"

Shackleford scrubbed his hands over his face. "Yeah. Is that what you want to hear? She told me she wanted me to kill Pauline for her. But I never intended to. I took the money—why wouldn't I? Who's she gonna complain to if she never gets what she paid for? The Better Business Bureau? And when Pauline disappeared, yeah, I let Natalie think I did it. But I didn't."

For the briefest moment the passion in Shackleford's plea made Tom wonder whether the man could be telling the truth.

Tom was about to press on when the door opened and Dennis Murray stuck his head in. "Sorry to interrupt, but could I talk to you for a second?"

When Tom joined him in the hallway, Dennis said, "I just found out something that might shed some new light. I heard from the cops in South Carolina who checked out that private mailbox that's rented in Amy's name."

"And?" Tom's heartbeat kicked into high gear.

"It's billed to somebody else, the name doesn't mean anything to me, but the bills go to a post office box in Washington, D.C. All the mail that comes into the South Carolina address is remailed to the Washington address. And several times a year something comes in from Washington to be remailed with the South Carolina postmark."

"Oh, man." Tom clapped a hand to his forehead. "And who do we know who lives right across the Potomac from Washington?"

Mary Lee.

Chapter Forty

Tom sent Shackleford back to the jail, collected his notes from every interview he'd conducted through the day before, and returned to the conference room with Willingham, Brandon, and Dennis.

"Let's look at the whole picture," Tom said. "Natalie McClure admits she hired Troy to kill Pauline, but he claims he took Natalie's money then didn't do the deed."

Willingham snorted. "Likely story."

"Let's suppose he's telling the truth for once in his life."

"Aw, come on, Tom," Willingham said.

"Just consider it. If he didn't kill the women, he knows who did. And I'd stake my life on him and O'Dell being the ones who got rid of the bodies. What did O'Dell's mother say?" Tom opened the folder of notes and sifted through the sheets. "Here. On the night Pauline disappeared, Rudy came home hours later than usual and told his mother Pauline was dead—*and the girl too*. He said Troy, quote, made him do something horrible, unquote. But he wouldn't tell his mother what."

"Assuming Shackleford didn't do the murders," Dennis said, "why would he get involved at all? Did he care enough about anybody to dump the bodies for them?"

"Not likely," Tom said. "But he might have done it for money. The only people in Pauline's life who had the money to buy that kind of cooperation were the McClures and Mary

Lee. Now that we know about the post office box, I'm leaning toward Mary Lee."

"My lord, Tom," Willingham said. "You think the girl killed her own mother?"

"That sort of thing has been known to happen," Tom said. "If she killed Amy too, that explains why she would write to Holly and to Amy's parents, pretending to be Amy, making the whole family think Amy's alive."

Brandon and Dennis both nodded.

"We don't know whether Mary Lee's the one renting that P.O. box in Washington," Willingham said. "And we won't know for sure unless we force the Postal Service to tell us. We'd have to go through the U.S. Attorney up there for a warrant."

"It all fits," Tom said. He let his imagination run loose, pictured the very reserved woman he'd met in a lavish McLean house sinking an ax into her mother's skull. Not an easy image to conjure, but anybody was capable of anything, given enough motivation. "She got Shackleford and O'Dell to hide the bodies, and she left for college the same night and pretended she'd actually left a day earlier. Nobody ever doubted her story. I think my father accepted it at face value. I haven't found anything in the old file to make me think he suspected Mary Lee."

"Well, maybe there's a reason," Willingham said. "He was a better judge of people than you are, and he knew she was innocent."

Or he was predisposed to be blindly protective of his lover's daughter. "If Mary Lee's writing letters, pretending to be Amy, that means she knows Amy's dead. How would she know if she wasn't involved in the killing? And why would she conceal Amy's death?"

"This is pure guesswork," Willingham said. "Meanwhile, we've got a McClure locked up for the same murders you're trying to pin on Mary Lee."

"Natalie McClure's guilty of conspiracy to commit murder, at the very least," Tom said. "Her confession doesn't mean we have to close our minds to other possibilities." Before the sheriff could interrupt again, Tom went on, "Ed McClure had a reason to be furious at Pauline, and he had the money to pay Shackleford for disposing of the bodies. If he's Mary Lee's real father, and Mary Lee knows it, she might protect him."

"Now you're calling Reed Durham a liar?" Willingham said. "He told you the girl was conceived by artificial insemination."

"That's what Pauline told him. Doesn't mean it's true."

Willingham threw up his hands in exasperation.

"Mary Lee would've been upset," Brandon said, "if she found out her real father was some stranger who jerked off in a cup."

"Wait a minute." Tom flipped the pages in the folder, hoping something would jump out at him. He stopped when he came to an account of his interview with Bonnie and Jack Watford. He skimmed the interview notes, went back and read a couple of quotes a second time. "Let's think about Bonnie and Jack. Seems to me they felt a lot of resentment toward Pauline. Still do, even after all these years. And Bonnie was at Pauline's house right before the disappearance. Screaming at Pauline about something, but Mrs. Barker couldn't make out what it was about. Let me find—"

He shuffled papers and found the account of his last interview with Mrs. Barker. He read it quickly. The scenario taking shape in his mind was so far-fetched that he didn't dare put it into words. Not until he was sure it was possible. He pushed back his chair and rose. "Hold on a minute. I need to make a call."

⟨⟩⟨⟩⟨⟩

"Hey, Tom," Reed Durham said when he answered the phone. "I heard about Natalie McClure. I am flat-out amazed, but I guess we should have suspected something like—"

"Reed," Tom interrupted, "I need some information."

A brief silence. Tom could envision Durham bracing himself to deflect intrusive questions. "I'll help if I can," he said, his tone turning brisk.

"Where was Mary Lee born?" Tom asked.

"That's what you want to know? Florida. Palm Beach, I believe."

"How did Pauline and Adam happen to be in Palm Beach when the baby was born?"

"Well—" Durham paused. "What's this about?"

"I don't have time to explain. Why were they in Florida?"

Durham hesitated, and Tom knew the lawyer was trying to figure out what kind of trap he was walking into. "It was winter," Durham said at last. "Pauline was having a lot of morning sickness and backaches and so forth. She wanted to be in a warm place."

"How long was she down there?"

Another silence, this one stretching out. Tom tapped a pencil on his desktop and waited.

"About six months, I guess," Durham said. "Adam wasn't with her the whole time, he had his work at the bank, but he flew down a lot. She was about three months pregnant, I guess, when she left. That's a hard time for a lot of women. My wife—"

"Pauline was in Florida from the third month of the pregnancy until after the baby was born?"

"Right."

"Tell me this. Did you ever see Pauline looking pregnant?"

"What kind of question is that? She started wearing looser clothes, and… Well, no, I guess I never saw her really heavy. Why?"

"Thanks." Tom dropped the receiver into its cradle.

Back in the conference room, he faced the sheriff's displeasure. "What are you up to?" Willingham said. "Who'd you have to call in such a hurry?"

"I'll explain everything." Tom leaned his palms on the tabletop and swept the three men with his gaze. "We know Mary Lee isn't Adam's daughter. What if she's not Pauline's daughter either?"

Chapter Forty-one

"Now you're not making any sense," Sheriff Willingham said. "Pauline gave birth to Mary Lee. How could the girl not be her daughter?"

"If she'd given birth in Mason County General," Tom said, "and she'd seen a local doctor throughout her pregnancy, I wouldn't question it. But she went off to Florida before the pregnancy was even showing, and she came back with a baby."

"So what?"

Tom repeated what Durham had said and Willingham lost his inclination to argue. "I'll be damned," he murmured. He frowned at Tom. "Then whose baby was it? Mary Lee's got to be related to the Turners. She looks just like them."

"She's related, all right," Tom said. "Here's what I think happened. Adam and Pauline couldn't have children. But Pauline's sister Bonnie was a baby-making machine. She had four sons and a daughter, one right after the other, when she was in her teens and early twenties. I've heard from several sources about Bonnie's emotional instability, her bad nerves. She was overwhelmed. Maybe when she got pregnant again, a sixth baby was the last thing she and Jack wanted."

"And along came Pauline to take the kid off her hands," Brandon said.

"Right. We're probably not going to find any records after all these years, but I'd bet anything that Bonnie Watford was in Florida with Pauline, and she probably used Pauline's name when she saw a doctor and when she had the baby."

"But why go to so much trouble?" Dennis asked. "Why didn't Adam and Pauline adopt her sister's baby? Or some other baby."

"Because Adam's mother wanted *real* grandchildren. She wouldn't have accepted an adopted baby. Robert told me the only reason the elder Mrs. McClure tolerated Pauline was because she was the mother of her grandchild."

Willingham slumped back in his chair. "Okay, let's say all this is true. What does it have to do with the murders?"

"I think it's the reason for the murders," Tom said. "Maybe Bonnie and Jack regretted giving up their child. They wanted some contact with her, but Pauline wouldn't allow it. When I talked to Bonnie and Jack, Bonnie said something like 'I just wanted to see her now and then, but Pauline treated me like poison.' I thought she was talking about seeing her sister, but she might have been talking about her daughter."

Willingham frowned. "I don't know, Tom. This is all pretty hard to believe."

"Another thing," Tom said. "Pauline sent Mary Lee to boarding school and wouldn't tell anybody where she was. From the time Mary Lee was twelve, she spent almost no time in Mason County. Everybody says Pauline was trying to protect her from the fuss the McClures stirred up about the girl's paternity. But maybe she was hiding Mary Lee from her real parents."

"What are you thinking?" Dennis asked. "Bonnie or Jack killed Pauline? But why would either of them kill Amy? Maybe Mary Lee found out the truth and flew into a rage and killed Pauline? Why would *she* kill Amy?"

Brandon said, "Mary Lee thought Amy was trying to take her place with Pauline. And she felt threatened after she found out she wasn't really Pauline's daughter."

Tom shook his head. "I'm not sure who did the murders. Shackleford's one possibility. Mary Lee already had access to a trust fund, so she had money to pay him off. He could have killed O'Dell too. But if Shackleford's not guilty, I'm convinced he knows who is. Let's get him back in here."

⟨⟩⟨⟩⟨⟩

Troy Shackleford, in handcuffs, halted in the conference room doorway and surveyed the uniformed men. "I'm not talkin' anymore without a lawyer."

"Sit down, Troy." Tom pulled out a chair. "Listen to what I've got to say before you decide whether to talk."

With an elaborate sigh, Shackleford sank into the chair. "I'm all ears."

Tom took his seat across from Shackleford and switched on the tape recorder between them. "If you don't cooperate, you'll be arraigned tomorrow morning on capital murder charges, based on what Natalie McClure told us. You meet us halfway, tell us everything you remember about the night Pauline died, and we might reconsider. If your story jibes with what we already know."

Shackleford's eyes narrowed. He didn't answer for a long time. His gaze roamed the room, his breathing rasped. When his eyes met Tom's again, he drawled, "You don't know a damned thing. There's a lot of stuff you're never gonna figure out, 'cause you don't know the right questions to ask."

Tom smiled. "We know that Jack and Bonnie Watford are Mary Lee's parents."

Shackleford's mouth dropped open. "Well, I'll be damned," he said slowly. "You're a real detective after all, Deputy Dawg."

Tom wanted to whoop in triumph at this confirmation, but he said coolly, "We also know Rudy O'Dell helped you hide the bodies."

Shackleford shifted in his chair, ran his tongue over his lips. "Rudy's dead. He ain't been tellin' you nothin'."

"He told somebody else about it. That'll be good enough. You waited too long to kill him."

"I didn't kill Rudy. And I told you, I took Natalie's money but I didn't kill Pauline."

"Prove it. If you don't, Natalie McClure's going to put you on death row."

"What kind of a deal am I gettin' out of this?"

"Tell us your story and we'll decide what it's worth."

Shackleford looked down at his bound wrists and didn't answer.

Changing tack, Tom asked, "Did you know from the beginning that Mary Lee was Bonnie and Jack's child?"

"Naw." Shackleford wiped the back of one hand across his mouth. "I didn't hear about it till the girl was a teenager. Jack got drunk one night and told me. Amy wasn't but two months old when Bonnie got pregnant again. And her already a nervous wreck. Jack didn't want any more kids, but Bonnie wouldn't get rid of it. So Jack sold it to Pauline and Adam. They all went down to Florida and Bonnie had the baby and Pauline and Adam's names went on the birth certificate. "

A tide of revulsion rose in Tom, disgust with Jack and Bonnie, Pauline and Adam in equal measure. "But Jack and Bonnie kept trying to see Mary Lee, didn't they?"

"Not at first. They got a chunk of cash to move out of state, but after nine, ten years—before Adam died—they come back home. And the trouble started. Bonnie wanted her little girl back."

Tom could imagine the panic Pauline and Adam felt when the Watfords reappeared. "But the McClures wouldn't let them see Mary Lee."

"Adam paid 'em to get lost again. They left for a while, but Bonnie kept comin' back, tryin' to see the girl. Jack couldn't control his own wife. When Adam died, Pauline had to send Mary Lee off to boardin' school to keep Bonnie away from her. Bonnie was already nuts, but it made her crazier, not bein' able to see the little girl Pauline took away from her. And Pauline made it worse by takin' a shine to Amy. She ought to've had more sense."

"Bonnie felt like Pauline was taking her other daughter away from her too."

"Oh, yeah," Shackleford said. "That was the last straw. They had a big fight about Amy spendin' so much time at Pauline's and puttin' on airs like she was better'n her own family. So it was all set to blow. Pauline was just askin' for it."

"What do you remember about the night of the murders?"

"Didn't happen at night," Shackleford said. "It was afternoon, late. I was fixin' the light over the kitchen sink and Rudy was out cuttin' the grass when they walked in, Bonnie and Jack and Amy."

Tom's vague mental picture of the murders dissolved and a fresh one sprang up, but he didn't know whose hands had held the ax. "Go on."

"Bonnie heard somewhere about Mary Lee comin' home for a visit before she headed off to start her first year at college, and her and Jack and Amy hightailed it out to Pauline's place, hell-bent on seein' Mary Lee and tellin' her the truth."

"What happened when they showed up?"

Shackleford placed his hands on the table, the cuffs rattling when they struck the wood. He grinned, but his dark eyes were cold. "Things got out of hand. People got killed. I can tell you who killed who, but I got more to offer too. I can give you a juicy little morsel that'll make you drool like a dog sniffin' a bitch. I'm keepin' it to myself, though, till y'all guarantee in writin' to let me off on the murder charges."

"No guarantees till we know what you're offering," Tom said.

"Well, then," Shackleford said, rising, "if you gentlemen will excuse me, I'm startin' to miss my deluxe quarters in your fine facility. I'm done talkin'."

◇◇◇

Rachel studied Joanna's enclosed porch with a critical eye. "Yeah," she told Holly. "We'll have to improvise, but this will do. Help me move the furniture out of the way."

The supplies Rachel had ordered would arrive the following morning, and as long as no patient needed emergency surgery, she'd be able to carry on at Joanna's house for a week or so, until the parts of the clinic that hadn't been burned were cleaned up and made usable. Soon she would have her insurance payout and could begin rebuilding.

Holly's eyes had a faraway look and she answered in monosyllables when Rachel spoke to her. Watching Holly's face, Rachel could track her emotions, the grief and anger and bewilderment that crashed through her in relentless waves.

After they set up a card table for small animal exams, Rachel touched Holly's arm. "Don't force yourself to work if you're not up to it."

Tears filled Holly's eyes. "But you need to be ready, and it's my job to help you." Her voice caught on a sob. "I can't believe Mama's really dead."

Rachel pulled the girl into a hug and patted her back. She desperately wished she could do something to help Holly, but no one could reach into another's heart and ease the anguish of loss. The raw misery of her grief for her own mother would never leave her completely. If that was what losing a loved one could do to you, she'd thought more than once, perhaps it was better never to feel deeply. But love couldn't be kept at bay. It invaded her heart whether she welcomed it or not. She loved this girl who had become such a huge part of her life in only a few days. And although the possibility terrified her and made her feel like a traitor to Luke, she knew she was falling in love with Tom.

Holly clung to Rachel and sobbed. When she'd exhausted her tears, she stepped back and pulled tissues from her jeans pocket to blow her nose and dry her face. "I keep worryin' about Grandma. She must feel as bad as I do, and she's all alone without me to help her."

Oh no. Holly couldn't be thinking of going back. "She has your Aunt Bonnie," Rachel said. "They'll help each other."

Holly pushed hair off her damp cheeks and shook her head. "Aunt Bonnie's kind of… She's not real steady, you know? She's probably fallin' apart, and she won't be any help to Grandma."

"Holly—"

"I ought to go see her and make sure she's all right."

Rachel bit back the words that wanted to pour out, the warnings, the pleas. She had no right to make Holly's decisions for her. But she couldn't let Holly be drawn back into her old life, and that would surely happen if Mrs. Turner got her alone for even a few minutes. "Why don't you call her? That'll make her feel better and it'll set your mind to rest."

Holly chewed her bottom lip and considered. Rachel held her breath. At last Holly shook her head again and said what Rachel dreaded hearing. "Maybe I ought to go stay with her a while. I know you need me to work, but Grandma just found out my mama's dead, and she needs me too."

"Please listen to me." Taking her by the shoulders, Rachel made Holly look at her. "You know how it'll turn out if you move back in with your grandmother. You might plan to stay a few days, but she'll never let you leave again. You'll lose your chance for a life of your own. I understand how you feel, but you have to think of your future." Rachel paused, then added, aiming shamelessly at Holly's most sensitive spot, "Isn't that what your mother would want? A better life for you?"

Holly wrapped her arms around her waist and rocked back and forth, head lowered. "Yes. And I don't want to go back there to live." Her head came up. "But I ought to go see how Grandma's doin'."

Rachel imagined Mrs. Turner grabbing Holly and refusing to let go, whining that family came first, playing on Holly's guilt until she gave in and stayed. Grief couldn't be rushed, and Holly would probably be riding an emotional roller-coaster for weeks to come. Her grandmother would give her no peace or comfort. Rachel almost wished the Shacklefords weren't in jail, so she could argue that venturing into their part of the county was too dangerous.

"Listen," Rachel said. "You hardly ate any lunch. Come in the kitchen and I'll make you some hot chocolate and toast and we can talk about this some more."

Rachel was mixing milk and cocoa in a saucepan when the doorbell rang. "I'll get it. It's probably Deputy Duncan. He should come in and warm up."

She opened the front door, not to the deputy who was guarding them but to a stunning woman with black hair and blue eyes who looked a lot like Holly as well as like photos of Pauline Turner McClure that Rachel had seen in the newspaper.

"Dr. Goddard?" The woman's brow creased with a slight frown. She began pulling off a white leather glove one finger at a time, changed her mind, tugged it on again.

Another of Holly's relatives, Rachel thought with a stirring of apprehension. This one must be rich. Her coat was white cashmere, her gloves looked like kidskin, and she'd arrived in a red Jaguar, which sat on the driveway. Deputy Grady Duncan, lost in admiration, circled the sports car slowly. "Yes, I'm Dr. Goddard. May I help you?"

"I'm looking for my cousin, Holly." The woman peered through the screen, her gaze shifting beyond Rachel. "Oh. This must be her."

Holly was coming up the hall, her step hesitant, her half-smile quizzical. "Who...?"

The woman opened the screen door, moved past Rachel, and swooped Holly into an embrace. "It's me, sweetheart. Mary Lee."

Rachel watched in amazement, struck by Holly's stiffness and the look of confusion and alarm frozen on her face. What was going on here?

Mary Lee released Holly from the hug and held her by the shoulders. "I know you haven't seen me since you were a little girl." A smile flitted around Mary Lee's lips but didn't take hold. "My goodness, look how much you've changed. If you weren't so much like your mother, I wouldn't recognize you either."

Rachel stared. Hadn't Holly said that she'd never met Mary Lee? That Pauline had kept all the Turners away from Mary Lee? Holly had been a small child at the time, though. Could she have forgotten?

Holly backed away, putting several feet between herself and Mary Lee. She looked at Rachel with a question in her eyes, but Rachel had no answer. She didn't even know what the question was.

"Why'd you come?" Holly asked Mary Lee.

"To take you home with me, sweetheart." Mary Lee moved closer and grasped Holly by the shoulders. "Our grandmother called and told me somebody shot at you and she's terrified that you're not safe here. She begged me to come get you, and of course I agreed immediately. I knew I had to take you away from here before you get hurt."

"Wait a minute," Rachel said. "You can't appear out of nowhere and expect Holly to leave with you."

Mary Lee threw her a warning look. This woman wasn't used to being thwarted. "I'm sure the whole family appreciates what you've done for Holly," she said, "but she'll be better off with me now."

"No," Holly said, the word flat and final.

"You can't stay here, sweetheart. I'm afraid for you. And I can give you everything you need. You can go to college, or—"

"No." Holly edged toward Rachel. "I'm not goin' anywhere with you."

Rachel was ready to throw the woman out, but Mary Lee's eyes filled with tears and she raised a trembling hand to her forehead. "I'm sorry. You must wonder what's wrong with me, bursting in this way. Could we sit down and talk? I'll try to make a little more sense."

She'd have to make a lot more sense if she expected to walk out of here with Holly. "Do you want to talk to her?" Rachel asked Holly.

"Please." Mary Lee smiled at Holly. "I didn't mean to scare you."

Holly wavered, but in the end she nodded. She stayed close to Rachel as they walked into the living room. Instead of joining Mary Lee on the sofa, she sat on the arm of Rachel's chair and leaned against her shoulder. Holly's body felt rigid, tensed for flight, and when Rachel looked up at the girl's face, she saw the hyper-alertness of a hunted animal. Holly was scared to death of Mary Lee.

"Oh, gosh," Rachel exclaimed, feigning dismay, "we left the hot chocolate on the burner." She rose and caught Holly's hand. "Come help me."

"No," Mary Lee said, "stay with me. We have a lot to talk about."

"She'll be right back." Rachel forced a smile. "Make yourself comfortable. We'll bring you something to drink."

"I don't want—"

They were already out of the room. In the kitchen, with the door closed, Rachel asked, "What's wrong? Why are you so afraid of her?"

Holly's voice was a fierce whisper. "That's not Mary Lee! That's Amy."

"My God. How can you be sure? You haven't seen either of them since—"

"I never met Mary Lee in my life! And look at her eyes. She's got these gray rings around the blue. Amy's the only one in the whole family with eyes like that."

"But why would she claim to be Mary Lee?"

Holly pressed her hands to her head and leaned against the wall. "I heard them talkin' about it that night at Grandma's house, talkin' about hidin' the bodies and figurin' out how they could get away with it. My mama was cryin' and sayin' they'd all burn in hell for what they did. Grandma always said I didn't hear anything, I just imagined it and I couldn't tell anybody because people would think I was crazy and makin' things up, but I heard them, I know I did."

"Oh my God," Rachel said, her breath tight in her throat. "You mean—"

Holly looked at Rachel. "They killed Aunt Pauline and Mary Lee. "And Amy went to Mary Lee's college and took her place."

⟨⟩⟨⟩⟨⟩

Following the aborted interview with Shackleford, Tom waited in his office for the Commonwealth's Attorney to arrive, listen to the tape, and tell him what they could reasonably offer to make Shackleford spill everything he knew. Tom planned to pick up Bonnie and Jack Watford after seeing the prosecutor. By tonight he would probably be in Fairfax County, where he would ask the local police to assist him in picking up Mary Lee for questioning.

He was slumped in his desk chair, wondering how much of the truth about Mary Lee his father had known, when the phone rang. Rachel was calling.

"Why are you whispering?" Tom sat up straight. "What's wrong?"

Rachel's voice was quiet but urgent. "There's a woman here claiming to be Mary Lee."

Tom shot out of his chair and sent it rolling backward into the wall.

Rachel went on, "But Holly swears the woman is Amy. She says Mary Lee's dead and Amy took her place. And now this woman—Amy, Mary Lee—she's here and she's determined to take Holly away with her."

"Tell Grady Duncan I want him to stop her if she tries to leave. I'll be there in twenty minutes."

Chapter Forty-two

When Rachel and Holly reentered the living room with four mugs of hot chocolate on a tray, they found Amy pacing in front of the cold fireplace. She still wore her coat and gloves, as if she intended to leave any second.

The mantel clock told Rachel five minutes had passed since she'd talked to Tom. Fifteen more minutes and he would be here. She had to keep Amy in the house till then.

Placing the tray on the coffee table, Rachel asked, "May I take your coat?" She wondered if Amy was hiding a gun under it.

"No, thank you. I'm fine." Amy returned to the couch and sat with her hands clasped in her lap. Her purse hung from her shoulder by a golden chain. After Holly took a chair opposite, she said, "I've been very concerned about you ever since...since all this started."

"You never called me or anything," Holly said.

"I should have. I'm sorry."

Rachel held out a mug and saw with dismay that her hand was shaking. "Have some chocolate. It's the perfect thing for a day like this. It's nice and hot."

Amy's quick little frown of irritation matched the edge in her voice. "No, thank you. Really. I don't care for any."

"Okay, if you're sure. I made a cup for the deputy. He must be freezing out there. I'll tell him to come in and warm up." Rachel headed for the door.

"No, wait," Amy said. "Can't Holly and I have some privacy to talk?"

Rachel pretended not to hear, and she was unlocking the front door before Amy could say anything else. She stepped out into a blast of icy wind. Duncan saw her wave and climbed out of the cruiser, unsuspecting, a smile on his face.

"Come have something hot to drink," Rachel called. She waited till he'd clumped up the front steps to the porch and stamped the snow off his boots. She leaned close and whispered, "I can't explain right now, but Tom's on his way to arrest this woman and he wants us to keep her from leaving. She might be dangerous, so don't alarm her. Act as if you just need to warm up."

Duncan's expression turned grim and his right hand shifted to the pistol on his hip. He nodded.

When the deputy entered the living room, Amy's mask of composure fell away for a split second to reveal pure, wide-eyed panic. But she quickly hid her fear with a tight little smile.

Rachel's heart thumped so hard and fast that she felt breathless, lightheaded.

Duncan dropped his bulk onto the sofa next to Amy. She leaned slightly away from him. He yanked off his gloves, stuffed them in his jacket pockets, and rubbed his palms together. "Man, it's colder than a witch's—" He caught himself and broke off with a cough. "Real cold."

He downed his hot chocolate in three gulps and accepted the cup Amy had refused. Holly, her gaze never leaving Amy, clutched her mug so tightly that Rachel could imagine it cracking under the pressure.

A few more minutes at the most, and Tom would be here. *Come on, come on, drive faster.*

What did Amy's sudden appearance mean? Holly had said the whole Watford family was involved in the cover-up, but she wasn't sure who'd actually killed Pauline and the real Mary Lee. This elegant woman would have been a teenager at the time. Could she have committed those horrifying murders? Had she killed Holly's mother too? And what fate did she have in mind for Holly?

"I know you'll be happy with us," Amy said, her smile frozen on her face. "We have a big house. You'll have all the privacy you need. If you want to work with animals, we'll you get into a training program."

Rachel watched over the rim of her mug. Holly set her drink on the coffee table, untouched, and stared at Amy with cold, unforgiving eyes. "I'm stayin' right where I am."

"Sweetheart, you aren't safe here. You have to come home with me."

"She's given you her answer," Rachel said.

"This is between Holly and me. I'd appreciate it if you—"

The doorbell rang.

Rachel jumped up. *Tom. Thank God.*

She set down her mug and started for the door, but Deputy Duncan rose and said, "I'll see who it is." He gave Rachel a look so freighted with conspiratorial meaning that she was afraid Amy would realize something was about to happen.

He strode out of the room.

Her whole body thrumming with tension, Rachel stood waiting for Tom to walk into the house and take control of this insane situation. Instead, she heard Jack Watford's unmistakable voice, loud and demanding. "We come to get Holly."

Holly leapt from her chair and grabbed Rachel's hand.

At the same instant, Amy bolted off the couch, banged her knees against the coffee table, and upset one of the mugs. Hot chocolate splattered her white cashmere coat, but she didn't seem to notice. Her eyes fixed on the doorway, she stumbled toward a corner.

"It's okay," Rachel told Holly. *Don't panic, don't panic.* "Deputy Duncan won't let anything happen."

"You can't come in here," Duncan was saying. "Just get back in your truck and go home."

The sounds of a scuffle followed, and Jack appeared in the living room doorway with a black-haired, teary woman at his side.

"Aunt Bonnie," Holly whispered.

Amy's parents. Murderers? Amy's accomplices?

"Come on, Holly," Jack said.

"No!" Holly cried. Her hand tightened painfully on Rachel's.

Duncan hustled around Jack and Bonnie to block their way. "You people are trespassing, You get on out of here right now or I'm putting you under arrest."

Bonnie Watford craned her neck to see around the deputy. "Holly, honey," she whined, "you need to be with your family. Your grandma's real tore up over all this bad news. She needs you to come home."

Rachel fought to stay calm and give away nothing of what she knew. Wiping a sweaty palm on her slacks, she said, "I'm sorry Mrs. Turner has to go through this. I'm sure Holly will call her later."

"That girl's goin' back where she belongs," Watford said.

"Something the matter with your hearing?" Deputy Duncan said. "I'm giving you one more chance—"

"She's not going anywhere," Rachel said. *Tom, where are you?*

"Get your coat on, Holly," Watford said. "We ain't goin' without you."

"Leave her alone." Amy stepped from the dim corner and into the light.

Bonnie squeaked in surprise. Watford stared at Amy. "What the hell are you doin' here?" he said. "I told you I'd take care of this."

Rachel pulled Holly off to one side. God only knew what might happen next. These crazy people could kill each other for all Rachel cared. Her only concern was keeping Holly safe.

"She's going home with me," Amy said.

Watford shook his head. "We're takin' her."

Duncan gripped Jack's arm. "Nobody's taking that girl anywhere."

"Amy, sweetheart," Bonnie cried. "My baby girl." She darted past Duncan and tried to throw her arms around Amy, but Amy dodged the embrace and bumped into the fireplace mantel.

"No, I'm Mary Lee," Amy said. "Remember? Aunt Bonnie, I'm Mary Lee."

"It's so good to see you, baby." Bonnie reached out and Amy cringed from the touch on her cheek.

"Bonnie! Shut up!" Watford jerked his arm free of Duncan's grasp and started across the room. "Watch what you're sayin'. She's Pauline's girl, Mary Lee."

Duncan fumbled with his holstered gun.

Rachel shoved Holly behind a chair, pushed her to the floor, and crouched beside her. What the hell was taking Tom so long?

Grabbing Bonnie by the arm, Watford wrenched her away from Amy. Bonnie twisted and squirmed but couldn't get free. "She's my baby girl! I want my daughter back."

"Let go of her and get your hands up," Duncan ordered. Gun drawn, he advanced on Watford.

Watford thrust Bonnie aside, seized the fireplace poker and whacked Duncan across the wrist. Duncan screamed in pain. The pistol went flying and landed with a clunk ten feet from Rachel. Watford slammed the poker against Duncan's temple. The deputy fell unconscious on the floor.

On her knees, Rachel scrambled for the gun. As her fingers closed around it, Watford's foot connected with her arm and knocked her off balance. He stooped, his black eyes meeting hers, and snatched up the deputy's gun.

<><><>

Tom and Brandon sped north toward the horse farm with two deputies following in a second cruiser.

"That's what Shackleford was holding back," Tom said. "Mary Lee's dead, and Amy took her place. She went off to freshman year at college and there was nobody around to say she wasn't who she claimed to be. As long as she didn't come back to Mason County, she could get away with it. The whole damned family was part of the cover-up."

"Not Holly," Brandon said.

"No. But she knew bits and pieces, and the rest of them were afraid she might put it all together. Sounds like that's exactly what happened when she came face to face with Mary Lee— Amy."

"Amy wouldn't kill Holly, would she? Not right there in Mrs. McKendrick's house." Brandon fidgeted, cracked his knuckles, stared out the window.

Unable to reassure him, Tom said, "I can't even guess what these people might do." What was happening? Was Grady Duncan in the house? Was he quick enough, sensible enough to keep things under control? God, why hadn't he assigned somebody younger and stronger to guard Rachel and Holly?

When they reached the farm gate, Tom pulled to the side of the road and the second cruiser stopped behind his. Everyone got out and the deputies huddled around Tom for instructions. "Go over the fence here and through the trees, stay out of sight as long as you can. Brandon and I are going in the front. I want one of you outside the back door and one at the front, ready to grab her if she gets away from us. Let's go."

As soon as he and Brandon cleared the stand of evergreens inside the fence, Tom saw the pickup parked behind Duncan's cruiser. "Jesus Christ, Watford's here."

He broke into a sprint across the snow-covered lawn, Brandon keeping pace. They slowed when they reached the house. With Brandon following, Tom crept up the steps and onto the porch. He'd seen no movement at the windows to indicate they'd been spotted. He eased open the screen door and silently thanked Joanna for keeping the hinges oiled. The main door, he realized, was standing open a couple of inches, and that sent a fresh ripple of apprehension through him. What the hell had happened here?

In two seconds Tom was in the living room doorway, Brandon behind him. Tom saw Grady Duncan inert and bleeding on the floor near the fireplace. Rachel sat on the couch, an arm around

Holly's shoulders, and Jack Watford stood above them, pointing a pistol at Rachel's head.

Heat fueled by fury rose in Tom and washed through every muscle. "Jack!" Tom yelled, leveling his gun at the man across the room. "Drop it!"

Watford whirled, the pistol wobbling in his hand, seeking a target.

"Lay the gun on the floor, Jack."

Watford steadied his gun hand with the other, took aim at Tom.

Tom didn't take his eyes off Watford's pistol, but he heard a gasp from one of the women, a muffled sob from another. "Rachel, Holly," he said, "get up and come over here. Bonnie, Mary Lee—I guess I should call you Amy, shouldn't I?—the two of you get out of the way."

Rachel and Holly started to rise, but Watford caught Rachel's arm and pulled her against him. He pressed the pistol to her temple.

Tom's body went cold, his mouth dry, and dread squeezed the air from his lungs.

"You let her go!" Holly cried.

"Holly, please," Rachel begged in a whisper. "Be quiet." Her eyes met Tom's with a fierce intensity. Not a plea but a promise that she would stay calm, she wouldn't do anything to make Watford pull the trigger.

"Let her go, Jack," Tom said. Jesus Christ, why had he told Rachel to move? "You want to come out of this alive, don't you? Let her go and lay the gun on the floor."

"You're not takin' me in," Watford said. "I'll blow her head off first."

"If you hurt her, you're dead." Tom tightened his clammy hands around his pistol and imagined a target in the middle of Watford's forehead. But if he shot Jack, the man's finger might pull the trigger reflexively and Rachel would die. "You can come out of this alive or dead, your choice."

Watford looked left at his terrified wife, right at Amy, who clutched her stomach as if in physical pain. "We're gonna walk out of here," he said, "and nobody's gonna stop us."

"The house is surrounded by armed officers. You can't get away."

"You tell 'em to back off!" Watford tugged Rachel closer to him, his arm across her waist, pinning both her arms. "I'm takin' her with me, and you're gonna tell 'em to back off or I'll shoot her."

Tom kept his voice calm. He was not going to lose Rachel to this lunatic. "There's nowhere for you to go now, Jack. It's all out in the open. The murders. Amy taking Mary Lee's place."

A moan tore from Amy and she bent double. The gold chain of her purse slid down her arm and hooked on her wrist. "Oh, God, what's going to happen to my children?" She raised her tear-streaked face to Watford, then Bonnie. "Look at all the people you've hurt. Why did I let you drag me into this?"

"You was damned happy to do it at the time." Watford's lips curled with contempt. "You always wished you was Pauline's daughter. Well, you got what you wanted, the money, the good life. And all you had to do was keep your mouth shut."

Amy spun to face Tom and cried, "He made me do it! He said he'd kill me if I didn't do what he said."

"He never would have!" Bonnie rushed to her daughter and enveloped Amy in an embrace. "I wouldn't let him hurt my little girl."

Amy shoved Bonnie away. "You're a monster just like he is! You killed my sister. She was your daughter too, and you choked her to death right in front of me."

"She hurt me so much." Bonnie plucked at Amy's coat sleeve, only to have her hand pushed away. "I just wanted her to love me. I was her mother, but she acted like I was nothin' but trash. She said all those hateful things, and I just couldn't stand her talkin' to me like that."

"You're crazy, you've always been crazy," Amy said. "How could you expect Mary Lee to love you? She didn't know she was your daughter. You thought she'd fall into your arms when you told her."

So that was what happened. Tom imagined the chaotic scene, the horrified disbelief on the real Mary Lee's face when she learned her whole existence was a lie. He kept his eyes on Watford, alert for any sudden action to stop the family's dark secrets from spilling out of Amy and Bonnie.

"Well, you know something?" Amy went on. "I feel the same way she did. I'd rather be dead than be your daughter. Are you going to murder me too to keep me quiet about what you've done? Or maybe you'll get *him*—" She spat the word in Watford's direction. "—to kill me with an ax like he did Pauline."

Bonnie slapped her in the face and knocked her sideways. Amy raised a fist to hit back.

"That's enough!" Tom barked.

Amy's hand hovered, then dropped.

"Stand against the wall," Tom said. "Both of you."

"Shut up," Watford said. "You're not givin' the orders here."

The mantel clock chimed the hour. One. Two. Three.

Holly, who'd been scrunched into a corner of the couch, looked up at Watford and demanded, "Which one of you killed my mama?"

"Your sorry mother was gonna turn her own family in," Watford said. "You want to know what a connivin' little bitch she was? She tried to fool me, told me she was gonna do what I said, get on a bus and leave and keep her mouth shut. She even got me to drive her to the station and watch her get on the bus. Then soon as she thought I was gone, she got right off and run into the alley straight toward the sheriff's office. If I hadn't caught up to her—"

"You killed Jeannie?" Bonnie said, her stricken eyes on her husband. "You swore to me last night that you didn't have anything to do with it."

He was an ax murderer, Tom thought, and his wife was upset because he lied to her. For a wild second, Tom felt like laughing.

"You killed my mama." Holly rose from the couch. "You're not gettin' away with it."

"Shut up and sit down or I'll kill you too," Watford said. "You're no better than your mama."

"Holly," Tom cautioned. "Sit down."

She didn't seem to hear. She moved to the hearth, picked up the iron poker Watford had dropped, and advanced on him. "And you're not hurtin' Dr. Goddard."

When Holly raised the poker, Watford loosened his grip on Rachel and turned the gun on Holly. Rachel hooked a foot around his ankle and shoved her elbow into his stomach. He grunted and the gun went off, the noise exploding in the room.

Tom lunged. The carpet seemed to suck at his boots like quicksand, yet he reached Watford by the time plaster started raining from the ceiling.

Tom knocked Jack to the floor and fell on top of him, a knee in his stomach. Jack got his pistol up and pointed it at Tom's face. Pressing one hand hard on Watford's throat, Tom raised his gun and cracked the butt into the man's wrist. Bone crunched. Watford uttered a strangled scream and dropped the pistol. Brandon scooped it up.

Doors banged open as the other deputies stormed into the house from front and rear. Boots pounded through the hallway. Bonnie screamed when the men burst into the room with guns drawn. She cowered at the approach of the Blackwood twins, but as soon as they touched her she started slapping and kicking. They grabbed her by the arms and forced her against the wall.

"Get your hands off my wife!" Jack yelled. He bucked, trying to throw Tom off him.

Tom gripped Jack's injured wrist hard enough to make the man let loose a wail of pain. "Settle down and shut up," Tom ordered, "or I'll break something else."

Where was Rachel? He glanced around and found her huddled with Holly, safely out of the fray.

Just then he spotted Amy trying to edge along the wall to the door. "Stop her!" he called out, and Brandon sprang at her. She surrendered more meekly than Tom expected, sobbing as the cuffs clicked around her wrists.

Tom snapped cuffs on Jack and left him to the deputies. He bent over Grady, whose eyes fluttered open when he heard his name.

"I let them get in the house," Grady said in a hoarse whisper. "My fault. Sorry…"

"Don't worry about it," Tom said. "Don't talk. I'll get an ambulance." Darla was going to be furious, and she'd give Tom all the blame for her husband's injury.

After he called for an ambulance, Tom stepped back into the living room and looked for Rachel. She stood at the fireplace now, gripping the mantel with both hands. Sweat soaked her hair and her face was chalk-white. She was the most beautiful thing he'd ever seen.

Chapter Forty-three

"What a gorgeous morning!" Rachel stepped out of Tom's truck into two inches of fresh snow. Soaring spruces and pines around the church parking lot looked like a Christmas card with their dusting of white and decorations of red cardinals and blue jays. "It's wonderful to feel free again."

Tom rounded the rear of the truck. "Thanks for coming with me. I drive out this way all the time, but I haven't been to their graves since they were buried."

They walked past rows of headstones, their boots laying down the first footprints in the new snow. The Bridger family plot was on the far side of the cemetery.

During the drive, Tom had stayed quiet, and his hands had gripped the steering wheel as if he were bracing for an ordeal. Rachel was bursting with questions, but she'd allowed him his silence. Now, walking with him toward his family's graves, she was relieved when he spoke.

"You'll be glad to know Jack Watford admitted setting the fire at the animal hospital. You don't have to worry that somebody else is still running around free."

"Good. I'd love to put all these crazy people out of my mind forever." Rachel knew, though, that a long time would pass before she stopped thinking about the real Mary Lee, who'd grown up not knowing who she was. What had the girl felt in the last moments of her life, when the truth was so brutally laid out for her? The echoes of Rachel's own past stirred up memories that ambushed her at odd moments and left her aching and empty. At times she was tempted to tell Tom about her life, but she couldn't bring herself to do it. She might never allow him that close.

She had to focus on getting through the immediate future. Perry Nelson's hearing loomed ahead, only a few days away, and she would have to be strong to confront him in court. She also had to prepare herself to face Luke again, because she knew he would seek her out when she went home for the hearing. Until she saw him, she couldn't be certain whether she would let herself be drawn back into her old life or resist and keep moving forward, away from the past.

A gust of wind swept snow off the nearby trees and it fell over them in a wet, cold shower. Rachel tugged her coat collar around her neck. "Would you believe Shackleford called and asked Holly to visit him in jail? She said no."

"Yeah, I heard," Tom said. "I've told the jailer to restrict his phone privileges. He says he wants to be sure his daughter knows he didn't kill anybody."

"Oh, right, Mr. Innocent Bystander."

"He helped hide Pauline and Mary Lee's bodies, but Bonnie killed Mary Lee and Jack killed Pauline and Jean. Jack hasn't admitted to killing O'Dell, but we found O'Dell's rifle hidden in the Watford house and it had Jack's prints on it. Mrs. Turner says after O'Dell shot me, he went to Jack for help, and he was so out of control that Jack was afraid he'd crack and spill everything if he got caught."

"So Jack killed him with his own gun."

"Right. He used the same gun to shoot at you and Holly, and he probably left the shells at the site so we'd think O'Dell did it."

They paused and watched a mockingbird, with a red berry in its beak, land on a headstone in a flurry of scattered snow. The bird gulped and its throat bulged as the berry went down.

"Why did Shackleford help hide the bodies?" Rachel asked. "Why didn't he turn Bonnie and Jack in?"

"Jack knew about the deal with Natalie McClure and threatened to pin the murders on Shackleford and Natalie. I think Shackleford was glad to see Pauline dead, but to hear him tell it, he ought to get a medal for trying to stop the killing. He claims he pulled Bonnie off Mary Lee, but it was too late, the girl was already dead. Then Pauline ran out the back door screaming for help, with Jack right behind her. Being the noble fellow he is, Shackleford tried to go to her rescue. She grabbed the ax from the woodpile to protect herself from Jack, but she was shaking so much she couldn't hold onto it. Jack snatched it, Pauline ran into the woods, Jack went after her... You can imagine the rest."

All too well. Rachel shuddered at the image of an ax coming down on the woman's head.

"How's Holly doing?" Tom asked.

"She's completely adrift right now," Rachel said. "She can't stop wondering whether her grandmother knew Jean was dead all along and covered up for Jack."

Tom shook his head. "No, I'm convinced Mrs. Turner believed Jean was alive. She told me she was scared to death of both Jack and Shackleford. We're not charging her with anything. She did what she had to do to stay alive and keep Holly safe. By the way, Reed Durham and the prosecutor want to have a meeting with Holly. I told them I'd arrange for you to bring her in."

"For heaven's sake, hasn't she given enough statements? Why does she have to go through that again?"

When Rachel glanced up at Tom, his lips twitched as if he were suppressing a smile. "It won't be too rough this time. They need to clear up one more thing."

Rachel stepped in front of him to make him stop and look at her. "What thing? What's going on?"

"Oh, it's nothing much." Tom absently studied the treetops before bringing his gaze back to Rachel and allowing his smile to break through. "Just a little matter of Holly's multi-million-dollar inheritance."

Stunned, Rachel stared at him for a moment. Then she gave a short laugh and said, "You're joking, right? It's not very funny, Tom."

"It's true. Holly's getting Pauline's estate, once the courts get it away from Amy."

"But how?" Rachel said as she tried to sort through the various inheritance possibilities in an insane situation like this one.

"It's in Pauline's will. Everything was supposed to go to Mary Lee. But if they died at the same time, and they did, it would all go to Pauline's sister, Jean, and her daughter, Holly. Jean's dead too. Holly gets it all."

"Oh, my god," Rachel said, beginning to believe it. "That's fantastic." Tom, grinning at her excitement, took her arm and they moved on. "Think what this will mean to her. She can go to college— She can do anything she wants to. She can have the kind of life she deserves."

Rachel laughed out loud with pleasure of this surprise, but she fell silent when she saw that Tom had stopped at a double headstone. He crouched and brushed away drifted snow to reveal the names of his parents, John and Anne. Next to this site were the graves of Tom's older brother, Chris, and his wife, Carol.

Rising, Tom slapped snow from his gloves. He looked down at his parents' graves for a long time before he spoke in a voice hoarsened by unshed tears. "I guess I'll never know the whole truth about Dad and Pauline. I want to believe Reed Durham, but I keep thinking that he's got plenty of reason to lie about it."

"You can choose to believe the best of your father," Rachel said. "For your own sake."

Tom nodded. "I know he loved my mother, to the day they died. And he was a great dad to Chris and me."

"That's all you need to know. That's all you'll ever need."

They stood in silence for a moment longer, then turned and walked back to the truck, retracing their footsteps in the snow.

To receive a free catalog of Poisoned Pen Press titles, please contact us in one of the following ways:

Phone: 1-800-421-3976
Facsimile: 1-480-949-1707
Email: info@poisonedpenpress.com
Website: www.poisonedpenpress.com

Poisoned Pen Press
6962 E. First Ave. Ste. 103
Scottsdale, AZ 85251